Strapped
FOR
CASH

Taking down the
aristocracy, one prat
at a time.

Andrene Low

1

All this effing white! Jeez, Martin might just as well have popped his clogs already. Cue the sodding harp music.

Brenda hates hospitals with a passion and adding to this misery, her arse hurts, thanks to a chair designed to ensure any visit is brief. It hasn't been upholstered: the bloody thing's been panel-beaten.

Holding the clammy hand of her elderly lover, Martin McGowan, she can't help but feel responsible for his current condition. It had been her idea to try that particular position and it was only due to her rough and ready mouth-to-mouth that he hadn't snuffed it on the spot. Although, he'd assured her while they were waiting for the ambulance that he wouldn't have minded kicking the bucket in such a spectacular fashion.

The one thing she's thankful for is that it didn't happen while they were in London, with Martin's heart having the decency to remain ticking until after their return from the UK.

A vision in white pops her head inside the door of Martin's private room. "She's on her way."

"Bloody hell, I'd better go." Brenda disengages her hand

and is unable to stop herself from wiping it on her jeans. A quick kiss to Martin's forehead confirms this is also covered in a fine sheen of cold sweat, though how anyone could feel chilly in Melbourne in the middle of a stinking hot February is beyond her. If anything, it feels even hotter inside the air-conditioned hospital than it had outside where there had at least been a lacklustre breeze.

Thoughts of longer goodbyes are forestalled when they both hear Mrs McGowan's strident tones at the other end of the ward, already ordering people about.

"You'd better go, or we might have another heart attack on our hands," says Martin, grimacing.

Brenda isn't sure if he's referring to his harridan of a missus or if he's experiencing more chest pains. Either way, she punches the call button before hightailing it out of the room, managing to disappear into the patient lounge just along from his room without being spotted.

Waiting in hope Mrs McGowan's visit will be of the brief variety, Brenda stares out the large window that allows unforgiving light to flood the room. If it hadn't been an emergency, Brenda doubts Martin would be in a public hospital but the ambulance had come here and so here he stays. His bitch of a wife hasn't stopped living up to her reputation since the first hospital corner had been tucked in using a T-square and protractor.

She's flipped through all the women's magazines and is down to reading pamphlets on prostate health before she decides to bail. Bloody woman's arse cheeks must be iron.

After a steadying breath, she readies to make good on her escape, releasing her long, dark hair from the ponytail high up on the back of her head and draping it artfully around her face. Pulling her jacket on to cover her skimpy red boob tube, with head down, she hurries past Martin's glass-windowed room as fast as her platform shoes and ankle-trapping flares will allow.

It's not that she's worried about having a showdown with Mrs McGowan but she'd prefer to avoid anything that might upset Martin.

She'd take that cow on in a heartbeat.

Taking a quick sneaky peek into Martin's room as she speeds past, she's pleased to see a nurse taking his pulse. If nothing else, this will gag the pile of Crimplene and pearls that's spread like cottage cheese over the visitor's chair.

Brenda's surprised at how upset she is over Martin's ill-health. Sure, he'd started out as a meal ticket, but she's come to care for the old codger. Even the sex hadn't been too bad, although she'll be cautious about that in the future. It wasn't as if either of them wanted to risk necrophilia.

Near the double doors fronting the ward, she hears Mrs McGowan's cut-glass tones. "For goodness sake, if you haven't managed to find a pulse by now, he doesn't have one."

Freezing, Brenda listens hard. Unable to hear the nurse's response, she retraces her footsteps to one side of the door to Martin's room. On hearing him trying to placate his wife, she slumps back against the wall.

"How much longer must I suffer visiting my husband in this, this ...?"

Brenda can clearly envisage the expression that must be pasted on the woman's face. It's the 'poo under the nose' look she uses at the least provocation and Brenda's borne the brunt of it in the past. So what if she was caught swimming in the McGowan's pool in her undies? Martin hadn't given a hoot.

The distinctive rattle of the clipboard being unhooked from the end of Martin's bed follows, then the sound of charts being flipped.

"It looks as though it'll be another week," says the nurse, her voice firm. She adds "Maybe even longer," and Brenda hears a touch of glee.

"For goodness sake, this simply won't do! I'm going to arrange a transfer right now."

The visitor's chair screeches in relief and Brenda knows she'll never make it out of the ward in time. Luckily there's a door right behind her and, without hesitation, she opens it, walks in and closes it quietly before sliding to the side so she's not visible through the tall skinny viewing pane. Her hopes the room is vacant are dashed when a creaky and rather hopeful voice says, "Are you here to give me my enema?"

———

Parking in the side road up from the flat, Brenda turns off the engine and yanks on the handbrake. The realisation that with Martin in hospital and unable to remind his accountant to pay the rent–that she might have to fork out herself–anchors her in the seat.

Maybe she can resurrect the previous arrangement with Stefano? Tapping her teeth with her viciously long red nails, she mulls over her choices. Under normal circumstances, she wouldn't give a rat's about shagging Stefano, but something about it doesn't feel right.

"Damn!" Brenda thumps the steering wheel hard. "Don't tell me I need to get a job?"

On this depressing thought, she gets out of the car and locks it before clomping down the road to the empty flat. Used to having lots of people around when she'd spent a couple of months in London over Christmas, she's finding its echoing qualities a tad bloody boring. It's even worse with Martin temporarily out of the picture.

———

Come rent day, Brenda's still undecided. Martin's accountant hadn't paid the rent as usual to the landlord and she hadn't liked to bring it up at the hospital. The upshot is, Stefano's on his way to collect, one way or another, so she's flogged a bracelet rather than pick up some bar work. But she's still loath to hand over cash without it being life or death.

As an insurance policy of sorts, she's put fresh sheets on the bed and dressed with care. Cut-off jeans, singlet top, no bra. No knickers either and, boy, had that done damage to her pubes. Pulling the flap to one side, she can still see some poking through the zipper, letting her know stripping will be as depilatory as dressing had been.

Stefano's trademark rat-tat-tat at the front door makes up her mind. The money is in her back pocket. She can do this. It only takes this short walk to the front door to change her mind. She's wrong, she can't do this and looking at Stefano, she's not sure she wants to take the cash route when other 'roots' could be so much more fun.

It's the first time she's seen her landlord in months. With Martin's accountant taking care of the rent, there'd been no need for his fortnightly visits. She'd forgotten how bloody good looking he is, even if he is crowding fifty. The Italian blood and accent are a big part of his attractiveness but his innate sense of style doesn't hurt either, although he's dressed far more casually than she's ever seen, with faded jeans fitting his toned frame snuggly. His dark green t-shirt is also fitted, leaving Brenda in no doubt about how she'll settle the rent.

Leaning casually against the door jam, he crosses his legs at the ankles, an eyebrow raised. Brenda switches into rent mode, sauntering the last few steps until she's standing hard against him, her breasts squishing out the top of her tank in down payment. It's one he accepts with alacrity, scooping her up and marching unerringly towards the bedroom where he tosses her into the middle of the bed.

"Long and slow, or fast and dirty," says Stefano, giving her the option.

Brenda pretends to consider this dilemma, even though there's no need. Thoughts of being able to go for it without risk of killing her partner, or simply popping his hip, make her grin excitedly before ripping off her top and flinging it at him. She rips down her zipper, in a 'removing a plaster' kind of way, but can't help a small yelp escaping. It doesn't slow her in arching her hips off the bed to rid herself fully of the cut-offs.

"Fast and dirty it is," says Stefano, stripping as quickly as she has.

————

She's on the edge of another blinding climax, only her second of the non-faked variety so far this year, when the sound of the gate opening cuts through the sexual haze that's wrapped tightly around her. Part of her is aware the front door is still wide open, while a much smaller part is having too good a time to give a rat'sarse. She's panting like an A+ Le Mars student, when there's a knock at the front door.

Stefano looks up from his position between her legs, "Are you expecting anyone?"

"No, no, no," says Brenda, "don't stop!"

Ever the conscientious landlord, he doesn't.

"Is there anyone there," calls out a cultured male voice from the vicinity of the front step.

"Yes, yes, yes!" yells Brenda, the last more of a scream.

"She'll be coming in a minute," yells out Stefano, and indeed he's true to his word.

With the last of the climax still pulsing through her body, Brenda drags herself clear of Stefano and although it takes only a moment to pull on her dressing gown and walk through to the front door, it's not fast enough for the visitor. A grey-haired besuited gent is already making his way back along the path, a large carry bag gripped in one hand.

"Can I help you?" she calls out to him.

He turns and glares at her as if she's done something wrong and this makes her wish she'd left him to it. Missing out on the post-coital glow so she can be frowned at is something she can do without. A year ago she'd have let him leave, concerned he looked too official for anything good to come of it, but hanging out with Martin means her lifestyle of late has been impeccable, with the statute of limitations on anything that had gone before surely over.

Obviously, she's wrong.

"Miss Brenda Munro?"

For god's sake!

"Who is asking," says Stefano, coming up behind her only wearing a towel.

His appearance makes the legal-looking arsehole, even more irate. "I'm Denis Kellerman, Martin McGowan's lawyer."

On hearing who their visitor is, Stefano leaves them to it.

"He's not? Is he okay?" says Brenda, her hands gripping the front of her dressing gown tighter than necessary.

The look of censure coming from the suit at the bottom of the steps flips to one of comprehension. "Mr McGowan was fine when I saw him at the hospital this morning. I can see you're concerned about his welfare."

That he waves his hand towards her relative state of undress, makes her bristle. If there's one thing she's learnt from Martin, it's how to deal with officious jerks like this.

"In answer to your question, yes, I am Brenda Munro. Perhaps you'd like to inform me of your business here?" Her tone and stance are now altogether less relaxed than they were and she's pleased to see him struggle with the change. Jumped-up old bastard.

"Then, this is for you."

He stomps up the front stairs and hands her the David Jones carrier bag. Without uttering any pleasantries or instructions, he retraces his steps and plods down the path.

She's closing the door and locking it, when she hears the gate slam behind him.

Peering inside the bag while walking back to the bedroom, she's surprised to see a present and an envelope, both with her name on them. Any thoughts of opening them are squashed when she spots Stefano lying in the middle of the bed, ready for another round. She's not sure she's up to it. Sleeping with an older gent for ten months has her well and truly out of practice when it comes to sex. If she was to risk another climax like the one she'd just experienced, she might end up in the hospital bed next to Martin.

"Long and slow," says Brenda, dropping first the carrier bag and then her dressing gown.

———

Stefano is still in the shower, using all the bloody hot water no doubt, when Brenda drags the carrier bag off the floor and onto her bed. She retrieves the gaily wrapped present but leaves the envelope languishing in the bottom of the bag. It doesn't take her long to rip the gift paper away, but her excitement dies when she sees it's a shoulder bag and one that's big enough to nick more than a couple of glasses. It's nice and all, being Louis Vuitton and a match to the large trunk he gave her for their trip to London, but it's not like she doesn't have a dozen handbags already.

And it's stuffed full of the paper the manufacturers use to pad it out to its fullest. She knows from experience that once the bag is a withered shadow of its store-bought plumpness, her rubbish bin will be overflowing.

She decides she may as well gut the damned thing now, and

unzips it in readiness. The zipper on top isn't halfway along when she's assailed by the stench of mothballs. She's coughing and pushing it away when she spots money peeking out.

Any thoughts of asphyxiation are out the window as she whips the zipper fully open. Freed from their confines, wrinkled notes spill over the edges of the bag and onto the bed. By the time she's emptied the main chamber and all the side pockets, there are an awful lot of one-hundred-dollar bills on her lap and scattered around the bed.

She's rolling in them and having a lovely Scrooge McDuck moment when Stefano walks back in unashamedly naked.

"Good god, what is this?" he says, gesturing to Brenda, who's holding up bundles of notes and letting them flutter down onto her body.

"I'm rich!" says Brenda, cuddling a large armful of notes close to her chest, inducing a coughing fit.

"Who is it from?" says Stefano, starting to dress.

"Martin! He's such a sweetheart."

Shoving the crumpled notes to one side, Brenda leans over and grabs the carrier bag in readiness for filling it with her booty.

"There is bound to be a price," says Stefano, sounding less chipper than usual.

"Trust me, I know that."

Brenda has already shoved the first few handfuls of notes into the carrier bag when she spots the envelope with her name in Martin's scrawl on the front.

One of her talons makes quick work of opening it to see a piece of paper and airline ticket sitting snuggly inside. Leaving the ticket where it is, she removes the letter and after unfolding it, scans its contents.

A sob escapes, and she isn't sure who's more surprised, her or Stefano. Brenda doesn't like giving into girly emotions, and sure as hell not when she has an audience. She struggles to control her tears but this is made difficult by Stefano demanding to know what has upset her so.

"It's nothing," says Brenda, hoping to dodge an emotional dialogue, especially one that involves discussing one lover with another. It all feels too much like an Olympic tryout for comfort.

"We've known each other for a couple of years and this is the first time I've seen you shed a tear when onions weren't involved." Stefano crosses his arms, indicating he won't be fobbed off.

Brenda is annoyed she'd opened the envelope in front of him. She is so out of practice when it comes to keeping multiple guys on leashes at the same time. It's an art, manifestly one she's lost.

"It's from Martin. He said he wants to make sure I'm looked after when he's gone."

"Is he close to ... ah ..." Stefano's words dwindle away awkwardly.

"No! He says if he gives me the money now there's less chance of his wife getting her hooks into it. If he leaves it to me in his will, she'll contest it and that'll hold it up for bleeding months."

"How much is there?"

"Not sure, I was too busy enjoying it."

Together the two of them make quick work of straightening the money into neat bundles and counting it.

"One hundred thousand. That is a lot of money," says Stefano.

The glint of speculation in his eyes is blinding enough that Brenda carefully slots all the money in the bottom of the carrier bag. She talks about banking it, but he advises against this.

"Why? I don't trust sodding banks either, but this dosh will be a damned sight safer in a vault than under my bed."

"If I were you, I'd get it out of the country. If there's even a small chance of him, um, going soon, you need the money as far away from the widow as possible."

"That's what he said too," admits Brenda, pulling the airline ticket out of the envelope to see where it can take her.

Careful examination does nothing to clarify this, and so she hands it over to Stefano.

"It is a round-the-world ticket. Keep heading east, or west, you can have as many stopovers as you like." He looks more closely. "It is good for a year."

2

S till transfixed by the airline ticket, Brenda hears Stefano say "One stopover should be Zurich."

"Zurich?"

"Yes. You need a Swiss bank account."

"Hah! No way will the old battle-axe be able to get her dibs on the cash if it's locked away in one of those."

That's if Swiss banks are as tight-lipped as they are in the movies. Brenda hopes this is the case but it wouldn't be the first time she'd been misled by Hollywood.

"Find one with an office in England or the States," says Stefano, interrupting the Bond movie flickering away in her head.

"How do I do that?"

"Easiest way is to dress like you mean business, walk in and ask."

"They'll see I mean business when I hand that lot over." Brenda pats the carrier at the side of the bed.

"You cannot do that."

"Why not?"

"Because there are rules about how much money you can leave the country with."

At this revelation, Brenda sees red and abuses the government and bureaucracy in general. It takes a while for her to get this out of her system. She still hasn't finished when Stefano interrupts.

"I do not make the rules. I only know how to bend them."

This comment ensures she gives him her full attention.

He outlines a plan to see the money safely out of the country but it's not one she's happy with. The thought of handing that much money over to him is enough to make her break out in hives. It's not that she doesn't trust him; it's more that she doesn't trust his associates, many of whom spend an inordinate amount of time either acting as bookies, at the bookies or at the track. Their idea of a big investment usually involves the Melbourne Cup.

Unable to decide right then and there, she asks to sleep on it. She sure as hell intends to look at other options before handing it all over. For one thing, she needs to confirm how she goes about booking flights on this unusual ticket and check exactly how much money she can take with her personally. Come to that, she's not even sure where she should go, other than Zurich.

Not that it takes long for her to decide, London being the obvious choice. She's been there before, Jennie her old flatmate still lives there and, with luck she'll be able to stay with her, especially now Sam and Chris are living in Italy.

Brenda again calculates the time difference before picking up the receiver. It takes all her concentration to dial the incredibly long number that will connect her to Eadie's place in west London; it takes a couple of attempts to get it right. After a series of clicks and dead air, it rings at the other end. And rings. And rings.

It's answered just as she's steeling herself to hang up. The line is atrocious, with a killer echo, meaning Brenda is replying at the same time as Eadie's second greeting crackles through.

Hopeless! "Hang on, I'll call you back, back."

She does so, with better luck and while it's still not a brilliant connection, at least now Eadie is only saying everything once. They discuss the weather and how everything is, while Brenda waits until it's polite enough to cut the old lady off.

"Is Jennie there?"

"Still abed at this hour."

"Oh, oh, I'm so sorry. Must have got the bleedin' time zones wrong."

"Stop berating yourself, gal. It's ten in the morning and high time the pair of them was up."

This news has Brenda in a flurry of indecision. Maybe she should bypass Jennie and go directly to the source? The silence is awkward; she makes up her mind.

"Eadie, I'm coming to London in a few weeks." Her voice catches in her throat before she can continue.

"But, of course, you must stay," says Eadie, eliminating the need for Brenda to throw herself on the old girl's mercy.

"Thank you. Thank you so much." Brenda allows her head to drop back, before continuing. "I'll be a model guest."

The rest of the call is devoted to when she'll be arriving and how pleased Eadie will be for some extra company.

Within minutes of sitting opposite a travel agent, who looks to have never left the country, let alone her desk, Brenda has a teetering pile of brochures stacked in front of her.

"Of course, London is nippy at this time of year," says the agent, in a knowledgeable voice. The fact she's looking at a book that highlights everything there is to know about London, rather blows the effect.

"Yes, I know, I was there a couple of months back," says Brenda, unable to stop herself sounding smug. "My, ah, gentleman friend and I flew there first class on Qantas."

The agent's demeanour changes at this snippet and sensing extra commission, she asks "And will you be upgrading your ticket for these flights?"

"Hell, no! Not if I have to pay the dif."

The agent gasps and Brenda knows she's sworn, again. Martin has tried to break her of what is simply a bad habit, but with little luck. It's something she'll need to be aware of if she wants to be taken seriously when cold-calling on Swiss banks.

While the agent might not have much international travel under her belt, she's a mine of information on everything from visas to how much money Brenda can take with her. It's a depressingly small amount meaning she'll have to hand over almost all her 'hope money' to Stefano for him to deal with on her behalf. A quick side trip to a bank, one other than her own, on the way to the travel agents, confirmed that to transfer the money by legitimate means would be slow and cost a lot in fees. Plus there'd be evidence she'd actually received the dosh if Mrs McGowan ever got her tits bent out of shape.

The fees would be more painful than anything Stefano would charge and, anyway, hadn't she already covered his fee in the scratcher, going for it over the past few days? Her gut is sure as hell feeling flatter for all the unaccustomed 'ball crunches'.

With her flights booked, Brenda's next visit is to the British Consulate to organise a visa. The chap behind the grille also suggests she gets a work permit, making her snigger although she turns this into a cough. With the bulk of her money safely stashed in Switzerland, it would look strange if she didn't look for work in the UK and she's smart enough to know image is king.

It's touch-and-go for everything to fall into place over the next two and a half weeks. Her visa and work permit come through worryingly close to her departure date and she's relieved not to have to change her flights. She's been in to visit Martin every day and is pleased he hasn't yet moved to a private hospital, as his wife has been badgering for. Brenda can't help but laugh when she hears this is because the nurses on his current ward are stalling all they can, following his instructions. He knows full well if he's incarcerated in a private hospital, it will be difficult if not impossible, for Brenda to visit him.

She tells him of her plans and he agrees with everything, even if he's nervous about her putting her faith in Stefano to get the money out of the country.

"You should have let me take care of it for you," says Martin, through his oxygen mask, a new addition since she'd last visited him.

Not wanting to point out she hadn't wanted to bother him because he's looking like shit, she goes for a neutral, "Oh, well, it's all settled now," before returning to stroking the back of his hand.

After a few moments of this calming motion, he admits if he were to transfer it through his usual channels, it would leave a paper trail for his wife that was a mile wide, thus vindicating Brenda's decision to go with the Stefano option.

Her tears are genuine when she kisses him goodbye for the final time. There are promises to meet up in London, but Brenda has a sad sense this will never happen. Looking back at him as she's leaving the room, a feeling that this will be the last time she'll ever see him washes over her. It's enough for her to return to his side for another a hug and a kiss beneath the oxygen mask – involving a lot more tongue than is safe for someone with a ticker on the fritz.

Riffling through the contents of her relatively tiny, but incredibly colourful, suitcase, Brenda hopes she's got enough stuff to get her through the next few months. While it would be fantastic to take her large Louis Vuitton trunk to England, the excess baggage charges would wipe out a large chunk of her traveller's cheques. It's still come in handy, though; she's packed everything she's leaving behind in it, with Stefano promising to look after it for her. She only hopes he's not stupid enough store it at the family home where his wife might stumble across it.

She's sick to death of sharing the men in her life. There's always someone in the background threatening to kybosh her fleeting sense of security. And she has felt genuine security in this flat, perhaps for the first time in her life. Her parents were, and still are, useless. Growing up with the constant worry of making the rent or even eating at times has forged Brenda into the survivor she is.

A final check around the flat and she knows it's time to move on with her life. Stefano is taking her to the airport, due in no small part to her disinclination to hand the bag of money over to him, yet. She's keeping control of it until the last possible moment, enjoying its protective presence.

———

She's checked in and received her boarding pass before she finally hands the carrier bag over to him. Even then, he has to prise her fingers away from the handle, all the while spouting platitudes about how he has her best interests at heart and that he'll look after her. It's only when he says that even with him taking the bulk of it, she's in possession of more money than she's ever had before, that peace descends. He's right of course and when she takes into account the accessories she's draped in, Brenda knows she's good for at least three or four months without having to work. Even without a protector.

Travelling to Zurich is no fun when you're flying economy. This is the first time she's flown long distance without being cocooned in first class as she had been on her previous trip to London. It takes a day of being horizontal before she's ready and able to traipse around banks until she finds one that has an office in London.

For a non-travelled travel agent, the homely girl behind the desk at the agency in Melbourne does herself proud on Brenda's accommodation in the Swiss city. It's a chocolate box chalet with a plump and motherly frau ruling the roost. The duvets are thick and snuggly, making it doubly hard for Brenda to drag herself out of bed on the day she's set aside to sort out a bank account.

She dresses in the grey suit as recommended by Stefano, for all the good it does her. She can't even get past the guard at a couple of banks and when she does get in the door at another, they're quick to steer her back towards the entrance. Frau Schwegler takes in her dejected air when a foot-sore Brenda clomps into the guest haus, late that afternoon.

Fortunately for Brenda, the woman is a marvel of Swiss efficiency and knowledgeable about how to be taken seriously by the local financial institutions. Indeed, Brenda has no trouble when calling on her first bank in the morning. She hasn't dressed any differently from the day before but is now wearing all her trinkets. Every single blasted one of them. She feels like a walking jewellery store and is on edge about being mugged, but it works a treat in getting her in the front door and, more importantly, speaking to someone in a suit. That the bank has an office in London is down to pure dumb luck.

After depositing half her available funds into the newly opened account, she leaves with a record of that and the account details for Stefano that she immediately sends to him in a telegram.

Delaying her departure, she visits the bank daily to check on progress but the balance remains worryingly in shit-out-of-luck territory. With the bank having a branch in London, and Frau Schwegler chewing through her funds as fast as she's chewing through the bloody fattening food the frau is constantly serving up, Brenda gets the hell out of there before her arse ends up the consistency of half-melted fondue.

This arrival in London is different from her last visit. Even though the flight from Zurich to London is a reasonably short one, Economy does evil things to a person's body. No one is supposed to sit jammed up like that for more than half an hour tops. Also missing is the chauffeur-driven limo pick-up at the airport. For once, Brenda is glad she's not dragging the Louis Vuitton chest around; it's difficult enough lugging her one small bag through Heathrow to the tube for the trip to West London.

A couple of dodgy-looking characters offer to help, but Brenda is nothing if not streetwise. A filthy look and invective-laden 'no' sends them on their way–without her bag in tow. She snaffles a black cab at Turnham Green, elbowing a punk out of the way to achieve this. Stopping outside the familiar house in Chiswick, she's warmed by the sense of homecoming she experiences as she drags her bag over the threshold, the front door is unlocked as always in deference to Eadie's arthritis and her inability to undo the mechanism.

This complete disregard for keeping the crims at bay will have Brenda looking for a good spot to hide her jewels and spare change; it's far too easy for anyone to walk in off the street and help themselves.

"Is that you, Brenda?" warbles out of Eadie's sitting room, off to the right of the hallway.

"Sure is. Hope that decanter's full. I'm bloody parched," says Brenda, throwing her puffer jacket in the direction of the coatrack and walking into the chintzy sitting room where the old lady spends most of her days.

The welcome she gets isn't what she expects.

"Where on earth have you been? I've been worried sick!"

That Eadie's eyes look suspiciously moist reinforces the old lady's concern. It throws Brenda. Hells bells, not even her parents care this much.

"I got held up in Zurich."

"You should have called," scolds Eadie, leaving Brenda struggling for a suitable response. "But you're safe and that's all that matters."

Brenda sits tentatively on the couch but doesn't relax, just yet.

"You look like you could use a little something. Unfortunately …" The rest of Eadie's sentiment dies as she looks at the empty decanter in disgust and Brenda knows her own expression is comparable.

"Has he been holding out on you again?" says Brenda.

"The little pipsqueak thinks he can wean me off it by taking ages to top-up the bloomin' decanter."

The pipsqueak in question is Mark, who at six foot three is hardly little, but who singlehandedly looks to be trying to dry out his auntie Eadie.

"Is he around?"

"No, he and Jennie waited as long as they could but they had to leave."

"Where are they off to?"

"Italy, staying with Chris and Sam."

"How long for?"

"Six months!"

"Six months!" says Brenda, unsure what effect this will have on her continuing to stay here. "When did they decide that?" Jennie hadn't said anything about it in her last letter.

"It was last minute. Chris managed to secure a contract for Mark and Jennie was agog at thoughts of all those art galleries. I'm just pleased you'll be around to keep me company."

With this immediate worry allayed, Brenda allows herself to relax a little. "How long have you been living on fumes?"

Eadie eyes the decanter and Brenda can see fierce calculations going on. "Three hours now!"

"Just as well I arrived when I did!" says Brenda, standing. "I'll be right back."

The flagon of sherry is on the shelf in the cellar exactly where she remembers, although the level of this bulk supply isn't exactly healthy, either. Something she'll remedy the next day.

Back in the sitting room, she doesn't bother with the decanter and instead pours healthy glasses for herself and Eadie directly from the flagon. She places it on a newspaper on the floor, as it's too big to sit on the small mahogany table with the decanter and its tray.

They toast each other like old friends with a "Here's mud in your eye", and polish off their glasses in one go. Brenda tops them up again and, having taken the edge off their thirst, they contentedly sip their second and subsequent refills.

Brenda brings Eadie up to speed on her situation as she hadn't bothered with any details in the phone call. On reaching the part about handing the bulk of the money over to Stefano, Eadie doesn't have to say anything. Her expression more than communicates that she thinks Brenda has seen the last of her nest egg.

"But what else was I supposed to do? I checked it out with

the bank and they were going to take ages and charge a bleeding fortune for the privilege."

"You're wearing the answer to your problem," says Eadie.

Brenda runs her hands over her outfit, and her face creases in confusion. It's not until her hands encounter jewellery that the old lady smiles

"Damn," says Brenda, mentally thrashing herself for being so stupid.

"I've worn a fortune through customs in the past. Gold is the best option, twenty-four carat, if you can."

At Brenda's questioning look, she carries on. "The purer the gold, the brighter and shinier it is. If it looks cheap, no one takes any notice of it."

"Melt it down and flog it off!"

"Well, too late now. You'll have to hope your chap comes through."

Brenda knows Eadie is only saying this out of sympathy.

After putting Eadie to bed, Brenda drags her suitcase up to the room she'd used last time and unpacks. She's delighted to see the Christmas decorations are still in place, giving the room a festive feel, even though the yuletide season has long since gone.

With everything stowed away, she settles for a snooze. This is more to do with being tired from travelling than alcohol consumption. There wasn't enough sherry in the house to take care of both her and Eadie's capabilities, even though Brenda had collected all Eadie's secret stashes following directions from the old girl.

First thing in the morning, she'll head to the local off-licence to buy a couple of flagons of sherry. Brenda is in full agreement with Eadie on this subject. The old lady is an adult and if she isn't allowed to deal with the pain of her arthritis by ending each day half-cut on cheap fortified wine, what's the point of living?

Despite being tired, sleep doesn't come. Brenda is unable to stop thoughts of Stefano lying naked on a bed somewhere, rolling in her money. She's angrier with herself than she is with him. She should've known better. She's mid-stew when it feels as if someone's chucked a sack of spuds on the bed next to her.

"Gidday, Charlie," says Brenda, to the enormous black and white cat as he collapses on top of her and purrs strongly enough for her to feel it throughout her body. "I missed you, too."

She squeezes the monster hard enough to make him squeak, but not a single claw pops out. They have an understanding and a strong bond. Something she's never experienced with an animal before. She likes the non-judgemental nature of their relationship, with neither of them expecting much of the other.

As the weeks pass, Eadie, Charlie and Brenda settle into a comfortable routine. Early on, Brenda had phoned the bank to see if her money had turned up but being Swiss, nothing short of a face-to-face visit and maybe a blood sample would coerce them to release that sort of information.

She's therefore faced with a long tube trip every time she wants to check in with them. What starts out as a daily exercise soon becomes 'weakly', as all hopes of the money coming through from Stefano, fade. Despite the temptation to do so, she doesn't empty out the account. That money would stay there as a 'tits up' fund to cover her worst-case scenario.

With each shake of a bank official's head, Brenda's blood pressure climbs a couple of points. Even living cheaply at Eadie's she's noticing her bog standard British bank balance free-falling into 'oh, shit I'll need to get a job' territory.

"What does Stefano say he's done with the money?" says Eadie.

"I can't get hold of him. If he keeps dodging me, I'll ring the bastard at home and screw what his missus thinks."

"Maybe the threat of that will be enough."

"Good point. I'll ring him at the office tonight, our time. If whoever it is who answers won't put me through, I'll say I'll phone him at home later."

"In the meantime, maybe you should give some thought to a job?" says Eadie, adding, "Just in case," when she sees the look of horror Brenda's giving her.

Receiver jammed hard against her ear, Brenda listens to her call ringing all the way over in Melbourne at what is the next morning according to the calendar and the clock.

Her call is answered promptly and as expected, Stefano is not in. Brenda has lied through her own teeth enough in the past to spot this behaviour in someone else.

"Really? That's okay, I'll phone him at home tonight."

While the chap on the other end is still gagging, she slams the phone down.

3

R ather than return to the sitting room, Brenda paces backwards and forwards in front of the hall table, staring at the phone and daring the bloody thing to ring. She's rewarded not long after.

"Hello, Stefano."

"Ah, baby, your voice, it sounds so good. I have missed you."

"I've missed you too, Stefano. But I'm missing my money a lot more. Where the hell is it?"

It takes Brenda a second or two to cobble together his stuttered reply. The upshot is that there was an opportunity he couldn't pass by and so he's invested it for her.

She presses him on the details, but his answers are vague enough that she knows a horse race, or more than one, is involved.

"If you've lost my sodding money, I am going to come back home and call round to see your wife, wearing nothing but a smile. Are we straight?"

Not surprisingly, Stefano suddenly has trouble with what has been up until this point, a crystal-clear connection; but Brenda knows the sounds of a slippery bastard scrunching up paper right next to the receiver when she hears it. This is followed by the disconnect tone. Despite clenching her teeth *hard*, she's unable to stop herself from screaming like a banshee, her screeches of frustration echoing back to smack her in the face. She's so angry she wants to smash something. Preferably Stefano. The telephone bears the brunt of it, but being industrial in design, it survives the overzealous hanging up of the receiver.

"Gone?" says Eadie, to her when she thumps herself into the couch.

Its cushioned softness does nothing to take the edge off her anger and so she drums her heels into the carpet with better results. "He said he's invested it for me."

"Oh, dear."

"His idea of an investment usually involves a blasted bookie."

"Is he successful?"

"Bloody useless. If there's a candidate for the glue factory in the line-up, it's a given that Stefano will put all his money on the nag."

An uneasy silence follows as they mull things over. The quiet eventually dissolves Brenda's anger sufficiently for her to face her current predicament. Luckily for her, she'd armed herself with a work permit for appearance's sake, even if thoughts of going back to full-time work fill her with dread. She's enjoyed being one of an elite circle, that of a kept woman, for the last ten months and it's been wonderful. Sure, she's been bored at times, but no more so than if she'd been stuck in a cruddy office job.

She doesn't know how she'll break the news to Martin that she's lost the money he's given her. Maybe when she's come to terms with it herself?

"What can you do?" says Eadie, mirroring Brenda's own thoughts.

"Office job. Behind a bar. Something like that."

"I didn't ask *what* you'd do, but what *can* you do?" At Brenda's lack of comprehension, she expands. "What are you actually good at?"

Brenda thinks on this for a moment and after a couple of false starts, eventually comes out with, "Does screwing old guys out of their hard-earned money count?"

Apparently it does.

But Eadie's plans are altogether more grandiose than anything Brenda is thinking of. "Why bother with one-on-one when you can pass your skills on to others?"

———

Okay, so I've got The Initial Approach, The Tackle, Make Him Pay, The Next Encounter and, my favourite, The Hook, Line and Sinker." Brenda taps her pen against the pad. "Any other classes you can think of?"

"My goodness, yes. They'll need to study deportment, etiquette, table manners and elocution."

"Hello, what?"

"Elo-cu-tion," enunciates Eadie. "Rounding vowels, not dropping aitches, that sort of thing."

"Some old geezer isn't going to give a toss about their language if they're dressed the right way."

"While a fine bosom might be all it takes to keep your Aussie chaps on the leash, it's rather different here in England."

"Yeah, from what I've heard, over here they prefer you actually use a leash."

"Jolly good point. We need to apprise the young ladies on what to watch out for."

Brenda's mulling over whether this is so they can find them or avoid them, when Eadie continues.

"We'll also need a reasonably up-to-date copy of Burke's."

In answer to Brenda's blank look, she adds, "Burke's Peerage. It's a who's who of the well-to-do."

"You are kidding me?"

"Not at all. The English aristocracy is proud of their heritage and so don't quibble to see it all there in print. It also stops inbreeding."

Seeing that Eadie is visibly wilting, Brenda clicks the Biro a final time and hooks it through several pages of the pad. "Right, I don't know about you, but I'm knackered."

"I am rather done in." Eadie double checks she's finished the glass of sherry in her hand before putting it down clumsily on the side table. "If you wouldn't mind?"

Brenda doesn't need to be asked twice and helps Eadie to her feet and through to her bedroom, although offers of further assistance are refused.

Brenda is halfway back through the sitting room when Eadie calls out, "Wake me for breakfast and we can get on with our planning straight after that."

Brenda still thinks lesson plans are overkill but the old girl won't be dissuaded and seeing as it's her house and all.

———

Standing and stretching the kinks out of her back, Brenda says, "Are you sure it's going to work?"

"I don't see why not. The odds of covering your costs are a lot better if you teach others and take a cut, than trying to make it on your own."

Eadie appears unaffected by both the prospect of the teaching syllabus and the hours and hours they've spent thrashing out plans for each of the disciplines. Brenda has to hand it to the old girl though, she hadn't even thought about role-play, but it would be perfect for teaching the subtleties of flirting with geriatrics. Any subtleties being wasted if they were short-sighted and deaf as a post.

"And you're okay with turning this place into ah, a finishing school?" Brenda waves her hand around, unable to come up with a better description for what Eadie is suggesting she do to earn a living. Brothel had sprung to mind, but been rejected.

"Of course. It'll keep my mind off other things."

The pain the old lady lives with is well known and anything that can be done to make life more bearable is a good thing in Brenda's books.

With three live-in students, there's a heap for Brenda to organise before classes get underway in earnest. Furniture is the priority with the few odds and sods stored down in the cellar of no use, consumed by cold and damp. To keep costs down anything she buys will be second-hand; antique in all but price.

The students will live on the vacant second floor, a sort of no-man's zone that exists between the floor Brenda's bedroom is on and the attic space that is Jennie and Mark's domain. Looking at the state of those stripped-bare rooms, Brenda knows there's a lot of hard graft ahead to get them to a point girls will pay to live in them.

Still, anything is better than sitting around stewing about her lost cash and it'll sure as hell be better than being at the beck and call of some tyrant of an office manager.

Leaving Eadie safely propped up in bed, Brenda heads to her own. Charlie thunders up the stairs after her, passes her and is ensconced in the middle of her bed by the time she arrives.

"Move over, ya fat bastard!"

While Brenda's words might technically be harsh, her tone leaves Charlie in no doubt that he's okay to keep pummelling the eiderdown with those dog-sized paws of his. His goofy look slides into place, prompting Brenda to lean over and drop a smattering of kisses on top of his head.

She doesn't pull away, waiting instead for the second part of their nightly ritual. True to form, he whips his head around and licks the underside of her chin. Brenda gets ready for bed but sees this is an exercise in frustration. Keyed up about Stefano losing her money and the stack of things to do to get ready for Munro's (charm-them-out-of-their-cash) School, she knows it will be a while before she can shut down enough to sleep. Shame it's already after midnight.

Sure enough, no sooner has she switched off the light than her brain goes into overdrive, with anger at the forefront of her emotions. Mostly she's angry for being stupid enough to give her money to that arsehole, Stefano. She'd always thought of herself as being street-smart.

"Guess that's what living the high life does to you."

Charlie's only response is to stretch out more; apparently there are spots on his tummy she's missed while idly running her hand up and down his length.

After anger comes sadness. People say money can't buy you happiness but Brenda had sure as hell enjoyed the security it provided.

The relief at not having to shag a string of old guys, or report to a grey moron in an even greyer office, had been wonderful.

She's back to facing uncertainty in her life, and she hates it.

A few tears escape, making her give herself a psychological kick up the rear end. If anything, she needs to harden up if she wants to survive the next few months. Maybe Eadie is right and it's time to forge her own path. To be mistress of her own destiny and some other crap Eadie had rambled on about that made Brenda's eyes glaze over.

Rule number one of the school will be "Don't take everything". Apart from it being unethical, it'll also avoid them being hounded by relatives who can see their inheritance being syphoned away. The same rule will apply to any jewellery that looks to be heirloom.

Counting her own stash of jewellery as it jumps over an imaginary pawnbroker's counter, eventually sends her to sleep.

———

It's only because Charlie doesn't have a snooze function that Brenda is upright before nine the next morning.

"Jeez, I wish you had opposable thumbs, ya little whinger," mutters Brenda as she staggers down the stairs after the persistent feline.

He looks chipper compared with her ragged reflection in the mirror that backs the hall table.

She stops long enough to drag her fingers through her hair several times, in a vain attempt to beat it into submission, and is still tying the cord on her dressing gown when she stumbles into the kitchen.

She slams her eyes shut in response to the sunshine streaming into the room, unaware Eadie is at her usual spot at the table, until the old lady says, "Goodness. Are you not feeling well?"

"Couldn't sleep."

Brenda opens her eyes wide enough to sort out Charlie's kibble. At least this will put an end to the ankle-high interference he's currently running on her.

"I'll top up your milk after I've had a cuppa." The look of disgust this gets her makes her laugh. "Ya impatient little bugger."

The stop button on Charlie's whinging effectively hit, Brenda feels it's okay to pour herself a cup of tea. She picks up the pot to find it empty. Eadie's managed to prepare some toast, although it doesn't take a trained eye to see the toppings look like concrete laid by a dodgy contractor.

Guilt smashes down the last of Brenda's lethargy as she grabs Eadie's knife and spreads the butter and marmalade right out to the edges. A pot of tea follows.

"How do you get dressed in the morning? says Brenda, intrigued and concerned in turn.

"Very bloomin' slowly."

"Yell out if you ever need help. Won't you?"

Eadie's mumbled response leaves Brenda none the wiser but knowing how independent the old lady is, she doesn't push it.

"Have you given any more thought to the enterprise?" says Eadie, before taking a bird-sized bite of toast.

"Why do ya think I'm sporting these? Took freaking ages for my damned brain to shut down."

"Where will you start?"

"Cleaning. And that's all down to me, unfortunately."

"Flo could help."

"Who's she?"

"The char who comes in three times a week to help me out."

Having never seen hide nor hair of anyone called Flo, Brenda's at a loss. Maybe the old girl has imaginary friends.

"Six a.m., Mondays, Wednesdays and Fridays. For years."

"Six in the morning. That'll be why I've never seen her."

"She helps me shower and keeps my bedroom and bathroom tidy. It's my one concession to arthritis."

"If I have to pay someone, I'll need to get my hands on more dosh." Brenda absently plays with the diamond bangle on her left wrist, prompting Eadie to speak.

"There's a reasonably honest dealer in the High Street and you're wearing a small fortune right there."

"I was going to flog some other stuff down the nearest pub."

"Goodness me, no. Not only is that likely to have the local constabulary at our door, but you'd only get a pittance in return."

After cleaning up the breakfast things and settling Eadie in her sitting room, Brenda is back in her bedroom. Reaching up, she pats around on the top of the mausoleum of a wardrobe until she hits pay dirt. She grasps the velvet bag and lifts it clear of the carved front piece.

Emptying the contents onto her bed, she's mollified by the number of pieces she's accumulated over the years.

She carefully picks through the pile, sorting them into pieces she loves, those from Martin and thankfully, the biggest pile by far, being the stuff she thinks is shit.

After selecting her most hated pieces from the shit pile, she stuffs the rest of it in the bag and tosses it back on top of the wardrobe. Hopefully, she'll raise enough that she doesn't have to sell something she loves, like herself.

4

The pawnshop is an easy find with its ubiquitous three balls hanging out front as proud as any dog. The interior is hidden behind barred and grimy windows; the accumulation of road dust and old rain on the surface as effective as any frosting or pattern.

Luckily, the small antique shop next door gleams in the half-arsed spring sunlight. Packed to the gunnels with furniture, crockery and paintings, Antique Alley has more than a few animal heads hanging from the walls like a high-flying suburban zoo.

"Kirsten?" says Brenda, to the woman seated behind a glass cabinet crammed with jewellery and small pickpocket-sized knick-knacks, who's engrossed in a doorstop-sized book.

Her head snaps up in response and she slams the book shut. "That's me."

Brenda is all set to flog the ugly jewellery, when the woman says, "Blasted buzzer must be on the blink again."

She clambers off her tall stool, lifts a section in the counter and joins Brenda. "Be with you in a tick, need to tweak it so no one sneaks up on me."

There's no look of censure with this statement, so Brenda doesn't feel the need to apologise for being the sneakee. Not that she would anyway, not when she's about to negotiate with the woman.

After fiddling with a few exposed wires and swiping her hand backwards and forwards in front of it, Kirsten is rewarded with a no-nonsense buzz.

"You must be Brenda," she says, her hand coming up into a shake position as she slips between a roll top desk and a tea trolley.

"I am." Brenda grips the woman's hand and recognises the firm shake of a formidable opponent. "I take it Eadie's phoned."

"She did. She's been dealing with the family for at least thirty years."

At Brenda's look of confusion, she continues, "Dad started the place, my brother and I inherited it when he passed."

This explains the woman's casual dress. It's not that she's untidy; more that she doesn't exude that poker-up-ya-bum edge that a paid employee might. On the plus side, it means there'll be no mucking about when it comes to doing a deal.

"Can I interest you in a cuppa? I'm having one."

"Yeah. Sure. Why not?"

On her first visit to London, Brenda had been gobsmacked at how many gallons of mostly stewed tea the average English person could put away. On that trip, she'd gone from refusing cup after cup, to being the one offering to put the kettle on. Now she's as big a leaf junkie as the most hardened Prisoner of Mother England as the English were known in the colonies. POMS for short.

Brenda is astonished when the owner selects an ornate, flowery set from one of the laden shelves and uses this for their tea break.

Kirsten spots the look. "I sold the last set I was using.

Woman wouldn't take no for an answer. The pot still had bloody tea leaves in it when I wrapped it."

Brenda joins in with Kirsten's laughter. "What do you suppose she thought when she went to make her first pot?"

"With the bargain she drove, she probably used them."

Settled on the sofa of a Queen Anne lounge suite that's part of a display and the tea assembled on a large price-tagged silver tray, they get to business.

"Eadie says you have a couple of pieces that are superfluous to requirements."

"That's one way of putting it," says Brenda, delving into the side pocket of her handbag. She drops the offending items into Kirsten's outstretched hand.

"My word, they're ..."

"Antique," says Brenda, hopeful of shining a monetary light on the necklace and bangle Kirsten is examining closely. She hasn't even seen where the eyeglass came from.

"I was going to say hideous," says Kirsten, dropping the eyeglass back into the front pocket of her jacket. "But worth a bob or two if we remove the stones and melt the rest down."

"That makes sense. They are bloody revolting, aren't they?"

Kirsten drops the offending jewellery onto the silver tray. "I've seen better looking bilious attacks."

After completing the tea ritual, Kirsten weighs the pieces and they agree on a price. At first, Brenda is disappointed but then twigs the sale is in pounds and after calculating the equivalent in Aussie dollars, enjoys the enveloping sense of relief.

"If you get stuck, I'd be happy to take that off your hands," says Kirsten, staring covetously at the diamond bangle.

"Not for sale. Sorry." Brenda's hand covers the piece protectively, "Sentimental value."

"It's also worth a blinking fortune. Might be best to put it somewhere safe?"

Brenda laughs off this warning, sure she can best most

muggers thanks to a childhood spent living in less than salubrious neighbourhoods. Not that this stops her from pushing the bangle further up her wrist and dragging her sleeve down to cover it when she leaves the shop. Thank goodness for winter woollies.

She'd hoped to receive cash for the sale, but Kirsten didn't carry that much money on the premises. Instead, she'd filled out a business-sized cheque and signed it with authority. After a quick trip to the bank to deposit it, Brenda's on her way home. She had planned on heading straight to the second-hand furniture shop but, call it paranoia, she's keen to put Martin's present to her somewhere safe.

She'd only been aware the diamond bracelet had slipped down her wrist again when she saw the bank teller's gaze latch onto it, her eyes widening longingly. Now Brenda's jammed it so tightly up her wrist that it'll take washing-up liquid to get it off.

───

In the sitting room, Brenda can see Eadie's position is unchanged from earlier, although the old lady is asleep and Brenda feels an unaccustomed emotion niggling away at her. For so long she's only had to concentrate on looking after herself, to the exclusion of all others, that it takes a second or two for her to recognise the feeling as compassion.

An element of fear edges in there, too. From what she's heard, Eadie was a goer in her youth. That someone who had been so edgy is reduced to this makes Brenda examine her own life. It would appear that no matter how firmly you grasp life courtesy of some old bloke's balls, this doesn't mean you'll have it by the short and curlies for as long as you feel you deserve.

"Jeez, that's deep," mutters Brenda.

"What's that," says Eadie, moving from sleep to consciousness faster than she can propel any other facet of her life.

"Nothing. Hey, do you have anywhere safe I can stow this?" Brenda holds out her arm.

"I was wondering about that," says Eadie. "There's a perfect place in the cellar."

Listening to the directions Eadie gives her, Brenda can't help but be more astonished at the life Eadie has led. Who the hell has hidden rooms?

On her way to the lower level of the house, Brenda retrieves her jacket from the coat rack. It had been as cold as a witch's tit down there when she'd collected the sherry and she isn't about to freeze her own off, in the process of squirrelling away the bracelet.

Leaving the door at the top of the cellar steps open, Brenda descends into the bone-chilling gloom. A wide arc with her hand is enough to locate the cord dangling from the bare bulb that hangs miserably in the middle of this first room. Following a similar process, Brenda makes her way through various other rooms until she senses she must be under the front door. If anything, it feels even chillier through here and the light flickering from the bulb above her is meagre and bleak.

Thankfully, it's enough for her to see the crack in the shelves in front of her exactly as explained by Eadie although a cursory glance would have missed it. Pulling on the middle shelf, Brenda is rewarded with the whole wall swinging towards her, squealing like a pig at a slaughterhouse in the process.

She stares into the gloom of this hidden chamber and is relieved to spot a cord hanging in the middle of the room. She walks forward and yanks hard on it, but rather than a bulb springing into action, a series of pulleys grind away and something lifts off the floor to her right, scaring the shit out of her.

"Bloody hell!"

Stumbling backwards out of the room, she waits for her heart to worm its way back inside her chest. This takes longer than she would have expected.

"Come on, ya stupid cow. Harden up!"

Shaking the tension out of her limbs, she creeps back into the room, with a lot less verve than her previous visit. Now that she can cross a central light off the list, she stands to one side of the doorway to allow in as much light as possible. Once her eyes have dilated to resemble a cat's, she sees matches and a candle on a shelf on the other side of the doorway.

Lighting this taper, she works her way around the room, igniting every wick she can find. The room goes from super creepy through to majorly creepy, before finally settling on just plain weird.

Brenda knows what the room is for, even if this is the first one she's been in. Although lit by a multitude of candles as it is, it's a toss-up whether the place is one of bondage or satanic ritual. Maybe a mix of both, if the large pool of wax beneath the straps on the rack device at the back of the room is any indication.

A fine layer of dust covers everything in the room, making it obvious the place hasn't been used for a long time. Hiding the bracelet in the spot Eadie recommended will be problematic because it'll leave telltale patches in the dust.

Brenda looks carefully around the room, crossing potential places off as she goes. She's close to running out of nooks and crannies when she stumbles on the perfect place, slipping the bangle over a hook that holds a selection of tattily bejewelled handcuffs and chokers. There's nothing better than hiding it in plain sight.

Find everything okay?" Eadie pounces conversationally on

Brenda as soon as she swings through the kitchen door into the hallway.

"And some," says Brenda, walking along the hall and into the sitting room.

"The dungeon could come in handy with the new setup."

"Might be best if you take those classes. With my luck of late, I'd end up relieving some old codger of his tackle."

Eadie winces before admitting Brenda might be right on this point. "Hopefully, your gals will be able to get away with a simple bit of slap and tickle rather than anything too advanced."

"Right," says Brenda, reluctantly. "Do you have everything you need? I'm off to check out furniture shops."

While Brenda is happy to buy second-hand furniture, the mattresses must be new. Having experienced bed bugs first hand as a child, it's not something she wants to inflict on any of her students, let alone anyone who is honourable in name only. While the plan is for any shagging to take place off the premises, who knew what might happen.

"Before you go out and get everything, it might pay to have your students lined up."

"Good point. Friggin' useless to get this lot," says Brenda, tapping her pen against the pad that features an ever-growing list, "if I can't convince any chicks to sign up."

"We'll need to give thought to recruitment grounds," says Eadie, staring into space as though working her way around an imaginary London and ticking off spots where likely targets would hang out.

"I reckon I hit pubs in the snobby areas."

"Goodness me, no. The best options are more likely to be society gatherings."

"Sure, once we've got the girls trained up a bit, but if we want to find sheilas who have no bloody clue what they're doing wrong, pubs will be best."

"Of course!" Eadie shakes her head as though she's unable to believe she's made such a rookie mistake. "Maybe around Belgravia?"

———

It takes Brenda a couple of trips into town to select the pubs. They're full of the men who've spawned the Hooray Henrys who gad about the better neighbourhoods as though they own them, which they probably will one day. Women are thin on the ground in the two establishments that make the final cut, with those who are there having a hungry, hopeful look, the sort of mien that has old blokes looking for their walking sticks in readiness to scarper.

Brenda decides a Friday night is best for her recruitment drive. Bloody useless for picking up old guys, but perfect for finding girls who are trying and failing.

———

Pushing open the doors that bisect the building's corner, Brenda is struck by a barrage of society accents and a fug of cigar and pipe smoke. With its base notes of Deep Heat and dodgy prostates, the atmosphere is injurious.

A quick scan of the bar is all it takes for Brenda to spot a potential student.

The girl doesn't manage tiny, only short, a height that fails at cute. Her red hair clashes woefully with a pink suit that wouldn't be out of place on Barbara Cartland. The contrast is awful. The suit is badly cut and hides any curves the girl might have, which doesn't help.

The redhead has latched onto an old bloke who's actually wearing a monocle.

"Jeez, he's like something out of a Jeeves' story," mutters Brenda, quietly.

Given the number of hi-fi-sized hearing aids on show, she needn't bother. It also explains why everyone is shouting at each other.

Circling the bulk of the crowd, she makes her way to the end of the bar and orders a water. As far as she's concerned, this is work and she'll be damned if she's going to fork out for sugary crap that'll only have her breaking out in zits the size of small change.

Glass in hand; she sidles her way through the crowd unobtrusively. She's dressed down for this occasion, wearing a severe black trouser suit and high-necked starched white blouse. With her long, dark hair scraped back into a no-nonsense ponytail, she looks school teacherish. No makeup is the final touch on this no-frills ensemble.

It's only when a couple of old chaps check her out with interest that Brenda realises the disciplinarian edge to her get-up might appeal to those who like a jolly good spanking. Luckily, they assume a submissive posture when she glares at them, allowing her to move past without further interaction.

Edging up behind Red and the Jeeves' character, Brenda settles in to listen to their conversation. It takes but a few moments of earwigging to confirm that Red is Irish and bloody useless at hooking, let alone reeling in any male. The girl offers to buy the next round and monocle man accedes; it's all Brenda can do not to call the girl an idiot and him a cheap prick.

Brenda spots her opportunity and follows Red when she goes for the drinks, even managing to squeak in next to the girl at the bar. Hearing what's ordered, she's pissed off and surprised in turn. The old guy is drinking Scotch older than the girl, who's settled for lime and soda. Hearing what the bartender asks as payment for the two drinks, she comprehends the girl's Spartan choice doubtless has more to do with fiscal constraints than any desire to keep her wits about her.

"That's bloody expensive," says Brenda, tapping the glass of amber fluid in which the tide is sitting at full low, never mind halfway out.

"It's the turd one, too." Reinforcing the financial strain this is imposing, she has a nervous look in her purse.

"Has he forked out for any drinks yet?" says Brenda, unable to keep the astonishment off her face or to hide her knowledge of the participants.

"He left his wallet at home."

"Sure he did," says Brenda, her tone reeking of disbelief.

Disgruntlement is writ large on the girl's face, but before she can voice her feelings, Brenda pushes on.

"You're going about it the wrong way."

"What do you mean?" bristles the girl.

"Watch and learn," says Brenda, before swinging back towards the cheapskate.

Red totters in Brenda's wake, and nearly runs into her, when Brenda stops halfway there.

"I'm Brenda Munro, by the way."

"Paula Dunphy."

Names sorted, the two girls swap places and press on, before popping up in a small gap next to Red's target. Red introduces Brenda as an old friend and the three of them settle into amicable chitchat. It doesn't take much gentle grilling on Brenda's part to work out the old guy is bloody loaded and the bar is a regular haunt, leaving her in no doubt the reason he isn't carrying a wallet is because he runs a tab.

Seeing he's close to finishing the dribble of liquid gold left in his glass, Brenda deliberately sculls the rest of her water and looks at him expectantly. While he's staring at the ground to avoid eye contact, Brenda indicates to Paula that she should drink up. She does so promptly and even crunches loudly enough on an ice cube for the target's head to pop up.

He still doesn't offer to buy, so Brenda goes for the jugular. "I'm so sorry. It must be so hard getting by on a pension."

"A pension," splutters the cheapskate, one foot already in the stirrup of the saddle on his high horse. "I'll have you know, I've left—"

Brenda cuts him off before he can trot out the wallet-at-home line.

"Goodness. How embarrassing. We didn't realise."

At his look of utter confusion, Brenda goes in for the kill. "Some establishments can be so finicky these days about running a tab."

She deliberately leaves the rest of this sentiment dangling in the middle of the three of them, but it's at eye level and bloody hard for him to ignore.

His face flushes at the realisation that if he goes for either of the options Brenda's offered him, he firmly labels himself as poor, rather than the cheap bastard he is. It's a step too far.

"What are you drinking?" he grumbles.

Brenda orders a double of the same Scotch he's drinking. Paula does the same, and his face takes on the hue of under-cooked rhubarb with the eye muscles clutching tenaciously to the monocle twitching enough to lose their grip, leaving the eyepiece dangling uselessly on its safety cord.

While he's on his way to the bar, Brenda turns to Paula "And that is how it's done."

"That was amazing. This is the second time I've met him and he's pulled the wallet con both times."

Looking through the crowd, Brenda sees he's at the bar, placing his order. The drinks safely poured, Brenda suggests she and Paula go somewhere quieter.

"But what about our drinks?"

"That's not a drink. It's nail polish remover."

"Then why?"

"I suspect it's the most expensive drink on offer," says Brenda, grinning broadly before taking Paula's hand and dragging the girl towards the door. They're pushing their way through it when they look back to see the old chap standing where they'd recently been, three glasses held awkwardly against his chest, scanning the bar looking for them. When he finds them, they both blow kisses in his direction. Realising their actions have been identical, they burst out laughing.

The doors are still swinging closed when Brenda sees him knock back one of the glasses of scotch with a complete disregard for the number of years and amount of effort involved in its production. She suspects the other two will follow in quick succession.

Convincing Paula to sign on as the first student is surprisingly easy and Brenda knows this is all down to her demonstrating the correct technique for dealing with an older monied gent. Seeing something first hand is always an easier sell than gabbing on about theory.

"When can I move in?"

"Two weeks. I need to finalise a few things first." A few things? There's a shit load needed to get those rooms looking less like something out of Oliver Twist.

"Great. I'll give notice at work tomorrow and tell my landlady to shove it the day I move."

"Notice?"

"Well, I haven't got any holidays owing and it's a shit job anyway."

"What about the boarding house?"

"It's a flea pit."

Brenda bites hard on her lip to stop herself from speaking. No pressure to make it work, then?

5

The next evening Brenda dresses as though on the pull and has to bat the old guys away when they settle like flies at a barbecue, but it also assists in the recruitment of her second student, Stephanie McLean.

Stef is the wrong side of six feet in her flats and lacking in curves; she's also subconsciously erected enough safety barriers that she resembles roadworks. Her accent is Bow Bells and rough enough to have Brenda feeling positively cultured in comparison, even with her tendency to swear.

Stef hasn't been doing too badly and can at least get the older crowd to buy her drinks and the occasional meal, but not much more than that. A quick look at the bracelet she's jangling ostentatiously and Brenda can tell by the green stain on Stef's wrist that it doesn't have two carats to rub together.

All it takes to arrange for Stef to come to the house to check things out before committing is to inch up the sleeve on her tight-fitting top, to reveal the diamond and platinum monster that she'd retrieved from the dungeon earlier that evening.

This takes place in the ladies – testament to Brenda absorbing the paranoia shown by others that her bracelet is too expensive to wear as an everyday piece. The way Kirsten at Antique Alley had gone on about it, made it sound as though she should employ an armed guard.

———

Finding the third student proves more problematic, to the point Brenda is teetering on whether to give up or go ahead on the off chance she'll fill the final vacancy before the start of term. She and Eadie had both laughed fit to bust after Eadie came up with that scholastic name. For Brenda, who had hated school passionately, it was especially hilarious to know that she'll be in the position of teacher. Or is that teacher of positions? Maybe both.

"You should go ahead," says Eadie, nursing her third sherry of the evening.

"But with only two of them paying board, I barely cover the cost of Flo. No point doing it if I'm running at a loss."

"You've got a week, plenty of time to find another gal. Maybe try other establishments."

Brenda had stuck to the same two pubs she'd originally selected, but could see the wisdom of looking further afield.

"To hell with it. I'm gonna do it. Maybe go down-market with the pub and get someone with grand ideas."

———

Armed with details of a suitable shop, next morning, Brenda is off on a buying spree. By the end of the day, she's purchased beds, wardrobes, bedside tables and dressers for three students. She's also kitted out the 'common room' with a nice lounge suite, coffee table and sideboard that she's bought off Kirsten at mates' rates. The furniture is old enough to pass as antique but not old enough to attract antique price tags which,

Brenda suspects is why the proprietor of Antique Alley wanted rid of them. The mattresses and linen are new.

Knowing everything will arrive in two short days, Brenda gets on with recommissioning the rooms on the second floor. They'd already been stripped bare years before her arrival, making them easier to clean than if they'd been chock full of half a forest of furniture. She's also relieved that Eadie has said she's spoken to Flo, her char, about helping with this mammoth task.

Brenda is scrubbing the windows in the future common room at the front when she spies a rain slicker making its way along the pavement before the coat turns and walks up the front path. Brenda knows there's a human under all that hurricane-strength yellow, but from this angle, it's impossible to see who.

Stopping polishing, she climbs off her chair and is on the first-floor landing when she sees their visitor walking up the stairs.

"Hello, love. I'm Flo and you must be Brenda," says the woman, by way of greeting.

Her hair is pure white and cut pixie-short, while the overly large dark-framed glasses magnify her eyes to more than twice standard issue, so that they dominate her face. But if she lives up to her reputation, they also allow her to spot dust at thirty paces.

The woman's short enough that her head just reaches Brenda's chest; Brenda wonders where you'd buy child-sized flowery housedresses like the one hanging off Flo. It's topped with a clashing pattern apron, the bib of which is as flat as the iron had left it, suggesting Flo struggles to fill an A cup.

Her stockings, unlike the woman, are substantial; three-hundred denier at the least, with none of their elastic properties in use. Flo's sneakers are also on the loose side, floating on her feet and providing enough ballast that she could stay upright in a blizzard if she wanted to, or simply take in a spot of skiing. While small like Eadie, there all comparisons end. This woman exudes physical strength and capability.

She grips Brenda's hands in a no-nonsense shake, leaving her fingers feeling like they've been holding fully-laden plastic shopping bags for a couple of hours. The woman's fingers have the characteristics of high-tensile steel cables.

"We're up on the second floor. I've got all the cleaning crap up there," says Brenda, flexing her hands.

"Let's get to it." Flo rubs her claw-like mitts together before shooting up the stairs at a speed that leaves Brenda's head spinning.

"I hope she cleans as fast as she climbs," says Brenda, to the empty landing.

A quick look on the second floor finds Flo tutting over Brenda's bucket of cleaning gear.

"You weren't kidding when you called this lot crap, were you? This won't do at all." Flo shakes her head slowly to reinforce what she must consider second-rate equipment for a professional like herself.

"Sorry. That was all I could find downstairs," says Brenda, unable to believe she's apologising to a cleaning lady about the tools of the trade.

"Not your fault, love. I hide all the good stuff. Back in a jiffy."

Brenda is alone seconds after this is uttered. "Good stuff?"

She thinks about it for a second, but cannot visualise what this would equate to in home cleaning products. Unable to come up with anything, she clambers back on the chair to continue scrubbing away at the years of grime on the common room windows.

Flo doesn't reappear and Brenda doesn't go looking for her. More than likely she's been delayed by the Queen of Sherry on the ground floor.

The windows are clean enough to have doubled the light in the room and Brenda readies herself to work on those in the room on the other side of the landing.

Her arms and shoulders are aching at the unaccustomed work and if it weren't for the impending furniture deliveries, she'd give all this sodding cleaning a miss for the rest of the day. She hasn't worked this hard in living memory. If ever.

Shrugging away her stiffness, Brenda picks up her bucket of not-up-to-snuff cleaning supplies and trudges across to the other room.

The windows are sparkling. In fact, they're so clean it doesn't even look as though there's glass in them. The side windows overlooking the drive are in a similar state. The same goes for the bedroom at the back on the left.

Brenda runs into Flo in the back-right bedroom where the cleaning demon is finishing up the last pane of glass. She's polishing it furiously with what looks like screwed up newspaper.

"Yesterday's Sun. Best polishing cloth going," says Flo, before giving the pane one final flourish and stepping back to check on the overall result.

Satisfied, she swings in Brenda's direction. "Right. What shall we do next? Walls?"

"I need to have another go at the windows I've finished. Mine aren't as shiny as these."

"I'll go give them a buff with the sports section."

Flo whips past Brenda, at a speed no slower than when she'd first arrived. Just watching the woman makes Brenda feel more tired than ever.

"What the hell's she on?" Brenda leaves the room with a bemused expression that's settling in for a long stay.

Flo never does slow down. Just keeps up at a speed worthy of the Road Runner. Her energy levels don't flag either. Brenda gasps in relief when Flo finally jumps up from her hands and knees, tosses her scrubbing brush in the large metal bucket that's been her constant companion and says, "Righty ho, love. I need to 'ead 'ome. My Bert will 'ave my tea on the table bang on six."

She and the bucket disappear seconds later, leaving an exhausted Brenda in their wake. With the need to keep up removed, Brenda sinks in a pile on the floor, uncaring that it's wet. Her hands feel raw and her knees as if someone's given them a right going over with steel-capped boots. She can't focus on any other individual body parts, with them having merged into a goo of knackered tendons and overstretched muscles. She's sure even her bones are hurting.

It's only with a conscious effort that she prises herself off the floorboards and takes herself to bed for twenty, no make that thirty, winks before dinner. She leaves the bucket of dirty water where it is, knowing she's got her hands full simply getting downstairs.

Waking the next morning, Brenda finds she's still dressed from the day before, reeking of cleaning products, old sweat and hard graft. Even turning her head to see what time it is, takes more energy than she's ready to spare. Focusing on her bedside clock is also hard work, but she's rewarded with seeing it's only seven.

"Thank god for that!" she says to Charlie who's climbed onto her chest and is sniffing her experimentally. He stops and stares fixedly at the ceiling, and it takes Brenda a moment to hear what it is that's caught his attention.

"The woman's a machine."

Each thump abrades Brenda's conscience until she's ready to scream. She considers taking a shower to wash away the smell of pine and the stiffness from her muscles, but isn't sure she can stand the weight of all that water without giving into gravity.

"Want to go and make me a coffee?"

Charlie's response to this request is to look at her as if she's nuts before getting on with his morning ablutions.

After a stiff-legged trip down the stairs, Brenda stands in the kitchen, trembling. Dammit, her legs are only just holding her upright. She's staggering around getting her breakfast when Eadie's voice breaks through the wall of pain.

"You didn't try keeping up with her, did you?"

Brenda drops her head limply in response.

"Goodness, Flo could clean for England. You must be shattered."

6

After breakfast and going back to bed for a couple more hours' sleep, Brenda feels almost human enough to get back to cleaning. Twenty minutes soaking in the Olympic-sized bath, with water hot enough to de-bristle a pig, and the worst of her aches and pains have gone.

She needn't have bothered getting out of bed.

"What do you mean, you've finished?"

Brenda watches Flo pick up her supposedly top-of-the line cleaning gear, guarding it as if Brenda is about to sneak off with something. Given the lack of labels, she can only surmise the various concoctions are of Flo's own design and involve lash-ings of sulphuric acid. No one can clean as fast as this woman. Dusting with paint stripping thrown in for good measure is more like it. Brenda does have to admit, though, the rooms positively sparkle.

The floors are gleaming but need carpets, because even with all Flo's acid-fuelled elbow grease, the pale patches where rugs had once sat are still discernible.

The only thing to do before the furniture rocks up the following day is to put the curtains back up. The windows in the various rooms are enormous and having seen the size of the drapes in her own room, she knows installing them will be exhausting.

It's a huge relief when, as she's taking her cleaning products away to no doubt hide them, Flo informs Brenda that she'll be staying on for the rest of the day and she knows which curtains and rugs go in which rooms.

"Why did Eadie take them away in the first place?" says Brenda when they take a break between loads from the cellar. That the break is purely for Brenda's benefit grates, but she's unable to keep up with the indefatigable Flo without them.

"Was worried about moffs getting at 'em," says Flo, ripping the plastic away from a pair of minty green curtains, signalling an end to their break.

The smell of camphor hits Brenda and she knows those curtains are not only free of 'moffs' now, but they're safe for another ten years, at least. The second floor is officially out of bounds to moths and asthmatics. Make that anything with lungs. Brenda hopes the toxicity dies down overnight.

By the end of the day, curtains hang at all the windows and the rugs have been unrolled in the rooms, although their ends are still curling in a trip hazard. Brenda hopes they'll settle down before the furniture arrives.

Next morning, Cockney chatter interrupts the filthy dream Brenda is having about Stefano. This pisses her off no end. First, that she'd been dreaming about the idiot who has squandered her money on glorified pet food and second, the dream sex had been getting interesting. Dragging a spare pillow over her head does nothing to staunch the volume of Flo's badgering instructions to the furniture delivery crew. She can't help but smirk when Flo questions one chap's strength and offers to help. Even through the barrier of the heavy wooden bedroom door and a flock-load of feathers, Brenda can hear the male outrage at this suggestion.

Huffing with annoyance, she throws the pillow to one side. All these early mornings are a pain in the arse. She's not at her best before the crack of ten thirty.

"What the hell time is it, anyway?" she grumbles to Charlie, who is oblivious to the banging, crashing and swearing currently coming from the stairs.

Groping about on the bedside table, she finds her small clock and picks it up and holds it in front of her face. Only after wiping the sleep from her eyes with her other hand can she focus.

"Eight-o-bleeding clock."

From her experience so far, London didn't stir much before nine. To get a delivery this early in the sodding day was unheard of.

"Screw it. No way I'm getting up this bloody early."

She clunks the clock back down on the bedside table and rolls away from the door, dragging her pillow up and over to encase her head. She holds it firmly in place, relieved this takes the edge off what she imagines is complete bedlam out in the hallway.

Waking much later, she's overjoyed to find the house blissfully quiet. It remains this way while she showers and maintains its silence when she walks downstairs to breakfast. Entering the kitchen, Brenda finds Eadie and Flo talking up a storm over a cuppa.

With Charlie's breakfast sorted, Brenda sets about getting her own. Her brain teeming with random thoughts, it's not until she drops into a chair at the table that she focuses on their conversation. It takes a moment of concentration before she can work out what they're chattering about.

Rather than discussing denture cream and support hose, the subject is menus for a week. Eventually up to speed, Brenda interrupts.

"Are you talking about meals for the girls? Because I sure as shit can't make the crap you're talking about."

"Good lord, we're not letting you near the kitchen," says Eadie, "Ptomaine poisoning is the last thing we need."

"I'm not that bad!"

"It's not your calling, dear," says Eadie, patting the back of Brenda's hand to soften the blow.

"I'm bloody useless in the kitchen, too," says Flo, chortling. "Bert won't let me do anything but the dishes. Apart from porridge that is. It's my speciality."

"Then who are we gonna get to knock together the highfalutin grub you two were yacking about?"

"Bert," say Eadie and Flo in unison.

"Bert. As in your Bert?" Brenda looks at Flo for confirmation.

"That's the one. Retired, but he's a dab hand in the kitchen. Going barmy at home. He'd be 'appy to make lunches and dinners."

Brenda's chomped through a second round of toast with tea to suit, before they've finalised all the details around meals and cleaning. Brenda's relieved to have all the hard graft taken off her hands and suspects it'll be nice to be looked after, even if she is the one paying for it all.

It's Friday night and Stef and Paula are due to move in on Monday. Brenda looks at herself critically in the mirror; this is her third choice of outfit and she thinks she might finally have cracked it.

The denim jumpsuit is designer but not so high-end as to stand out like the proverbially damaged digit. Black platform shoes and a fitted black bomber jacket complete the look. The whole outfit cost a fortune, but is understated enough not to draw too much attention in the pub she's selected for tonight's recruitment sortie.

Checking the contents of her handbag, a beeping out front catches her attention. That's the one drawback of the City Barge pub, it's out of the way on the Strand on the Green next to the Thames River; catching the tube there, or even a bus, isn't possible. On the plus side, it'll be full of people looking for action as it isn't in the main swing of things.

The cab is of the black variety, so the driver has undergone 'The Knowledge', meaning the trip is completed quickly, avoiding traffic because the driver knows all the shortcuts. The routes taken by the independent mini cabs tended to be more 'scenic' in nature.

Pushing open the glass-panelled front door to the pub, Brenda is embraced with a wall of warmth and sound, with the former more welcoming than the latter.

The bar feels vastly different from when she'd scoped it out earlier in the day. Gone are the middle classes having a quiet lunch or beverage. It's filled to the rafters with people washing away the angst of their working week. The more stressful the week, the greater the number of pints.

The crowd is balanced in terms of gender, meaning the odds of Brenda finding their third pupil have been tipped in her favour.

Moving into the mêlée, Brenda is careful to skirt around any big groups and deliberately ignores eye contact. Her hearing, on the other hand, is at its highest setting, eavesdropping on any conversations nearby.

Because the bar is so full, she doesn't bother getting a drink, instead completing slow laps of the room until she's isolated the best girl to approach. She wades over to the bar and orders a single G&T in a tall glass; alcoholic, but not enough to cloud reason.

She moves through the mob, inching her way closer and

closer to her target. The girl looks similar in height to herself, but Brenda can't yet see if her quarry is in heels or flats. The girl's blonde curls have an electrocuted edge to them, with the strength of curl meaning no matter how hard she tries, she'll never end up with longer hair, just a bigger afro. And while that might look good on Michael Jackson, it looks like shit in this instance. Without it, the girl could look stunning. As it is, her face is so crowded by hair, it looks a couple of sizes too small for her body.

Her most striking feature, her large, dark blue eyes, appear to struggle to take in the world.

Making out she's been pushed from behind, Brenda stumbles into a gap next to the mountain of hair, glaring over her shoulder at an imaginary assailant, before turning back to the girl. "Sorry about that. The bloody place is like a zoo."

"Isn't it just? I've already worn a couple of drinks." She looks at her clothes in disgust, prompting Brenda to follow her gaze.

The girl's outfit is as hideous as the hair. A couple of drinks sloshed down the front have probably improved it even if it's hard to see any evidence of spills. They picked dark tweed for school uniforms with good reason. The twinset atop the travesty of a skirt is dark tan, though it's edging dangerously close to poo in colour and Brenda's long lost gran had worn a fake suede jacket similar to the one hanging without benefit of darts from the girl's boobs. If she has a waist, Brenda can't tell.

It also explains why the girl is alone, with any males in the vicinity making sure their backs are towards her, even if this means closely examining pillars and walls.

Maybe this girl is a step too far? She doesn't look to be particularly interested in attracting the attention of anyone, let alone keeping hold of them and relieving them of coin by way of lavish meals, jewellery and holidays abroad.

Maybe Brenda could simply work on getting this girl a date. Would someone even pay for that sort of help?

For Brenda, who's never had trouble finding dates, ever, this looks like a long shot, but she's conscious that without this third pupil, she faces having to use her 'tits up' money, or worse, cancelling everything and – heaven forfend – getting a job.

Sure the girl needs help, but would she be willing to sign up simply to achieve that goal?

Yes. She would.

In fact, Rosie Keeler, as she's introduced herself, is so keen to sign up that Brenda regrets her snap decision. The girl is puppy-about-to-go-for-a-walk eager and literally bouncing on the spot, although how she achieves any elevation with those ugly brogues is one for the scientists.

The misgivings pile up when Rosie lets it slip that she's still living at home. The last thing Brenda needs is concerned parents snooping around.

"This might not be the best place for you," says Brenda. She doesn't get any further, instead having to deal with Rosie, who looks to be close to tears.

"I'll tell Mummy I'm staying with friends in the country." Rosie's tone is pleading with an edge of desperation.

Brenda opens her mouth to continue letting the girl down gently, something that's out of character for her.

"I'll tell them anything you want, so long as you take me on."

Brenda thinks Rosie's handwringing is over the top but sees the girl isn't even aware of her actions. Instead, the girl's whole attention is focused on her. Jeez, talk about pressure.

Holding up her hand to stop the avalanche of entreaties and promises, Brenda closes her eyes to give herself space to think. At most, all the girl needs is a makeover and lessons on how to chat to guys. A month tops should do it. Time enough for her to scout around for another proper student.

"Okay, you're—"

Rosie throws herself at Brenda, wrapping her free arm tight around Brenda's neck, choking off anything else she might have to add. Crunchy curls smother Brenda and they wear each other's drinks.

Disentangled, Brenda scribbles her details on the back of a beer mat and hands it over to Rosie. This is quickly tucked in the inside pocket of a truly battered handbag when a couple of Sloane Rangers shove in next to them.

Brenda turns to give them an earful.

"Rosie, we're ready to go now," says one, a slight slur in evidence.

"Drink up, driver," says the other. No slur here, just a lisp that appears more affectation than impediment.

Rosie looks at her glass but the amount left there is pathetic.

"Come on, you're nearly done. We're tired," says the first.

"Friends of yours?" says Brenda to Rosie, drawing the attention of the other two.

"Sorry. Brenda this is Gemma and Marie, old school chums. Marie, Gemma, this is Brenda, ah, a friend of the family."

"A friend? Really?" says number two, her voice purposefully spiteful.

Brenda looks at the new arrivals closely. Dressed like someone's auntie on the pull, belligerent and ready-to-rumble. No, as tempting as that might be, there were far better methods of revenge.

"I'd better go," says Rosie, apologetically, ready to follow in the wake of the other two who are barging their way through the crowd towards a back exit.

"For god's sake, don't say anything to them about what you're up to!"

"But I have to give them my number, they might want me to drive them somewhere," says Rosie, doubt playing in her eyes.

"Tough. They'll have to deal with it."

"But."

"If you leave the course to ferry those two bitches anywhere, our deal is over."

Brenda knows she's coming across as scary but thinks the only way she'll stop Rosie giving into the demands of the other two is by being a truckload scarier than they are.

The promise that Rosie makes is so solemn that Brenda knows she'll keep to it. The girl leaves looking like a whipped puppy, although Brenda isn't sure if this is down to her threat or the 'friends' who are continuing to carp from the other side of the bar that she's not moving fast enough.

Mission complete, Brenda goes in search of a cab and finally gets home after seeing more of west London than necessary, courtesy of a minicab driver who apparently has less idea than she does of where he's going.

"How'd you get on?" says Eadie, when Brenda walks into the sitting room.

Brenda fills her in on the latest recruit and is worried when the old lady shares her misgivings. Explaining the way in which Gemma and Marie treated Rosie as their personal lackey, she too thinks Brenda's plan for revenge is perfect.

7

R osie, ever eager, is the first student to arrive. The travesty of a suit she's wearing lets Brenda know she'll have her work cut out. Funny, she'd never thought of mould as a colour, but it's one that does sweet bugger-all for the girl.

There's not much chitchat on the climb to the second floor, although Rosie gushes politely when shown her room and carefully places her green leatherette suitcase on the end of the bed.

"It's so quaint. It's like a doll's house."

Stef arrives next and is as different from Rosie as is possible. She comments on everything, knowing to the penny what anything and everything would make if you flogged it 'dahn' the market. Even Charlie, who's sitting outside Brenda's bedroom door, has a value, although Stef doesn't confirm whether this is as sausages, a pair of slippers or a pet.

She too is pleased with her room, even if the 'apples' might get tedious. Flo confirms later that rather than referring to fruit, the girl is using a short form of Cockney rhyming slang for stairs. Apples and pears if you're being formal, apparently.

Last to arrive is Paula, red hair a bird's nest and face flushed to match. "Bejeezus, sorry I'm late. Got off a stop too early and decided to leg it rather than wait for the next tube."

Brenda's wondering how the girl has managed to lug all her stuff from Turnham Green when she spots the wheeled suitcase waiting behind the girl, like a patient hound. It's not until the girl is dragging the case into the hall that Brenda sees it's actually a bog-standard case with a couple of roller skates taped to the bottom with bucket-loads of electrical tape.

After a brief introduction, Brenda leaves the girls to unpack and get to know each other before going to check on Bert in the kitchen. She finds him whistling away as he goes about setting up everything how he likes it, in tandem with getting dinner underway. With nothing for her to do, she leaves him to it.

Brenda's pottering around in her bedroom, enjoying time to herself before lessons the next day, when a loud gong echoes through the house. A quick check of her watch and she knows exactly what it is, even though she hasn't heard it before.

There's a festive feel in the formal dining room when Brenda enters. Eadie reigns supreme at the head of the table with the three girls already having claimed what Brenda thinks will be their assigned seats for the rest of their stay. Brenda takes the only spare spot set to the right of Eadie. Candlelight flickers on cutlery that has been recently polished and Brenda suspects no one other than Flo could have achieved that level of shine.

"Why on earth are we eatin' so blimmin' early?" says Stef.

"Bert needs to be away at a reasonable hour and if we eat this early it also means we don't end up off our tits if we go to an evening event," says Brenda, by way of explanation.

"But surely a lot of the functions we'll be attending will be catered?" says Paula.

"They are," says Eadie, "but one thing you'll learn about the rich is that while they're happy to provide plenty of turps, there's never enough food to mop it up."

Rosie doesn't say anything. Instead, her gaze follows the conversation around the table, taking everything in and processing it.

During the meal, they all get to know each other better, but it takes coaxing from all of them to get anything out of Rosie. It's something Brenda will have to work hard on, if the girl's to have a hope in hell of getting a date, let alone getting laid.

But I can't cut it! Gemma and Marie say it's my best feature." Rosie's hands are gripping her mountain of hair as though to stop anyone nicking it.

"I'll bet they did," says Brenda.

"They're bleedin' lyin' fru their teeth, whoever they are," says Stef.

"Not working for you," pipes up Paula.

Seeing Rosie's eyes fill, close to spilling over, Brenda continues. "Your eyes are your best feature."

"Really?" says Stef, "didn't realise she 'ad any."

Brenda walks casually behind Rosie and after disengaging the girl's hands from the pillow stuffing of a hair do, scrapes the hair away from the girl's face.

"Wow!" says Paula.

"Flipping 'eck," says Stef.

"What?" says Rosie, expecting the worst.

"They're amazin'," says Stef.

"Gorgeous," confirms Paula.

"And hidden by this lot," says Brenda, yanking gently on a couple of handsful of static frizz.

With Rosie finally conceding that she could do with removing a few split ends, Brenda phones Kirsten at the antique shop and asks for a recommendation. While Eadie is a mine of information, she's not up to speed on cutting-edge hairdressing.

According to Kirsten there isn't anything local, unless you're after an overcooked perm. Something Rosie doesn't need. Fortunately, the shop owner knows of a couple of other places for them to try.

"I can't go to the place in Richmond," says Rosie, emphatically.

"Why not?" Brenda favours this establishment, as it is only a couple of stops away on the tube.

"It's where I go now," says Rosie.

"Bloody 'ell. You pay for that?" says Stef, undiplomatically.

At the flat, narrowed look that Rosie's eyes take on, Paula backs up Stef's sentiment. "She does have a point."

"Hang on a second," says Brenda. "Let me guess, Gemma or Marie always go with you to the hairdresser, don't they?"

"No!" says Rosie, indignantly.

"But?" prompts Brenda.

After a long and awkward pause with the others all staring at her, Rosie is forced to respond. "Fine. The hairdresser is Gemma's cousin."

"I'm startin' to dislike these two," says Stef.

"They sound mean," says Paula.

"I've met them and they're complete cows," says Brenda, because she knows Rosie is too soft to say anything. "Okay, Hammersmith it is."

Brenda calls the salon and because it's Tuesday, there's an appointment available that afternoon.

Shelly's Hair & Nails is within spitting distance of the tube station. Brenda accompanies Rosie for the trip and Stef and Paula stay home with Eadie to work on their elocution. Paula simply needs to soften her accent so it's easier to understand, while Stef's propensity to drop consonants and strangle vowels make her sound more like a 'barra' boy than someone able to mix and mingle at society events. Brenda's unsure how much Eadie will be able to improve on that.

Pushing open the glass front door to the salon activates a string of tiny bells that tinkle their arrival to the owner.

Brenda's not often surprised, but she is now. With a recommendation from the middle-class Kirsten, Brenda isn't expecting someone with a punk hairstyle and outfit to match. If the salon hadn't been recommended, she'd execute a swift U-turn and it's only by clamping her hand on Rosie's arm that she stops her pupil from doing exactly this.

"Bleeding hell! What happened?" says Shelly, if the label on her apron is correct, when Brenda drags Rosie out from behind her.

Seeing Rosie's hackles rising, Brenda wades in. "It's a natural curl, there's just too much of it. Needs a trim."

"Right. A trim," says Shelly, weakly.

"Yes! I don't want any more than this off." Rosie holds up a hand with her thumb and forefinger indicating that removal of more than a millimetre or two in length will be met with a complete meltdown.

"We can leave the length. I'll thin it out so the curls are more defined," says Shelly, in an effort to allay Rosie's fears.

"Yes!" says Rosie, relaxing a bit.

After Shelly, who looks to be a 'sole proprietor' in the truest sense, shampoos and conditions Rosie's hair, Rosie settles into the only chair in the salon. It's an antique job that looks as though it started life in an establishment with a red and white striped pole out front.

"There's no mirror!" Visibly horrified, Rosie tries to regain her feet.

Shelly puts a hand firmly on either shoulder and holds her in place. "Relax. I can see what I'm doing without a mirror," she says, laughing.

This does nothing to soothe Rosie's nerves. "It's just that ... I don't want ..." Her words peter out and she's unable to finish.

"Oh, I get it." Shelly spins the chair so her client is facing her. "This is how I like to have my hair. That doesn't mean it's the only style I know. Besides, you'd never pull it off."

Brenda can't help but smile at this sentiment, but keeps looking at the magazine she's flicking through. Better to leave Shelly and Rosie to sort this out on their own.

Attention caught by an article, Brenda is absorbed and it's not until she no longer hears snipping, that she looks up. She's gobsmacked at the amount of hair on the floor under the barber's chair. She knows it's all Rosie's because the floor had been pristine when they'd entered.

Even with all of that lopped off, Rosie still has a reasonable amount left on her head. The difference now is the curls have room to bounce and aren't in danger of choking each other to death. Shelly swings Rosie in her direction with a triumphant "Tadaa!" and Brenda's amazed at the difference the cut has made. For the first time, it's possible to see Rosie's eyes and they look gorgeous, in a face that is in proportion to the hair above and the body below.

"How does it look?" Rosie rummages through her handbag without waiting for a response, finally pulling out a compact in every sense of the word. She flips it open and attempts to see herself in it. A huff of frustration informs the others that it's not up to the task.

Without a word, Shelly steps around the chair and opens a decorative panel on the wall, revealing a large mirror. She swings the chair around so that Rosie can see her new do in its entirety.

"Wow!" says Rosie, leaning forward in the chair, slowly getting to her feet, turning her head first to one side, then the other. Eventually, she's close enough that she bumps her nose into the mirror and pulls back sharply. There follows an interrogatory lifting of her eyebrows as she looks at Shelly's reflection in the mirror.

"Because this way, I get to cut your hair how I think it should be, not how you think it should be."

Brenda can see that Rosie is about to argue this approach, but when Shelly gives her a hand mirror, she spins so she can check out the back of her new haircut. That it looks as fabulous as the front is borne out by the lack of any further arguments.

Rosie pays for the cut, and Shelly suggests to her and Brenda that they pop next door and see Alison before heading home.

Rosie is a little more compliant entering the shop next door, but when it becomes apparent the clothes in there are all second-hand, she digs her heels in, even after it's pointed out the stock is vintage and designer. Brenda's also impressed the place doesn't smell of old people. Breathing in deeply, all she can smell is the faint whiff of dry-cleaning fluid.

Brenda fingers the cuff of Rosie's fake suede jacket, unable to hide her look of disgust. "You mean to tell me, you've had this from new? Maybe Alison will let you swap it for something less octogenarian?"

"I can't do that. It was my gran's."

"Sentimental value."

"More like she'd go mental if I got rid of it."

Brenda, who had been assuming the old lady had already snuffed it, is about to voice her opinion on this before deeming it a complete waste of bloody time. The silent approach works when coupled with gentle persuasion from Alison, the shop's owner, to at least give a couple of pieces a try.

To get things rolling, Brenda tries on a suit that looks to be from the thirties. It's in moss-green crêpe with the skirt finishing right across her knees. The military cut of the outfit is amazing and even though it's not her style, she's rewarded by a look of avarice in Rosie's eyes.

"Not for me," says Brenda, "maybe you should try it on? We're a similar size."

Actually, this is a wild guess on Brenda's part. She knows they're close to the same height, but because of how successfully Rosie hides her body from the world, who knows what size or shape the girl is.

After taking the suit off, Brenda tosses it over into the next stall space and gets dressed again. She's relieved when she pulls the curtains to see that Rosie has disappeared into the other changing cubicle. With the ice broken, Brenda hopes the biggest issue will be getting Rosie out of the shop.

This hope is dashed when she hears sobbing from Rosie's cubicle not long after.

The assistant and Brenda look at each other, both at a loss to know what could have caused the upset.

"What now?" mutters Brenda, under her breath before slumping against the wall. Increasing her volume so Rosie can hear her over her sniffling, she says, "If it doesn't fit, it's not the end of the world."

Brenda hears a sharp intake of breath from Alison and assumes it's because of her swearing, but the owner isn't looking at her, she's looking at Rosie, who's opened the curtains of her cubicle.

Pushing herself off the wall, Brenda swings around so she can see what all the fuss is about. She is over this bloody shopping lark in a big way. "Whoa!"

Any further response is choked off as Brenda looks at her student in the thirties' suit. It's an even better fit on the girl than it had been on her. Rosie runs her hands down the sides of the skirt as though to smooth any wrinkles. She repeats the process with the front of the jacket, but nothing is out of place.

"It's as though it was tailor-made for you," says Alison.

"It's not too revealing?" Rosie's voice is a confliction of nerves and hope.

"If it was okay for the thirties, you're hardly gonna be arrested now, are you?" says Brenda, exasperated.

This is not an emphatic enough response for Rosie, who turns to Alison for a second opinion.

"Not revealing at all. It's fantastic on you!" says the owner, bouncing from foot to foot.

Floodgates opened, the next hour is spent in a flurry of trying on clothes. Even Brenda, who'd had a gutful of shopping up to that point, is caught up in the excitement. She'd never had a Barbie when she was little, but imagines it would have been a lot like this.

The door is shut and locked while they're still under cover of the small awning that protects it from the worst of the weather. Rosie is in her new green suit and both of them are holding onto a large number of carrier bags. Other than her gran's jacket, Rosie has binned all her other clothes. Something that is guaranteed to upset Gemma and Marie, who had, apparently, spent a lot of time choosing them for her. The 'open' sign hanging on the glass front door next to them is flipped to 'closed' and the descends into darkness not long after.

"We can go shoe shopping in the morning," says Brenda.

After a questioning look at Brenda, Rosie looks at her feet, then back at Brenda. "Absolutely!"

The girl is beaming, something that's not missed by a couple of lads walking by. They wolf whistle, and Brenda is unable to stop laughing at the complete lack of response from Rosie, courtesy of her years of being invisible.

"You've got so much to learn," says Brenda, nudging Rosie in the direction of the tube station.

The trip home isn't a pleasant one, caught up as they are in the rush hour. It gets to the point Brenda is even envious of Rosie's brogues. She might have to look for lower heels on the shoe shopping expedition in the morning.

They arrive home for dinner with only fifteen minutes to

spare. Even then there's a small delay in eating as the others gush about Rosie's haircut and demand an impromptu fashion parade.

Once it's finished, Rosie is left in no doubt that her new look is awesome and that after dinner, her fellow pupils have every intention of trashing the contents of her wardrobe upstairs.

"Maybe you can give all the tat back to the ugly sisters?" says Stef.

"Who?" says Rosie.

"She means Gemma and Marie," says Paula.

"Now that I'd like to see," crows Brenda.

With the amount of laughter and the quiet that follows, the chances are high that Brenda will get her wish.

She'd had a rough childhood because people ostracised her through no fault of her own and she hated to see it deliberately orchestrated for someone else. In her case, it was because her parents were, and still are, criminals, petty and spectacularly unsuccessful ones. She isn't even sure if they're currently 'in' or 'out'. It had been a rare occasion when both of them were home simultaneously. Whenever their incarcerations had overlapped, she'd stayed with her Auntie Pat. She'd liked it when that happened and had always hoped they'd pull a big job together and get nicked for it. She'd shocked a department store Santa with that request when she was around seven or eight. After that, she kept her wishes to herself.

The only females in the house not present on the shoe-shopping trip the next morning are Flo and Eadie: there is no way Stef and Paula are going to endure 'electrocution' lessons while Brenda and Rosie gad about trying on shoes.

While Stef, Paula and Brenda only buy one pair each, Rosie is so lacking in anything that doesn't smack of Miss Jean Brody that she ends up buying four pairs. The assistant who sells the pair replacing the brogues asks Rosie if she'd like them disposed of.

Before the girl can respond, Brenda chips in, "Could you possibly package them up for us? We'd like to post them to someone."

This strange request forces the assistant back onto her heels, a question poised on her lips. But before speaking, she gets the message in Brenda's eyes loud and clear. "Absolutely I can."

"There's no need to wrap them," says Rosie, "I can hand them into a charity shop as they are."

"What? Your *friends* Gemma or Marie wouldn't want them back after going to all the trouble of helping you to choose them?" says Brenda, archly.

"Brown paper would be wonderful," says Rosie, without missing a beat.

The assistant is now grinning as hard as any of them.

They leave the store carrying a couple of large bags each with the load evenly spread between them. After a visit to the Post Office, they're missing one pair of brogues with the contraceptive abilities of bad acne.

Brenda had stopped Rosie from adding a return address, but when the officious little twit behind the counter had insisted, a quick flick through the Yellow Pages to find one led to much hilarity, with Rosie laughing as hard as any of them.

8

The next week is a whirl of elocution, grooming and chatting-up lessons. But Brenda has trouble convincing the girls that her chat-up lines will work.

"Guys are really that gullible?" says Paula.

"'Course not," says Brenda, but on seeing the looks of confusion all round, presses on, "but because they can only concentrate on one thing at a time, if they're staring at your boobs, they won't hear what you're saying, anyway."

"What if they're not on show?" says Rosie, her tone clearly indicating hers are going to be tucked up tight.

"In that case, you simply pull out 'old faithful'."

Brenda pauses until she's certain she has their attention. She widens her eyes and says earnestly "But what about you? You look so successful. I'm sure your life will be far more interesting than mine."

"And that drivel works?" says Stef, sceptically.

"On the old guys, definitely. You've called them successful and fascinating and indicated you want to listen. You've made out they're still important."

"Isn't that cruel?" says Rosie, uncomfortably.

"Not if you listen to them, it isn't," says Brenda. "Sometimes it's years since anyone's taken notice of them and that includes their bloody money-hungry relatives who mostly sit around waiting for them to kick the bucket."

"But what about, ah, you know, the other?" says Paula, fanning her face.

"That particular problem doesn't often pop up," says Brenda.

There's a moment's pause before they all laugh, even Rosie, although she's scarlet and her laughter is nervous.

Once the hilarity dies down, which takes a while, they split into pairs and practice their chat-up techniques. Each taking turns at playing the crusty old chap.

After dinner that evening, the girls traipse upstairs to the common room, while Brenda and Eadie settle in the sitting room. The early dinnertime means it's not yet late enough for bed.

"They'll be ready for their first outing soon," says Brenda.

"Really? I'm still having a devil of a job with the elocution. Paula's coming along nicely, but I doubt I'll ever stop Stephanie sounding like anything other than the Cockney she is."

"I'm used to it now. Maybe if we glam her up enough, she'll get away with it. It's not as if she's looking for a marriage proposal."

Any further discussion is interrupted by the phone ringing.

"I'll get it," says Brenda, unnecessarily, given Eadie's incapable of jumping up to answer it and Bert and Flo have left for the day.

"Hello?"

"May I speak to Brenda, please?" The man's voice is deep and cultured without being snobby.

"May I tell her who's calling?" says Brenda, unwilling to identify herself to a stranger.

"Julian's the name."

The name means nothing.

"May I tell her what it's about?" says Brenda, calmly, even though the thoughts swirling around in her cranium are chaotic and unsettling.

"I'm interested in taking lessons."

This has all the scenarios she's been picturing crashing in a big old heap at the base of her skull. A guy taking the sort of lessons she's offering? She wouldn't have picked that in a million years. Gay?

"I don't believe she has any places available at present," says Brenda, picturing the only spare room in the house. If anything, the room that's diagonally across from hers and that fronts the house is in even worse shape than those on the second floor had been before Flo attacked them.

"I'll pay double!"

Now Brenda can really smell a rat, although she's also intrigued. "Perhaps it might be best if you met up with Brenda, to discuss it."

"Perfect."

They make arrangements to meet the following evening at the City Barge pub, where she'd recruited Rosie. It's close but not too close.

Next evening after dinner, Brenda changes for her meeting with Julian. She deliberately dresses blandly, not wanting to give away any clues about the nature of the lessons on offer. She has no idea what he's found out about the school and has no intention of blurting it out to any Tom, Dick or Julian.

While technically not illegal, there were those in society who might deem it immoral. Mostly the relatives set to inherit.

Scanning the bar, Brenda compares all the males against the description Julian had provided her with. No one comes close.

"Where have you been all my life?" says a deep voice over her shoulder, scaring the crap out of her.

She spins to give him a piece of her mind. The last thing she needs is some lame bastard trying to hit on her when she's here on business. She doesn't get a chance to spit out, "Hiding from you!"

"I'm Julian. Julian Stables," he says, holding out a hand, with beautifully manicured nails.

Brenda automatically takes it and shakes. "Jeez, with a name like that I hope you're hung like a horse!"

A beautifully shaped eyebrow shoots up.

Shit. That last thought must have come out louder than she'd meant it to.

"I take it you're Brenda?"

Rather than respond immediately, she assesses him. While not outwardly gay, the signs are there if you know what you're looking for. For one thing, no straight bloke wears a pink shirt in public. That'd be enough to get the crap beaten out of you in some parts of Brisbane. His jacket is a deep burgundy and tailor-made, if the snug fit is any indication. His pants are dark grey with black brogues finishing the look.

At over six foot, he has that whole equestrian thing going on; as though someone's spent hours giving him a right going-over with a curry comb. His physique is most decidedly thoroughbred.

It's only when that damned eyebrow of his pops up again, she twigs she hasn't answered him.

"Yes. I am."

With her identity confirmed, he lets go of her hand, which

she hadn't been aware he was still holding. *Damn it, his hands are smoother than mine.* This makes her feel masculine in comparison. It's not often she's knocked off-balance like this.

Noting he's studying her just as minutely, Brenda drops her own examination down a gear, using sideways glances and sneak peeks rather than a full-on stare. He continues with what feels like a professional assessment of her, although she isn't picking up that he's formed an opinion. Yet.

"Let's find a table." He places his hand in the middle of her back to steer her in the direction of an empty booth off to their right, but when Brenda arches her back to break contact, he drops his hand to his side.

"After you," he says, gesturing towards the booth with his other hand.

Each taking a side of the booth, they slide in. It's then she sees that his dark brown hair, rather than slicked back with copious amounts of Brylcreem as she's assumed, is pulled back into a long ponytail. Gay and a hippy, could it get any worse?

She's still mulling over this development, when his blue eyes lock onto her, effectively pinning her to her seat.

"Tell me about the curriculum," he says, without preamble in a deep baritone that smacks of a public school education.

Rather than potentially incriminate herself, she turns it back on him. "Why don't you tell me what you've heard?"

Outlining what he knows about the setup has Brenda seething. Someone had been thorough in her gossiping, with Julian aware of every bloody facet of the operation.

———

Who the hell blabbed about me!"

That Brenda's volume and tone are only challenged by the crash of the common room door smashing against the wall, is evident by the trio of shocked faces.

"Who was it?"

With no one putting up their hand, she glares at each of them in turn. "Rosie! What the hell were you bloody thinking?"

"I ... ah ..." The girl stutters to a halt.

"I told you at the beginning that if you said anything to anyone, we were done!"

"But I didn't ..." Tears crowd Rosie's lower lashes.

"Obviously, you did." Brenda crosses her arms and stands rigid.

Damn the girl for blabbing. This could be the end of things unless she can get another student and she sure as hell isn't taking on a bloke she knows sod all about. Julian Stables is too bloody good looking and too smooth to need lessons on picking up old blokes. Something is off and Brenda can still smell rodent, even now.

"You can leave in the morning." Brenda's pulling the door closed behind her, when she's stopped cold.

"If she goes, I go," says Paula, loud enough for Brenda to hear through the door.

Brenda reopens it in time to hear Stef say, "And the same goes for me'n'all!"

"What?"

"You 'eard me," says Stef.

"Hear hear," says Paula.

A snivelling and red-eyed Rosie is jammed between them.

"You're serious?"

"Damned right, we are," says Stef, her accent back to pre-elocution days.

Paula signals her assent to this.

Brenda only has seconds to decide how to proceed. She turns away from the three on the couch and pinches the bridge of her nose in hopes of arranging her thoughts and wanders out into the hall for space to think. No contest. It's either deal with Rosie's lack of discretion or find an office job. The thoughts of nine-to-bloody-five are enough to bring her out in a cold sweat.

She redirects her pacing to take her back into the common room. "Fine. You can stay, but for god's sake, don't say anything to anyone else! And that goes for you two as well."

The response is immediate with vows of silence mixed in with crossed heart gestures.

"Are you going to let Julian sign on?" sniffles Rosie, not dry-eyed yet.

"I'm not sure."

Walking into Eadie's sitting room, she doesn't even have a chance to pour her first sherry before the old lady starts grilling her on what had happened upstairs. Apparently the volume had been such Eadie had been able to hear two floors below.

Rather than explain what all the fuss had been about, Brenda pours herself a glass, sculls it and pours a second.

"Bloody Rosie went and told her cousin Julian all about us and now he wants to join up."

"Accidental?"

"Hardly. He seemed to know the bloody lot."

"And he still wants to enrol?"

"Yeah. I don't get it. He's a reasonably good-looking bloke and suave as hell. He sure doesn't need my help picking up old dudes."

"He's gay?"

"Not obviously ... but he must be to want to sign up for what we're selling. He even offered to pay double when I said I didn't have space."

"Something's off," says Eadie, emphatically.

"Yep, I smell a big old dirty rat."

"Still, they do say that you should keep your friends close and your enemies closer."

"And what we're doing isn't technically illegal," says Brenda.

"Up until they sell any jewellery and we take our cut, all we've done is charge them board and lodgings."

"With a small profit," says Brenda, who has set the amount the girls pay each week so that she makes enough to cover her day-to-day expenses.

"If the lad is willing to pay double, perhaps."

"I'm meeting up with him again tomorrow night back at the same pub."

"He doesn't know our address?"

"I'm hoping not, but Rosie looked so guilty, I reckon he knows everything about us, including what we had for sodding breakfast this morning."

"If you do end up taking him on, you'll have your work cut out getting that front room up to snuff. I think the wallpaper might be jiggered."

Brenda's onto her fifth sherry before she's finished a lengthy list of purchases and chores that will need attending to before Julian can move in. Even taking Flo, the cleaning dynamo, into account, it will be three or four days' work. Brenda's relieved that other than paying for stuff, she can leave everything else up to Flo and Bert to handle.

———

The mood at breakfast the following morning is unsettled, something Brenda thinks will take a day or two to dissipate.

"Rosie, can I catch up with you after breakfast?" says Brenda, jangling the uneasy atmosphere even further.

Rosie's eyes widen, while Stef's narrow. "Remember what we said. She goes, we go."

Paula and Stef leave for their morning elocution lesson with Eadie; it's only Rosie and Brenda in the kitchen, although Charlie is sitting on the chair next to Brenda, looking hopeful.

With good reason: the crumbs surrounding him proof of the success of his technique.

"I am sorry. He backed me into a corner and wouldn't leave me alone."

Having seen Julian in action the night before when he'd badgered her at the pub, Brenda has no doubts that Rosie wouldn't have stood a chance against him.

"Other than him being your cousin, what else can you tell me about him?"

"He saw me talking to you that night we met at City Barge. He wanted to know who you were. I couldn't tell him you were an old friend, he knows them all. Gemma and Marie told him that I'd said you were an old friend of the family. He wouldn't let it go."

"Go on," says Brenda, sliding a titbit of toast along the table in Charlie's direction.

"He overheard me talking to mummy about heading to the country for a month to stay with friends and put two and two together."

"For a cousin, he appears to spend a lot of time at your place."

"He stays with us when he's in London."

"Where does he usually live?"

"He's got a place on the Isle of Wight."

Brenda has no idea where this is, and really, she couldn't give a rat's arse. "Go on."

"On leaving the room, after mummy said I could go, he was all over me, firing questions at me about what and where."

"You had to ask for your mother's permission to go away?"

To Brenda, who's been a free agent since she was about twelve, if not younger, the concept of asking your parents for anything at the age of twenty-two is inconceivable.

"Of course. If I hadn't, they'd have been just as likely to have Scotland Yard on the case. Daddy knows people."

"Okay, fair enough," says Brenda, who's disconcerted that Rosie's dad knows someone in law enforcement. "So, what does Julian do?"

Rosie looks momentarily perplexed. "I don't know."

"You're kidding, right?"

"That's so funny – I don't have a clue what he does. He's always on holiday when he stays with us. I've never even thought about it before."

Brenda gets what information she can out of Rosie. The things she does know are that he's always immaculately turned out, never untidy and never had a girlfriend that Rosie knows of.

───────

Definitely gay," says Brenda, to Eadie after the elocution lesson is over and they're about to go into lunch.

"You'll be taking him on?"

"Don't see any reason not to and it might be safer in the long run."

"True. He's hardly likely to spill the beans when he's mixed up in it himself."

───────

It's very, ah, pink," says Julian, as he lowers his suitcase to the ground inside the door of his new bedroom.

"You don't like it?" says Brenda, neutrally.

Even she'd been surprised at the décor Flo had organised. Brenda knows this is down to the briefing she'd given, in which it came up that Julian was maybe not as masculine at one would imagine.

The limp-wristed pose that Bert had struck was sufficiently

out of character to have Brenda and Flo giggling like schoolgirls.

Julian spins back towards Brenda. "I don't like it. I love it!"

His response is just camp enough to both put Brenda at her ease and strangely, have one small warning bell tinkling away in her subconscious.

Brenda runs through meal times with him and explains where everything is.

"See you at lunch," says Brenda, before leaving him to settle into the Barbara Cartland suite.

9

Life in the house falls into a routine, with Stef and Paula spending their mornings with Eadie and her dreaded elocution lessons, while Rosie and Julian have it easier, their speech already perfect. Julian makes the most of his freedom by popping out whenever he can, promising with hand on heart not to say anything about the setup, period. She's given up pushing him on where exactly he's off to because it's a waste of sodding time. He's a slippery bastard, even if he's excruciatingly polite about it.

Sitting with Rosie and Julian while they're finishing their breakfast; Brenda decides to broach the subject with him, again.

"Julian, I'm still not sure there's anything I can show you that you don't already know." She keeps her tone neutral despite her inbuilt sense of preservation soaring off the scale.

"That's not quite right," he says, leaning back in his chair, crossing his legs and removing a piece of lint from his pristine grey trousers, "I've already learnt far more than I expected to."

Brenda's not sure if it's the words themselves or the emphasis he places on some that has the bell at the top of her self-preservation gauge clanging loud enough to be heard by everyone in the kitchen. Unfortunately she's unable to argue the point further without looking paranoid.

A quick shufti at the kitchen clock and she knows that if they don't haul arse, there's no way she'll have time for that morning's session on Rosie's self-esteem before the others finish with the female equivalent of 'enry 'iggins.

This basically involves a lot of shopping, because the main thing holding Rosie back is a wardrobe that wouldn't look out of place on Margaret Thatcher. Even Julian has more fashion sense. Another thing he and Brenda agree on is that the so-called friends, who have been advising Rosie on what to wear, don't have her best interests at heart.

Sliding hangers back and forth in Top Shop, Brenda nabs more dresses for Rosie to try on. They've given up on the sales assistants who are more interested in giving the mannequins a run for their money than helping customers.

Brenda arrives at the changing room at the same time as Julian and they both shove their finds through either side of the red velvet curtain, eliciting a squeak from a surprised Rosie.

Knowing how many outfits have gone into the cubicle, Brenda suspects it's rather crowded in there.

"You wanna hand out any crap you don't like?"

"Oh, yes!"

This is followed by a lot of rustling from behind the curtain followed by the red velvet poking out in a bum-shaped bulge before it flattens out with a shriek when Julian pinches it.

Soon after, both Julian and Brenda have their arms laden with rejected clothes. Rather than put them back on the racks, they march over to the main counter and dump the lot on its glass top. After the dummy behind the counter comprehends these aren't purchases, her pasted-on smile comes unstuck.

"Brenda!"

This one word is so brim-full with excitement that she's

back to the curtain in double-quick time, leaving Julian to point out to the assistant that it's *her* job to put all the clothes back, not the customer's.

"Any good?" If it were anyone else, Brenda would simply jam her head around the curtain, but Rosie has already let her know that she doesn't enjoy her space being invaded like that.

Rather than answer, Rosie pulls the curtain aside, walks out and performs a twirl for Brenda's benefit. Julian returns from his altercation with the help and stands next to Rosie, and Brenda is unable to stop her bark of laughter.

"Bloody hell! It's Ken and Barbie." Her laughter continues, drawing even more annoyed looks from the two in front of her. Their faces crease into scowls, eliciting more snorts and guffaws from Brenda. Grabbing an arm apiece, she drags them over to stand in front of a big mirror.

The two of them stare at their reflection for a beat or two before Julian says, "I see what you mean."

He smiles, and Rosie follows suit. She strikes a 'Barbie' pose and 'Ken' joins her; the three of them enjoy the joke, drawing looks of censure from a dummy on her way to refill the racks.

Rosie still buys the dress because, while it is Mattel in nature, it suits her to perfection.

Once again the lunch hour turns into an impromptu runway show as Rosie parades around in her new clobber. Julian's commentary is fashioned on Frankie Howerd and has them all crying, including Bert and Flo.

After wiping away more tears, Brenda claps to get everyone's attention. "After lunch, we'll be learning about jewellery and in particular signs of good quality and what's complete arse."

At Eadie's raised eyebrows, Brenda gives herself an internal shake. While she isn't running a proper finishing school, she and Eadie have agreed it might look better if she tones down her language a tad in front of the students. Brenda's finding it tough going; she's battling years of this bad habit, although she'd had practice when dating Martin McGowan as he wasn't keen on her cussing. Thinking of him, she wonders how he's getting on.

This leads her to reflect on the money he'd given her and the subsequent loss of those funds because of that useless bastard, Stefano. It's not until she clocks the expressions of those around the table that she thinks some of this thought has been more vocal than she'd intended.

Rather than explain her strange behaviour, Brenda addresses her students. "We'll meet in the front hall at two. Don't be f... late."

———

A stream of beeps announces Brenda and her students' presence to Kirsten at Antique Alley. Brenda is particularly pleased at the arrangement they've agreed upon whereby, in lieu of cash for these classes, all Brenda has to do is ensure her students give the woman first right of refusal on any items they want to 'liquidate'. Kirsten has agreed to deduct Brenda's commission from any sales and pay this to her direct, thus keeping the students out of the loop on that altogether.

"Please have a seat," says Kirsten, indicating a mismatched collection of wingback chairs crowding a battered military chest. The top of this is cluttered with a selection of boxes large and small. There are also two jewellers' loupes sitting on a velvet-lined tray.

At the end of the session, Brenda has learnt as much as any of her students. Obviously, it's not possible to take a jewellers' loupe on a date, but they've gained enough knowledge about overall design and what constitutes quality craftsmanship to know when to say, "Thank you," and when to say, "I couldn't possibly," and hold out for richer pickings.

While they wait for their return taxi, the students mill about outside giving Brenda a moment to catch-up with Kirsten.

"Where can I get my hands on one of these?" Brenda uses the loupe to examine the ring on her right hand, confirming Martin's taste is impeccable and his bank balance healthy.

"I can get a new one for you if you like, or you can take that one you're using for a tenner."

Brenda pulls it away from her eye and looks at its battered and scratched nature.

"Sounds good to me," she says, before dropping it into the depths of her bag and grabbing her wallet. While the exterior might not be beautiful, the lens is still perfect and that's all Brenda's interested in.

Dinner out of the way that evening, it's show-and-tell on the jewellery front with everyone, except Brenda, dragging out any baubles they have in their possession so they can put their recently acquired gemmology knowledge into practice. Even Julian has cufflinks and a tie pin he wants to have a closer look at, although he's mum about his benefactor.

Stef pulls the loupe away from her eye and drops it and her prized bangle on the table with a clatter. "That cheap bastard!"

There's a mix of responses from the others as they examine their own finery, ranging from delight to dismay. There are also a few items put to one side for cashing in with Kirsten.

A week's more intensive study and Eadie and Brenda agree the students are ready to put their new-found knowledge into practice. The two of them have undertaken a lot of research to pinpoint the best hunting grounds for the fledgling crew, narrowing this to a pub in the City of London. This should provide easy pickings and no competition in the way of wives and relatives.

"If we're lucky, there might even be retired gents at this one," says Eadie.

"Won't they all be at their clubs?" says Brenda, who has enough understanding of London society to be aware of these hallowed institutions.

"Not always. Sometimes they like slumming it. And anyway, there's no club worth its salt to be found in that part of town."

Eadie had confused Brenda when she first talked about 'the City of London'. Wasn't it all the city of London? Apparently not. The 'City' is the original area settled by the Romans complete with a wall and not to be confused with Greater London.

The City is also where the rich and would-be rich 'toil' away in banks, stock brokerages, oil companies and the like. Even if the money isn't technically 'old', it'll still spend like it is and that's good enough for Brenda and her students.

Because of the distance they're travelling, they decide to catch the tube rather than a cab and for this reason, the girls all wear flat shoes for the journey, their killer heels safely stowed in baby-sized handbags. Julian doesn't need to worry about this and is only weighed down by a wallet that he stows safely in the inside pocket of his spick-and-span hunter-green jacket. Brenda is envious of how nice it must be to move about so freely.

Close to their intended hunting ground, they pile into a small wine bar tucked down a side alley. If it weren't for the large barrel sitting next to its front door, it wouldn't have been visible from the main street, but it's the perfect place to have a calming glass of wine and for the girls to swap shoes and to carry out a final application of lippy and spray of perfume. While all of this is going on, Julian tidies the folds of his paisley cravat that Brenda thought looked perfect already.

"Announce your presence subtly, don't asphyxiate them," Eadie warned before they left the house. This advice is particularly pertinent to Stef, who has a more-is-better approach to fragrance.

Walking beside Julian and behind the other three, Brenda is pleased to take in a mix of floral scents from the girls and a spicy blend from Julian without feeling the need to cough. Their levels are perfect.

Seconds after their arrival in The Lord Raglan, of missing arm and sleeve fame, Brenda can see any subtlety will be lost on the customers in this establishment. The place reeks of pipes, cigars and hops.

The only thing to give the smell a run for its money is the volume of the place. It's wall-to-wall cultured accents and liberal brayings of "Haw, haw, haw" from patrons laughing at their own jokes.

In unspoken agreement, the five of them split up. It's been agreed Brenda will only get involved if her students need help; otherwise they're on their own. A lime and soda in hand, she plonks herself on an upholstered stool at one end of the bar, from where she'll keep an eye on proceedings.

There aren't too many females in the bar, with those in evidence dressed in such a way as to announce them as office workers on their lunch breaks. Brenda looks briefly at her watch and starts an internal countdown. Sure enough, when it hits five to two, without exception, all the 'office girls' chug back whatever is left in their glass and leg it, leaving the way clear for Brenda's students to work their magic.

The gents left behind appear less concerned about returning to work with many looking as though they're settling in for the rest of the day. In the case of a couple of old purple-nosed chaps in a corner booth, Brenda suspects any trips home are infrequent and brief.

Julian is quickly deep in conversation with the old pair, with the three men laughing up a storm. She wouldn't have picked the old guys as being gay, looking far too civil service, but never say never.

Brenda sees Stef and Paula have already latched onto a couple of middle-aged chaps who have 'banker' written all over them. Perhaps not the best option if the key characteristic you're after is generosity, but not a bad start.

She spots Rosie and is unable to stop a heartfelt sigh. For all the effort Brenda has expended on building up the girl's self-worth, she's standing there like a wallflower at a school social. It's the kiss of death if she wants anyone to approach her. Brenda's already off her bar stool and on her way to the rescue, when she stops.

Rosie's been approached by an elderly gent of small stature, with a kind face. This could be just what she needs. She retraces her steps and hitches herself back up on her perch to await developments.

Once again, looking around to see what the others are up to, she's pleased to see they're getting on famously, with all three of them having been bought drinks; doubles by the looks of things in Julian's case. They might need to get a taxi home after this.

Brenda's looks back at Rosie and shoots lime and soda out of her nose. "That dirty old bastard," mutters Brenda, to herself, again sliding off her bar stool.

"Look after that, will you?" says Brenda, to the barman, not waiting for a response, already on her way to the rescue.

He may well have looked affable and kind, but the lecherous old bugger has backed Rosie into a corner and has his grubby mitts all over her. Looks like an elf but acts like a troll!

The expression on Rosie's face makes it obvious she's not

enjoying the mauling and isn't sure how to deal with the situation. It's something Brenda will make sure she covers in class
tomorrow. "Rosie, I've been looking all over for you," says
Brenda, insinuating herself between groper and gropee. With
her back to the old guy, Brenda whispers, "Go to the bar, I'll
join you there."

The corner location proves perfect for Brenda giving the
old codger a right bollocking about manhandling her 'cousin'.
Rather than be apologetic, the old guy's gaze locks onto her
boobs as if they're magnetic. That they're level with his eyes
doesn't help. He raises his hands to follow up, but she smacks
them away, hard.

"Diplomacy's bloody lost on you isn't it, ya little bugger,"
hisses Brenda, pressing in on him, her hands gripping his
braces.

―――――

Standing next to Rosie at the bar, Brenda takes a sip of her lime
and soda. "Starting tomorrow, we're going to cover how to deal
with creepy little bastards like him."

"I didn't want to be rude."

"If someone is groping you like that and you haven't said it's
okay, hell, yes, you can be rude."

Rosie doesn't look convinced.

"Look, go and check out the rest of the place. Try the
upstairs bar. I'll be up in a tick to see how you're getting on."

With Rosie off, hopefully to greener and less troublesome
pastures, Brenda checks on the other three. They're going spectacularly if all you're after is free drinks. Stef's, and even Paula's,
laughter is giving the 'haw haws' a nudge in volume and Julian
has buggered up the folds of his cravat, even if he's pristine
otherwise.

Finishing the world's longest-lasting lime and soda, Brenda

slips off the bar stool again, and completes a circuit of the room. Surreptitiously pointing at her watch as she passes her students, she gets looks of confirmation in return. At the top of the stairs, she has a quick looksee to find Rosie. Spotting her, she can't help a sigh. Trust Rosie to latch onto the youngest and poorest looking bloke up here.

Sure, Rosie has only signed up to help with her self-esteem and dating prowess, but Brenda wants better for her than this.

"Hey, Rosie, the rest of us are heading off now."

"Uh, oh, okay," says Rosie, realising she's been sprung chatting to someone who's unsuitable. She looks across the table at what Brenda would describe as a bloody boring sap. His demeanour screams schoolteacher, and maths at that. He'd been no challenge to the girl a month back, before all the time and money spent on her makeover.

"I'd better get going." The girl looks so disappointed Brenda can't help another sigh escaping. She might well prove to be a hopeless case after all.

Leaving her to it, Brenda walks back downstairs and is pleased to see the other three chatting together next to the door. She hasn't long been next to them when Rosie pops up next to her, looking suspiciously happy.

They're about to go through the door, when a cultured voice nearby cuts through the clutter of the bar.

"Is anyone interested in unhooking Clarence's braces from that wall sconce? His kit sticking out like that is putting me off my jellied eel."

The 'haw haws' increase in volume.

"Brenda, you didn't?" Rosie's mouth is as agape as her eyes.

"The creepy little bastard lunged at me. It was self-defence." Brenda's voice is a study in mock outrage that fools none of them.

10

The invitation sits like a Basildon Bond illuminated lettered challenge on the coffee table in the sitting room. Brenda and Eadie look at it with speculation.

"Are they ready for something like this?" says Eadie.

"Who bloody knows? Their strike rate at scrounging drinks is high if today's trip to the Churchill Arms in Belgravia is any indication. We had to come home in a blasted cab."

Brenda's still smarting at how much this had cost. Apart from her cut of the board and lodging, she's only received a pittance from the tat her students have sold through Antique Alley, with the pieces being more brass than gold.

"This event might be a good one, though," says Eadie.

"Why, especially?"

"It's borderline respectable, so the chaps attending will more than likely leave their wives at home."

"That could work," says Brenda, slowly.

The event is a week away, leaving plenty of role-playing time to hone everyone's skills. Brenda still despairs of Rosie chatting to anyone over thirty, but on the bright side, she pays her rent on time and in cash to boot.

Brenda holds the invitation up and flaps it. "How did you manage this?"

"Host's an old acquaintance of mine, otherwise we wouldn't have had a snowball's." Eadie can be brutally honest at times.

"In that case, I say we go for it."

Mind made up, Brenda wastes no time in letting her students know of the forthcoming event. The invitation is pinned to the notice board in the common room and is never far from anyone's mind after that.

Because of the formal nature of the event, the main problem facing them is what to wear. Julian already has something suitable, but Brenda and the girls need kitting out.

"What about the second-hand place next to *my* hairdressers?" says Rosie, having firmly claimed Shelly as her own.

Brenda closes her eyes to recall the interior of the shop. As she mentally scans the racks, she remembers longer items being tucked away at the back. Because Rosie had been after daywear, they hadn't ventured there.

***

No sooner has breakfast been inhaled the following morning than the girls are ready to head to Hammersmith.

"Mind if I tag along?" says Julian, his face showing as much excitement as any of his classmates.

"'Course you can," says Brenda.

Julian's sense of style could come in handy, especially with him being at ease in the sort of company they hope to attract the coming Saturday evening. Brenda has yet to see a gay man who doesn't dress beautifully.

There's a kaleidoscope of flash frocks on offer in Alison's shop, but Brenda finds herself looking at those at the darker end of the racks. She garners enough looks without dressing like a walking bloody billboard and wants her students to be the centre of attention at Saturday's shindig, not herself.

She's holding up a dark purple dress, examining it for flaws, when Julian walks up next to her.

"Why do you always dress like someone's died?"

"Life's simpler that way." She's deliberately obtuse, not wanting to open up to one to her students and especially not to him.

There's still something about Mr Perfect that doesn't ring true. For one thing, all he's learnt from her so far are pointers on jewellery, and that was Kirsten at Antique Alley's doing. If she were him, she'd be after a refund by now.

Realising she's not going to elaborate, he moves his attention back to the velvet gown. "You going to try it on, or simply look at it?"

Rather than respond, she moves away from him and over to the curtain-style cubicles. From the relative quiet towards the back of the shop, the scene here is one of chaos, although the owner isn't fazed and has even been caught up in the excitement. No doubt she's calculating how much money she'll take.

Paula is spinning around, arms wide as she demonstrates the length of the fishtail in the gown she's chosen. She comes close to beheading a mannequin before she stops long enough for Brenda to examine it more carefully. Looking as though she's about to resume her twirling, Brenda stops the Irish girl with an imperious, "Stand still!"

The effect is immediate and Paula freezes as if she's playing a childhood game of statues, allowing Brenda to check the dress from all angles. The bottle green colour is a perfect foil for the girl's red hair and pale skin and the strapless fishtail gown fits her curvaceous figure to perfection, with no need for any alterations.

The dresses will cost enough, without having to pay for them to be altered. It's an issue that causes Brenda to bemoan the fact that Sam, and her amazing dressmaking skills, is in Italy with her fiancé, Chris. On the plus side, if they'd still been living with Eadie, it would have been impossible to get the school up and running.

Brenda's even more pleased that Mark, Eadie's nephew is also out of the way. He'd have a conniption if he knew about Eadie and Brenda setting up the school. It's something they'll have to deal with when he and Jennie return in around four months.

Even with the second-hand shop offering a reasonably cheap alterations service, time is not on their side and so the less tweaking required, the better.

Stepping from one of the cubicles in an apricot confection, Stef's expression says louder than words that she's uncertain about it.

"Good god, that's ugly," says Julian, saving Brenda the trouble.

"That, ah, doesn't, um, do anything for you," says Brenda, as diplomatically as she can. This is so against nature that she speaks haltingly as she stumbles to string a sentence together that isn't laced with profanities.

"That's a relief," says Stef, "I was worried you were going to like it."

The curtains on the second changing room remain hanging limply, letting Brenda know Rosie will need coaxing into showing them her gown.

"Come on, Rosie, show us what you've found." Brenda tries hard to keep irritation out of her voice. The timidity is wearing thin, but as the teacher, it's not appropriate for her to show it.

"Coming, ready or not, cousin." Julian steps up to the curtains and grabs them in readiness to rip them open.

She must be standing there in her undies rather than fully dressed if the squawking from inside is anything to go by.

"If it doesn't fit, we've got plenty of others in stock. There are even more out the back," says Alison.

"Owww!" Julian yanks his hands away from the curtain and rubs his knuckles vigorously. "Did you clip me with a hanger?"

The curtains are parted by Rosie, armed with a heavy-duty wooden hanger and, more interestingly, fully dressed. Less surprising is that she looks close to tears.

Brenda is unable to stop herself from gritting her teeth. It's as though the smallest thing and the girl is white-knuckling it in the front carriage of the emotional rollercoaster. Standing back, she leaves the others to deal with it. Not being able to smother her exasperation enough, she'd only make matters worse.

"You can use the cubicle over there if you like," says Alison, pointing her to curtains and a curved rail suspended from the ceiling on the other side of the shop.

"Ta, thanks."

Leaving Julian playing Henry Kissinger and the others adding their support, Brenda stomps off toward the other changing room.

Whipping the curtains closed she strips and then slips into the gown to a background of the ongoing negotiations with Rosie.

"Wow!" While the colour might be subtle, the overall effect is anything but. No need to worry about taking the dress in, but if she was to buy it, she wouldn't be able to eat for the rest of the week. As it is, closing the side zip without ripping her armpit to shreds is a close run thing.

"Wow, what?" says Julian, from disturbingly close by.

The man moves like an Indian scout, sans moccasins.

Brenda bites off her initial retort. "Never mind me. Go help the others."

She listens, but as she doesn't hear him move, jams her elbow into the curtain where he'd been standing. She comes up empty but still hears a sharp intake of breath meaning she must have been damned close.

"Julian, can you please go and assist the others."

This time, she hears him leave but only because his muttering is louder than his footfalls.

Satisfied he's gone, she swaps clothes and goes back to the other cubicles. It doesn't look as though Rosie has moved. Stef, on the other hand, is sashaying around in a dark burgundy gown that suits her perfectly, even if it's on the loose side around the waist. Seeing her looking at it, Alison asserts the alteration is an easy one with the dress ready in a couple of days at worst.

Okay, that's two of them sorted. Brenda swings back in Rosie's direction, ready to do battle. She can see nothing wrong with the front of the dress and so is at a loss to account for the girl's obvious distress.

"Give us a twirl." Brenda spins her finger in the air to reinforce this request.

The girl is frozen in place, forcing Brenda to move closer so she can look at the dress from all angles. Standing right in front of Rosie with her possum-in-the-headlights expression, Brenda sees the girl's reflection in the mirror in the changing room.

"Hell, no!" says Brenda. "You've bloody near got builder's crack.

At her outburst, relief floods Rosie's face. The other three crowd in for a closer look, forcing the girl to stagger back into the cubicle where she wastes no time yanking the curtains shut. It's as close to slamming as possible when dealing with drapes.

"What was wrong with that one?" says Stef.

"A bit of skin never goes astray," says Paula, from the safety of her reasonably modest-by-comparison dress.

Not wanting to get into a discussion, Brenda hands the purple velvet to Alison to rehang and starts hunting the racks for a suitable grown for Rosie. If the girl chose that arsehole-revealing number herself, she doesn't have a bloody clue.

Brenda is a whirling dervish as she flicks her way along the rack, examining, rejecting and choosing. All those making the cut are tossed at Julian to feed into the cubicle; Rosie has no issues with him playing handmaiden due to his relative status.

Brenda knows she's hit pay dirt when a squeal of delight comes from behind the curtains. Her relief is shared by the others now that all of them are sorted in the clothing department. Even Julian has managed to find a beautiful vintage waistcoat and matching cravat that Brenda suspects will make him look like a dandy from a bodice-ripper.

The curtain is opened and an ecstatic Rosie steps from it and pirouettes for all to see.

"It's fabulous. Get it off and let's get the hell out of here," says Brenda, well and truly over the expedition.

She thinks she might have overstepped the mark when Stef looks at her sharply, but the girl follows in Brenda's stead. "Yep, it looks amazing. Get the bloomin' thing off and let's go home. I'm blinkin' famished."

"Looks lovely," says Paula.

Julian simply gives her a thumbs up, before ushering her back into the cubicle and closing the curtains.

Stef's dress has been pinned at the waist and left for alteration and Paula is carrying a large bag with her dress stowed safely inside. Julian simply has the waistcoat and cravat draped over one arm. Brenda looks longingly at the purple dress draped over the counter but decides Saturday night isn't about her. She'll pick something up from Chiswick High Street.

They're rallying themselves outside in preparation for hailing a cab, when Julian says "Bloody hell. In the rush to leave, I forgot to pay. Back in a mo."

True to his word, he's back in under a minute, having spoken briefly to Alison, grabbed the large carry bag she's given him and thrown notes on the counter. He's still stuffing his purchases into the carrier when he rejoins them.

His timing is as impeccable as the rest of him as he appears at the exact moment a cab dropping off a fare stops next to them.

―――――――

By Friday morning of that week, both Stef and Brenda are getting antsy. There's been no sign of Stef's altered gown even though it should have been delivered the previous afternoon. A panicked call to Alison reassured them, but they're still on edge. No dress, meant nothing appropriate to wear, with the alterations place closed at weekends. It's today or never.

Brenda looks at her watch again. Eleven forty-five. The alterations place is pushing it on the morning delivery. If the bloody dress isn't there by twelve, she's going to give Alison a right rev up.

As the minutes tick by to midday, Brenda is so annoyed, she's looking forward to making the call. Luckily, Stef and Paula are still in their elocution lesson with Eadie in the dining room, while Julian and Rosie are out on a family errand. She won't need to watch her language, not that she could, she's so riled.

"Alison's."

"It's Brenda here. Again! Where the hell is that bloody dress?"

There isn't an immediate response but Brenda can tell by the hollow tone the girl hasn't hung up on her.

"For god's sake! It hasn't arrived yet? They could have made the sodding dress in this time." Alison sounds as annoyed as Brenda, which goes some way to appeasing her.

The two of them are in the middle of quite the character assassination; when there's a timid knock at the front door.

"I don't believe it. I think it's arrived. Hang on a tick."

Brenda drops the receiver on the hall table; wrenches open the door and glares at their visitor. In response, the pimply youth holding a large garment bag stumbles back off the step. She follows him and yanks the bag from his limp grip.

"Next time, don't go via sodding Glasgow!"

He's still standing there, mouth drooping and face flushed to the extent he appears blemish-free, when she slams the door on him.

After hanging the bag on the coat-rack, Brenda picks up the receiver. "Got it!"

"Thank bloody hell for that," says Alison. "Good on you for giving him a bollocking. The little shit is always late. I've even had dresses arrive smelling of fish and chips."

"Useless prick."

11

No sooner has Brenda slammed the door on the world's most useless delivery boy than she's yelling out for Stef to come and grab the dress so she can try it on. If the bloody thing doesn't fit, they're scuppered and need to come up with a Plan B damn fast.

Stef wastes no time abandoning her elocution lesson and racing upstairs to put the dress on. She models it for all to see, and the dining room is awash with 'oohs' and 'aahs'. The dress looks incredible, with the improvement far exceeding the small alteration required to achieve it.

That afternoon, Brenda and Eadie drill the team on techniques for engagement, luring and going in for the kill. With these terms bandied about, it sounds as if they're going fox hunting the next day rather than attending a society knees-up.

Brenda's less enamoured with her own dress and doesn't deem it worthy of a fashion parade. It's a black halter-neck with an A-line skirt and was the plainest one she could find.

That it's polyester only adds to its utilitarian nature. She plans to wear the best of her jewellery in hopes of nudging it into acceptable territory.

The day of the 'do' and the house is a flurry of activity. After breakfast, the kitchen takes on the air of a nail studio. Even Julian allows Paula to give him a manicure, not that he needs it, although he draws the line at polish. Instead, he lets her buff his nails until they gleam.

Brenda paints her own nails a deep crimson, making them look long and lethal. Whether she'll need to resort to using them remains to be seen.

The arrival in the afternoon of Shelly, the girl who'd transformed Rosie's mop, converts the kitchen from nail bar to hair salon. With her salon open on Saturday mornings only, she's more than happy to make a house-call for the four girls in the afternoon. Especially as they're all paying cash.

Less concerned about her own appearance, Brenda lets the other three go first. This way if they run out of time, she can simply scrape her hair up into an unforgiving bun.

But she needn't have worried; Shelly flies through Stef, Paula and Rosie's hair. It's not until they go to dress after a dinner so early it almost counts as afternoon tea, that trouble arises.

Brenda is upstairs, ready to don the polyester 'dream', but it's no longer hanging in the freestanding mahogany wardrobe that dominates her room. In its place hangs the purple velvet dress that she'd last seen at Alison's second-hand shop.

"What the hell?"

Apart from this, Brenda is gobsmacked and initially at a loss for words, but several more 'what the hells' follow. It's intelligent comment that's lost to her.

Not for long.

"Bloody Julian!"

Apparently, it wasn't just the waistcoat and cravat he'd paid for when he went back into the shop. Draping the velvet dress carefully over the end of the bed, Brenda dives into her wardrobe in search of her missing dress. She shoves every- thing to one side wrenches a hanger over to the middle and then to the other end. She's on the fourth one when she realises that this metal-on-metal action is causing sparks, something to be avoided in a wardrobe as old and dry as this one.

"Damn it!"

She uses every bit of her anger to wrench clothes out of the wardrobe and toss them in the general direction of her bed until there's quite the pile. She then grabs the top item, sees in seconds it's not what she's after and tosses it over her shoulder before moving on.

"Fuck it, fuck it, fuck it," says Brenda, when Charlie is finally visible again.

Wrenching on her dressing gown, she storms across the landing and hammers on Julian's door.

He opens it wide, takes in her outfit and, not missing a beat, says, "It's understated. But I like it."

"Where is my dress?"

That Brenda hasn't peppered this with profane adjectives is testament to the tight control she's exerting over her fury, although the effort is making her jaw hurt. The muscles in the rest of her body are also bunched for action.

Before he can respond, Brenda senses the arrival of the girls, down from the second floor.

"Why aren't you dressed?" says Stef. "We don't want to be late."

Backed up by badly rehearsed prompting from Rosie and Paula, Brenda swings in their direction to find conspiratorial grins pasted on all three faces.

"So, who's got my dress?"

"What's wrong with the purple beauty," says Julian, reversing Brenda's opinion that he isn't involved.

"You mean apart from the fact it doesn't fit?" Brenda throws in his general direction.

"Shit!" says Stef, her smile faltering.

Paula and Rosie are also appalled rather than amused.

"What have you done?" Brenda is unable to do anything about the volume at the end of this question.

"We swapped it," whispers Paula, nerves sending her Irish accent into full lilt.

"You swapped it?"

"For the purple one," says Rosie, coming clean for all of them.

"Julian, you clod," says Stef, scowling at him. "You said it looked amazing on her."

Brenda frowns, considering this statement, before she turns back to him again. "But you didn't see it. I never showed it to you."

At his guilty look, she has to grit her teeth and fight to keep her arms pasted to her sides. Bloody curtained cubicles.

Leaving them standing where they are, Brenda stalks back into her room. Her muttered diatribe starts on the landing and continues long after she's shut the door to her room and ditched her dressing gown.

"This had better bloody fit."

Brenda drops the dress over her head and contorts to do up the side zipper. It starts sliding up smoothly enough but jams a couple of inches from the armhole.

"I hate these things," says Brenda, into her armpit.

She tugs on it gently but the bloody thing doesn't budge. She gives it a harder tug and automatically sucks in her breath when it releases and yanks up to the top, narrowly missing skin in the process.

"That's weird."

Brenda straightens and looks at her reflection in the wardrobe mirror before running her hands over the dress. It's looser than it was in the shop. She scans the side seams, failing to find any signs of an alteration.

Stepping into her shoes, Brenda thinks back over what she's eaten that week. She continues her examination of the menu while applying her lipstick and collecting her evening jacket and bag.

"Those sneaky little bastards!"

She has to include Flo and Bert in this conspiracy. The two of them worked as hard as the others to make sure she hadn't been able to nab seconds. Every time she'd eyed-up the final spud, one of them would swoop on it. If she'd asked if there was more pud, a straight-faced Bert had told her there wasn't any left.

Refusing to play the Cinderella role thrust upon her, Brenda stalks down the stairs. The compliments flow but she holds her hand up to halt them mid-gush.

"Invitations?"

In answer to this, the heavy-bond cards pop up one after the other, although Paula takes a while to find hers in a bag with more compartments than the Orient Express.

"I'll be with you in a moment. I need to catch up with Eadie."

She's pushing open the door to Eadie's sitting room when jaunty beeping announces the arrival of their cab.

"Go out and wait. I'll be there in a mo."

To say her students look disappointed is the proverbial understatement. That their cunning plan has been greeted with anything but gratitude leaves them poleaxed.

"I thought you'd decided to wear something plain?" says Eadie, a full glass of sherry forgotten halfway to her mouth.

"It was the plan, but that lot," Brenda jerks her thumb in the general direction of the street, "liked this one better. So they swapped it without my knowledge."

"Ah."

"Dumb bastards. It's gonna make it bloody difficult to walk about unobtrusively checking on their progress."

Brenda isn't being vain, only pragmatic. She knows the effect she has on old geezers. It's been her main means of income for the last few years. In the gorgeous purple dress, she'll spend most of the night beating off unwanted advances, rather than playing the role of discrete tutor.

"Let's hope the evening isn't a complete washout," says Eadie.

"Yeah. You got everything you need?"

Brenda has already checked the decanter looks healthy.

"Tiptop," says Eadie, toasting her.

Brenda is closing the door behind her when she gives last minute advice through the gap. "Remember to get yourself to bed before you get hammered."

A snort is enough to let her know what Eadie thinks of this advice.

The tension in the cab is uncomfortable and doesn't dissipate as they near their destination, a club in Kensington.

"Look, it was a wonderful thought," says Brenda, shattering the awkward silence, "Problem is that I *wanted* to blend into the background tonight."

"But why?" says Rosie, her forehead crinkled in confusion.

"So I could circulate and keep an eye on all of you without anyone seeing what I was up to."

"But what's the point of that when we're all arriving together?" says Julian, pointing out a flaw Brenda hasn't thought of.

Thinking on her feet, even though she's seated, Brenda pauses for mere seconds. "Because, I'm dropping you off, then getting the cab to circle the block before dropping me off."

There are thumbs up from all of them to this strategy.

Hoping to sneak inside and blend in with the crowd proves to be impossible when the dead-flash-looking bouncer at the door insists on seeing her invitation. He calls out her name, the volume guaranteed to be audible even to those who've left their hearing aids at home, and she knows any hopes of sneaking in are busted.

Because the elite of London is relatively few in number, any new blood is guaranteed to generate interest. Not only do all the males in the crowd openly stare at her, they move in for a closer look with the effect that the room feels as though it's shrinking. Brenda experiences a moment's panic. Bloody dress will be the death of her.

She's weighing up her options when someone gently takes her hand and drapes it over an arm. Recognising the cologne, Brenda relaxes, but she's also annoyed he's linked the two of them together after she's gone to the trouble of being dropped off separately from the others.

"Relax. I don't know you, I've simply moved quicker than anyone else to claim you," says Julian, under his breath.

Once clear of the forward scrum, he unhooks her arm and is soon swallowed up by the crowd. And what a crowd.

Tightly packed as it is, Brenda feels she may well be able to move through the mob without attracting too much attention. With the age of most of the gents in the room in the vicinity of sixty plus, she'll be too close for them to focus, without dragging out their bloody reading glasses.

Not bothering with a drink she'll only end up wearing, she starts slow laps of the venue. Rather than one big hall, several rooms link together, although she sees there are large sliding panels which can open them up, if required. What is surprising is how tatty the place is. But only if you look closely and you're sober. The place would show its age and look tawdry in the harsh morning light.

The first of her students she spots is Paula and Brenda can't help a small grin. The three old guys circling her are so small and wizened they look like chimps off to a high-end tea party. All that's missing is the excited 'eeping' and a tyre swing.

Stef too is surrounded by geriatrics, jockeying for position and if any of her students are capable of whipping them into a frenzy, it's this one.

It's only on the third circuit that Brenda finds Rosie.

"For god's sake!"

Heads turn in her direction. Brenda feigns innocence, reminding herself to keep her sodding voice down.

Pushing her way through the mob towards her most trying student, Brenda rehearses her opening line.

"It's Rosie, isn't it?"

"Ah, yes." Rosie stammers, with her colour heightening to match her gown.

Turning to her companion, whom Brenda has recognised from their class trip to the Lord Raglan, Brenda says, "Will you excuse us?" We haven't caught up in ages."

The maths' teacher is still stumbling through a reply when Brenda pulls Rosie behind her into the midst of the crowd.

Forgetting about keeping a distance from her students, Brenda works the room with Rosie in tow. The two of them prove quite the attraction, given their vastly different demeanours.

Brenda has spotted Julian on several occasions although he's never on his own; he's always cornered by one of the dozen or so older ladies present. Sure, some of these old birds have money in their own right, but not as much as the guys usually do.

Leaving Rosie chatting happily to a couple of not too grabby gents, Brenda does another circuit so she can check on the others.

She stops cold when a large 'gentleman' deliberately steps in front of her, proving he's anything but.

"I've been watching you," he says.

"Bully for you," says Brenda, stepping to one side to move past him.

He sidesteps to match and grabs both of her arms to hold her in place, but rather than feel scared, her anger spikes.

Leaning in as if to whisper something smutty, Brenda sees his expression change, with him under the misapprehension she's acquiesced.

"If you don't take your sodding hands off me, I am going to knee you so hard you'll be able to wear your dick like a tie and your balls for earrings!"

Rather than stumble back as she expects, his eyes darken. Great, just her luck to get one of those sick B&D bastards! Jeez, they're thick on the ground in London.

"Name's Wallace, and I think someone is in need of punishment."

"Wallace who?" says Brenda, already suspecting the answer.

"Smythe-Brown."

Bloody hell! Eadie's nemesis and a total wanker! Something his son Rupert had inherited.

Looking at him closely brings it home to Brenda what an amazing artist Jennie is. She's only ever seen a painting of the creep hanging onto her and in that, he'd been depicted in the throes of ecstasy. But even without the facial contortions, he's easily recognisable. The strawberry-like nature of the old drunk's nose had been spot-on in the painting. His man-breasts, prominent in the composition, are straining against the front of his dress shirt.

Brenda knows without looking down, that he's sporting an erection and all because she abused him. Sad bastard.

"Meet me outside the ladies in five minutes," whispers Brenda, directly into his ear. She bites the lobe, hard, and is rewarded by his sharp intake of breath.

Swallowing the bile filling her mouth, she wriggles out of his grasp and steps away from him. After a coquettish wave, she turns her hips, spins on her heel and is swallowed by the amorphous crowd.

The last she sees as she goes in search of the others, is him swaggering and elbowing his way through the mob on a doomed trip to the ladies.

Let the stupid wanker wait.

They compare notes on the trip home, with all of them in possession of a good number of calling cards and promises of lunches and fun times aplenty.

Even Rosie has collected a couple of cards, although Brenda is dismayed to see one of them is dog-eared and covered in pocket lint. No prizes for guessing to whom that belongs.

Out of courtesy to Eadie, any chatter stops when they pull up in front of the house. After the students have disappeared quietly upstairs, Brenda eases open the door to the sitting room. The room is dark, but she can see the light is still on in Eadie's bedroom.

"Eadie, you awake?" She whispers just loud enough not to wake the old lady if she's fallen asleep with the light on.

"Come on in."

Brenda walks into the bedroom to find Eadie propped up in bed and very much alert.

"How did you get on?"

"Quite well, if the number of cards collected is any indication."

"Even Rosie?"

"Yeah, even her, for all the good it will do if she simply keeps them in her handbag like before," says Brenda, "I ran into an old friend of yours?" Her tone is deliberately neutral.

"Oh, yes?" Eadie's eyes are alight with curiosity.

"Wallace Smythe-Brown," says Brenda, preparing herself for the reaction.

The interest in Eadie's eyes morphs into something altogether more lethal.

"With any luck, the stupid prick is still waiting for me by the ladies."

After an initial bark of laughter, Eadie turns serious. "You be careful. It's all very well to play merry hell with Rupert's life as you did, but Wallace is a different kettle of fish."

"Hey, if he wants me to beat the crap out of him, I'm happy to oblige."

"No, no. You've got him all wrong. Wallace is subservient to no man, let alone a woman. He's pure evil."

Because of her earlier dealings with Rupert Smythe-Brown, Brenda has some knowledge of the family and knows Wallace isn't a nice chap. But evil?

Brenda only appreciates how obvious her thoughts must be when Eadie reiterates, "Yes! Evil! Black to the core! Trust me, I know."

12

The next morning, Brenda mulls over the events of the previous evening. She's pleased with the progress shown by Stef and Paula but despairs of sorting out Rosie. Even though the girl is only taking the course to learn how to get a date, the blokes she targets are those she might have been successful with before the make-over and lessons. Much as Brenda would be happy to take her money and say nothing, she feels an obligation to see the girl land someone better than the drip she'd been speaking to last night.

Moth-eaten best describes Rosie's current interest. If he was any more of a pill, you could slap a label on him and call him a prescription. He looks to be just shy of thirty and is already missing half his hair.

"That's sodding careless," says Brenda to Charlie, who's glued to her side. "Isn't it, big boy?"

Charlie chirps his concurrence, confident in the knowledge that his own hair coats most surfaces in the house, despite Flo's best efforts.

Brenda still doesn't know what to make of Julian. She hadn't seen him chatting to a single eligible bloke last night. If he's as keen on success as he'd made out at the interview, he needs to stop hanging around with all the old biddies. Maybe he's still lurking in the closet? Maybe this is why he signed up?

If he is getting ready to come out, what better way to do it than while you're out of your usual surroundings?

"Ooooh," says Brenda to Charlie, "That'll rip the family's undies."

This time, Charlie doesn't respond, instead stretching out and rolling over so his belly is an open invitation. It's one she accepts.

By the time he's had his fill of tummy rubs, it's close to breakfast time if Charlie's meowing and kneading are any indications.

It's Sunday and Brenda doesn't bother dressing for breakfast, instead pulling on her dressing gown, sliding into her slippers and dragging a brush through her hair to hammer out the worst of the tangles.

She's crossing the landing towards the stairs when the bathroom door opens and Julian emerges. He's only wearing pyjama bottoms and Brenda gets a good eyeful of muscled, hairless chest sitting above a six-pack.

Luckily, he's still half asleep and doesn't notice he's been subjected to a visual frisking.

"Morning," is mumbled in her direction before he disappears back into his bedroom.

"Such a waste," whispers Brenda to Charlie, who's on his sixteenth lap of her ankles as though winding her into action.

While not interested in hooking up with a guy who's closer to her in age, she can still appreciate the packaging, even if he is off-limits in more ways than one.

The chatter from the kitchen is audible before she's halfway down the final flight, with the debrief to Eadie apparently underway. The amount of laughter is testament to the evening having been a success.

Hand on the swing door in readiness to push it open, Brenda pauses when Eadie asks Rosie how she'd fared.

"Well, there is this one guy," says Rosie.

Brenda closes her eyes and holds her head against the door softly enough that she doesn't push it open. The coolness next to her forehead disappears, and she opens her eyes in time to see the door swinging back in her direction. Charlie has waited long enough.

A quick backwards jerk of her head avoids the impact, as does the fact she's still holding up her hands. Pushing the door open, she's met by pandemonium, lots of arm gestures, with all the women in the room talking simultaneously. On the plus side, at least Bert and Flo aren't working today. Those two could talk the leg off a donkey and it's zoo-like enough as it is.

"Thank god I didn't drink last night," says Brenda, for all the notice it receives.

If she wanted to grab everyone's, or even anyone's, attention, she'd need to tap dance starkers in the middle of the bloody table. A further nudge to her ankle reminds her that she's in possession of opposable thumbs and that Charlie is in danger of starving to death. So focused is he on his empty bowl that he's oblivious to a scene chaotic enough to make most felines hide under the nearest furniture.

She's dispensing kibble when Julian enters, still in his pyjamas but also wearing a cherry red smoking jacket that has 'fag' written all over it. Brenda can't help a chuckle when his eyes dilate and he holds his hands up to cover his ears. Strange, he didn't look as though he'd drunk that much last night. Before she can quiz him on it, he spins around and exits with his need for silence outweighing that of food and coffee. She's borderline herself.

A quick look at the table confirms there's a Matterhorn of toast as well as a pot of tea and the percolator. Despite her conversion to tea by the bucket-load, she lifts the percolator to check if there's enough for a cup and is surprised to find it heavy and maybe even capable of two cups.

Settling into a spare seat, she grabs snippets of the multiple conversations taking place around her, although in most cases they're more like monologues.

Putting her fingers to her lips, Brenda whistles loud enough to be heard by a sheepdog several paddocks away. It's loud enough to stop all the ladies at the table.

"One at a time, please. This racket is doing my bloomin' head in."

Working around the table, Brenda hears from each of them how they feel the previous evening went, now they've had time to sleep on it. She makes mental notes along the way, because she can't be arsed getting pen and paper. The main theme is that they need to work on 'going in for the kill'. While there have been offers of lunch and the like, none of them have received any firm invitations. Except Rosie. Much to Brenda's annoyance, the maths teacher, Brian, is meeting up with Rosie for lunch later that day.

"Promise me one thing," says Brenda, and once she receives a thumbs up from the girl, continues, "Don't you go paying for it."

Rosie has "but" already forming when both Eadie and Brenda hold a hand up to stop her.

"Did he invite you?" says Eadie.

"Yes. But—"

"No buts. He invited you, so he pays," says Brenda, hoping her tone will put an end to the discussion.

The girl sits in mutinous silence, but Brenda can see her acquiescence has come too easily. A quick look at Eadie and Brenda can tell the old lady shares this opinion.

With no classes that day, the morning is spent eating a leisurely breakfast and clearing up. Brenda is relieved the girls pitch in with this because, technically, they could have left her to it.

With the kitchen once again sparkling, Stef, Paula and Rosie disappear upstairs to get ready for their various outings. While Rosie is off to her lunch, Stef and Paula have decided to visit the British Museum. At first, Brenda thinks this must be for intellectual edification, but they let it slip they're going to have a crack at practicing their new-found skills.

Homework off their own bat? I am impressed," says Eadie, about to partake of her first sherry of the day.

Brenda has poured this for her but hasn't bothered with one herself, adhering to her own rule of not drinking before lunchtime. A childhood spent watching her parents drink themselves into oblivion before eleven every morning has put her off. That's not to say she's averse after lunch, but neither does she want it to rule her life as it had once.

"So tell me," says Eadie, interrupting herself with a sip of fortified wine, "Now that Rosie has a date, she's achieved what she set out to. Hasn't she?"

"I guess so, but she hasn't hinted that she wants to leave, yet."

"Will Julian leave when she does?' muses Eadie.

"Hmmm. It makes a hell of a lot more sense him signing on to keep an eye on her, than for anything I can teach him. Unless ..."

"Unless what?" says Eadie, her eyes alight with curiosity.

"Well, I've been wondering if he's getting ready to open the closet door. From the inside."

"No better time to experiment, than when you're in a new environment."

"He'd better hurry up, though. If he keeps up his current pace, he'll still be with us in five years."

"I can think of worse things." Eadie takes a healthy swig from her glass, emptying it in the process.

They're working on a lesson plan for their 'kill session' the next day, when they hear all the others clattering down the stairs; a rich baritone informs them Julian is up and about, too. After the front door closes, Brenda hops up to check on what everyone is wearing given their targets that afternoon.

"Bloody hell! Jeans!" says Brenda.

"That's not good. Totally inappropriate for a lunch and they'll send the wrong message at the museum."

"Not the girls. Julian!"

"Now that is a surprise. He's always struck me as too much of a Tory to dress like the hoi polloi."

"If I knew what you were talking about, I might agree," says Brenda, watching Julian saunter down the street.

So successful is the 'going in for the kill' lesson that the students want to put what they've learned into practice immediately. The only thing coming up on the social calendar is an opening night at the Michaels' Gallery that Wednesday.

"The place where Jennie will hold her solo exhibition? The one where we glued Rupert Smythe-Brown to the front window? That Michaels' Gallery?"

"That's the one," says Eadie, unable to stop a follow-up guffaw. "Hell's bells, that was funny. The look on Wallace Smythe-Brown's face is one I'll cherish until my grave."

"I suppose the creepy bastard will be there?" says Brenda, referring to the elder Smythe-Brown.

"More than likely. The whole blasted family has well and

truly enmeshed themselves in the art world. Even if they've had to resort to larceny and forgery to achieve it."

"Whoa." Brenda is surprised at Eadie's venomous expression. "I thought us forcing Wallace to pay over the odds for those hideous B&D acrylics had evened the score?"

"Not even close," says Eadie, "That bastard made my life a living hell for years and all because of something he thought I'd done."

It doesn't require too much prompting for the full story to come out.

"I can understand why you're so angry. Especially being innocent, and all."

"He ruined my career, and stole my best work," says Eadie, summing up her twenty-minute rant.

"But couldn't the cops get your paintings back?"

"Hardly. The old boys' network is above justice in this country. Also, I couldn't push it because I was guilty of painting that insulting portrait of him, as he thought."

With the exhibition only a couple of days away, there's a flurry of activity around the house as they spend hours cramming with role play.

"But I was the man last time," says Paula, her nasty whine blending uncomfortably with the soft Irish lilt.

"Fine, I'll be the man," says Stef, pantomiming rearranging her imaginary balls before walking with bowed legs over to stand in front of Rosie.

Rosie dissolves into a fit of giggles she's not likely to recover from in the short term.

"This is serious," says Brenda, her hand clamping down on Rosie's shoulder, although she'd love to join in with the merriment. "You have to know how to react to any number of openings with your rehearsed lines. The more you practice, the more natural you'll be."

Rosie's eyes widen and another peel of giggles escapes. Brenda turns in time to see Stef twisting the ends of an imaginary moustache "And you stop that."

"Sorry." Stef tips her imaginary hat in Brenda's direction and stands still, her mien so falsely serious that Rosie loses it again.

"Gah, I give up," says Brenda, part of her aware that the longer they take to get it, the longer they have to stay, paying her rent. Even so, she makes sure they keep up with the role play for another hour until they're all word perfect with their responses and able to steer the conversation in whatever direction they choose. Not always easy when dealing with older gents with a tendency to waver when it came to concentration.

Even more time is spent on what they're going to wear. The event isn't formal, allowing the girls to choose appropriate outfits from their own and each other's wardrobes.

Even Eadie knows what she'll wear, although her attendance is kyboshed on the day when it dawns wet and cold, leaving her joints clamouring for attention.

"Might be best if people don't see me with you, anyway," says Eadie, from the nest of pillows in her bed. "I'm still out of favour in some quarters thanks to Shit-Brown."

At Brenda's look of anger, she continues, "I couldn't give a rat's on my own account, but better if you and the students don't have to deal with any fallout. And more importantly, it might be best he doesn't connect the two of us. He might try to get to me through you."

Piling out of the cab around the corner from the gallery, Brenda spots a chauffeur-driven Roller glide by. Taking heed of her sixth sense, she pulls back into the depths of the cab, even though she gives herself a mental shake for the Mata Hari behaviour. She revises this when she walks around the corner and sees who the Rolls Royce is ejaculating.

The others wait too, unconsciously circling her and thus hiding her from Wallace Shit-Brown. Rupert, the younger Shit-Brown, follows his father from the car, making Brenda especially glad of her human shield.

"Bugger," says Brenda, spotting the little Hooray Henry, following his dad into the gallery. Rupert must have sacs the size of melons to show his face here after the humiliation to which Jennie and Brenda subjected him. Never mind that he's entering an establishment where the owner knows all about the extortion whereby he'd forced Jennie to forge paintings on his behalf. The rich are a law unto themselves.

"All good?" says Julian.

"Yeah," says Brenda pausing long enough for the Shit-Browns to enter the premises, "All good."

Rupert had been blindfolded the night he'd been glued to the plate glass window and has no idea what Brenda looks like. He knows nothing about her and she's dressed differently. For one thing, she's not sporting a mask on this occasion.

Still, she has no intention of tempting fate by talking to him and will avoid him like the plague. She's not sure, though, how she'll deal with Shit-Brown senior. That the old bastard is still in possession of a goodly number of Eadie's paintings has her blood boiling.

While the police seem loathe to carry out justice, someone needs to sort that odious bastard. Still, it wouldn't be the first time Brenda had taken the law into her own hands. It also wouldn't be the first time she'd seen the police fail to mete out punishment to the true culprit. Hell, spending time in borstal for something she didn't do was evidence of that. Sure, she'd hot-wired cars heaps of times before that night, for the sake of convenience, but not on the one time she'd been fingered for it. *Screw you, Janie Nielson.*

Letting the others go ahead, she hangs back. She'll have to be careful how she plays it with the older Shit-Brown. With no idea yet of how she'll get retribution for Eadie, she can't agree to anything. Non-committal is the best way to play it with S-B; even better if she plays hard-to-get.

Immediate plan of action sorted, Brenda enters the gallery and hands her invitation to the chap behind a table that's groaning with glasses of wine, poured and ready to go.

"Do you have any water?"

This simple request puts him in a right tizzy; he looks at her as though she's a sandwich short of a picnic.

"Water?"

"Yes. You know. That clear stuff. Comes out of a tap."

"You don't want a lovely glass of Gewurztraminer?" he says, trying to put her off a drink that will involve him in shifting more than three feet.

"If I wanted wine, I would have asked for it. Wouldn't I?" says Brenda, overtly polite, even though her underlying message is anything but.

He's not giving up his favoured spot this easily, though, and spotting a passing waitress, clicks his fingers to get her attention. Brenda suspects this irks the girl as much as it does her. A feeling the girl can't keep off her face.

He instructs the girl to get Brenda's water and the waitress's attention swings to her. Rather than take it on the chin, Brenda gets herself on side by saying, "Yes. The chap behind the table is having trouble with his legs holding up all that, ah, muscle."

Brenda says this loudly enough that the jumped-up twit hears it. If the expression sported by the waitress is any indicator, her intended target is currently grinding a couple of layers of enamel off his gnashers.

"Come with me, I'll sort that for you, immediately," says the waitress, fighting to keep a smile from surfacing.

Once they're far enough around the edge of the crowd to be

out of his sight, the girl turns to Brenda, "Thanks for that. The obnoxious little twerp needs taking down a peg or two."

"Is he your boss?"

"Hah. No. He's on the same rate as me. He just struck it lucky by being selected to run the front table and collect the invitations."

"If I were you, I would have snapped his bloody fingers off."

"The night is young," says the waitress. "Right, I'll get that water for you."

While waiting for the world's most difficult drink, Brenda scans the room. She easily spots her four charges and is pleased to see them all interacting with what look to be rich old dudes.

"Here you go," says the waitress, handing over a glass brimming with water and ice, "Let me know if you need a refresh."

Slipping into the crowd proper, Brenda works her way around the room. Her progress isn't aimless, anything but. Pretending to look at the featured artist's work, Brenda eavesdrops on each of her students in turn, while keeping an eye on Wallace and his son.

She's not worried about running into Wallace but feels it's safer to give the younger Shit-Brown a wide berth.

Brenda's on her second lap when she notices a tight-knit group at the back of the gallery. The participants are tittering about whatever, or whoever, they've surrounded. With all the students doing what they're supposed to, she feels unencumbered enough to check out the spectacle.

Peering over a shoulder into the huddle, Brenda has to hold back a snort of laughter. The 'sculpture' wouldn't look out of place in a sex shop. Yes, she can admire the skill involved in its creation, but unless the 'biggus dickus' of a trouser python takes batteries, it's useless in her books.

"Like what you see?" whispered into her ear causes her to

convulse hard enough that she nearly spills her recently refreshed glass of water.

Turning, she isn't surprised to see Wallace Shit-Brown invading her personal space and trying his damnedest to clock her nipples.

"I've seen bigger," says Brenda, dismissively.

"I waited a long time for you the other night." His tone lets her know he's less than happy about it.

Flicking her gaze slightly to the right, she's happy to see his earlobe is still looking red where she'd chomped on it. Maybe she'd even him up tonight and leave him waiting somewhere else. Nothing would challenge the arsehole more than this, if he's used to getting his own way as Eadie says.

Moving away from the porcelain phallus, Brenda isn't surprised when he shadows her. Initially merely irksome, it escalates to bloody annoying. Her attention should be on her students, not this lecherous old creep. She needs to make a plan for how to deal with him so she doesn't have to waffle on to him like this at future events.

It gets to the part of the evening where a lot of the work is sporting sold stickers, and Brenda gives her students the pre-arranged signal to let them know they should wrap up their current conversations and make their way to the door.

Brenda knows from experience that it looks better if you depart before the dregs and leave your target wanting more.

She's making her own way to the door when Wallace blocks her way in what appears to be his signature move.

She keeps moving until she's hard up against him. Going up on tiptoes, she drops her head to the side as though to whisper sweet nothings into his hairy lug. He drops his head to the other side to give her better access. Gormless twit.

"Go over and wait for me by the dildo and I'll show you what I can do with it."

With the majority of the stupid old bastard's blood heading

south, Brenda chomps hard on his earlobe ensuring he'll be wearing a matching pair.

He doesn't immediately move, so she looks up at him through her lashes. "If you hurry, you could be biting someone yourself."

She clicks her teeth together before smiling broadly, relieved when he stalks obediently towards the rear of the gallery.

She wastes no time in leaving with the other four and is even happier when Julian hails a cab. Despite the temptation, she doesn't look inside the gallery to see if there are now two big dicks standing next to the storeroom doors.

13

They're home from the gallery a lot earlier than they'd be from any other function and Brenda is paying for the cab when she sees the sitting room curtains twitching. The cab tootles off into the night and she joins her students on the path so they can enter together, but knowing Eadie's still up and about, she doesn't bother lowering her voice when she bids them goodnight before opening the door to the sitting room.

"It looks like I'm going to have to deal with Wallace, one way or another."

"Why's that?"

Brenda is unable to hide a look of disgust marching across her face. "I suspect he won't give up until he's marked me like a dog spraying its patch."

"Hmmm." Eadie isn't any more forthcoming than this, leaving Brenda in no doubt the old lady wants nothing more to do with the man, even if it is indirectly.

"How many of your paintings did he nick?"

"Thirty, or so."

"Thirty! We'll need a van."

"No! I don't want you anywhere near that revolting man. As much as Rupert is submissive, Wallace is cruel."

Despite a lot of variations of the same question, Eadie doesn't budge, so after confirming the old lady is set for the rest of the evening, Brenda calls it a night. She'll get the dirt, one way or another. It might involve sherry, lots of it.

She's nearing the top of the stairs when Julian pops out of his room, the timing letting Brenda know he's been waiting for her.

"You should be careful of Wallace Smythe-Brown."

"You know him?"

"Only by reputation and it's not good."

"He's into a bit of B&D from what I hear, consenting adults and all that."

"B&D's okay, it's the S&M you want to avoid. Rumour is he's a sadist of the highest order. Women have been hurt."

"Oh." This new development will need to be taken into account with any plan she comes up with.

"If he ever tries to slap cuffs on you or tie you to anything, run like the clappers."

His warning delivered, Julian leaves her standing on the top step and unsure of herself for the first time in a good few years.

The week following the exhibition and Brenda doesn't leave the house. Rather than hiding from Wallace, she hasn't had any need, with all the students out enjoying lunch dates, dinners and private parties and generally reaping the rewards of their efforts.

Stef and Paula are being treated like royalty by the middle-aged gents they've hooked, but Julian is less than forthcoming about his activities. As long as he keeps paying cash and twice as much as everyone else for his board and lodging, he can do anything he bloody likes.

Rosie is also circumspect about what she's up to, but Brenda has no trouble working out that she's meeting up with the blasted maths' teacher again. If the silly girl wants to pay for the pillock's lunches, good luck to her. Brenda makes a note to catch up with Rosie to see if she needs to continue the course now that she's mastered the art of getting a date.

With time on her hands, Brenda schemes to get Eadie's paintings back. Just because she'd said no to their retrieval didn't mean Brenda would obey. Unfortunately, no matter how convoluted her plans, they all end up with her being with Wallace Smythe-Brown. On her own.

There's no doubt she could do a lot of damage if she tried hard enough, but she might get hurt in return. If she can minimise the odds of that happening, she's happy to delay until every loose end is tied up.

After filling the rubbish bin in her bedroom with failed plans, Brenda goes in search of company even though she suspects it might only be Bert, Flo and Eadie who are in. She's swinging around the newel post at the bottom of the stairs when a good old wad of mail is fed piecemeal through the slot. Most of it drops into the wire basket hooked on the inside of the front door.

Picking up the dropped pieces and retrieving those in the basket, she makes short work of sorting the mail into piles on the hall table.

It's no surprise that the students each get a good amount of mail. The invitations arrive in ever-increasing numbers, confirming for Brenda that her teaching strategy is bang on. Certainly the students say they've never been invited to this many functions in the past.

That there are a couple of letters for her is a surprise.

Taking them into Eadie's sitting room, she sits on the sofa and examines them.

Of concern is the one from a law firm – if the multitude of surnames is any indication. There's a Melbourne address in small print under the logo. She pops it to one side and looks closely at the plain brown envelope with a fair old line-up of Aussie stamps covering the top third. Flipping it over, she's none the wiser with no return address showing.

"I find it's quicker to open the envelopes," says Eadie, who has been quietly watching Brenda.

"Hmmm. Question is, do I need to know what's in here?"

"Only one way to find out," says Eadie, unable to stop impatience colouring her words.

Brenda slides her finger into the gap at the end of the flap and slides it along, ripping a ragged hole as she goes. Peeking through this gash at the contents proves useless. She pulls a single sheet of paper free and flips it open, making quick work of reading the contents.

While the ink might be blue, Brenda sees red. She has to read it three times before she's sure of the meaning. She opens her mouth to speak, twice, snapping it closed again, both times without uttering a word.

"Everything all right?"

"I have no bloody clue."

A slight elevation of one of Eadie's eyebrows is prompt enough for Brenda to elaborate.

"It's from Stefano."

"And?"

"He's raving on about another investment that will make up for the last failure. One that's too good to resist."

"I take it that by now he'll have given up resisting, and it's your money he's investing."

"Bingo." Brenda wipes her hand across her mouth before

forming a fist and holding it hard against her lips. This is all that's between her and a total verbal meltdown.

"Maybe it'll pan out?" The lack of conviction in Eadie's voice is something Brenda's feeling herself. That there are no distinguishing marks on either the envelope or the letter itself, tells her that while the investment might be gold, it's also dodgy as all get out. That Stefano has only signed the letter with a bold 'S' and a lot of kisses is evidence he's keen to avoid anything that might incriminate him.

"I'm surprised there was anything left after he'd settled with his bookie. I wish I'd realised what a total bloody disaster he was *before* I handed the money over."

"If the school pans out, it might not matter in the long run."

Silence descends on the room as Brenda steels herself to open the second letter. She hasn't yet received a letter from a solicitor that she's enjoyed and never one she's benefitted from. The only thing in its favour is that it's not a window envelope.

Mind made up, she hurries to open the envelope, managing to rip the letter itself in her haste, but not enough for her to miss the gist of the correspondence.

"Dead?" stutters out Brenda.

"Oh?" Eadie gets no further.

"Martin," says Brenda, looking at Eadie through a veil of tears.

"Your elderly gent from Melbourne?"

"He was more than that," says Brenda, crushing the letter in her hands, "So much more. He was the first person to ever believe in me and treat me with respect. He was more of a father figure than that useless prick who's still shuttling between prison and the latest hovel masquerading as home. Martin made me feel safe."

Seeing Eadie preparing to speak, Brenda mumbles, "Excuse me," before lurching to her feet to reach the sanctuary of her bedroom before she disintegrates.

She's curled in a tight ball under the covers when Charlie climbs out from under the bed, covered in dust bunnies, and worms his way in, right next to her, jamming himself tight against her aching chest. She curls her arms around him and gives him a squeeze of thanks that results in a small squeak.

"Sorry."

Leaning down and kissing the back of his neck, she receives a small lick to her arm in return. This small gesture of love is her undoing with any locked-in emotions promptly shown the door. While giving into them for a moment, she quickly reins her feelings back under her control. But a few seconds later, a loud sob breaks the silence she's fought so hard to achieve.

What the hell is wrong with her? Martin was a meal ticket, nothing more. She keeps telling herself this but it fails to take. Her world is a darker place for him no longer being part of it. It wasn't the money; it was that he believed in her, the first person ever to do so. What if ...? Brenda's unable to face that stark reality, hiding from it by stuffing her face in Charlie's side and breathing in his calming scent.

A couple of hours of this and she's feeling scoured, while Charlie is decidedly damp in places. But at least her hard exterior shell is back in place, albeit showing damage in places.

"Sorry, buddy. I didn't mean to use you like a hanky." Brenda smoothes his eyebrow whiskers back, hard, how he likes it, distorting the shape of his eyes in the progress.

A gentle knock at the door puts an end to this mutual appreciation session. Charlie's head pops up and he eyeballs the door, ready to protect his mistress. Damn it, she'd been so busy sniffling she hadn't even noticed there was someone out there courtesy of the creaky boards.

"Stand down, Tiger. We're all good."

"Who is it?"

"Julian. Are you okay?"

Bloody hell, just what she needs, the resident gay hand-maiden drooping all over her.

"Yeah, I'm fine," says Brenda, her forced jocularity stymied by her voice cracking halfway through.

"Sure you are."

Even though he hasn't bought it, Brenda can't help but feel she's had a lucky escape when creaking on the landing indicates he's gone back to his room. Even without them, she would have known this because Charlie's head has dropped back to the comfort of her arm, it's weight indicating he's already well on his way to falling asleep.

Scrabbling around on her bedside table with her free hand, Brenda locates the lawyer's letter so she can read it all the way through. She didn't get past the first sentence downstairs.

A quick skim of the contents and a chuckle bubbles up, although she's laughing at the irony of the situation rather than anything she's read. According to the lawyer, Mrs McGowan is aware of Brenda's windfall and intends seeking its return through the courts.

"Hah, good luck with that, you old trout. If I can't get my hands on it, you're out of luck."

The letter goes on to say that Mrs McGowan's legal matters are dealt with by a rival firm and following strict instructions from Martin, they will not be revealing Brenda's location. She can't help but smile. Boy, he's shafting the old tart, even from the grave.

She had made his life a living hell and it was only due to them largely living separate lives that he'd hung in there for the sake of outward appearances.

Looks like he'd had no qualms about all hell breaking loose after he'd popped off.

Martin's demise tinges Brenda's world with grey. Even with Stefano appropriating her nest egg, she'd felt safe knowing Martin would help her out, no matter what. She gives herself a right mental kicking. For someone who's had to look out for herself since before puberty, to be suckered into a false sense of security like that, is lame. 'Everything is fleeting. Rely on no one.' She needs to refamiliarise herself with her own maxim if she's to survive.

Leaving Nurse Charlie comatose under the covers, Brenda levers herself out of bed and stumbles over to the wardrobe to check the damage in the age-spotted mirror on the door.

"Shit! I look like a panda!"

Grabbing cotton pads and eye makeup remover, she blots till she looks less like something you'd pay to see before reapplying her makeup to restore her public persona. No way she's going downstairs without it.

She walks into the dining room in time to hear Paula say, "We need one of those motorised chair-lift thingies."

At thoughts of forking out more dosh, Brenda tenses. Damn Stefano and his useless bloody cash management. With access to her money, it would have been a no-brainer. Without that, it would be better for her to pay Sherpas to carry the visiting octogenarians up and down to the common room, if this is what Paula's referring to.

Not wanting to impose on Eadie's personal space, it has been agreed that any visitors to the house will be entertained in the common room on the second floor. But this has proved problematic for their more ancient callers. Even with chairs strategically placed on each landing, it sometimes took upwards of ten minutes for their hearts to settle after the climb. That a lot of them fall asleep during this process is hardly conducive to lively entertainment.

"My old man's got a mate who can get you one on the cheap," says Stef, looking at Eadie.

"Dented from where it's fallen off the back of a lorry?" says Julian, voicing Brenda's own thoughts.

"Hey, if it's hot, it'll keep the old codgers warm on the way up," says Stef, whose laughter is joined by that of the others.

"It would be nice to have access to the whole house again," says Eadie, wistfully.

Brenda knows for sure the only time Eadie has left the ground floor in recent years was when Mark and Chris had carried her up to Jennie's studio at the top of the house. Apparently, this had been a painful process and not one the old lady would wish to repeat any time soon.

"Can you get prices?" says Eadie, to Stef.

"You leave it with me." Stef wriggles her eyebrows to indicate the stair chair's pedigree will be hotter than Hades.

During this discussion, Brenda has been conscious of both Eadie and Julian looking at her, gauging how she is. The last thing she needs is for either of them to smother her with sympathy; that would end her self-control for sure. Luckily, the slight shake of her head at Eadie is enough for the old girl to lean back in her chair. She repeats the process with Julian and is relieved when he also stands down.

"Do you want to invest in something that long term?" Brenda forces the pair's attention back to the stairlift.

Eadie's shrug in response to this query isn't the confirmation she's after. Brenda isn't keen on forking out for a poor man's elevator and doesn't think Eadie should either. What if they can't get any more students after the current lot graduate? Apart from board and lodgings, they aren't exactly rolling in dough.

She claps her hands to get everyone's attention. "I'm heading to Antique Alley in the morning if anyone wants to join me or has anything they want me to sell on their behalf."

With any luck, there will be a trinket or two forthcoming that will help boost Eadie and Brenda's bank accounts by way of commission on the sales.

Brenda is heartened when Stef, Paula and even Julian,

promise to give her items in the morning. The head shake that Rosie gives is no surprise. Unless old maths' books are suddenly in short supply, there's no way they're making any extra money out of Rosie and her chosen target.

The following morning, before showering and dressing, Brenda retrieves her bauble bag from the top of the wardrobe and upends it onto her bed. She makes short work of sifting through it all, flicking disposable items to one side. Lifting a beautiful heart-shaped pendant, she's unable to stop a small choke escaping. It was one of the first things Martin had given her. At the time, she'd been disappointed, knowing he could afford better. Now it's priceless.

Replacing everything but a bangle and a pair of sapphire earrings, Brenda is about to return the bag to its hiding place when she pauses. It is too bloody obvious. Looking slowly around the room, she rejects one spot after another. Then she clocks how deep the hems on the drapes are. Lifting one of the curtains, she's pleased to see the hem is open at the side, providing the perfect spot to hide her plunder. She removes the bulkier items from the bag and slides them into the gap, then follows with the bag itself, the smaller pieces still inside. She drops the curtain back into place, happy with the result. Sitting as it does, partially behind the wardrobe, her hidey-hole is as good as invisible.

At breakfast, Brenda is pleased to see the little stash of jewels in the middle of the table. Stef and Paula have a couple of pieces each that, when liquidated, will cover their costs for a few more weeks. Brenda is still surprised at how easily they'd put their other lives on hold to attend lessons and live on site. Barmaiding and temp office work aren't exactly careers, but still.

Julian has only added two items to the pile, although being cufflinks they technically count as one. But what a one it is. The size of the diamonds makes Brenda examine him in a whole new light. He must be king of the blowjob to garner goodies like this. He spots her looking at him and deliberately makes a show of licking marmalade off the end of his finger. It's all she can do to keep po-faced before turning to look elsewhere. Anywhere will do, even at her plate. What the hell is it about some gays that they could be total male sluts? Still, no more than straight guys if Wallace Smythe-Brown is anything to go on.

"Julian?" says Brenda, looking him in the eye again.

"Yes?"

"Are you able to get your hands on a van?"

He's still formulating a response when Eadie speaks up from the end of the table. "No! Brenda, I categorically forbid it."

Julian clams up given the firmness of this statement.

Rather than quell any discussion on the matter, all the students are agog with curiosity, their heads swinging back and forth between Eadie and Brenda, hoping for clarification.

"I can," says Bert, already peeling potatoes for their lunch and seemingly oblivious to the tension mounting at the table.

Brenda is relieved at both finding a means of transport and also having the attention of the group diverted away from herself and Eadie and their covert discussion. Not that it lasts long.

"If I hear you've gone ahead with anything, I will be cross!" Eadie's tone brooks no argument.

The students' gazes swing back in her direction, and she tosses a subtle head shake to them, effectively telling them that she'll discuss it later.

"I saw that," says Eadie, her tone that of someone supremely pissed off that she's been taken as slow mentally, purely because she's not as physically capable as she once was.

"Fine, I'll leave it be," says Brenda, holding her hands up in surrender and hoping like hell Eadie doesn't notice she's got her fingers crossed.

The change of subject Brenda dumps on them is clunky but it works: everyone is keen to move on and clear the air of anything that might cause indigestion. Brenda's first to leave the table, eager to get to the antique shop and clear a profit. Classes are now few and far between with any help more than likely given at actual events, or in response to specific questions.

Stef follows her out into the hallway but when the girl opens her mouth, Brenda holds a finger up to her lips and looks pointedly in the direction of the kitchen. Eadie is no slouch in the hearing department.

Rather than heading out the door as she'd planned, Brenda walks upstairs, but it's not until she and all her students are safely in the common room on the second floor that she brings them up to speed with what Wallace Smythe-Brown had done all those years ago. She's thought long and hard about involving them, but if being involved is their choice, her conscience will be clear. Until they commit, she's not giving away any details of her plan; mainly because her plan is too sketchy to deserve the title.

"We can't let 'im get away with that!" says Stef, suitably riled and showing she, too, has developed a soft spot for Eadie.

The others, even Rosie, all vouch their support in whatever way they can; Brenda can see love for the old lady downstairs is universal.

"We can discuss it after I get back from Kirsten's," says Brenda.

She's leaving the common room when Julian confirms he can get a van. Stef adds, "An' me an' all," and Brenda knows there'll be no shortage of vehicles, although the van supplied by Julian is more likely to come with keys.

14

W alking along Chiswick High Street, Brenda's surprised how few people are about. A quick glance at her watch shows it's gone nine. Surely the shops should be up and running by now? Her steps falter as she takes a closer look at those she's passing. It appears to be fifty-fifty between those open and those still locked up tight, their interiors dark and unwelcoming.

Deciding she can live with these odds, she continues on to the antique shop even if her pace slows unconsciously. It's therefore with relief that she pushes on the door at Antique Alley and meets no resistance. It opens easily with her presence acknowledged by the buzzer. Looking around, she can't see hide-nor-hair of the proprietor.

"Hello?" She calls out, loudly enough for the buzzer to feel inadequate.

There's groaning in response from the depths.

Brenda walks further into the shop, expecting to find someone lying on the ground. What she finds is Kirsten, sunk low in a large armchair, nursing a nearly-empty mug of coffee and what looks suspiciously like a boomer hangover. Sniffing experimentally, Brenda detects the faintest whiff of second-hand alcohol.

"Good night was it?"

Kirsten looks briefly at Brenda, grunts, and after sitting up slightly, gulps the dregs of her coffee. She perches the mug back on her tummy and once again retreats into the chair.

"Want me to sort out a top up for you?" says Brenda, her motives not entirely altruistic. If she can help the woman feel less like death, she'll be able to take care of everything today, rather than having to come back.

The only response is Kirsten holding out her mug. Before Brenda can ditch her handbag on a spare seat and grab it, the mug has gone from trembling slightly to suffering from full-on palsy. Good thing it's empty.

Mug in hand, she stands next to a curtained doorway. "Through here?" A grunt confirms she's on the money.

The room she enters is storeroom-cum-kitchen-cum-everything, and it takes a moment for her to locate what she's after. The fridge is so old she initially mistakes it for stock. The jug is less of a museum piece, but not modern by any means.

Brenda pops her head back through the gap in the curtain.

"Any sugar?"

"Fridge," comes the croaky reply.

"Fridge?"

"Ants."

Nodding at the logic of this, Brenda retreats and reopens the fridge. She's checked through half a dozen containers before she finally finds one with sugar inside. She'd passed over the old enamel pot with 'LARD' embossed on the front on her initial search. She thinks briefly about asking how many spoons the patient wants, but decides she needs a couple at least.

Looking at the size of the souvenir spoon that's in use, Brenda adds an extra spoonful of both coffee and sugar.

"Sorry the tide's out," says Brenda, holding the mug out. "Didn't want you spilling it."

With nothing else to do, she shoves her handbag to one side and sits down. If the woman keeps drinking her coffee at the current speed, she's in for a good long wait.

The owner is on her third coffee before she advances from grunts and monosyllabic answers through to incomplete sentences.

"What the hell were you drinking?"

"Vodka. Sipper bottles."

"Sipper what?"

After a huge sigh, as though she's bracing herself to utter a complete sentence, she says, "Friend bought them in Russia. Bottles have sipper tops to avoid wasted time."

"Jeez. Wasted is right." Brenda shakes her head slowly as she mulls over what a mess the woman must have been the night before, and the inevitable carry over to this morning.

Dating Martin had halved her own consumption, as he wasn't keen on her getting trolleyed. It still happened occasionally, but no longer regularly.

"Damn it," mutters Brenda, to herself as this thought reminds her of Martin, reminds her he's gone, reminds her she's skint, which reminds her why she's here.

"Are you in any state to look at some bits and pieces I've got to sell?"

"Give me a ..."

"'nother coffee?"

"Minute or two."

It's more like twenty but Brenda guesses the woman's space-time continuum is seriously screwed up due to alcohol poisoning.

"What have you got?" Kirsten looks up at Brenda for the first time. Her eyeballs look like they've been cleaned with a Brillo pad.

"Bleeding heck, can you even see?"

"Enough." She holds out her hand, prompting Brenda to pass the goodies. The hand is trembling but doesn't waver into Parkinson's territory and, so, after retrieving the jewellery from the bottom of her handbag, Brenda drops the small, and nondescript, brown paper bag in the woman's palm.

Given the state she's still in, this involves more hand-eye coordination than she's capable of and the bag drops noisily to the table; the hangover victim winces mightily.

The woman doesn't move after this, appearing to be in a light sleep. Brenda leans over to pick up the bag in readiness to leave, but she's beaten to it. Slowly uncurling the top of the bag to minimise the rustling, Kirsten empties the contents into her lap before sifting through them.

Sitting back in her expensive, but bloody uncomfortable chair, Brenda settles in to wait while Kirsten assesses each piece.

Those provided by Stef and Paula are deemed fairly average, but good enough that Kirsten will take them off her hands. The same goes for the earrings and ring Brenda is ridding herself of. However, the woman's demeanour changes markedly when she looks closely at the cufflinks.

"Where did you get these?"

It's as though she's been given pure oxygen, so quickly does she slough off any remaining hangover.

"From one of my students. Julian."

"Are they his to sell?"

"I guess so. He's too bloody posh to have nicked them. Why?"

"I've seen these before. But I'm damned if I can remember where."

Putting effort into trying to remember proves too much for her and eventually she gives up.

"Can't take them. Sorry." She drops the cufflinks into the

paper bag and hands it back. "Can you get my calculator for me?"

"Sure. Where is it?" says Brenda, before adding, "On the counter?"

She gets a nod in return, which is followed by a grimace, the small movement no doubt sloshing her brain all over the show.

"And if you could grab a pen and my cheque book too?"

Brenda finds the calculator and pen easily enough, but the location of the cheque book isn't obvious.

"Cheque book?"

"Third drawer down, right-hand side. Under the stack of vintage postcards."

What should have been an hour's trip, is extended by several more – Kirsten's hangover eating into Brenda's morning. By the time she's deposited the Antique Alley cheque for her own items plus the commission on Stef and Paula's, it's crowding lunchtime.

Opening the front door, Brenda sniffs appreciatively.

"Stew!"

While it might not be everyone's cup of tea, the hearty brew that is a speciality of Bert's, is a firm favourite of hers. His dumplings are light and fluffy, unlike the hand grenades her mother produced on the odd occasion she'd been sober enough to finish cooking a complete meal. Growing up, Brenda's dinners had regularly consisted of roast meat with bread and butter because when it came to sorting out the veggies, gravy and the like, her mother had been too smashed to cope.

Following her nose, she walks through to the kitchen, where Bert and Flo are tucking into their lunch, and from there into the dining room.

"I didn't think you were going to make it," says Eadie, "What took you so long?"

While filling her plate, Brenda gives them the abridged version of that morning's events.

"Did you manage to flog everything okay?" says Stef.

"Sell, dear," says Eadie, automatically correcting the girl's speech.

"Yeah. Sell," says Stef.

"Almost everything," says Brenda, her gaze swinging in Julian's direction.

"No?" says Julian.

"No. Kirsten wouldn't take them. Said they looked too familiar and thought they were hot. Anything you'd like to share?"

"They're from a well-known designer. Maybe that's it," says Julian, airily.

"Hmmm," says Brenda, the smell of rat momentarily putting her off her lunch.

Paula's "How much?" is echoed by Stef.

Brenda rattles off what the various items have sold for, less her commission, without regard for privacy. If the girls are asking here, they mustn't give a toss about keeping the sales figures secret, so why should she?

"Excellent," says Stef, through a mouthful of dumpling.

"That cheap ..." says Paula.

The rest of her oath is masticated along with an overly large piece of beef, rendering the girl quiet for a moment. After a large swallow, she continues, "The way he went on about it, I expected to hear someone had run off with the blimmin' crown jewels."

"The more they talk a piece up, the cheaper it usually is," says Brenda, leading to questioning looks from her three female students.

"If the piece can't speak for itself, your cheapskate will do the talking for it. Unfortunately, they'll say anything to get their end away."

"You don't have a high opinion of men, do you?" says Julian.

Because his expression is neutral, Brenda isn't sure if there's a challenge buried in there, or not. Rather than go into details, she simply winks, sending him a response that's just as veiled.

———

Following through on her promise, Stef organises the installation of a stairlift. Rather than falling off the back of a lorry, it's come from a house in Mayfair that the new owners are gutting. All Eadie has to pay for is the installation and, from the sounds of things, that's at mates' rates, too. On the downside, there's only enough rail to take it as far as the second floor. Enough for Eadie to join in with festivities in the common room but not enough to visit Jennie's studio at the top of the house.

Three days of noise and builders' cracks later and once again, Eadie is mistress of almost all her domain. To celebrate its opening, there's a ribbon-cutting ceremony and drinks in the common room. It's a slow trip up. Eadie has to get off on the first floor and change over to another chair to complete her journey and so, on achieving the second floor, she's already had three glasses of champagne. This is courtesy of Julian who has walked next to her, topping her up when necessary.

Thinking ahead has also seen the installation of grab rails in the second-floor bathroom, not only for Eadie, but also to accommodate many of their elderly visitors; especially those with a drinking problem, which appears to be most of them.

———

Looking at Shelly's reflection in the mirror sitting above a counter cluttered with hairdressing paraphernalia, Brenda holds her breath.

The scissors in Shelly's hand are open and ready to cut. "You sure about this? Because you sure as hell don't look like it."

"I think so," says Brenda, wondering if she shouldn't have allowed Shelly to leave the mirror covered, after all. Better not to see the damage as it happens.

"I promise, I won't take off any more than I have to, but you have to get rid of these split ends." Shelly holds up a section of hair that ends in a frizzy ball, demonstrating the obvious.

Even a trim makes Brenda nervous, meaning it's something that only happens every couple of years, tops. Otherwise, it's a case of her snipping off the individual split ends as and when she spots them.

"That's what my mother used to say, too."

"And?" says Shelly, her reflected gaze agog.

"She'd overcorrect half a dozen times, I'd lose a good six inches, and it'd still be crooked. As a kid, I constantly looked like I had my head tilted to one side."

Shelly is unable to stop a snort of laughter at this revelation but stifles it when she sees Brenda doesn't share her amusement.

"That's not going to happen here."

Brenda doesn't relax until the cape is removed and she's paid. She's pleased in that there's been so little taken off that it's hard to even tell she's had a trim and when she holds the ends of what amounts to her super long fringe together under her chin, they're the same length, something her mother had never been able to achieve. The ends then taper away on either side to reach halfway down her back.

"See you in three months?" says Shelly, when Brenda is stepping outside.

"Maybe?"

Out on the footpath, Brenda finds herself in a localised tornado. It passes on, but rather than her hair metamorphosing into a bird's nest as usual, it flattens back down again, sleek and smooth.

Seeing Shelly looking at her through the plate-glass window, Brenda opens the door again. "See you in three months."

There's a lot of head swinging on the tube ride home as Brenda enjoys the feeling of swishing her hair without fear of it tangling.

Her lightness of heart darkens when she sees an ambulance parked outside the house. From walking briskly, she progresses to running, only one word rattling in her head as she does so. "Eadie!"

The house is in an uproar and it doesn't take long for Brenda to follow the noise to Eadie's bedroom. It's a squeeze fitting in, with all four students present, along with Bert and Flo and two ambulance medics.

The old lady is laid out on her bed, wearing one of her best frocks and even pearls.

The medics fuss over their patient, checking for a pulse and slapping one of those inflatable blood pressure things on, wrapping it around a couple of times given the frailty of Eadie's arm.

The medic wastes no time pumping this up and placing his stethoscope against Eadie's arm, and listening briefly. With a sigh, he drags the stethoscope clear of his ears in a manner that smacks of defeat.

"Can you all please leave," he says, swinging towards the audience crowded around the end of the bed and over to Brenda, who's still just inside the doorway.

The others all file out of the room, tears already in evidence. Brenda stands her ground.

"Is she ...? Has she ...?"

"What?" The medic says in confusion, although enlightenment follows. "She's still with us. But I couldn't hear a thing with that lot carrying on."

Standing quietly, Brenda watches as the two medics go through the process of examining her beloved mentor.

"Everything looks to be normal," says the medic on the far side of the bed.

"Madam, can you hear me?" he says in a voice loud enough to be heard by someone who'd shuffled off the mortal coil a couple of weeks earlier.

Eadie shows signs of coming around but when finally conscious, she appears confused and wants to know what's going on. The medics explain she's had a turn, but looks to be okay now.

The medic on the far side of the bed is already packing his bits and pieces into a large hard-sided case in readiness to return to the ambulance. The medic closest to Brenda starts unwinding the blood pressure cuff, but Eadie places her other hand on his, to stop him. She pauses long enough that his colleague has left the room. It's only then she speaks.

"Would you be willing to give my young charges first aid classes, in case something like this happens again?"

"I, ah ..."

"I could pay cash," says Eadie, her voice suspiciously tremulous. "It would mean so much to me."

"Yeah. All right, love," says the medic, proving yet again that cash is king.

"You can arrange all the details with my niece."

"Niece?" mouths Brenda to Eadie, while the medic finishes packing up the blood pressure kit.

The wink she receives in return has her close to laughter and it's only by exerting strong control that Brenda stops herself from losing it.

Walking back into Eadie's room after waving the ambulance off, Brenda is in awe of the old lady's Machiavellian streak.

"You crafty old bugger," says Brenda to Eadie, who has ditched the pearls and is already sipping on a glass of sherry that must have been hidden in the bedside cabinet while the medics were there.

"I thought it would be good if the students learnt the basics given the age of their visitors."

"Good point. I'll sit in on those, too," says Brenda, unable to stop herself recalling the night she'd had to resuscitate Martin.

15

L ooking at her notes, Brenda reads through the details again. It will take weeks to have Wallace Smythe-Brown frothing at the mouth enough that he lets his guard down.

The input from Stef and Julian has been invaluable, and even Paula has offered good ideas. Rosie's contribution has been the biggest surprise.

While not wanting to take part in the actual operation, she's come up with a couple of suggestions that tag her as being a master strategist. The old crud won't know what's hit him when they've finished with him.

The only thing they haven't sorted out is the final sting, but the early part of the plan is kicking off the coming weekend when they're all attending a house party in the country that Julian has managed to get them invited to. This event has the place in an uproar with all the girls fussing over what they're going to take and Eadie phoning around in hopes of uncovering the guest list.

Eadie's under the impression that this is so Brenda can work out targets for the various students but in reality, it's to confirm whether the fat bastard will be there as they've been led to believe.

Refolding the master plan, Brenda puts it back on her bedside table and goes to see how Eadie's getting on. Still on the phone, if the cord traversing the hallway is any indication. Following it into the sitting room and plonking herself on the couch, she waits for Eadie to wrap up the phone call. From the old lady's responses to whatever she's being told by her informant, the pickings will be good if the string of 'reallys' that goes on for a good couple of minutes is any indication.

"That is interesting," says Eadie, "Toodles, Ursula, see you soon."

With the large toad of a phone once again guarding the hall table, Brenda reclaims her spot on the couch so she can get an update and is ready with the pad and pen.

She looks hopefully at Eadie. "It sounds like this weekend could prove profitable?"

"Absolutely! Interesting mix, though."

"How so?"

"Eclectic." Eadie glazes over as she goes through an internal guest list only she's privy to. "I doubt Lady Preston has a clue what she's set herself up for."

"For god's sake!" says Brenda, becoming increasingly frustrated. "Spill."

Eadie looks at Brenda, surprised as though only just realising she's got company. "Sorry, I was a million miles and many years away."

"So?"

"As I said, interesting mix. Tories, landed gentry, movie stars, the usual slap-and-tickle crowd and even a few who really, really, and I mean really, love their horses."

"You are joking?" says Brenda, after she twigs what Eadie means.

"I wish I were," says Eadie, shaking her head, "It's beastly."

Realising what she's said, she starts to chortle. Brenda can't help but join in and the two of them have tears rolling down their faces.

They're spluttering to a halt, when Brenda says, "I hope I don't get saddled with any of them."

"Neigh. I hope not."

They have to resort to wiping their eyes with sleeves and corners of cardies before they finally run out of equestrian puns.

"Any worthwhile targets going?" says Brenda, after reining in her laughter.

"Yes, actually." Eadie's face is once again all business and she goes through listing potential guests for each of the girls with the exception of Brenda, who is to undertake her usual role of overseer.

"What about Julian?" says Brenda.

"Couple of options for him. There's Henry Newton. Camp as a row of tents but able to afford considerably better."

"And?" prompts Brenda, when Eadie doesn't continue with the second candidate.

"Lord Partington."

Eadie says nothing else, so Brenda winds her hand in the air to let Eadie know she needs to elaborate.

"Outwardly straight as a die. Inwardly, he's fitted a lock to the inside of the closet door, in case he's tempted. Worth a bloody fortune, though. And he's single."

"Obviously."

"Not always. Best accessory a gay Tory can have is a wife. If she manages to squeeze out a couple of little ones, so much the better."

Brenda adds Lord Partington to the long list, "That it?"

"I couldn't get all the names, but," Eadie wrinkles her nose, "Wallace and Rupert Smythe-Brown will also be present."

"Bloody excellent, I can have some more fun at his expense."

"I don't like the idea of you being in the same room as that repellent man. If anything were to happen to you, I'd never forgive myself."

The look of concern currently marring Eadie's usually placid features does funny things to Brenda. Shit, her parents hadn't even shown this much concern for her welfare. She's not sure she's comfortable with the pressure.

"I'll be fine, it's not like I'll be on my own with him." The 'yet' that follows this declaration is only audible inside her head.

Despite her assurances, Eadie's face remains stoic in its worry for an age before finally relaxing. "You might be all right in this instance because Genevieve, their mother and grand-mother will also be present."

"And this will be enough for them to behave?"

"Goodness me, yes. The woman's a gorgon. She'll bite their bloody heads off if they act up."

"Excellent," says Brenda, as though pleased Wallace will be on a short lease held by his mother but, in reality this could screw up the initial stages of their plan.

"I'd better go brief everyone," says Brenda, wasting no time in pleasantries.

Throwing the pad and pen in the general direction of the hall table, she's achieved the third step before Eadie has a chance to speak. "You'd better not still be thinking about tangling with that abhorrent man, because if I hear about it ..."

Rather than grit her teeth at Eadie's mental capabilities, Brenda starts laughing and is still chortling away when she walks into the common room.

Julian's in there, reading. But he's on his own. She picks up the small bell off the table inside the doorway and gives it a good old shake in the general direction of the landing.

She's rewarded with the doors to the girls' bedrooms opening, almost simultaneously.

"Fire?"

"Visitors?"

"Lunch already?"

"Nope. Briefing on the house party this weekend."

Waiting until they're all settled and Julian has bookmarked his page, Brenda does a quick run-through on who will be present, although she doesn't bother mentioning the whole horse-rogering crowd for fear Rosie, and maybe even Paula, will dig their heels in and refuse to attend. Even if they were to don saddles and bridles, Brenda doubts those sick individuals would give them a second glance.

"Are you still planning on catching the train down?" says Julian.

"Yes. Why?"

"After you asked me about a van the other day, I got to thinking it could come in handy for other stuff in the meantime."

"It'd better not be 'ot!" says Stef, drawing amused looks from both Julian and Brenda.

"Hardly," says Julian, but, on seeing they aren't simply going to take his word for it, continues, "Old school mate of mine has a transit van and he's off to the states for a couple of months. Said if he leaves it parked outside his place, it'll be a chassis on blocks on his return."

"In that case, it'd be bloody brilliant if you could grab it," says Brenda.

"I take it there's more?" says Rosie, looking at the sheath of paper Brenda's still holding.

"There is indeed. These are potential targets for each of you along with any particular peculiarities or hints on tracking. But there's no need to stick religiously to your lists. If you see someone better, go for it."

"Give 'em 'ere," says Stef, her hand already extended.

Rustling through the pages, Brenda pulls one free and passes it over to Stef, who wastes no time in scanning the page, given her list consists of one name only. "Brilliant. I've half-reeled the old duffer in already." Stef slaps the piece of paper against her other hand, "That all?"

At confirmation from Brenda, the girl returns to her room.

Paula is next to leave although rather than take Brenda's word as to the suitability of the applicants on her list, she's got the tattered copy of Burke's tucked under one arm.

Rosie runs her finger down her piece of paper scanning the half dozen names on it. That she smoothes her finger over one name in particular, arouses Brenda's interest.

"Anything I should know about?"

"No, no, no, everything's fine," says Rosie, staring at the note. "I'd better, ah, I've got to, ah ..." Without managing to stutter what it is she needs to do, she leaps to her feet and disappears in a flash.

Julian and Brenda look at each other, their reactions similar.

"What the hell was that about?"

"Who was on her list?" says Julian.

Brenda skims her master list, reading off any names with an 'R' next to them, before looking at him for a response.

"Know a couple of them, but I'm drawing a blank on the others."

None the wiser, Brenda takes a deep breath and hands a folded sheet of paper over to him. She doesn't wait to see if he's happy or not, but scarpers, leaving him to read them on his own. This is the first time she's openly acknowledged his being anything less than masculine and so thinks it's better if she gives him space.

She needn't have bothered when she hears him laughing

before she's halfway back to her bedroom. He appears delighted with the two names he's been given.

Looking down at the road through the window on the landing, Brenda is shocked at the state of the Transit van they'll be travelling into the country that morning.

Rather than the tatty beast she's been expecting, it being a loaner and all, the van is immaculate enough that it could even be brand new. No surprise Julian's mate hadn't wanted to leave it parked on the street if his neighbourhood is as dodgy as he'd made out.

Of concern is the fact there are no windows in the back, although there is a small skylight in the roof. Without that, the trip into the English countryside would be a dark affair for those riding in the back.

On the upside, it will be perfect for carting a lot of paintings around in a month.

"Everyone ready?" yells Julian, from the landing.

Brenda turns away from the van and skips back up to her bedroom. She's all ready to go and had finished packing the day before. It had taken her ages to decide what to take, with the final selection being a fine line between attracting Wallace's attention and blending into the background so she can keep an eye on her students.

While everything in her bag is fitted and revealing in places, it's also black, grey or denim; including her undies, even though these are still sexy rather than utilitarian. To be expected when she hasn't had to fork out for her own lingerie in years.

Brenda smiles as she remembers the one time she'd try to buy a couple of pair of comfy undies for that time of the month. Martin had looked so horrified when she'd picked them up, that she'd immediately dropped them again. Hell, she misses the old coot, and it's only by imagining him alive and well back in Melbourne that she hasn't fallen to pieces.

Altered reality firmly back in place, she grabs her bag and joins the others on the landing. She goes through a last-minute check with everyone that results in Paula rushing back to her room to get her curling tongs that she'd left to cool so she could pack them.

Dumping their bags in the hallway downstairs, they all file in to say goodbye to Eadie.

"Do you have everything you need for while we're gone?" Brenda feels a smidgeon of worry at leaving the old lady to fend for herself.

"You'll be gone for all of three blooming days! And besides, Flo and Bert are moving in to keep me company and help with meals and bits and pieces."

"Where are they going to sleep?"

"They're going to top and tail in the bed in Jennie's studio."

"Why don't they sleep in my room, or Sam and Chris's? What's wrong with Mark and Jennie's bed?

"They wouldn't dream of it. I suggested that, but they refused."

While trying not to laugh at thoughts of the Cockney couple jammed together in the bed on the top floor, she makes a mental note to slip them something extra to cover for this, even though they'll refuse because they're doing it out of love and not for gain. The choice of gift will be a tricky one.

———

Jeez, can you slow down?" Brenda's unable to keep the profanity out of this request because she's shit-scared.

"I'm going the speed limit," says Julian, looking over at her.

"Don't look at me, look at the bleeding road. If you can call this glorified sodding footpath a road."

Julian shakes his head, but duly eases off the accelerator enough that Brenda's knuckles regain their colour. The closer they get to their destination, the narrower the road becomes until the hedges on either side are getting quite the trim, courtesy of the commercial grade wing mirrors.

Brenda's sure things can't get worse when she hears frantic beeping from behind them. "You have got to be joking?"

Brenda sees a sliver of low-slung sports car every now and then in the wing mirror on her side of the van, as though the driver is contemplating undertaking them if he spots a big enough gap.

Luckily, they come upon a driveway into a paddock and Julian's able to pull over enough to allow the lunatic to pass.

"Arsehole," says Julian, in a move so out of character that Brenda's mouth drops open.

He's looking down on whoever it is scraping past them. "That figures. It's your mates the Shit-Browns."

Brenda smirks at Julian, who's taken up the cause whole-heartedly on Eadie's behalf. The sports car finally pulls in front far enough that the occupants are visible and Brenda isn't surprised to see that Wallace is driving. He's accelerating away when he casually raises his hand and gives them the finger.

"He's toast," says Brenda, already revising the sting plans to make things even more uncomfortable for the elder Smythe-Brown.

"Hell, yes," says Julian, his expression evil enough that Brenda is sure it mirrors her own.

"Are we stopping for lunch soon?" says Stef, leaning over the front seats. "I could murder a ploughman's."

"There should be a pub in the next village," says Julian, "we can pull in there."

A chorus of cheers comes from the three in the back. While

Brenda had worried the girls would be uncomfortable stuffed back there, they'd been anything but because of a double mattress and mountains of pillows. Even with all the bags loaded, there'd been enough room for them to stretch out and the snoring ricocheting off the walls like machine gun fire, proof they'd been comfortable. Brenda's sure as hell grabbing one of those spots for the trip home.

The hedges being set farther apart is all the warning they get that they've reached civilisation. Just as Julian had said, there's a pub. Actually, there are two of them, which is amazing given the size of the village.

Julian eases the van into the car park of the pub on their side of the road, drives through it and leaves again.

"What?" says Brenda.

There are cries of disappointment from the three students now leaning over the front seat.

"Didn't you spot a certain sports car in there?" says Julian, looking in both directions, before driving across the road and into the car park of the pub on the other side. Brenda isn't surprised when he parks the van right around behind the pub itself.

"How are we going to manage at the house?" says Brenda.

"We'll park around the back. Jerks like him never drive around there."

"Why are we hiding around the back?" pipes up Rosie.

"Because we don't want Wallace Smythe-Brown to associate us with the van, in case he puts two and two together after the sting," says Brenda.

There are 'ohs' of comprehension from the back at this revelation.

Bloody hell. It's like something Jane Austen would dream up," says Brenda, looking at the house in the distance.

They're currently crawling along the driveway having passed through the main gates miles back.

Conscious of being late, Brenda asks Julian if he can't speed up a bit.

"I would, but I'm waiting until Wallace and Rupert have had time to park and go inside."

It's because of those two lushes that they're running late now. Despite taking their time over lunch to allow the Smythe-Browns to hit the road and leave the way clear for them, they'd had to kill another hour after eating.

From the way Wallace had been weaving when he'd left the pub, they'd expected to come upon a crash site for the rest of the journey. The fact the pair have only just arrived indicates that having a skinful slowed him down.

No sooner have the two upper crust gits entered the house, than Julian floors it with a resultant spray of gravel. The Transit van is surprisingly peppy for what is essentially a delivery vehicle and they've soon shot down the drive and around the back of the old country pile.

Not long after nipping around the side of the humungous house, they're near the front doors when a large Rolls Royce pulls up in perfect alignment with the bottom step. Brenda stops dead, forcing Julian to do likewise, as he's right behind her.

"What?" he says, over her shoulder.

"Won't it look odd that we're arriving on foot?"

"One thing you'll learn about the English aristocracy is that odd is commonplace." He nudges the back of her legs with his bag as a gentle prompt. "Off we go."

They're already on the steps before the uniformed chauffeur has time to open the door so his occupant can disembark. Because 'get out of the car' is far too mundane a description to describe how the old lady exits the vehicle. It's laughably regal, but any smile is wiped off Brenda's face when Julian gives her a sharp nudge in the side.

She's readying herself to give him a right ticking off, but his expression and negligible head shake stop her. He leans in close enough to whisper, "Genevieve Smythe-Brown," without risk of the woman hearing.

What the hell is it about this bloody family that they seemed to be running into them like flies around shit? Brenda hopes there aren't any more of them lurking in the woodwork.

Rather than clamber up the steps in front of the woman, Brenda and her students stand to one side allowing her to enter before them.

The old lady acknowledges this, although Brenda thinks the woman expects nothing less than deferment to someone of her higher social standing. Little does she realise it's so they can all have a good gawp at her.

This gawp is returned when the old lady clocks Julian. The transformation from dragon to simpering deb is completed in a blink and Brenda's sure she hasn't imagined the small chuckle from Julian. A quick shufti in his direction confirms it. Bloody hell, he might need to borrow her doorstop at this rate.

Purchasing and packing doorstops had been at Eadie's insistence and while all the girls had thought it ludicrous, Brenda already sees the benefit of such an old-fashioned piece of kit. Julian might be lucky to last the weekend with his gayness unsullied if the predatory look in the old lady's eyes is anything to go by.

As if realising she's drooling in public, the woman moves on again and it takes all of Brenda's resolve not to burst out laughing when she sees a small Chihuahua, dragged in the old lady's wake like a canine water-skier. Not that water-skiers ever wore this much jewellery; the poor mutt is struggling under the weight of stones slung around its neck in a collar of sorts.

It looks ancient, even in dog years, with fur that's sporadic at best. As if sensing the scrutiny, it turns on Brenda, top lip curled back in a snarl, showing her that a couple of visits to the orthodontist wouldn't have gone astray, either.

"Come along, Countess, and do stop dawdling."

Hard on the pair's heels, is the chauffeur laden with three suitcases.

"I don't reckon we've packed enough," says Paula, looking down at her one small weekend bag.

"But *you* haven't brought your own sheets and towels, have you?" says Julian.

"You're kidding?" says Brenda.

"Nope."

"Jeez, if I end up with bed bugs I am going to be so pissed off!"

16

W alking into the hall proper, Brenda doubts bed bugs will be an issue, with the air redolent of Pledge and general cleanliness even if there are undertones of 'old pile'.

Genevieve and the moth-eaten dog are seen being whisked up to 'their' room, in as much as anyone in their eighties or nineties is able to 'whisk'. The old lady isn't moving much faster than the ancient dog and not as fast as her bags that have disappeared from view, presumably to be lugged upstairs via the back of the house; Brenda's seen enough costume dramas on the telly to know the drill.

She's isn't sure why, but she'd expected Lady Preston, their hostess, to greet her guests, but thinking on it, she can see how that'd be a pain in the butt for the woman. They're milling around their own pile of bags when a spotty youth in a suit older than he is, enters the hall through a door at the back. Rather than the half-arsed enthusiasm usually shown by someone his age, he's efficiency personified.

After giving him their names, Brenda expects to be checked off in some guest register or other but, demonstrating a mind that must be used more than outward appearances would suggest, he rattles off which rooms have been allocated to them and asks them to follow him.

"What about our bags?" says Julian.

"If they have tags on them, you're welcome to leave them where they are and they'll be sent up to your rooms," says the youth. "I can organise that for you, if you'd like."

Without consultation, they all retrieve their bags. It's not as though they're lugging Manchester around with them and it's as easy for them to carry their own bags as wait for some poor underpaid bastard to do it for them.

Walking up the sweeping staircase that dominates the hall, Brenda is conscious of being scrutinised by the friends and family hanging from the walls, even if they're long in the ground. There is the occasional portrait where the sitter is staring off into space, but the majority have eyes that follow their progress.

Arriving at their rooms at the back on the second floor, they're in no doubt they're on the lower rungs of the guest list. Brenda is the last to be escorted to her room, which is next to Julian's.

Her room is impressive even if it's not top tier. The spotty youth in the shiny suit had said hers was the Chinese room, but she hadn't been able to imagine what that might mean. During the trudge upstairs, she'd imagined something along the lines of a glorified Chinese restaurant with lashings of red and black and the smell of hot oil.

The room is nothing like this.

While a lot of the furniture is dark in colour and Chinese by design, this is offset by luminous fabrics hanging both at the windows and on the four-poster bed. The walls are covered in textured wallpaper, with a subtle bamboo pattern revealing itself only after closer examination. The cream carpet feels luxurious even though Brenda is still wearing her shoes.

The only thing the room doesn't appear to have is a bathroom.

"Jeez, does this mean I'm going to have to traipse down the hall to have a pee?"

The room doesn't reply; it is deathly quiet and even when she concentrates on listening, she can't hear anything.

"Weird."

It's only after Brenda's unpacked that she gives her bed the bounce test. She's mid-bounce when she notices a small envelope sitting on the pillow. She'd missed it earlier, obscured by the gorgeous bed curtains that even open, still enclose the space.

Skimming the note, Brenda is back on her feet. Walking over to the wall to the left of the bed, she starts pushing on it near the window and keeps working her way along until she's rewarded with a click and a panel opening to reveal a small, modern bathroom. Brenda can see the bathroom is a later addition. Sunlight beams in through a skylight in the ceiling, bouncing off the shiny tiles that cover every surface. Without that light source, the room would have been pitch-black.

A quick check of her watch lets her know she has plenty of time to shower before dinner. She's about to fall back onto the bed for ten winks when she stops at a slight angle. If the plumbing here is anything like she's encountered in other buildings in England, the hot water tank will be woefully inadequate. Tensing her thigh muscles, she propels herself back to standing.

"No way I'm getting caught with a cold shower."

Her ablutions are rapid and no-fuss up until she's safely washed the conditioner from her hair. It's only then she relaxes.

She stiffens when she senses movement right next to her. She tenses even more when her shower turns from hot to freezing cold in a heartbeat. Her string of profanities as she jumps clear of the icy blast does nothing to help with her recovery from the shock.

"Sorry!" comes back Julian's voice through the wall.

His hardly muffled apology makes it obvious the new walls are thin in comparison to their original counterparts. She makes a mental note to close the bathroom door before bed. With walls this thin, she'll be able to hear Julian taking a slash and that would hardly be conducive to sweet dreams. Jeez, she'd even be nervous about dropping a 'silent but deadly' unless she was right next to the window.

Any hopes they can sit where they like at dinner are quashed when Brenda spots the calligraphy written cards sitting at each place setting. Her students make short work of finding their own and each other's places, leaving her wondering where she's sitting.

Julian clears his throat, making her look in his direction. He points down at the setting next to him and then at her. Working her way purposefully through the aperitif-quaffing crowd, eventually she stands next to him.

"Shit! That's not good," says Brenda, quietly, after spotting who she's stuck next to. Sure, she wants to work on the set-up of Wallace Smythe-Brown but she doesn't want to spend an evening next to the turd. That nose of his could put a girl off her dinner.

She's about to ask Julian if it's okay etiquette-wise to move places, when he leans forward, pockets Wallace's name card and replaces it with his own. Leaving Brenda standing there with a bemused expression, he strolls towards the far end of the ridiculously long table, leans forward, and metaphorically puts Wallace in his place.

Seeing the gent in question enter the dining room, Brenda moves from behind her seat at the dining table and over to the periphery of the crowd where she can keep an eye on him without him being able to return the favour.

He makes a beeline for what was his seat, confirming for her that he's had some influence on the seating plan and he sure as shit knows her name. The reddening of that cratered nose of his when he spots his name card is no longer there lends further credence. He's already picked up Julian's card when her student arrives back from his trip to the other end of the table. Although unable to hear what's said, she's in no doubt as to what's happening when Julian takes his name card from Wallace and pops it back on the table. Wallace doesn't exactly storm off in a huff, but his rigid posture says he's not happy.

Brenda is unable to stop a small snigger. "Game on," she whispers to Julian, who has joined her.

"It will be an interesting weekend that's for jolly sure."

Any further conversation is halted when a serious and ostentatiously liveried gent announces that dinner will be served and would everyone please take their seats.

A high-class scrum ensues as guests wander aimlessly around trying to find their spots. As well as those who don't have a clue where they're sitting, there are a few stand-out guests who, like Brenda and her students, either already know where they're sitting or have slipped someone a twenty to sit in a particular spot.

Looking in Wallace's direction, Brenda can see him exchanging serious words with one of the waitresses. The two of them turn in tandem to give Julian the evils.

It's at this point that Genevieve toddles up and stands next to her son and the waitress. Looking down at her place setting, and the one next to it, her face hardens and she, too, turns on the waitress. More heated words result in the waitress snatching the card from the setting next to Wallace's and marching around the table to the place to the right of Julian.

With an expression that clearly says 'this is all your fault', she replaces the card with Genevieve's, grabs the card of whoever was supposed to sit there and takes it back to Wallace's end of the table, where she slams it down, before making a hasty exit in case she's started a round of the world's poshest game of musical chairs.

Julian shrugs in Wallace's direction, causing the arsehole's face to darken. Wallace moves his gaze from Julian to Brenda, and unsure how to play it, she concentrates on placing her napkin on her lap rather than commit herself in any one direction.

Having finally tottered her way from the far end of the table, Genevieve stands regally behind her new chair. This puts paid to Julian and Brenda discussing Wallace in any way, shape or form. Julian pushes his seat back so he can get to his feet and help the old lady to sit, but, before he can do so, a uniformed lackey moves in to assist.

Dinner is a long, drawn-out affair consisting of bland course after bland course, with salt apparently in short supply in the kitchen. Brenda has never been so bored in all her life. The old chap to her left is either profoundly deaf or rude as hell, both of which mean conversation is impossible. Julian has been nobbled by Genevieve and their conversation is spirited, with a lot of laughter ensuing. Some of this is loud enough that it warrants Wallace glaring at his mother to silence her. He fails miserably and Brenda can't help but side with Genevieve, mentally egging her on to be even more of an embarrassment to her son.

Julian half-heartedly spears a greying piece of broccoli. "Do you suppose this green, and I use the term loosely, was over-cooked when it left the kitchen, or if it happened in transit?"

"I'm glad Eadie gave us a head's up," says Brenda, salivating on thoughts of the stash of snacks back in her room.

"Bert has spoiled us," says Julian, dropping the broccoli to join its compadres.

Unable to rearrange the stodge on her plate any more artistically, Brenda gives in and drops her knife and fork with an unexpected clatter. It's as though she's broken a spell, with cutlery connecting with crockery in a wave around the table.

Thinking things can only improve with dessert, Brenda is hugely disappointed. The nearest living relative of custard appears to be snot. Even wallpaper paste would be farther up the culinary chain of evolution than this insipid gunge. The stewed plums drowning in this sea of pus give her plate the appearance of something left over after surgery. The plate should be kidney-shaped and stainless.

Looking at the mess in front of her, the few meagre mouthfuls she'd forced down of the main, clamour for release. She's swallowing deeply and wondering if it's okay to scarper when Julian picks up her side plate and puts it over the organ transplant, hiding it from view.

The announcement that coffee is being served in the drawing room evokes a palpable sense of relief around the room. Brenda would much prefer to deal with Wallace than continue to avoid looking at uneaten desserts. Jeez, even her mother had been able to knock together something better than this. While pissed! Just watching those few brave souls who are happily shovelling it in, makes her feel queasy.

A few seconds in the drawing room and she's pounced on.

"That was bad form of your friend," says Wallace, his breath warming her ear and inducing small spasms of revulsion.

Brenda jerks her head away. "Excuse me?"

If she wants to reel him in, innocence will be how she will make him desperate for a good old bout of rumpy-pumpy. If it's obvious she's avoiding him, she risks him tiring of the game and moving onto some other poor unfortunate. If they can't hook up simply due to circumstances, this will frustrate him but, more importantly, keep him keen.

"Let's you and I have a little chat," says Wallace, the darkness of his eyes telegraphing he has something more carnal in mind.

Planting his large paw in the middle of her back, he steers her towards the doors and it's all she can do not to shake him off and karate-kick him in the nuts. Bopping him in the nose is off the cards; she doesn't want her fist anywhere near it. As it is, she doubts she'll ever eat another strawberry without gagging.

"I'm gasping for a coffee," says Brenda.

"I've got something far more stimulating in mind."

Gross.

"Oh, Brenda! It's terrible!" Rosie blocks her progress with a display of hand wringing, tears and general woebegone that is worthy of an Oscar.

"Whatever is wrong?" says Brenda, grabbing the soggy lifeline by stepping forward and drawing the girl into her arms and thus breaking contact with Wallace.

"I'm sorry, but I need to look after my friend," she says, looking back at him.

Wallace's jaw clenches tight enough that it pulls on his ears. If the chatter in the room wasn't so loud, the accompanying graunching would no doubt be audible.

Brenda fights to stop a smile from surfacing, but it's touch and go; she drags Rosie's head closer so the girl's riot of curls covers the twitching of her lips.

"Of course," says Wallace, through gritted teeth, before bowing briefly and storming from the room.

"Thanks for that," says Brenda.

"You're welcome!" Rosie's tone is positively chipper, compared with her earlier demeanour.

"You should be on the stage. How the bloody hell did you manage to cry on demand like that?"

"I think of dead pets," says the girl, once again thinking on dearly-departed companions of the fluffy variety if the welling up is any indicator.

"Handy trick."

Seeing the girl is heading towards another bout of tears, Brenda thinks of the best way to divert her. "Wasn't that pudding truly disgusting?"

"I've had worse," says Rosie, after a small hiccough.

"Jeez. How is that even possible?"

"Boarding school," says Rosie, as though this should explain everything.

Leaving Brenda none the wiser, the girl wanders off in search of a cup of tea.

The rest of the evening is uneventful with Wallace not reappearing but then, neither does their hostess. What an oddball. Meanwhile, the dishonourable and reprehensible Rupert holds court in one corner of the large room and, as easily as she could, Brenda can't be arsed taking the little todger down a peg or two. No challenge there.

Because the plan for the weekend is to continue reeling in targets or even the initial hook-up, all five of them repair to their bedrooms en masse, which works to dislodge most of the hangers-on. Simply running up the stairs gets rid of the rest.

Brenda is especially glad the others are with her when she sees Wallace lurking in the hallway on the second floor. That the creepy codger is annoyed when he sees her entourage is an understatement. His expression steers more towards lethal and Brenda grasps what a handful he'll be when she ends up alone with him. She's relieved when he stalks off down the stairs.

Even with him gone, Julian sees her to her door and only moves when she's finally jammed her doorstop in place. She hasn't even finished her third chocolate bar before someone,

Wallace, attempts to open her door. Finding it barred, he gives it a good shove and the sound of splitting wood reverberates around the room. Inching closer to the door, Brenda is disturbed to see the doorstop has moved slightly and there's even a tell-tale gap showing between the door and its frame.

"No you sodding don't," mutters Brenda, under her breath.

Running at it full tilt, she chucks all her weight against it and is rewarded with a bang, then a grunt, then a thump. The moans that follow serenade her as she jams the doorstop firmly back in place.

There's only one reason someone's head would have been that close to the door, bloody peeping tom. A quick gander through the keyhole confirms it is Wallace she's lobotomised. An even quicker scan of the room and she spots the perfect thing to stuff up his spying. Thank you, Chinese, and your love of screens. As tempting as it would be to blind Wallace with a blast of hairspray through the keyhole, this way isn't as obvious.

She's only just unfolded the screen in front of the doorway when she hears Julian speaking out in the hall.

"Are you okay?"

The response from Wallace is a stream of invective directed at Julian and Brenda, evidence of the level of pain he's experiencing. Apart from the contusion, Brenda imagines only a good hand-job will stop Wallace's balls from matching his blood.

Thoughts of this have her so fit to bust that she runs into the bathroom and slams the door rather than give herself away.

***

Wallace isn't at breakfast the following morning.

Nor lunch.

Or dinner.

It's only when Rupert is doing the rounds on Sunday morning trying to hitch a ride back into the city, that it dawns on them that Wallace must have left early on the Saturday morning.

With any luck, he's sporting a couple of shiners.

17

The trip home from the country pile sees Brenda stretched out in the back of the van with Rosie and Paula, while Stef is up front with Julian.

"So, how'd you get on?" says Brenda, looking at Rosie and Paula in turn.

They both respond at once, forcing Brenda to hold up her hand. "Rosie, you go first."

"Well ... I think it went well. I've got another date with Brian, for dinner on Wednesday." Rosie's face is infused with pink, her voice laced with excitement.

Initially, Brenda screws up her forehead as she tries to work out who Brian is. Thinking about Rosie's enthusiasm, it can mean only one thing. Jeez, that maths teacher is well connected. Shows how drab he is that Brenda hadn't even seen him that weekend; she must have missed him amongst all that bland wallpaper in the main rooms.

"What about you Paula?"

"Un-fricking-believable," says the girl, bouncing more than can be attributed to the van's suspension. "I'm close to getting a sort of commitment out of Parker!"

"As in the Earl of Barnsfield?" says Julian, from the front.

"That's the chap. Loaded, dodgy ticker, no kids."

Brenda drags herself upright enough to high-five Paula, before subsiding back onto the mattress.

"What about you, Stef?" calls Brenda, in the direction of the front seats.

"Got a couple I'm working on. Should know more this week."

"Do you mean couple couple or couple?" says Brenda.

Stef swings around and leans over the back of her seat. "Huh?"

"Couple as in Mr and Mrs, or couple, as in two different blokes."

"The second one. I have to work out which one gives better odds."

"Why settle for one?" says Brenda.

She's immediately pounced on by all three girls. Could they do that? Was it ethical? Wouldn't that end in disaster?

Even Julian throws in a, "Like that's not going to blow up in your face," his voice tinged with brotherly concern.

"First off, if you're shagging 'em, it's one at a time."

At the look Stef gives her, she says, "Sorry, Stef, but those are the rules. Secondly, if you let them know you aren't seeing them exclusively, not only is it ethical but it can spur them on to greater generosity. It'll only end in disaster if both of them are at the same event as you and they think you're with them exclusively." Brenda is unable to stop herself from shaking her head as she recalls how she found out the hard way on that score. "That's what's called a clusterfuck."

"Technical term?" throws Julian over his shoulder, so he can keep his eyes on the road.

"You got it. A technical term." Brenda's words are interspersed with laughter.

Silence descends on the van as her students mull over this new development. Rosie is the one to break it.

"But we don't need to be dating more than one? Do we?"

"No. You don't," says Brenda, and is rewarded with seeing the tension ease. Being a virgin must be such a drag.

"What about you Julian? How'd you get on?"

Brenda isn't expecting any developments here. For one thing, she hadn't seen him so much as speak to the two chaps recommended by Eadie. On the occasions he wasn't beside her, he'd been deep in discussion with Genevieve Smythe-Brown, the pair of them either giggling conspiratorially about something or their heads close together in an obvious attempt to keep their conversation private.

His mumbled reply leaves her no wiser.

The van empty of luggage, students and lolly wrappers, Brenda pops into the sitting room to give Eadie an update.

"Did Wallace make it down?" Eadie's casual tone doesn't fool Brenda for a moment. The gaze aimed in her direction is all business.

"He was there on the Friday night but I didn't see hide nor hair of him after that."

"Did he give you any trouble?" Eadie's hands dig into the arms of her chair while she waits for Brenda to answer.

"Nothing I couldn't handle."

Brenda briefly describes the events around Wallace, finishing up with her smashing the door into his head. Rather than addressing Eadie's worries, it puts her into a spin.

"That was a big mistake, gal!"

"Why?"

"Because he's cruel and you've just given him reason to be

even crueller to you if you ever give him the chance. I'm so pleased you're not going ahead with the plan."

Brenda opens her mouth to respond a couple of times, but nothing appropriate comes up. "Is he really that bad?"

Eadie's shudder and the pain in her eyes is all the answer she needs.

"How did you find Lady Preston?"

Brenda's thrown for a second at this sudden change of subject, but answers, "I didn't."

At the look of confusion clouding Eadie's normally alert countenance, Brenda continues, "Only saw her at dinner on the first night. Other than that she was a no-show."

"How incredibly rude," says Eadie, before prompting Brenda to continue with the update.

The old lady enthuses at all the news, even Julian getting on well with Genevieve is greeted with delight.

"But if she's like that arsehole of a son of hers, wouldn't it be better if he stayed away from the mother rather than take on the role of gay handmaiden?"

"That's the thing, she's different. Yes, she might be a gorgon, but Wallace takes after his father. Now that man was a horror."

"More than Wallace or Rupert?"

"Hard to believe, isn't it? Genevieve damn near danced on his coffin after he was finally taken out courtesy of a hunting *accident*."

"Who pulled the trigger?" says Brenda, scooting forward in her seat.

"That's where it gets interesting. The police never found out. Mind you by the time the local constabulary got there, any clues had been obliterated by all the dogs, horses and aristo-crats milling about."

"Come on, spill! I'll bet you've got a theory." Brenda never ceases to be amazed at the level of gossip Eadie is privy to.

"Everyone thought it was Wallace ..." Eadie stalls.

"But ..." says Brenda, giving her a gentle nudge.

"That's just it. Genevieve got everything in the will. Apparently when the lawyer read that out, both Genevieve and Wallace were as stunned as each other."

"Didn't go according to plan?"

"Who knows? It would depend on who knew what was in the will. Either way, they both had bloody good motives."

Brenda spins her hand to prompt a continuance.

"Genevieve hated Henry with a passion. He was a womanising misogynist who insisted she stay stuck in the country to keep the way clear for his shenanigans in town."

"And Wallace?"

"It was all about money with him. The old bastard kept a close eye on spending and it crimped Wallace's lifestyle something shocking."

"Jeez, he must have been hacked off when his mum inherited the bleeding lot."

"Indeed! Actually, my money is still on Wallace having done the deed. He's got a vicious streak when he's backed into a corner and he always did like a flutter on the ponies. Maybe that caught up with him."

"Man, I'd be watching my back if I was her," says Brenda.

"She should be fine. She's far more generous than her late husband when it comes to settling with Wallace's bookies and I suspect she knows how Henry met his end. I should imagine she's got steps in place should anything happen to her."

"What an awful way to live," says Brenda, surprised to find herself feeling sympathy for Genevieve.

The Wednesday following the world's most boring house party, the table heaves with the trappings of breakfast. The only sounds are those of crockery, cutlery, chewing and slurping. Brenda's mouth is eventually empty long enough to speak.

"Flo, would you have time today to give the common room a bit of a blitz? We've got guests coming over this evening."

"Not a problem, love. I'll have the place sparkling," says the char perched on a bar stool that sits next to the end of the kitchen counter. Bert, husband and cook, is likewise perched next to her. The stools are a new addition and a good one. Refusing to sit at the large kitchen table with their employers, they used to stand next to the counter and wait until they could be of use. Eadie hadn't liked it, nor had Brenda, the two stools had been purchased and now everyone is happy.

"Thank you," says Brenda.

"Would you be wanting knick-knacks to go with your drinks?"

Wondering why they'd want small figurines and other dust-gatherers confuses Brenda for a moment. "Yes. That'd be lovely, Bert. Nothing too fancy, though."

The other development with the pair is that they're continuing to live on-site, at least until the current lot of students leave. They'd been finding the early mornings on the tube a bit much and so had fully moved themselves into the studio on the top floor.

Brenda suspects this might also have something to do with their son moving back home, eating them out of house and home and spending an inordinate amount of time in front of the telly. Not that he'll be watching it now. Bert retrieved the museum piece and lugged it up to the top floor. Good on 'em as far as Brenda's concerned.

The planning session for their first 'At Home' takes place that afternoon in the formal dining room. Eadie is not with them;

she's having a lie-down courtesy of a rum toddy prepared by Flo that necessitated a temporary 'no naked flames in the kitchen' policy.

"Right, let's run through who you've all invited. Stef, what about you?"

"I've invited old Cecil Percy-Ryder."

"Christ almighty, that's a mouthful," says Brenda.

"Apparently so," says Stef, before slamming her hand over her mouth.

The room erupts in laughter, even if Rosie's response is reserved. Most likely because the poor girl has no idea what they're laughing about and Brenda's stuffed if she's going to be the one to enlighten her.

"Paula, what about you?" says Brenda, when her own laughter is under control.

The Irish girl, on the other hand, is still gurgling away and so has to calm herself before she can respond.

"I've invited Parker."

"Excellent," says Brenda. "And thank god we had the stair lift fitted. Wouldn't be good form to have a fatality at our first 'At Home'."

"With the CPR capabilities in this room, it'll be the safest soirée in London," snorts Julian.

While he's the centre of attention, Brenda asks him who he's invited.

"Genevieve."

"Genevieve Smythe-Brown? As in the main target's mother?" says Paula, eyes agog. "Is that wise?"

"Yes, is that wise?" says Brenda.

Even though she's aware there's not a lot of love lost between mother and son, blood can prove a powerful bond. There's also the chance that one of them could slip up and alert the old lady to their long-term plan. Of more concern, though, is that Julian's invited a woman, thereby keeping himself firmly behind that closet door.

"I've thought about that, but it'll work in our favour, too. Ginny won't think anything of telling me if Wallace is out of town or what events he'll be attending."

The only response to this statement is for all the females to look at him and say "Ginny?"

"That's what she asked me to call her."

Shaking her head at this development, Brenda turns to Rosie and raises her eyebrows in a non-verbal request for the girl to announce who she's invited.

The girl turning pink, her mouth opening and closing like a goldfish, is answer enough.

"Brian it is." Brenda knows she's successfully hidden her annoyance when the young girl relaxes and excitement visibly makes itself at home. She'd hoped for better for Rosie, but if the girl is happy with a lowly paid maths teacher, all power to her.

"What about you?" says Julian, causing Brenda to turn in his direction to see who he's addressing.

"Me?" says Brenda, holding her hand against her chest.

He nods in response.

"Flying solo tonight. Same as Eadie. Otherwise, it's likely to turn into an orgy."

Rosie gasps.

"What's wrong with that?" says Paula.

"Yeah, a bit of group rumpy-pumpy might be fun," says Stef.

Brenda makes a note to keep an eye on that one.

Julian doesn't say anything about his preferences either way.

"Because we could end up with an aristocratic massacre on our hands," says Brenda, pointing out the obvious and, once again, forgetting not to swear in the process.

"Good point," says Paula. "Last thing I want is for Parker to shuffle off before I get some decent jewellery out of him."

Stef sighs dramatically before speaking. "I suppose so."

The sense of relief in Rosie's demeanour is palpable.

Sneaking a look at Julian, Brenda is none the wiser. Jeez, she'd hate to face him across a poker table.

———

Dinner that evening is early enough to damn near qualify as afternoon tea but works in their favour by giving them enough time to primp and preen for their guests.

Brenda isn't so concerned with her own ensemble, aiming for neat and tidy and, more importantly, comfortable. She goes for what Martin used to affectionately call her ninja look.

"Damn!" Brenda looks up to stop any tears in their tracks and save her make-up.

That Charlie chooses the same moment to attack his own tail, chasing the appendage round and round on the bed, trans-moggie-rifies any potential tears into laughter.

"Ya daft bastard!"

As if realising he's been caught doing something stupid, he rolls into a sitting position and looks embarrassed, but covers it by studiously licking his paw and cleaning behind an ear.

"Good luck with that technique," says Brenda, laughing, letting him know he's been busted.

———

The first guest to arrive is Genevieve. She's done up to the nines in what must be the octogenarian equivalent of an outfit designed to pull. There's a lot of crêpey cleavage on show, with the ostentatious ropes of pearls draped around her neck smothered by folds of skin in places.

Bert is about to close the door when Countess the Chihuahua totters into view, following a sharp jerk on her leash. She's just as mouldy as Brenda remembers, the jewels strung around her neck the only thing that distinguishes her from a junkyard dog.

The dog has only just made it into the hallway when Charlie pushes open the kitchen door at the other end and stalks out to see what's going on. Countess transforms from shivering and timid to pulling on her leash in an effort to reach the cat and rip it to shreds, but if Charlie's concerned, he doesn't show it. Rather than become a fluffed-up spitting ball of mean, he growls deep in his throat; on seeing his bum winding up in readiness to launch himself at the interloper, Brenda jumps between the pair, all the while yelling at him to stand down.

"What a disgusting animal," says Genevieve. "Should be put down."

Brenda agrees on both counts although she's thinking about Countess, while slowly walking towards Charlie, forcing him back up against the kitchen door. Not that he's ready to go through it without a fight, if the way he's looking around her legs at his target is any indicator.

Before Brenda has a chance, the kitchen door's opened from inside to reveal Flo standing there with a slice of leftover meat from dinner. She waves this in Charlie's direction and has his attention in a flash. A quick look between the scrag-end of bejewelled meat in the hall and the superior cut sitting tantalisingly in his bowl and his mind is made up.

Brenda shuts the door on him, relieved he hasn't taken out the mangy apology for fur that's still baring its teeth at ankle height behind her.

Julian does a bang-up job of calming both Countess and Genevieve with a lot of pats and stroking involved. Seeing the old lady, with the mutt perched precariously on her knee, fade out of view on the slow stairlift, Brenda wonders if he knows he'll be expected to go pearl diving before the night is out.

Parker and Brian arrive at the same time; Brian walks up the stairs next to the old chap, who has insisted on being belted into the chair for safety. Given how sodding slow it is, Brenda thinks this precaution is hardly necessary but she's happy to comply with the decrepit codger's wishes to be 'strapped down good and proper'.

What does fascinate Brenda, listening to the two of them nattering away on their journey up to the common room, is that they appear to know each other.

While Brian might well be a lowly teacher, he's well connected. Must be son number three, four or more? Eadie had covered this in her lecture on the differences between being titled and being rich. One doesn't necessarily ensure the other.

Percy-Ryder is the last to arrive. He eschews using the stair-lift, asserting he's "Not dead yet," although listening to his breathing as he regally drags his aristocratic arse up the stairs, Brenda worries "yet" might be imminent.

With all the guests safely in or on their way to the common room, Brenda opens the door to the sitting room. It's empty but she can hear humming coming from Eadie's bedroom.

"You ready?" says Brenda, crossing the room and walking into Eadie's bedroom through the wide open door.

Eadie indeed looks 'hot to trot' and is wearing what Brenda has come to know is one of the old lady's favourites. The dove grey silk dress looks lovely on Eadie and the absence of buttons, a zip or belt, mean it's something she can slip on and off without her arthritis hindering her.

"Come on. Let's get this show on the road," says Eadie, passing her canes to Brenda.

Brenda holds her other arm out to help Eadie to her feet in a move their ambulance driver friend had shown them. He's teaching them so much more than CPR. They've already covered splints in case of broken bones, how to spot a stroke and what to do in the case of a seizure.

Apparently, he has some 'cracking' classes coming up presumably covering plastering anyone who falls while plastered. Whether this is due to an altruistic or avaricious streak has yet to be determined. Without a doubt, his favourite part of any class is when Brenda hands over an envelope of notes at the end.

At the bottom of the stairs, Brenda helps Eadie into the stairlift.

"Do you want me to do the belt up?" says Brenda.

"At the speed this thing goes? The only way I'm going to fall out is if I kark it because of old age."

Brenda hits the red 'go' button and the chair whirs into life and starts its asthmatic ascent.

"So, who have we got here tonight?"

"Right. Stef has invited a Cecil Percy-Ryder."

Eadie's pupils dilate to more than twice their normal size.

"What?"

"There's slap and tickle and there's Cecil. He's in a league all his own."

"Maybe you'd better bring Stef up to speed on that tomorrow?"

"That chap would happily have his balls chewed off by ferrets before he'd use his safe word."

"Thanks for that image!"

"Who else?" says Eadie, as though she hasn't just planted that disgusting image deep in Brenda's brain.

"Ah, Paula has invited Parker, Earl of somewhere or other."

"Good god, he's still alive? I thought that supposedly dodgy ticker he's always rabbiting on about would have given up the ghost by now."

"And, Julian's invited Genevieve." Brenda can't help her

misgivings about this from colouring her tone and it's something Eadie picks up on.

The chair crawls to a stop on the first-floor landing and while Eadie moves over to the chair that will take her up to the second floor, they quietly discuss the pros and cons of Julian's choice of partner for the evening.

"Hmmm," says Eadie, "let's see how it goes with that one."

"I'm starting to worry Julian's never going to leave the closet. He didn't go near either of the chaps you'd highlighted at the house party."

Eadie is momentarily lost in thought, but soon back in the here and now. "What about our young Rosie?"

"Brian," spits out Brenda, not needing to cover her frustration in front of the old lady.

"Brian who?"

"You know, I wouldn't have a bloody clue. Likes moth-eaten cardies and corduroy pants. Doesn't seem to own anything that isn't patched on the elbows. Generally scruffy."

"That means he's bloody loaded," says Eadie, before laughing.

"It screams maths teacher in my books."

18

After what feels an age, Eadie and Brenda achieve the second landing.

"You want to use the bathroom before we go in?" says Brenda quietly to Eadie.

"Excellent plan."

Brenda hands Eadie her canes and opens the bathroom door for her.

"Who was the genius behind putting hand rails in here?" says Eadie, who's using this bathroom for the first time.

"Stef's uncle. He got 'em from the same job as the stairlift."

Pulling the door closed, Brenda promises to wait on the landing so she can help her into the common room. By the time they join the others, the room's feeling snug, especially with Countess having her own chair. On the plus side, at least the dog is no longer snarling.

There's an easy familiarity amongst their guests, proof of them already having been acquainted. Not that this comes as any surprise to Brenda. They've only been to half a dozen soirées so far, but the guest list has a common thread throughout.

Looking at how closely the couples are jammed together, it's as well Eadie and Brenda are on their own, otherwise, they'd need to break out a crowbar and baby oil at the end of the night. Mind you, if the look Cecil is giving Stef is any indication, the old coot is already fantasising about the cockney girl using something like that on him later.

Awww, our first castration.

Stifling her laughter, Brenda gets Eadie settled in the only free armchair before sorting out drinks for the two of them. The mahogany sideboard is groaning under a startling array of alcohol with nothing teetotal on offer.

A quick sniff of the decanter and Brenda pours a sherry for Eadie and one for herself, putting the two glasses on the small table next to Eadie's chair. She retrieves the hard-backed chair from the landing because it doesn't look as if Genevieve wants to shift that overly accessorised fur ball of hers.

Rather than sit, Brenda says, "Can I get anyone a top up?"

There are head shakes all round, with the exception of Genevieve, who sculls the contents of her crystal tumbler and holds it towards the back of the couch so Brenda can walk around the crowd, rather than run the gauntlet of legs and the coffee table.

"Gin. Lots of ice."

The tone is autocratic, apprising Brenda she's been labelled as the help rather than the hostess, which doesn't make sense given they'd been at the same house party. Maybe the woman's simply a cold-hearted bitch?

"Not getting any younger here," says Genevieve, in the upper-crust equivalent of "Get a sodding move on", confirming Brenda's theory.

She's unable to stop herself from bristling; but that the woman's behaviour also irks Julian comes as a surprise.

"Ginny, you've not been formally introduced," says Julian. "This is Brenda, Eadie's niece from Australia." The lie rolls easily off his tongue, perhaps too easily. "Brenda, this is Genevieve Smythe-Brown.

Looking the woman dead in the eye, Brenda says, "Lovely to meet you," although the words scratch the back of her throat.

Rather than the courtesy being returned, their guest gives a thoroughly impolite *harrumph*, before stating, "That doesn't change the fact I'm not getting any younger," shaking her glass for added emphasis.

Realising the woman's an aristocratic old misery guts with nothing about to change that, Brenda walks around the back of the chairs in the most direct route, but before she can take the glass, Julian beats her to it.

He plucks it from Genevieve's hand, "Why don't I fill that up for you?" he says, before manoeuvring his way over to the sideboard.

The look Genevieve skewers him with is an interesting mix of pissed off and, disturbingly, arousal. Brenda understands the first but isn't sure of the second. Maybe it's a case of 'treat 'em mean and keen 'em keen'? The old bird is going to be so disappointed.

Once she's happily chugging away on the liver-damaging sized glass of gin Julian has poured for her, conversation starts up again, with the main topic being a dissection of the preceding weekend's house party.

At first Brenda, Eadie and their students are reserved in voicing their opinions but when it's obvious their guests aren't holding back, they join in with glee. As well as the more obvious character assassinations, the quality of the food also receives a lot of attention. The one person not mentioned is Wallace Smythe-Brown and his attempt to force his way into Brenda's room, although Genevieve does make mention of him having a silly accident and having to leave early.

Stef looks as though she's going to question this, but a

throat-clearing bark from Eadie and a subtle head shake from Brenda have her subsiding back next to Cecil.

There's a lull in the conversation after the fifth round of drinks, and Eadie takes the opportunity to jump in, "Brian, how have you been? I haven't seen you since you were in short pants."

The mousey chap, who's snuggling up to Rosie, blushes furiously, before spluttering out a reply, "All good, Miss Cadwalader, all good."

"And the family?" Eadie pumps him for a fuller reply.

A shadow flickers briefly over his expression before he replies, "Father's not doing so well, but mother and my sisters are tickety-boo."

"Tickety-boo?" says Brenda, under her breath. Who the hell speaks like that these days? He's like an escapee from Enid Blyton.

"I'm sorry to hear about Eamon. Please pass on my regards on to him."

When the next lull occurs, it's broken by Genevieve. Unfortunately, it's by her snoring, with the bejewelled flea-breeding facility on the seat next to her being similarly occupied and adding to the din.

"Time to call it a night," says Julian, turning towards his guest and no doubt being able to tell if she's still in possession of her tonsils.

Checking the other guests, Brenda can see they're drooping, too. Whether this is symptomatic of age or the large quantities of alcohol imbibed is a toss-up.

"I'll call for taxis," says Paula, jumping to her feet, none the worse for the number of drinks she's knocked back.

"I can drop everyone off, if you like," offers Brian, who's still alert and, more importantly, sober.

The stairlift is running hot by the time all the guests make it downstairs. It had taken considerable manpower to get

Genevieve and Countess strapped in and on their way. She'd lolled to the side and Julian opted to accompany her to avoid a nasty spill along the way.

She's the last guest to leave the house and with legs apparently now the consistency of rubber, this is only achieved with Brenda under one arm, and Julian under the other.

Seeing Brian's car, Brenda surrenders her half of the load with the result that Genevieve and Julian end up in a drunken heap in the front garden with the dog perched on them like a cake topper.

"Little help here," squeaks out Julian, who's taken the full weight of the elderly lady.

"Shit. Sorry" Brenda nudges the growling dog out of the way with her foot before dragging on one of Genevieve's arms with little success. It's not until all her other students pitch in that they're able to lever, push and generally manhandle the old lady back into a standing position. Giggling like a bunch of schoolgirls, the task wasn't made any easier by the dog ankle-tapping them.

They waste no time in shovelling the drunken old bird and her pooch into the back of the Brian's Daimler – the beast that caused Brenda's lapse in concentration. She'd genuinely been expecting an Austin Princess, or the like, and a tatty one; not the gleaming vehicle the girls watch until it disappears around the corner.

After a quick head swivel and obvious head count, Stef says, "I'm surprised Julian didn't wave goodbye."

"Bloody hell." Brenda swings back towards the house and looks down into the garden, "Are you okay?"

It takes the combined force of all of them to extract him from his weedy resting place. He's not drunk, but Genevieve landing on him as a deadweight seems to have dislocated his shoulder.

"Thank the lord we covered slings in the last first aid class," says Paula, fashioning one expertly on Julian. That's she's using a bright pink shawl means it's not textbook, but it will do until they can get him to A&E.

You okay?" Brenda looks down at Julian, tucked up in bed, a goofy grin on his face courtesy of the painkillers he'd been pumped full of at the hospital.

"Fab-u-luss," he manages to carefully enunciate, before adding, "but cold."

Brenda knows he's got pyjama bottoms on because she'd been the one to undress him and get him ready for bed. But the amount of strapping and a hospital-issue sling of the non-pink variety, meant she hadn't been able to get the top on him.

Even a tiny movement on his part and his shoulders are exposed. Hell, he's got a great bod; it's something she couldn't help but notice when stripping him. If he weren't gay, he'd be sleeping in his clothes.

"Got it," says Brenda, grabbing the pyjama top. "Hold up your good arm."

Julian tries to comply, but his brain and the limb appear disconnected, from all the dope flooding his system. In the end, she grabs the arm, feeds the sleeve over it as if to button the jacket up at the back, then pulls it across his front and tucks it around the back of him on the other side, effectively covering his chest, shoulder and the sling.

"Better?"

"S'luvly," slurs Julian, before giving into a drug-induced coma.

Leaving the bedside light on and his door open, Brenda heads to her own bed. She also leaves her door open, in case he needs her during the night.

Charlie is already there, having burrowed himself under

the covers while they were at the hospital. He acknowledges her presence by meowing, stretching, farting and curling back up into as tight a ball as he'd been in when she first pulled the bedspread aside.

"Phew! You stinky little bastard." Brenda flaps her bed t-shirt in his direction to clear the noxious fumes away from the vicinity of her pillow, before she pulls the shirt over her head and climbs in next to him.

Brenda has no idea what the time is when Charlie rudely awakens her by whacking her face repeatedly with one of his dog-sized paws.

"What!" She sits bolt upright, sending him flying. "Cut it out!"

Flopping back down, she rolls away from him and is close to going back to sleep, when he bites her ear.

"Owww!" She bats him away before grabbing her ear. "What the hell is wrong with you?"

The cat stomps over her, jumps to the floor and starts meowing loud enough to wake the whole household. He walks a couple of steps out of the room, all the time howling.

"Shut up, you'll wake Julian. And the dead."

Reluctantly, Brenda rouses enough to see what the daft feline is on about and follows Charlie to Julian's bed.

He's out cold, his face covered in a fine sheen of sweat and he's groaning.

Brenda grabs two of his painkillers and the glass of water from the bedside table but puts them back down again. There's no way he'll be able to swallow them while he's still lying down. Trying to prop him upright enough to swallow the pills, Brenda experiences flashbacks of dragging Genevieve out of the garden earlier. Except this time she's on her own and conscious of not hurting his shoulder.

She only feels a little guilty when she slaps his face, hard.

It works. He's awake but his eyes are swivelling randomly. Maybe she should have left him asleep?

"Hell, my shoulder's killing me."

"It must be hurting like hell for you to swear. Can you shift up a bit? I've got more painkillers for you."

Without responding, he tries to push himself upright by leaning over onto his good arm. From the string of cuss words and hissing, this manoeuvre comes at a cost.

"Hang on, I'll give you a hand."

Brenda runs around to the other side of the bed and climbs on. She puts her arm behind his shoulders and levers him up. She only realises how much this has hurt him when he groans and goes limp on her.

At first, she thinks he's having a breather, but he's out cold. "For god's sake!"

Making the most of him being unconscious, Brenda pulls him higher up the bed and grabs all the pillows and stuffs them behind him in hopes of propping him upright.

She fails miserably.

You have got to be bloody joking me?"

There's not enough water in the cylinder on the first floor for Brenda to stay in the shower long enough to get rid of all the kinks in her back. She was stuck holding Julian for the rest of the night, worried he'd collapse and do more damage to his shoulder.

It isn't until after seven that he wakes enough for her to help him swallow a couple of painkillers and settle him back down again.

She takes her time walking down the stairs, with her lower back twinging with each step down. The door hasn't finished swinging shut before the elderly crew in the kitchen are firing questions at her.

"How's the boy doing?" says Eadie.

"Cuppa?" says Flo.

"Bacon buttie?" says Bert.

"Better. Yes. Yes," says Brenda, to each of them in turn.

Lowering herself gingerly into her chair, Brenda is unable to stop a small gasp when her back spasms.

"Never mind Julian, what's up with you?" says Eadie, her face full of concern.

"Got stuck holding Julian upright after he passed out. I slept funny."

Brenda moves around in her chair until she finds a comfy spot, then figuratively glues herself in place to avoid any further pain.

She's doing fine until she has to pick up her cup of tea, this one small act sparking another spasm.

"Flo, would you be a dear and pop through to my room and bring my yellow pills from the bedside table?" says Eadie.

"Back in a tick," says the char, disappearing and reappearing again in short order.

She's putting the bottle down in front of Eadie, when the old lady stops her. "Not for me. Give one to Brenda."

"What?" says Brenda, without bothering to lower her teacup away from her mouth. She's found another comfortable spot and she's sticking with it.

Looking at the horse-tranquiliser-sized tablet that Flo has dropped onto her plate with a clatter, Brenda wonders whether she's meant to swallow it or insert the thing.

Flo puts a large glass of water on the table in front of her, giving Brenda the answer.

"I can't swallow something that size," says Brenda, into her half-full cup of tea.

"Not a worry love, I'm the same with tablets," says Flo, retrieving the yellow suppository.

She expertly crushes it between two dessertspoons and leaves the pile of chemical gravel in one of them so Brenda can take it directly off the spoon.

Her cuppa finished, Brenda braces herself to return it to the saucer. She's incredibly careful but is still unable to stop herself hissing in pain.

It's only with Flo's assistance that Brenda manages the crushed pill. The char holds the spoon next to Brenda's mouth so she can take the contents. She holds the glass of water for Brenda while she drinks enough water to clear her mouth of the multitude of sharp-edged and bitter pieces.

"You ready for ya bacon sarnie now?" says Bert.

"I'll wait until Eadie's pill has kicked in."

"Probably not a good idea," says Eadie, "Those yellow perils play merry hell with your tummy if you don't have something to eat right away."

"Yellow peril? What the hell have you given me," says Brenda, already feeling queasy, even if only psychosomatically.

"A painkiller which is faster and stronger than that rubbish the hospital prescribed for Julian."

Brenda is formulating another question, when Flo holds a bacon buttie wrapped in greaseproof paper right in front of her mouth. She wastes no time taking a greasy chunk out of it. This is followed by another, with Flo peeling the paper back as Brenda gnaws her way through the culinary delight.

She's half way through a second sandwich when she's aware that her back no longer hurts. Nothing hurts. She's delightfully numb and seemingly no longer in touch with the chair, table or even the earth.

"That's good shit," says Brenda, through lips that appear to be as numb as the rest of her.

19

Brenda regains consciousness on the couch in Eadie's sitting room and it takes a moment's hard thought to recall why she's stretched out like this.

"You're awake," says Eadie.

Brenda's disconcerted at how much relief there is in this simple statement. "What the hell was that you gave me?" says Brenda, referring to Eadie's horse tablet.

"A little anti-inflammatory painkiller, nothing to worry about."

It takes a moment for Brenda to grasp the curtains are drawn. She tries to focus on the clock on the mantelpiece. "What time is it?"

Eadie's reply is muffled.

"Sorry, what was that?"

"Ten-thirty."

"Great, I thought I'd slept the day away." She struggles into a sitting position and waits, as she seems to have left her head on the cushion. Once reassembled, she slowly gets to her feet. "Tell you what, my back feels right as rain." She moves experimentally and is relieved when this doesn't result in any spasms or the like.

"You want a cuppa?" She looks at the old girl in time to see her take a sip of sherry.

"Jeez, bit early isn't it?"

With thoughts of whether the old lady does have a drinking problem, Brenda opens the sitting room door. The hall is dark, the same as outside. She turns at such a rate she has to steady herself on the doorjamb.

"It's ten-thirty at night!"

"They don't knock me out like that," says Eadie, as though defending herself for drugging Brenda to the eyeballs.

"Now what the hell am I meant to do?"

It's close to the time she'd usually go to bed and having shaken off the last of the effects of the knockout pills, she's bloody wired. She'd go to the local pub, but even that'd be ready to close.

As if on autopilot, she climbs the stairs even if sleep is the last thing on her mind.

Seeing Julian's light is on reminds her of what had led to Eadie sedating her. His door's open so she pops her head in. "How you doing?"

Any further queries stagger to a halt. He looks half cut, his eyes open, but only just.

"Bloody hell." Brenda moves to his bedside where she sits down.

He tries focusing on her but fails miserably.

"How many did you take?" Brenda reinforces the importance of this question by putting her hands on both sides of his head so she can make him look at her. "How many?"

"Weren't working," slurs Julian.

"How many!"

Brenda is shouting at him to cut through the haze that's enveloping him.

"One," he manages to mangle out.

Hang on; the pills from the hospital hadn't been that potent. Brenda picks up the bottle from the bedside table to check the contents in case he's taken more by accident, in which case she'll be calling an ambulance.

Wrong label.

Yellow pills.

"Eadie!"

She's already at the door and on her way to give Eadie a right ticking off about drugging one of their students, when Julian mumbles, "So pretty," before his eyes roll up and he's out cold. Gentle snores follow.

"Jeez. Damn it," says Brenda, taking the top off the bottle, "if you can't beat 'em, join 'em."

———

Next morning at breakfast, Eadie is looking cagey. Brenda would admonish the old girl for handing out horse tranquilisers like candy, but she's feeling too damned good after an amazing night's sleep to ruin it with an argument. It's also occurred to her that a couple of them will have Wallace comatose, although she'd swiped half a dozen just to be on the safe side.

The wonder drug looks to have worked its magic on Julian, too. He's dressed and made it down for breakfast, though the sling is still in place.

"Everyone ready for the party at Lady Morehill's tonight?" says Brenda looking at her students.

A chorus of yesses is followed by an animated discussion by the girls on what they plan to wear.

"Are you up to it, Julian?" says Brenda.

"Yes! If I stay in bed any longer, I'll end up with a flat bottom."

"Perish the thought," says Eadie, deeming it safe to make her presence felt again.

In between mouthfuls of toast and sips of tea, there's an animated discussion of who's likely to be at the party that night.

"I take it the garden ornament is going," Brenda says to Julian, with an innocent expression.

"The what?"

"Genevieve."

It's only once all the laughter has died down, that he can answer.

"Yes, she's sending her Roller to pick me up."

"Can we hitch a ride?" says Stef, mirroring Brenda's own thought.

"Yeah, it's gotta be nicer than a blimmin' taxi," says Paula.

"You can all come with Brian and me if you like," says Rosie, tentatively.

Jeez, those drugs of Eadie's. Brenda feels she's still piecing together the last couple of days. "What's with that car of his?"

"It's lovely, isn't it?" says Rosie, missing the point.

"He rob a bank or something?" says Brenda, knowing full well that a car like the one Brian had been driving would be equal to five years pay for your average maths teacher. If not more.

Rather than answer, Rosie is looking at Eadie, who's laughing quietly, although her chuckles escalate into unlady-like guffaws and snorts.

"What?" says Brenda, looking at her, as though her stern expression will quieten the old lady.

"Maths teacher," stutters out Eadie, before pealing with laughter again.

Brenda doesn't bother with any further prompts, opting instead to simply glare at Eadie until she's got herself under control.

The students are also looking at the old lady with interest and a lot more patience than Brenda is feeling.

"It's just that Brian," Eadie wipes the tears carefully from her eyes, "is from one of the richest families in England."

"But he's the third son or something. Right?" says Brenda, sticking to her maths teacher theory.

"No. He's set to inherit a fortune when his father passes."

"Who else knows about him?" says Brenda.

"Mainly the older crowd. The family tends to keep to themselves in that big old pile of rocks they inhabit down in Devon."

The look Brenda gives Rosie is speculative enough that the girl looks discomforted. So much so, that she eventually squeaks out, "What?"

It's Stef who starts humming the wedding march, but it doesn't take long for the others to join in.

Rosie sits mute and scarlet, but Brenda can't miss the look of hope in the depths of the timid girl's eyes.

What a coup, thinks Brenda. It's also potentially far more profitable than simply screwing these rich chaps, figuratively or literally, and moving on.

Brenda strokes the sheer fabric of her midnight blue gown. It was the last thing Martin bought her. Wearing it to trap Wallace doesn't sit well with her. Looking up blocks her tear ducts, but it takes a couple of thumps to her chest put paid to the lump forming there. "Stop it. Stop it!"

The last thing Martin would want is for her to be all maudlin when she thinks about him. If wearing the dress to capture Wallace's attention is what's required, then so be it.

The plunging neckline and spaghetti straps mean a bra is out of the question. She could, of course, wear a strapless bra but thoughts of hitching that and her tits up from around her waist for the entire evening has her vetoing it. Happily, the seam that sits snuggly under her boobs stops them from heading too far south, especially with a stocking stuffed under each of them.

She's relieved that the dress fits, but she suspects this is down to having eaten nothing the day before but a couple of bacon sarnies. Being out cold for twenty hours is conducive to weight loss, it would seem.

Tonight is the first step in snaring Wallace and rather than fade into the background; she wants to stand out, even if this will garner a lot of unwelcome attention.

The deep vee of the neckline has her tits clamouring for attention, while her necklace is the perfect length to have the fire opal – the main feature – bang in the middle of her cleavage and begging for someone to come to its rescue.

She's also left her hair loose so that it hangs in a sleek waterfall down her back.

There is one thing she does want to check before they leave tonight: that this might swing open the door to Julian's own personal closet is a risk she's prepared to take.

There's no response to her first knock, but that might be due to its timidity. Brenda knocks again more firmly and this time, he opens the door.

His reaction on seeing her all gussied up to rope in Wallace isn't what she's expected. His eyes widen and he sucks air in through his nose.

"Is that wise?" He waves his hand vaguely in the area of his chest.

"Hey, you wanna catch a snake, you gotta use melons," says Brenda, laughing at her own ditty.

"True, but you still need to be able to control him," says Julian.

At his tone, Brenda second-guesses her strategy. "Damn it!"

Brenda shoves her hand under each boob in turn, retrieving her added 'oomph' hosiery and then roughly rearranges her boobs. She looks down to check her handiwork but has to complete some more squishing and smoothing to achieve perfection.

"Better?"

Julian has to close his mouth before he can respond.

"Anyway, I wanted to ask you something," says Brenda, recalling why she's at his door.

"Sure." He moves back and into his room in invitation for her to follow him in. He sits on the bed, while she sits in the armchair next to the window.

Now she's here, she's unsure how to proceed. Julian's eyebrows rise in query, letting her know she needs to break the silence to avoid this getting any weirder.

"I, ah, wanted to check what your plans are regarding Genevieve."

"My plans?"

"Well, she doesn't strike me as being your first choice." Brenda waves her hand around to indicate the sea of pink that surrounds them.

"Right," says Julian, understanding her inference. "I'm not after any sort of commitment at the moment. She likes my company and I don't feel any pressure in other areas."

His response is vague, leaving Brenda none the wiser as to his strategy. "That's counter to what you signed up for." Brenda pushes him for clarification.

"Not really."

"No?"

"No," says Julian, making a real show of tweaking his large and ostentatious cufflinks. He follows this up by straightening a large diamond tiepin that wasn't crooked, and Brenda knows her mouth has dropped open.

"She gave you those?"

"Delivered this afternoon."

"Well, screw me," says Brenda, in awe as she gets to her feet.

"I'm sorry, what was that?"

"Nothing," she says, airily.

20

S itting in splendid isolation in Genevieve's Roller, Julian leads the way to the party; the others follow in Brian's Daimler, having a far better time of it, with Brian even agreeing to crank up the stereo. Sadly his choice of music is out of the dark ages.

"I'm bringing a bloody mix tape next time we're out in this boat," shouts Stef to Paula and Brenda, who are sharing the expanse of dark green leather that covers the back seat. Rosie is riding shotgun.

"Bloody hell," spits out Brenda, when they pull up at the enormous mansion that is Lady Morehill's London crash pad.

With Julian safely on the front step, they inch forward until the Daimler is level with the steps and they get out and join him.

"Where's he going to park?" says Paula, as they watch Brian slowly drive away.

"He lives just around the corner, so he'll park at home and then walk back," says Rosie.

"Boy, he has the hots for you," says Stef, causing Rosie to go scarlet.

With the girl stammering to formulate a reply, the others back Stef's opinion.

"Why would you say that?" Rosie eventually manages to choke out.

"If he's driven from Belgravia out to Chiswick in rush-hour traffic, he's smitten," says Julian, confidently.

Rosie's only response is a nervous giggle as though she has trouble grasping the concept of someone being this keen on her.

"Relax and enjoy it," says Brenda, before propelling the girl up the stairs. "Come on you lot, it's too bloody cold to mill about out here." She especially is feeling it, because while she is wearing a coat, her dress is about as substantial as your average nightie.

"I was going to wait," says Rosie, digging her heels in.

"We can wait inside," says Paula, adding her weight to Brenda's to get Rosie moving again. "Bits of me are going numb."

If they're feeling the cold, Brenda suspects their numb bits pale when compared with the poor bastard at the top of the stairs charged with opening the door for new arrivals. He's rugged up in multiple layers, but it's easy to tell by the way he's stamping his feet, that the blood in them is solidifying. Hard to believe it's August and supposedly the summer. Damn, but Brenda misses the warmth of Melbourne.

They file through the front door and into a foyer that's positively tropical by comparison.

"Can we wait for Brian here?" says Rosie, hopefully.

"Might look odd," says Julian, backing up to one of the maids so she can remove his coat for him, which he's wearing cape-style to accommodate his sling.

"We'll wait for him just inside the door," promises Brenda, struggling out of her own coat, before handing it over. She takes the ticket she's given in return and tucks it safely in the depths of her evening bag.

With her shoulders bare, what had felt tropical only a moment earlier, is now feeling chilly. "Come on, I'm not freezing my tits off out here."

The atmosphere in the ballroom is overwhelming. It's far too hot and far too crowded and despite their intention of waiting for Brian inside the door, it's not long before they're absorbed into the room like ink on blotting paper. Brenda stays next to Rosie, but the others are soon lost to them.

"What if he can't find me?" frets Rosie.

"I doubt that very much."

Half an hour later and Brenda has doubts of her own. It's impossible to see more than a metre or two away due to the press of bodies.

"We need to move about," says Brenda.

"Mother always said to stay put if I was lost," says Rosie, remaining glued in place.

"That might work when you're five, but not now," says Brenda, unable to hide her exasperation. "You with me? Or not?"

Rosie doesn't commit either way and Brenda moves off with plans of completing a slow circuit of the large room. Never mind Brian, she needs to see what Wallace is up to. A quick glance over her shoulder shows Rosie is right on her heels.

"Fizz biscuit," mutters Rosie from behind Brenda, but loud enough that it's audible even amidst the babble of upper crust chatter.

"What?" says Brenda, turning back in her direction.

"My school chums," says Rosie, her eyes widening.

Following the direction of the girl's frightened stare, Brenda immediately recognises the two harridans forcing their way towards them. These spiteful bitches were the two responsible for Rosie dressing like her nana and lacking confidence after years of being worn down.

Seeing Rosie reverting to her former timid self has Brenda grinding her teeth.

"Well, what do we have here?" says the fatter of the two, looking Rosie up and down and not liking what she sees.

"Looks like a hooker to me," says the thinner one, who's been shoehorned into a dress that's an ugly shade of peach.

"We knew you'd disappeared, but going on the game is rich, isn't it?" says fatty, her tone vicious.

Rosie is close to tears and Brenda's hackles are up. Rosie's dress is as far from slutty as you can get. She's readying a mouthful when Brian pops up next to them and casually throws his arm around Rosie's shoulders.

Brenda isn't sure if this is because he overheard Tweedle Dum and Tweedle Dee's meanness or it's simply a general claiming of the girl as his. She suspects the former; Brian doesn't strike her as being the caveman type.

"This your trick?" says the thinner girl, who at best still rates as chubby.

With Brian on hand, Brenda happily stands back and watches developments in this live-action soap opera.

She's not disappointed.

"Excuse me?" Brian's timid demeanour drops away as he jumps to Rosie's defence. The girl herself is tongue-tied in the presence of the frumps who have years of experience when it comes to browbeating their slimmer and prettier friend.

"You must be paying by the hour," says the bigger girl, arrogantly.

"How dare you," says Brian, forcefully enough that Brenda can see chinks appearing in the armour of the two malicious bitches Rosie has the misfortune to know. "That's my fiancée you're running down."

"Fiancée?" spit out the two girls.

Unfortunately, Rosie and Brenda are shocked enough that they ask the same question, blowing Brian's ruse sky-high.

Brenda gives Brian his due, though. He isn't fazed for a second and retrieves a small box from his pocket.

"I'd get down on one knee but I'd risk being trampled." He fumbles as he flips open the lid of the small velvet box and Brenda worries that he'll drop the bloody ring. But when she sees the size of the rock, she doubts it would be hard to find.

"Do your parents know about this!" says the fatter girl, her eyes narrowed in spite and jealousy.

"No," whispers Rosie, so quietly that it's hard to hear her above the din in the room.

"Yes!" says Brian, forcefully, making all the girls stare at him. "I asked your father for permission, last night."

"And he said yes?" The thinner girl's voice is so full of glee that it's obvious to all that she thinks she already knows what the answer will be.

"I believe he's happy to have his daughter take up the title of Viscountess."

"Viscountess?" say all the females, although the evil friends don't sound as delighted as Rosie and Brenda.

"So?" says Brian, looking at Rosie, his eyes full of love.

"Yes. Yes!" says Rosie, damn near bouncing on the spot.

This is making it tricky for Brian to slip on the ring, so Brenda places her hands on Rosie's shoulders and keeps applying pressure until the girl stills.

The other girls are green. Possibly a mix of nausea and jealousy but before this can be determined they storm off in a huff.

"I enjoyed that," says Brenda. "Congratulations, you two!"

She hugs each of them in turn, made tricky by Brian refusing to remove his arm from around his fiancée's shoulders.

"You two should get out of here," says Brenda, to the loved-up pair, not that they notice when she strolls off to give them, and her, some space. Well, as much space as is possible in a sea of moneyed and titled extras.

She's aimlessly wandering through the crowd, turning

down offers from a glass of something right through to the other end of the spectrum completely, sick puppies, when "You are a very naughty girl," is whispered right into her ear and it's all she can do not to heave.

"Wallace," she turns to face him, at the same time putting distance between them. He moves immediately into her shadow, once again pressing hard against her.

She's bloody glad the updated plan involves two of Eadie's yellow pills. Thoughts of being alone with this creep while he's still conscious have more bile popping up in her throat.

"What happened?" says Brenda, as innocently as she can.

He looks confused until she places her hand on her own forehead reminding him he's still got a bulge up there. He's also looking suspiciously dark under his eyes.

"As if you didn't know, you little minx," says Wallace, his eyes giving her an altogether less jovial message.

She would have brushed this off once, but after pressing Eadie for details, she's now in no doubt about how cruel he can be. Even thinking about it has her nipples desperately trying to invert themselves.

Giving herself a mental shake, she embarks on the next tentative steps in driving this larcenous arsehole to frothing at the mouth to get his mitts on her. Not that this will happen on the night, because he'll be out for the count. Watching the movie playing inside her head, a broad smile slips into place, the cause of her joy misinterpreted by Wallace.

"What say you and I go somewhere quieter?" he says, his hand applying pressure to her back to get her moving, not waiting for a 'yes'.

Seeing the direction he's propelling her in pisses her off no end, but rather than voice objections, she takes the left-hand gap through the crowd whenever possible, meaning they miss the main doors by a good few metres.

"I'd love a drink," she says, taking refuge next to a Grecian urn that's defying gravity on a similarly challenged head-high plinth. Seriously, who would leave something this precarious in a room where you were going to have a knees-up?

"I've got drinks aplenty at my place," says Wallace, unable to keep a flash of annoyance from crossing his face.

"I'm not ready to leave yet," she says, inferring she'll leave with him at some stage.

It's all the encouragement he needs, "Bubbles or punch?"

She's sampled enough of the bathtub-gin that passes for punch in this town to know her gastric juices aren't up to the challenge. "Bubbles, please."

"Back in a tick. Don't wander off on me."

While his tone might be airy, the undercurrents make it clear she won't get away with ditching him for a third time. Not without putting the plan in jeopardy.

True to his word, he's back surprisingly quickly; it's obvious he'll be happy if she chugs the contents of her glass, throws the flute over one shoulder and insists they leave immediately.

In his dreams.

He wastes no time in polishing off his own glass but has to replace it with another as Brenda hasn't even started hers. After the third false start on her Champagne, she becomes aware of the tension and anticipation building in his body. It's out of kilter with them simply leaving early.

That slimy prick.

It looks as if everything Eadie has said about him is true. Fear and self-doubt cosy up together in the pit of her stomach. Were it not for the longing in Eadie's face whenever she talked about the missing paintings, Brenda would stick to her promise and shelve the plan. But she can't let him away with it. She just can't.

But that doesn't mean she'll calmly sip a spiked drink, either. She doesn't hesitate to nudge her shoulder into the plinth beside her.

The Grecian urn wobbles dangerously.

Then regains its equilibrium.

She gives her next nudge extra oomph.

The look on Wallace's face at seeing the urn heading in his direction is a lovely combination of horror and panic but at least he's no longer straining to grab her glass and forcibly pour the contents down her throat.

That he catches the urn without spilling his Champagne shows rugby must have been his chosen sport when younger. He's grappling to keep the urn from crashing to the ground when Brenda steps in.

"Here, let me hold your glass while you put it down. Damned stupid place to put a vase."

"Bloody lethal is what it is," says Wallace, putting the urn on the ground by the wall before reclaiming his glass.

Brenda takes her time drinking her bubbles, spinning it out long enough that it's gone flat and Wallace has had time to consume a couple more glasses.

It's not difficult to see he's subtly herding her towards a doorway at the side of the ballroom, obviously having given up on getting her through the doors to the foyer.

She's pissed off rather than surprised when he opens the door and forces her through it.

"Let's you and I have some alone time," he says, leaning in ready to slather his liver-like lips all over her face.

Two things happen.

Firstly, he takes her agitation as excitement.

Secondly, his eyes roll up in his head and he keels over backwards, hitting the carpet with a dust-inducing thump.

She's thinking she's killed another one until he starts snoring loud enough to have the crystals on a nearby Victorian lustre lamp gently tinkling.

"Effing bastard." She skirts around his bulk, leaving him to sleep it off.

Two quick circuits of the ballroom confirm Rosie and Brian have left as she'd suggested, Paula has also done a runner, no doubt without an engagement ring being involved, and Stef is nestled up to Cecil and wanting to stay put.

Julian, on the other hand, is ready to go, having already poured Genevieve into her Roller and sent her on her way.

"Did you manage to keep out of the garden?"

"No dislocations this time. Thank god!" He wiggles the fingers poking out the end of his sling briefly to demonstrate everything's still in working order.

Coats claimed, they wait in the foyer until a taxi turns up. There's no shortage pulling into the driveway of the mansion with the word out that there is a mob of rich and well-oiled people needing rides home.

After confirming the glass sliding panel is closed behind the driver, Brenda finally feels able to bring Julian up to date with her evening.

"Arsehole tried to drug me!"

"Tried?"

"Failed! I sent a bit of ugly bric-a-brac in his direction and while he was juggling that, I swapped glasses.

Julian's still laughing when she adds, "Yep, the help will be scraping him off the oriental rug in the morning. He went out like a light."

"Of course, he can't complain about you ditching him this time without admitting to one of the drinks being spiked."

"You got it."

21

The trip home is reasonably quick, with most of the inhabitants of London still stuck in the pub or congregating outside kebab shops rather than on the road.

"Eadie might still be up," says Brenda, seeing light sneaking through the sitting room curtains.

Without being sure, they enter the house quietly, both of them staying mum until Julian whispers, "Goodnight," when he's already halfway up the stairs.

Brenda waves, rather than saying anything and turns towards the sitting room door. Putting her ear to it, she's rewarded with the sound of a page being turned.

Knocking gently to give advance warning she's about to enter, Brenda drops all pretence of quiet when she opens the door and walks into the sitting room.

"Boy, oh boy, was tonight interesting," she says, as yet unsure if she'll let Eadie in on the Wallace segment of the evening's entertainment. With luck, Rosie and Brian's engagement will be enough to put the old lady off the scent.

Half an hour of non-stop chatter later and Brenda makes noises about going to bed.

"Did you see Wallace?" says Eadie, causing Brenda to mutter, "Shit," to herself.

"I heard that!"

Following a cross-examination that would have done Perry Mason proud, Brenda gives in and rattles off her adventures, even covering the urn-toppling stunt.

"The bloody todger is still pulling the same stupid malarkey! I'm so pleased you've decided to give up on that hare-brained scheme of yours to get my works back."

Rather than contradict Eadie and risk giving herself away, Brenda gives a noncommittal "Hmmmm hmmmm" in response.

"You're lucky you swapped drinks."

Even with a fairly good idea, Brenda's morbid curiosity gets the better of her. "Why?"

"Because about now you'd be waking up in the altogether in his dungeon, complete with hidden audience."

"Audience?" says Brenda, revulsion skittering up her spine.

"You think that's bad?" says Eadie, ignoring the comment about an audience, "He'd have been naked, too."

"And I'd be kneeing the bastard so hard in the goolies, he'd be wearing them like a sodding bowtie!"

"Tricky when you're chained up."

Brenda's still thinking on a solution to this conundrum that doesn't involve an acetylene torch, when Eadie continues. "It was having an audience that I didn't like, even if I was the one dishing out the punishment."

"Well, hang on, if there's an audience, I can just yell for help." Brenda allows herself to relax again.

"Hardly, when they've paid to see just that."

"But surely ..." Brenda pauses while considering other avenues of potential rescue.

"No help from that quarter. Any chap in a viewing room will stay quiet because the only way they're allowed in there is if Wallace has something on them. No, you'd be on your own as far as help goes."

The kitchen is thankfully quiet when Brenda stumbles in the following morning in desperate need of tea, and lots of it. She's had a crap night's sleep with back-to-back nightmares of finding herself unable to move while people just out of view whispered their opinions of her body and what Wallace should do with it. Thinking back on some of the more lurid suggestions propounded by her subconscious has her shivering, despite the warmth of the room.

Eadie is in her usual spot at the head of the table, while Bert and Flo are both perched on their bar stools next to the kitchen counter. Not that they stay that way for long; no sooner is Brenda sitting than a mug of tea is plonked down in front of her. It's so wonderful having these two around all the time now. As to where her students are, Brenda can hazard a guess.

"If Stef did spend last night with Cecil, I hope she hasn't done any lasting damage to the old guy's tackle," says Brenda, timing her comment perfectly with Julian's arrival into the kitchen.

He doesn't respond other than to grimace. It's an expression mirrored by Bert.

"Hmmm, I must catch up with her on that. Private tutoring might be in order," says Eadie.

The old girl is about to continue but a pointed cough by Brenda stops her.

"Is that everyone?" says Bert, his hand hovering above the frying pan with a piece of bacon ready to go.

"I yelled up the stairs loud enough that they would have heard me," says Julian.

"You mean Rosie didn't make it home?" Brenda is unable to

keep the surprise out of her voice. She would have bet her life on the girl staying a virgin until the bitter end.

"I wouldn't read too much into that if I was you. I should imagine young Rosie would have slept the night in one of the guest suites," says Eadie, confidently. "Lord knows that London place of theirs has enough of them."

***

It's Saturday afternoon before Stef makes it home. She appears happy enough even though she keeps muttering to herself about, "Weird shit."

Rosie arrives not much later but only so she can change out of her evening gown because she's going out to dinner with Brian. It doesn't take a rocket scientist to know she's still as pure as she'd been the day before. If she'd done the deed, she'd hang her head in shame rather than all the whistley and skippy crap she's subjecting them to.

"I guess she'll move out now," says Brenda, looking out the sitting room window at the girl climbing into the Daimler.

"Maybe," says Eadie.

"Why would she stay?"

"She's closer to Brian than if she was living at home and I should imagine she has more freedom to come and go here, too."

***

Paula crawls in on Sunday afternoon, but only to pack.

"You're leaving us," says Brenda, stating the obvious, while leaning against the doorframe and watching the girl try to cram everything into her patently inadequate suitcase. She's bought a heap of new clothes since being here and to expect them to fit in the bag she'd arrived with is a stretch.

"I am." Paula sits on her case and bounces up and down in a pathetic attempt to compress everything enough so she can shut it. "Parker has a place in Chelsea that he's setting me up in."

"Wow, do ya think that's a good idea?"

"Hell yes! I'm going to have him begging to marry me when I'm done with him."

"Good luck with that. I hope you've got a back-up plan."

"Sure do. I'm getting five hundred quid a month spending money. He's paying for everything else, though."

"Hell's bells."

"If it's okay with you, though, I'd like to keep paying board here for a while, just in case I change my mind."

This makes sense given the girl had told her last landlady to sod off. It also has the calculating cogs in Brenda's brain working at double speed.

Any long division stutters to a halt when she hears movement in Rosie's room and turns to see the girl taking her green leatherette suitcase down off the top of her wardrobe. So much for her staying on as Eadie had thought.

"I take it this means you're shacking up with him."

The girl spins in Brenda's direction, dropping the suitcase in a move reminiscent of an Olympic hammer thrower. Her gaze doesn't hold Brenda's for long, dropping to the floor and staying there.

It takes a second for Brenda to cobble together the flood of words sent in her direction. Something about Daddy cutting her off without a penny, blah blah blah, shame, blah blah blah, no daughter of mine, blah blah.

"So you're moving back home?"

Rosie rips her gaze away from the carpet and looks at Brenda. "I-I-I don't want to. Mummy's making me." The tears that had threatened throughout this exchange give up their tenuous hold on her lower lashes and dribble down her face, further enhancing the look of misery she's wearing like a charity shop cardigan.

"But you'll be allowed to visit us, won't you?" Brenda's confused at all this hand wringing. The girl can't be that attached to them, can she? She's only been living here a little over three months.

"I suppose so, but I won't have the same freedom to come and go as I please."

"Do you think you could stay on a little longer if Eadie spoke to your mum?"

"I suppose that would work. But why?"

Brenda's stumped as to what to say. She can hardly admit it's because Rosie paying rent when she no longer needs help is money for jam. "Ah, you've come so far, it would be a shame to revert now." It's vague enough that Brenda's not committing herself but concrete enough for Rosie to slide her suitcase back up on top of the wardrobe.

―――――

Taxi's here," bellows Stef, to the house in general.

Rosie skips down the stairs onto the first-floor landing, positively buzzing with excitement at this reprieve to what sounds like will be house arrest. "I'm so pleased Mummy agreed to let me stay on."

Story is Eadie's promised to keep a close eye on her between now and the Christmas wedding at Brian's country pile, his father's health permitting. Apparently, there'd been more than a little name-dropping by both parties in that particular conversation, as if to mark out their aristocratic patches.

Paula thunders down the stairs a second later, followed by Julian stepping out of his room.

"Have a great time," he says, confirming for Brenda that he's choosing not to partake in the girls' night out to see Paula officially off to enjoy the good life. Not that he looks like he'll be staying home with his clothes pointing to a night out. Possibly with the Gin Trap as Brenda thinks of Genevieve Smythe-Brown.

Eadie likewise is staying well out of this one, preferring to have a quiet meal at home with Flo and Bert. It will be quite the event, with the Cockney couple even agreeing to sit at the table for the occasion.

"Come on you lot, this is costing a bleeding fortune," yells Stef, prompting them to get moving.

The cab ride is the longest and most scenic Brenda has been on since arriving in London. These mini cabs are cheaper but you take a financial gamble every time you get in one. God knows where this restaurant is that Paula's been raving about. Brenda's starting to think about white slaving before the driver stops, presumably to offload them to his sellers.

She can't believe it when Paula sings out, "We're here."

Even when they're all out of the beat-up Ford Cortina and abandoned on the warzone of a footpath, Brenda can't see where they're meant to be spending the evening. No light spills out welcomingly from any doorways and there isn't a sign that she can see.

"Jeez, Paula, where the hell is this place?" Stef voices Brenda's own concerns.

"Mother Mary, it's safer here in Clapham than it was back in Belfast," says Paula, walking towards what looks like the entrance to a builder's yard. She applies pressure to the corrugated iron and scrap wood gate, swinging it open to reveal a small courtyard and another doorway. Brenda's pleased to see this door has light spilling welcomingly from it and there's even a sign, albeit homemade in nature.

"It's, it's lovely," says Rosie, surprise and relief evident in her uplifting tone.

They follow Paula in a teetering line across the high-heel-crippling cobbled courtyard and head inside where Brenda's own relief becomes permanent. She's not sure how the owners expect people to find the place, but it's obvious they do. People are crammed into every available nook and cranny in what feels like a Middle Eastern Bazaar.

Maybe it's only the immigration people and health inspectors the owners are trying to keep in the dark?

"Lord, I'd forgotten how hot the waiters are here," says Paula, pointing out a couple of well-built lads wearing nothing but baggy pants and a smile. "I wish, I hadn't told Parker to come now."

"Paula, you didn't?" says Brenda.

"I couldn't very well *not* invite him," says the Irish girl, "I was meant to be moving into the love shack tonight, I could hardly leave him there on his tod."

"Ladies, will you please follow me," says a hunky waiter who's popped up behind them.

"To the ends of the earth," is Stef's heartfelt response, and Brenda has to concede she's got a point.

It feels a though they're heading to the ends of the earth with the waiter leading them down several narrow corridors in a row, dimly lit by lanterns of an Eastern design which are on the shadowy side of bloody useless. At the end of the final hallway, they enter a room that is for their personal use. It's beautiful, with the walls painted a dark red with the occasional highlight of electric blue peeping out from the many niches that pepper the walls in a seemingly random fashion. Each of these holds a glowing candle, casting a soft glow up into their little space, then out into the room. Brenda suspects the fire department is also in the dark about this place.

There's an enormous lantern-style chandelier hanging above the single large table; the flickering light coming from this attests to the light being of the candle variety rather than two-forty volts. It's either been done for authenticity or the electricity's been cut off, if the place was connected in the first place.

The table under this fire hazard sits low to the ground on a Turkish rug, while big cushions with a similar design are scattered on all sides. Again this has either been done to set the mood or because they're too poor to afford chairs.

"Ladies, if you'd like to make yourselves comfortable," says their waiter, before bowing out of the room.

They haven't long been seated when Parker turns up. Brenda's more than a little ticked off. Tonight was meant to be a girls' night out, something that even Julian had picked up on; having a bloke along is bound to ruin the atmosphere. She's annoyed that the spot he chooses for himself in between her and Paula, crowding their corner of the table. The scene that ensues as he lowers himself onto his cushion is as good as any floor show. His joints creak so loudly that it sounds like someone's thrown a handful of lit firecrackers under the table.

On first sight, Brenda had envisaged herself lying back on the cushions like something out of the Arabian Nights, but with the wall hard against her back if she were to try that now she'd end up with her head in Parker's lap, a position already taken up by Paula's gently moving hand.

"Paula!" says Rosie, from across the table, this one word so full of censure that it has Parker gently removing the Irish girl's hand and putting it on the table, to the relief of the other girls.

Of interest to Brenda is her own reaction to Paula's hands being all over Parker in plain sight of the others. At one time, the pair of them could have shagged on the table for all she cared. It looks as though those days are in now in her past.

There follows the usual indecision on ordering for the table, with Parker taking over when it appears the girls are unable to agree on anything. That he's au fait with the menu points to him either having spent a lot of time in the Middle East or a lot of time in Clapham, at this particular restaurant.

The meal when served, is sumptuous, with piles of food covering the table to the exclusion of any elbows. True to form, Stef and Paula put away more than should be humanly possible in the way of alcohol while Brenda concentrates instead on the food, which is delicious. No way is she getting herself pissed in the back of beyond.

In the end, she needn't have bothered about being stuck in the boonies; Parker has arranged for his car to take them home after dropping him and Paula off at the place in Chelsea.

22

With Paula living in Parker's love nest in Chelsea and Rosie off visiting relatives with Brian, the house feels empty, although it's anything but quiet. As promised, Eadie is giving Stef lessons in advanced slap and tickle. The first time Brenda hears the sound of a whip cracking in the dining room, she nearly drops her cup of tea. The sharp bark of leather is followed immediately by the unmistakable sound of china smashing, proving there isn't room to swing a cat in there, never mind a cat-o-nine-tails.

Seeing Stef leave the room with the curled-up whip, she pops in to check on progress with Eadie. More than half a dozen ornaments have become casualties.

Brenda looks at the decimated crockery adorning the sideboard. "Jeez, maybe we should clear the room before the next lesson?"

"That lot? They're all bits and pieces I loathe, but they make for good target practice."

Brenda slides into the dining chair next to Eadie's. "I wouldn't have thought you'd need to be that accurate to tan someone's arse."

"Maybe not, but it's better if you've got enough control that you don't risk taking someone's eye out. Or worse."

There were worse things than blinding someone? "Oh, right."

"Are you going to find a student to replace Paula?"

Brenda takes a second to change direction and follow Eadie's lead. "I don't need to. She's still paying board."

"I hadn't realised."

"Yeah, she said she'll keep it up for a month or so. I can't decide if she's doing it to give us extra cash or she's worried it might not work out with Parker."

"Smart girl, either way," says Eadie, getting slowly to her feet.

With Brenda's help, she makes her way through to the sitting room so they can go over activities for the next week without risk of interruption. Apart from Stef's private lessons with Eadie, the girl is also taking advanced first aid classes with their tame ambulance driver, with a focus on lacerations.

"I guess if you're going to slap some posh bastard's bits, you need to know how to slap on a plaster too," says Brenda.

Thinking about this, she's unable to stop a burst of laughter, joined by Eadie.

"The girl does have a natural aptitude," says Eadie "could be a good career choice for her. If she can keep Cecil happy without killing or castrating him, she'll be able to get a job at any establishment in town."

It's something Brenda will talk to her pupil about because there's more than one way of making money out of these old guys and if you can do it without having to shag them, so much the better. While Brenda hadn't minded sex with Martin, this hadn't been the case with her earlier lovers and, after this long a break, she knows she'll never be able to go back to that way of life.

After lunch, Brenda catches up with Julian and Stef in the common room. She's armed with several sheets of paper and a plethora of coloured pencils, bought especially for the purpose.

"I've been giving the final parts of the plan more thought," she says, before scrawling Project S-B across the top of the first sheet. "We've got the perfect event coming up in two weeks."

"You mean the masquerade at the Colchester?" says Julian.

Stef claps her hands in excitement. "I've got a mask that'll be perfect."

Brenda's surprised on two counts. Firstly, that Julian is well connected enough to know about this invitation-only event and secondly, that Stef already owns a bloody mask.

Julian, has noticed her look of surprise and says, "Ginny is taking me."

"A friend gave it to me," says Stef, wriggling her eyebrows and causing a snort of laughter to escape Brenda.

After Julian changes the third item on their plan, Brenda swings the sheet of paper around on the coffee table and pushes the pencils to his side of the slab of oak.

"Are you sure?" he says.

"Knock yourself out. You're better at being devious than I am."

"Thank you. I think."

With Julian in the lead, the three of them rapidly nut out the main bones of the plan, with particular emphasis on keeping Brenda out of Wallace's mitts. They're still discussing the finer points when Rosie comes in after lunch at Brian's aunt's place.

"Hello," she says, kicking off her shoes and settling into one of the big armchairs. "What are you working on?"

"Fine-tuning the plan to get Eadie's paintings back," says Brenda.

"I thought that was all sorted?"

"Couple of new developments," says Julian, picking up their latest version and handing it to her.

Rosie studies it, goes to speak, then goes back to studying the plan.

"I can see a couple of issues."

"Really?" question Stef, Julian and Brenda simultaneously.

Brenda's forehead is crinkled in concentration when Rosie enlightens them.

"What about live-in staff? Also, your exit strategy is dicey. You need a couple of options up your sleeve there."

———————

The next ten days are spent with Brenda continuing to slowly reel in Wallace. By deft management, he's never able to drag her from any of the functions they attend and she puts on a good show of looking just as frustrated at the constant interruptions.

"What about this one?" says Brenda, doing a twirl in the middle of the common room.

Stef looks critically at the dress. "Not bad."

"There isn't much of it," says Rosie.

"Isn't that the idea?" says Paula, walking out of her mostly-unused bedroom.

"You're here," says Brenda, stating the obvious.

"Yeah, I got sick of staring at the wallpaper while Parker is catching up with his cronies. Thought I may as well pop over here for the day."

"So?" says Brenda, twirling again, "Will it do?"

She's turned to show them the back and has struck a pose with arms wide, when Julian pops into view on his way up to see what's being voted on.

"Good god!"

At first, Brenda interprets his tone as one of censure, but she's not sure, and her arms drop and cross over in front of her with no prompting on her part.

He walks around her looking at it from all angles. "He'll be frothing like a rat that's eaten soap when he sees this number."

He uncrosses her arms.

His brows knot.

After a lengthy stare at her chest that makes her feel strangely flustered, he says, "You'll need more socks."

"You're kidding?" says Brenda, looking down at her boobs, "If they're sitting any higher, I'll choke."

"We've only got one shot at this," says Julian, with this sentiment being backed by "uh huhs" all round. Even Rosie, which comes as a surprise to Brenda.

Thinking the dress has been agreed on, Brenda has already started down the stairs to her bedroom to change when Julian stops her.

"Do you have anything with colour in it?"

She turns and retraces her steps. "He's seen me in both the purple and the navy a couple of times now. What's wrong with black?"

"Too tame," says Stef.

"You always wear black," says Paula.

"Nearly all the women will wear black," says Rosie.

"Red!" says Julian.

"Red?" Brenda can feel herself going that colour at thoughts of dressing so blatantly. While she isn't afraid of standing out, she'd prefer to do so subtly, so she's passed a man before her looks kick him in the guts. Then it's up to her who she approaches, and not the other way around.

"I don't own anything red."

The shopping trip touch-paper is lit and truly alight well before they're all in the van and on their way to the second-hand clothes shop in Hammersmith.

After parking nearby, they descend on the place like a swarm of red-loving-locusts.

23

S tef is first through the door and wastes no time in getting things underway. Paula and Rosie stand waiting to be told what to do, while Julian lurks in the background.

"Red evening gowns?" says Stef, to the owner, Alison, who's sorting through 'new' stock.

"Who for?" she says, looking at Stef, Rosie and Paula in turn.

"Her," says Paula, hooking her thumb in Brenda's direction.

"This is going to be fun," says Alison.

"Says you." Brenda isn't looking forward to playing Barbie for this lot.

Her style of shopping for flash gear tends to be walking in with whichever old bloke she's got on the go at the time; they choose it, if it fits and they like it, they pay for it. It's led to some pug-ugly dresses hanging in her wardrobe, but if the old coot was happy, so be it.

Martin, on the other hand, had had impeccable taste and it's him she can thank for the most beautiful clothes she now owns. Before she can get too maudlin, Rosie frog-marches her over to a cubicle space.

"When did you get all bolshie?" says Brenda, before she's propelled into the imaginary space and the curtains yanked closed.

"Sorry," says Rosie, through the curtains, in her usual tone.

But there's nothing timid about how the first dress is shoved through the curtains with Brenda able to tell by the jewellery that Stef is the donor. Resigned, she makes short work of stripping off and trying the dress on.

"Hell, this is ugly!"

Without warning, Paula rips open her side of the curtains.

Stef follows suit on the other side and just like that, the cubicle space is reclaimed by the shop.

"Turn around," prompts Rosie.

Brenda spins, "As I said, sodding ugly."

With most of her students effectively having graduated, Brenda is no longer as careful about her language and the dress is hideous enough to warrant the use of profanities.

"Good lord." Julian's expression says it all.

It's the first time Brenda's ever seen his lip curl, but she's in agreement.

"Next!" says Rosie, clapping her hands like a ballet teacher.

The response is immediate. Stef shoves another dress at Brenda and she and Paula yank the curtains closed again.

Stripping off the ugly beast, Brenda stuffs it out through the curtains and tries on the next dress on offer.

"Too small," says Brenda, "Next?"

Six more dresses follow in quick succession and they have quite an assembly line going with all the dresses passed to Brenda already off the hangers and any zips or buttons undone.

'Too small' is followed by 'too orange,' 'too pink', 'too tatty', 'too prissy', a 'just don't bloody like it' that requires a second opinion and finally a 'just plain ugly'.

It's like the seven dwarves of shopping.

"This one's not too bad," says Brenda, with relief.

She's over this bloody shopping trip, so maybe her opinion that it looks okay is a measure of desperation.

The curtains open and she strikes a pose for the small audience.

The response is a Mexican wave of responses interspersed with non-committal 'hmmms' all round.

"Shit!" Brenda resigns herself to trying on more dresses. "Okay, give me the next one."

"That's all of them," says Stef, shoulders slumped in defeat.

Paula and Rosie look crestfallen, Julian's shell-shocked and Alison is still neck-deep in a large hessian sack full of what looks to be old rags, but her cry of glee still comes through loud and clear.

She shakes out a shapeless length of dark red fabric before holding it up. "This one's a pearler!"

"You kidding me?" says Brenda, looking at the hunk of cloth Alison's holding.

"Don't judge it in this condition. You'd be amazed what dry-cleaning can achieve."

Brenda takes the dress and is immediately enveloped by a stench that's reminiscent of forgotten swimming gear, minus the chlorine. She waves the dress about in vain hopes of airing it before she has to close the curtains.

Sure enough, no sooner have Stef and Paula closed the curtains on her than the smell becomes overwhelming.

"Screw this!" says Brenda, jerking the curtains open again. "Yell if it looks like someone's coming in."

She's not worried about the girls and Julian seeing her in her undies but doesn't want anyone else walking in and seeing how sheer they are. She removes the so-so dress and pulls on the rag that Alison is still gushing about.

"Can someone do up the buttons?"

Brenda swings away from them and looks at the dress critically in the mirror while she waits for Rosie to do up the myriad small buttons that run the length of the dress to just above her arse. Rosie's buttoning up around the nape of her neck before Brenda looks away from the dress to the audience so she can judge their reactions.

Stef and Paula look gobsmacked and Rosie is bouncing with excitement as she peers over Brenda's shoulder to check out the front of the dress in the mirror. Julian's reflection is strangely absent.

Brenda pirouettes in front of the girls. "So?"

There's a chorus of 'wow', 'amazing' and even a couple of 'stunnings'.

Brenda has to agree.

The dark-red satin dress fits her as though it's been made specifically for her, rare when buying second-hand. The style is old-fashioned enough to be way beyond out-of-date and there's even a slight corset effect with the stitching on the bodice. A small ruffle sits just above her bum that's as close to a bustle as you can get without a frame and a cushion being involved.

"Jeez," says Brenda, looking down at the square neckline. "I'm gonna have to tape my tits in place or risk a nipple busting out."

As if to prove her point, she doubles over, "See!" she says, after straightening.

At a cough from Julian, Brenda looks in his direction. He's moved down the back and is studiously picking through the one small rack of menswear.

"You want a man's opinion?" he says, focusing on the clothes in front of him.

"You're right," says Brenda, snapping her fingers.

She turns towards the front window and on her way to the plate glass tucks her nipples back into the top of the bodice. It's not long before a man passes and Brenda raps on the glass to get his attention.

She indicates the dress, spins for him and runs her hands

down her sides before giving him a questioning look and mouthing, "Well?"

With speech out of the question, he gives her a thumbs-up before moving closer to the glass until his eyes are as glazed as the window, which is why he bumps into it, his face immediately obscured by condensation.

"I think we can take that as yes to the dress and yes to me having to clean the window," says Alison.

———————

It doesn't matter how many times Brenda reads through the plan, there's still one vital element missing. She hasn't been able to get a bloody invitation to the masquerade. All three girls have managed to garner invitations because of their other halves and Julian has been on the guest list for weeks; but not even Eadie's influence has been far-reaching enough for Brenda to secure an invitation. She's going to kick herself when she finds out all that effort was so Brenda could get into Wallace's place to get her paintings back.

"Damn it!" Brenda thumps the much-thumbed sheet of paper down on the bed beside her, narrowly missing one of Charlie's eyes with the corner. "Sorry, mate."

Brenda needs to sort something out or the plan will be kyboshed. So busy is she looking for alternatives to an actual invitation that it takes her a moment to realise she's standing out on the landing.

"Student meeting, now," she yells in the direction of Julian's room, before thundering up to the second floor and repeating the summons.

———————

You can hardly nobble him in reception," says Julian, pointing out the bleeding obvious.

"I can ask Brian to see if he can organise something," says Rosie, tentatively.

Brenda immediately puts her out of her misery. "No. It's best Brian is kept out of it."

From the outside, it looks as though Brenda is doing this to keep this upstanding citizen away from their dodgy dealings. Truth be told, she's more concerned he'll try to stop them.

"My sister can get you in," says Stef, confidently.

"You've got a sister?" says Paula, who spends most days with them rather than sit alone at the love shack.

"Three, actually."

"How can she help?" says Brenda, who's also been unaware of any siblings.

"She works in the kitchens at the 'Col'. I can tell her to make sure she's working that night."

"That'd be bloody brilliant!" says Brenda.

In reality, sneaking in is the perfect solution.

In the lead-up to the masquerade, the house takes on a festive air. Paula and Parker often call in for drinks and Rosie, Julian and Stef are constantly visited by their – actually, Brenda isn't sure what the collective term is. While she'd bet her life Rosie's still a virgin, as to what's happening between Ginny and Julian, who knows. Whether he's been cornered into doing the nasty with the old girl, in return for all the trinkets she's showering upon him, is anyone's guess. As for Stef, she's simply whipping the crap out of Cecil's flabby old bits on a regular basis.

'Toffee-nosed arm candy' will have to do.

The Wednesday before the ball, they have a full dress

rehearsal with any kinks in outfits or hair sorted now rather than causing a ruckus on the night. Julian, as always, is immaculate with no need to fork out for a new suit. He does, however, have his hair cut. It takes a second for Brenda to see that it isn't tied back as usual, but is of military shortness, robbing him of his usual insouciance.

On seeing her raised eyebrow, he says, "Thought this might be harder to point out in a line-up."

"You don't have to do this, you know." Brenda's all too conscious of the risk her students are taking by being involved.

"It'll be a laugh. My life's become a tad predictable of late."

Predictable? This surprises her. If he thinks moving in here and learning how to fleece old guys of their spare cash is predictable, what the hell was he getting up to before?

———

The morning of the ball, Brenda wakes early and can't do a thing about the plan yet again assailing her brain. It's convoluted, worryingly so, and this means lots of opportunities for the whole thing to go tits-up. Involved are a heap more people than she'd like and the chain of events will have to be spot on if the plan is to come off without a hitch. She's calculated for every eventuality but if anything goes off the rails, it will have a domino effect. Without them having access to walkie-talkies or the like, it could end up a right SNAFU.

It's all these possibilities that are making her nervous and it's not a feeling she likes or is used to.

If it weren't for them recovering Eadie's stolen paintings, she'd say "screw it" to the whole venture. Maybe this is the cause of her nerves? If it were only her benefiting, she wouldn't give a rat's arse. This emotion is also an unfamiliar one.

A solid whack on her arm has Brenda back in the here and now.

"Is it that time already?"

Charlie backs it up with a plaintiff meow and, when she doesn't move fast enough, another whack to her arm. Bloody cat-o-larm doesn't have a snooze button either and she knows from experience that his whacks only get harder. After that, he'll be stomping around on her bladder or boobs for maximum effect.

"Okay. Okay!"

Brenda rubs the top of his head vigorously with her knuckles before throwing the covers to one side, covering him. His squawk is one of pure outrage.

"Hah! Payback's a bitch."

He's free by the time she's chucked on some sweats and had a pee and is waiting at the top of the stairs to accompany her down to breakfast.

"You're lucky I'm not having a shower this morning."

Back home in Aussie, she'd have showered now and again later so her hair was fresh for the hairdresser to put up. It isn't without reason that English plumbing has a shitty reputation. Cold showers sucked.

Brenda's surprised to find she's not the first down. The kitchen is abuzz with people, with Julian the only student not present. Even Flo and Bert are on deck today with a full-English currently being fried in copious enough amounts of lard to merit the term 'boiled'. The scrambled eggs sitting in front of Eadie look far more appetising, although their sheen suggests a good percentage of them is butter.

"Paula, I wasn't expecting you until later," says Brenda.

The girl yawns widely, before speaking. "Parker dropped me off on his way to the country to go kill something or other."

"Will he be back in time for this evening?" says Brenda.

"Yep. He hasn't gone far and from what I hear, the beaters make it pretty damned easy for them to bag a bird."

"Jeez, why don't they go to the supermarket like everyone else?" says Stef.

"Not enough blood and ammo, I suspect," says Eadie, after she's safely swallowed a mouthful of scrambled eggs.

The conversation dies off as Brenda and her students concentrate on their bacon, eggs, sausages and tomato to eat as much as possible before the fat congeals. Finished, Brenda suspects her stomach is now impervious to alcohol and will stay that way for a couple of bloody days.

Flo has cleared the plates before Julian makes an appearance. He looks like shit, something that Brenda voices.

"Feel like it, too," he says, his voice croaky.

"Back ya go," says Flo, marching in his direction like a force of nature. She spins him around and propels him back through the kitchen door and a Cockney running commentary on his state of health continues down the hall and up the stairs. The little woman won't be happy until she's tucked him back into bed herself.

"Shit!" mutters Brenda, to herself, although when she sees everyone at the table looking in her direction, it dawns on her she hasn't been as private as she would have liked.

While the three students sport looks of concern, Eadie looks confused but thankfully not suspicious. As far as the old girl's concerned, Brenda's ditched her plan and she prefers it stays that way.

"He'll be fine in a day or two," says Eadie. "I'm sure it's nothing life-threatening."

Brenda is calculating how this screws up the plan for that evening when Flo rockets back into the kitchen.

"That boy needs the tonic," she says, to Bert.

"Do yer think that's wise?" His brows are knitted so tight that he looks constipated.

"Flo, are you sure?" says Eadie, her face also creased with concern.

"If 'e wants to go to this party tonight like 'e says 'e does, the tonic it is!"

"Sounds like a bleeding miracle cure," says Brenda, looking between the three older occupants of the room.

"It would be better if he were there," says Stef.

She's backed up by Paula and even Rosie nods slowly.

"Right!" Flo rubs her hands together, throws open the cupboards and roots around in them until there's a pile of ingredients assembled on the counter.

She clicks her fingers before disappearing into the depths of the cellar. It's not long before she's back, a large bottle clutched hard against her chest.

Eadie notices it. "Good lord. What doesn't kill you makes you stronger."

"What is that shit?" Brenda looks at the dark viscous sludge clinging tenaciously to the insides of the bottle after being sloshed there on the trip up from the cellar.

"I'm not entirely sure," says Eadie. "But I won't be partaking of this particular remedy again, now I've seen what the raw ingredients look like."

"You've drunk this stuff?"

"I have. And while it might well taste like boiled down underpants, it works a treat."

Brenda's dwelling on what the flavour would be akin to, when Paula and Stef, who are on the side of the table closest to the stove where Flo is stirring away at a large pot like something out of Macbeth, start coughing.

"Sorry," trills out Flo, before tugging on the right-hand cord of the Xpelair fan.

Thankfully, despite sounding like a pack-a-day asthmatic, the fat-choked fan is soon sucking the worst of the miasma from the kitchen and sending it out into the garden where it will no doubt take out a good percentage of the local insect population.

The kitchen still stinks to high heaven, though.

"How about I help you through to the sitting room?" says Brenda, standing in readiness next to Eadie.

"I'll grab the door," says Stef, jumping to her feet.

"I'll, ah, go plump cushions, or something," says Paula, desperately.

"Um, I'll help you," says Rosie, out of obvious reasons for escape.

24

E ven from her bedroom, Brenda knows Flo has carried the brew into Julian's bedroom. The fumes off the damned stuff have the seek-and-destroy capabilities of an Exocet missile. The ensuing coughing and swearing soon after, warns Brenda that the brew doesn't improve in close quarters.

Poor bastard.

With Flo trudging back downstairs, Brenda waits a moment before opening her bedroom door and venturing out onto the landing. She's sure it's not her imagination that the air out here looks hazy. It's enough for her to pull her bedroom door shut to keep the air in there as pure as possible.

Bleeding heck, if it's this bad out here, god only knows what it's like in Julian's room. She knocks tentatively, with her tapping answered after a short pause. Bloody hell, he sounds as if he's been gargling bleach.

Stepping into his room, she immediately starts coughing, but rather than beat a hasty retreat, she marches purposefully over to the windows and opens every one of them, all the while trying not to take in too much air.

But she doesn't stop there.

Back on the landing, leaving his door wide open, she marches into the bathroom and opens the window in there before repeating the process in the sewing room, and Chris and Sam's room. The one room she doesn't include in this general airing out is her own, which still has the door closed tight against the persistent haze.

Only after the noxious cloud has died down, does she close the windows again. By then the temperature in Julian's room has dropped about ten degrees, but at least he's no longer in danger of asphyxiation. And, more importantly, neither is she.

"Was it bad?" says Brenda, looking down at him, lying prone and sweating as though in the final stages of a malarial episode.

His response is so croaky she has to lean closer to hear him, although she eventually gets close enough to hear his "God-awful."

"Are you going to be okay to go out tonight? Because I've gotta tell you, you look like shit."

"Great, that's how I feel," he rasps out.

"I'll check in with you again at lunch time. But if you're still like this, it's all off." Brenda doesn't wait for an argument from him and instead leaves him to succumb to the tonic while she goes upstairs to catch up with the girls.

"Are we cancelling it?" says Stef through the open door of her bedroom, the moment Brenda steps foot on the second landing.

"I can't see how we can proceed," says Brenda, walking into the common room and throwing herself on the couch.

It's not long before the three girls join her. They look at the plan for that evening but it doesn't matter how they reallocate the various tasks; without Julian, it simply won't work.

"Sod it all," says Brenda, collapsing back in her armchair. "When are we going to get another chance like this?"

"We're already past the end of the season," says Rosie,

knowledgeably. "Other than house parties, that might be the last big event for ages."

"Damn, I hope that shit of Flo's works."

The rest of the morning they spend in the common room working on manicures and pedicures, plucking eyebrows and general titivating because while the plan might be in jeopardy, the three girls are still going out that evening. Even Brenda is repainting her nails because while she's not officially going to the masquerade, she is unofficially. Well, she will if there's a miracle with Julian's health.

Not that making an effort will look strange to Eadie, with Brenda having told the old lady that seeing as she couldn't get an invite to the 'do' at the Colchester, she may as well head out to trawl for more students, given the current lot have pretty much graduated already.

The trip downstairs in response to the gong for lunch is slow because Stef, who's in the lead, still has cotton wool between her toes and is walking on her heels to save smudging the polish recently applied by Paula.

"Hold up, I'll just check on Julian," says Brenda, dreading what she's going to find but also resigned to the inevitable.

The door to his bedroom is slightly ajar but Brenda can't remember if she'd left it like that after airing out the fug, or if this is a new development. Knocking briefly, she pokes her head around the door and is surprised to find the bed empty. The bathroom door is open and she knows the only other place he can be, is downstairs. But he can't have improved that much. Can he?

They continue slowly down to the half landing where they're greeted by the smell of roast meat.

"Out of the way. We'll miss out on pudding at this rate," says Paula, reigning queen of chocolate, forcing Stef to the side so she can pass. She's followed by Rosie and Brenda, leaving Stef to hobble behind them.

They arrive in the dining room to find Julian sitting at the table with his plate already full to overflowing with roast beef and Yorkshire pud, leaving little room for anything else. He's not looking his usual perky self, but neither is he looking half-dead, as he had earlier.

"How do you feel?" Brenda's unable to keep the surprise out of her voice that he's even upright.

"Surprisingly good," says Julian, although his voice is still croaky. "I reckon another dose of that muck and I'll be good as new."

This last comment coincides with Flo entering the room with a huge platter of roast potatoes. After placing this carefully in the centre of the table, she says, "Righty-ho, I'll get some for you now."

But she hasn't gone far, when everyone at the table yells out, "No!" stopping her in her tracks.

"But the boy needs the tonic," she says, hands on hips and ready to fight for Julian's health.

"Your level of care is admirable," says Eadie, "but perhaps Julian could take the next dose outside."

It's only when Flo concedes that this might be a good idea that the people around the table fill their plates, knowing that they can do so without risk of suffocation by that foul smelling brew.

The meal over, the girls can't help but congregate in the kitchen and watch, through the safety of the glass, Julian taking his second dose of the heinous tonic. That his face turns an alarming shade of red moments after he's swallowed it is of concern, as is the coughing fit that consumes him.

"Jeez, it looks as though that shit is incinerating whatever the hell it is, out of his system." Brenda unconsciously shakes her head in denial at what she's witnessing.

"Who gives a damn, so long as it works," says Stef, eating a left-over spud.

"Where'd you get that from?" says Paula, looking at the golden piece of potato.

"They were in the roasting pan."

Soon, Julian and his borderline poisoning are forgotten as the girls hoover their way through the rest of the roast potatoes, although they leave a few for Julian to help him get the taste of that slimy shit out of his mouth. Even better is that they're the little crispy ones that they know he likes.

Julian walks in through the back door wiping his tongue on the sleeve of his shirt as he does so. "Gah, that truly tastes like boiled underpants, just like Eadie said."

"Here, this might help?" says Brenda, handing the roasting tray to him.

He wastes no time in shoving as many potatoes as he can into his mouth as though to beat the taste of aftertaste into submission. "Oh, god, that's better."

"Wow, that's amazing," says Paula.

"What is?" say the others, in unison.

"Your voice," she says.

"What about it?" says Julian.

"Wow, she's right," says Rosie, with this backed up by Stef.

"It's not croaky anymore." Brenda shakes her head at the efficacy of the stuff.

He clears his throat experimentally and must like the results if his wide grin is any indication. "Houston, we are good to go," he says, before laughing delightedly although this turns into another coughing fit, signalling that his recovery is tenuous at best but enough that the plan can proceed.

Brenda sees her students off in their various upmarket modes of transport, then walks into the sitting room so Eadie can see her outfit for the evening, surprised to see she's already rugged up in her dressing gown. "How do I look?"

It's the silk boiler suit she'd worn on a previous sortie to recruit students, of a quality that women would notice, but men wouldn't and so she's not expecting any objections.

"You look as beautifully turned out as always. It's such a shame you can't go to the Col with the others."

"Hey, no biggie. I'm as happy doing what I'm doing."

"What time will your cab be here?"

"Julian's letting me use the van so if I strike out at the first pub, I can easily get around to others."

Eadie's still nodding her assent to this plan when Brenda abruptly announces her departure. Lying to the old girl isn't sitting well in her stomach, with escape the only thing between her and antacids.

She checks the level of sherry in the decanter. "Good, it looks like you've got everything you need," and then hustles out of the house, and around into the driveway where she unlocks the van. She'd rather Julian was driving but he'd been collected by Genevieve's chauffeur-driven Roller earlier. Similarly, the others were going in tandem with their dates. To avoid raising Eadie's suspicions by changing in the driveway, she carefully backs out of the drive and motors a couple of hundred feet along the road before pulling to a stop.

Rather than risk climbing over the seats into the back and snagging her jumpsuit, she gets out and walks around to the back where she opens the double doors and climbs in. An elderly lady out walking her dog witnesses this, but that can't be helped. The damned woman sprang up from nowhere and rather than be caught loitering, Brenda decides it'll look less strange, although not by much given her boiler suit is not the kind usually seen on tradesmen, to simply get in and close the doors behind her.

Even so, looking out of the tinted rear windows she's aware

the old lady and her dog are both looking at the van with suspicion; especially the dog. Only once they've moved off does she set about changing. Her shoes and handbag she puts inside the large dark blue Colchester laundry bag that already holds her beautiful dark red evening gown. The jumpsuit she folds and pops into a plastic carrier bag to stay put in the van.

Down to her undies, she dresses again in a plain black uniform, white apron and a pair of shoes that would have given Rosie's brogues a run for their money in the ugly stakes. This ensemble has been 'borrowed' by Stef's sister from an open locker in the Colchester staffroom and while it is on the baggy side, Brenda doesn't plan on wearing it for long.

Even without the benefit of a mirror, she can still tell it's dreadful. But perfect if she's to walk in the back entrance of the hotel without anyone fingering her. She drags her hair up into a no-nonsense bun and hopes that if she keeps her head down, no one will notice the heavy make-up.

She's clambering over into the front seat when a black cab whizzes by so close that it clips the wing mirror, rocking the van as a result. What an arsehole. She'd give chase, but a quick look at her watch reminds her she needs to haul arse rather than play vigilante.

Brenda pulls into a loading zone at the back of the hotel that Stef's sister said would be safe to use and unloads herself and her carefully wrapped dress, shoes and handbag. They're under a couple of hotel towels Stef's sister had also 'appropriated'. Quite the klepto by the look of things. Not that Brenda can throw stones, given her past.

Head down, she walks purposefully through the staff entrance as though she has every right to be there; a minute or so later, Stef's sister falls into step next to her. Because of this, no one challenges them and once safely through the kitchens, they keep going until they're outside the women's restrooms in a side corridor with direct access to the ballroom.

"These lavvies aren't in use until afta the knees-up kicks orf," says Stef's sister, "you should be safe t'get inta yer clobber there." Without a backward glance, she legs it back to the kitchens.

So far, so good.

Brenda pushes open the door slowly, and pauses while listening for any movement in the cubicles, but it looks like Stef's sister is right. But rather than risk it, she puts the laundry bag down on the vanity and crouches down on the floor and takes a shufti under the doors to check for well-shod feet. Nope, all clear.

It's while she's hunkered down like this that the door opens behind her.

"No, that looks clean," says Brenda, before standing and grabbing her bag of goodies without looking around and legging it out of there before the new arrival can get a good look at her.

Shit, what now? These toilets weren't supposed to be in use yet. How the hell did that bird find her way around here? Rather than loiter in the hallway, Brenda walks down it, trying doors as she goes until she comes upon a door that isn't locked. She cracks it open and is pleased to see it's a storeroom and a far better spot for changing than a toilet cubicle with a lot less chance of dropping a shoe or her handbag in any wee on the floor, that's for sure.

Brenda flicks on the light and checks the floor as carefully as she can before putting the bag down and pulling the door shut behind her. She's almost in the dark again; the bloody useless bulb dangling above her must have been chosen purely for the lack of electricity required to power it. She wastes no time in stripping off the apron and sack-like uniform and kicking off those hideous, but surprisingly comfortable, shoes.

Pulling the red dress on over her head, she works it down her body and then zips it up at the side. Alison had suggested adding the zipper and a good idea it had proved to be. She'd never have been able to get the dress closed if she'd had to do up all those buttons.

She unpins her hair and shakes it out, before stuffing the maid's outfit into the laundry bag and putting it on an empty shelf. With any luck, the items will make their way back to their original owner, not that she cares one way or the other. A quick look in the compact mirror in the flap of her evening bag and she knows there is no way in hell she can refresh her make-up in here. She'd risk looking like a clown.

Still, now she's dressed appropriately, there's no reason why she shouldn't finish her make-up in the restroom along the hall. It's not like anyone she meets in there will ask to see her bloody invitation. Sliding the mask Stef had given her into place, she hits the light, plunging the room into darkness before pulling the door open wide enough to check the hall. It's empty so she wastes no time getting out and closing the store-room door.

Breezing into the Ladies like she owns it, Brenda's brought up short. The bird is still in there, sitting on one of the stools in front of the counter under the mirrors, a cane propped against her leg. Even with the mask, there's no mistaking those crippled knuckles.

She doesn't get a chance to ask Eadie what she's doing there before the old girl lets her have both barrels.

"I am most disappointed in you, Brenda."

Brenda's not sure what to say to this. First off, no one's ever cared enough to be disappointed in her before. Secondly, she's been caught red-handed, so there's little point in trying to bull-shit her way out of it. She doubts she'd get away with it, either. "Did you honestly think I'd let that arsehole get away with it?"

Eadie turns from looking at Brenda in the mirror to facing her, the stool she's sitting on creaking alarmingly as she does so. "That is not your decision to make, young lady."

"Looks like I've already made it," says Brenda, immediately regretting her flippant tone.

Eadie doesn't reply to this, instead looking hurt enough to make Brenda feel like a complete bitch. She's stuttering for something to say when Eadie presses on.

"I took the liberty of casting an eye over your plans and there are one or two weaknesses that need to be sorted out if we're to succeed."

Bugger. They should never have put in that damned stair lift.

"We're?"

"I thought you might need help, finding where things are."

"But Eadie," Brenda stalls, not sure how to break the new to the old lady that she'll only slow them down.

"Yes, yes, I know I'm not as fast as you young ones, but neither do I need to be when I know all the shortcuts."

Shortcuts? "Go on."

"If you leave the building the way you currently plan to, you risk running into others who are waiting to watch."

Brenda shakes her head at this, envisaging a perverts' waiting room, full of aristocratic wankers reading tattered copies of Playboy rather than well-thumbed National Geographics.

"Wallace used to make a tidy sum in the old days, charging other chaps to watch. Or even be watched," says Eadie, retrieving Brenda's plan from her Oroton handbag.

She smooths the crinkled sheets of paper flat on the vanity in front of her, but ever so slowly to spare her hands the worst of the pain. Even so, Brenda hears a couple of small gasps escape unbidden. That these are accompanied by Eadie's face tightening only reinforces what a bad idea it is for Eadie to tag along on this caper. But, on the other hand, if the cellar at Wallace's house is the labyrinth Eadie makes it out to be, it could save a lot of time overall.

It doesn't take them long to rehash the plan so that it ties in with the new 'intel' provided by Eadie. Actually, it makes the whole thing a lot more straightforward and this eases the worry that's been traipsing in 8-eye Doc Martens around the edges of Brenda's consciousness.

The only problem is how on earth do they update the others?

"Bloody hell, we need to get a move on, if we're going to let the others know," says Brenda, helping Eadie to her feet, occasioning all sorts of creaking and groaning. She does this with supreme care bit it makes no difference and Eadie's moan of pain cuts through Brenda like a knife.

"This is ridiculous. You're hurting here." Brenda lowers Eadie gently back down onto the small stool. "I've got an idea. Don't go anywhere."

The irony of this last instruction isn't lost on either of them. Despite the seriousness of the situation, they share a conspiratorial chuckle. Brenda nips down the still empty hallway to the storage room and retrieves the wheelchair she'd seen parked there when she'd changed earlier. The state of it leads her to believe it hasn't seen active service in about fifty years, but after a dust-off with the towels she'd hidden earlier, it's good to go.

Eadie on the other hand, is not.

"I am not going in that, that thing!" she says, in high dudgeon. "I am perfectly able to move around with my cane."

"Yes. You are," says Brenda, pausing while she carefully touches up her lipstick. "But not as fast as we need to, so you either get in the bloody chair, or I'm bloody leaving you here and going ahead without you." It's all she can do not to tap her foot, so annoyed is she with her elderly mentor. After what is a worryingly long internal battle, Eadie relents and allows Brenda to help her into the chair.

"I swear if anyone says anything about me being old and frail, I'll smack them with my cane."

"If anyone calls you old and frail I'll run the chair into their sodding ankles," says Brenda, eliciting delighted laughter from the elderly Boadicea she's pushing down the hallway towards the ballroom.

True to her word, Brenda ladders a good few pairs of panty-hose before word gets around 'not to mention the chair'. The other thing that makes it like the world's poshest demolition derby is staying out of Wallace's way and Brenda's immensely relieved the ballroom is as massive as it is, making this at least possible. The last thing they need is for him to link her to Eadie. They waste no time catching up with the others and it's with relief that Brenda hands Eadie over to Julian, although the plan is still for the old girl to stay out of that fat bastard's way.

25

For the first time ever, Brenda willingly approaches Wallace Smythe-Brown and boy, doesn't his ego just love it. Jumped-up prick. Not that he's like that for long after Brenda wrong-foots him by going on the offensive.

"You've been avoiding me!" she says, her lie so blatant that it leaves him stuttering for an appropriate response. "If you're not interested, say so."

"I hardly think that's fair, my dear," says Wallace, a hard edge to his voice.

Shit, better not push him too hard, thinks Brenda. Don't want him getting aggressive before I've slipped him those horse tranqs.

"I want us to have some alone time."

This statement has Wallace's eyebrows whipping up his forehead with enough speed to give him a fringe trim. He's blustering for a suitable reply when he turns away from her. At first, she thinks she's blown it, but it's Cecil and Stef who've captured his attention; Wallace's bulk initially blocking them from view.

"Say, old chap. Don't suppose I could use the playpen tonight?" says Cecil, bouncing on his toes as if to make more of himself.

"Of course, although you'll need to be gone by midnight. I might have need of it myself before I head off to the country for a spot of hunting," booms Wallace, with a lot of haw-hawing before delving into a pocket inside his jacket and retrieving a big old-fashioned iron key with a tatty bit of red ribbon attached to the cloverleaf end. He ceremoniously hands it to Cecil, before moving in to speak again. "Usual fee, my good man."

"Absolutely!" says Cecil, even more excited now.

Jeez, what the hell's the usual fee if he's getting this pumped about it? Watching, or being watched? It's not cash, if the gleam in Cecil's eyes or the speed with which he's drags Stef from the ballroom, are any indication.

Wallace swings back to face Brenda as though this interruption never took place. "So, you want some alone time, do you? I have the perfect idea."

Without waiting to be asked, he takes hold of her hand and, dragging her along after him, heads in the direction taken by Cecil and Stef. Honest to god, it feels as though her hand is stuffed in a pile of warm sausages and it's all she can do not to yank it free and wipe it on her dress. Swallowing her revulsion, she does neither.

Let the games commence.

They're bowling through the foyer and out the front doors of the hotel. Just as well she hadn't bothered with a coat because Wallace isn't going to waste time allowing her to collect one. After a lot of bellowing and general arm waving, his chauffeur-driven Rolls glides to a gentle stop at the bottom of the wide marble steps that front the hotel, where the porter opens the door for them. Brenda is bundled inside with that mountain of evening suit following.

He barks directions through a gap in the glass panel that separates them from the driver, slams it shut and crowds Brenda into one corner of the seat before the car is even moving. Damn, she hadn't thought he'd move this fast. Guess he's chucking etiquette out of the window after all those weeks of her egging him on. Or maybe he's a creep like Eadie says. Either way, she needs to put a stop to this or things will get out of control.

She goes for his genitals and squeezes hard. Nothing. Squeezing harder still, she finally gets him to pull those lumps of uncooked chicken he calls lips away from the make-up removal they're currently working on.

"Patience, my darling," she says to him, although the word 'darling' sticks to her tongue. Hoping to achieve just the right amount of indignation and contempt, she says, "Never in a car!"

"Quite right, too," he says, and Brenda can't believe her luck when he untangles himself from her and moves to the other side of the vehicle, putting a goodly amount of space between them.

Her relief is replaced by dread when she sees the cold calculation in his gaze as he looks at her. Lord knows what the bastard is planning and only fingering the yellow pills in the small pocket in her dress makes her feel as though she's still in control of things. Perhaps she should give him those now, because with the amount of fat he's carrying, who knows how long it'll be before they take him down.

"Is there anything to drink in this moving sitting room?"

"Indeed." Scooting forward on his seat, Wallace slides open a door in a walnut panel built into the back of the driver's seat and folds down a little table. Crystal glasses follow next, which he puts into the cut-outs that hold them in place while pouring enough whiskey into each of them to prepare someone for an appendix op.

"Thank you," says Brenda, taking the glass, but before he can make a lame toast, she pulls the smallest of the three yellow pills out of her pocket. "Think I need something to add an edge to the evening" and with him watching, she makes a production of swallowing it, downing her whole glass of spirits with a flourish.

"What was that?" Wallace appears both alarmed and intrigued, exactly as she's planned.

"Something a friend picked up in the States. They make everything so much more ..." She deliberately trails off and again using all her acting skills, shivers in delight.

"Got any more?"

"I do, but," Brenda pauses and looks pointedly at his crotch so he's in no doubt, "a big boy like you might need more than one."

Nothing like flattery of the genital variety to have a guy eating out of your hand, even when horse tranquilizers are on the menu. Watching Wallace gulp down the pills and finish his scotch, Brenda lets out a breath she hadn't been conscious of holding onto. Of concern is that he refills his glass to the brim with scotch and polishes that off, too. Who knows what that combination will do.

They arrive at his place not long after and Brenda is surprised to see it's where she'd collected Rupert Smythe-Brown from all those months ago, when she'd been instrumental in gluing him to an art gallery window. Here's hoping the little turd doesn't turn up anytime soon. It's been hard enough avoiding him at the various social gatherings. Although she'd been wearing a mask and affecting a fake accent that infamous night, her hair and body are both distinctive even to a product of generations of captive breeding like him.

Rather than stopping on the road outside, the chauffeur

drives the car ever so slowly through a covered portico to the right of the mansion.

Brenda waits impatiently while the driver pulls on the handbrake, gets out, walks around the car and opens Wallace's door, allowing the blubbery mountain of a man to exit the car. She's expecting him to turn and help her out, but no, he's off up the stairs leading into the side of the house, expecting her to follow.

Well, screw him. She waits where she is until he lumbers back down with obvious ill grace and shoves his hand inside the car, presumably for her to take it. Only when he stops flapping his fingers in a 'get a move on' gesture does she deign to put her hand in his; anything to give the drugs a chance to kick in.

No sooner have his sausage fingers closed around her hand, than she's as good as yanked out of the car. She falls on her knees on the first step in exactly the sort of position Wallace no doubt has in mind. Thankfully, the lush carpet that runs up the middle saves her from serious injury, not that she doesn't milk it for all it's worth.

So worthy of an Oscar is the show she puts on, that even the chauffeur rushes to help her but the look he receives from Wallace has him stepping back, quick smart. Without any obvious instructions, he closes the passenger door, narrowly missing Brenda and wastes no time, getting back into the car and leaving fast enough that the wheels give a small squeal of protest.

Now on their own, Wallace drops any semblance of civility and pulls Brenda roughly to her feet before hauling her up the stairs. That he's as strong as ever worries her. Surely two of those horse tranquilisers should be enough to take out a lard arse like this guy? They're near the top before she notices any difference. For one thing, she needs to help him open the door because his hand-to-eye co-ordination is sufficiently on the fritz that he can't get the key into the lock.

About sodding time.

Once inside, he's off again, taking her along for the ride. He makes short work of the enormous foyer, making for a wall like a missile.

"Wallace! Wall!"

But despite her screaming this at him, he doesn't take a blind bit of notice and if anything speeds up. Shit, this is going to hurt. Letting go of her with one of his hands, he holds it out in front of him and when he hits the wall, the resultant boom fills and echoes around the foyer. Rather than put his fist through the wall as she's expected, the whole panel swings inwards to reveal an exceedingly tatty hallway that must surely be the domain of the hired help or those with devious plans on their minds.

"Wallace, darling, where are you taking me?" says Brenda, so she can gauge how well the drugs are working.

He stops, swaying slightly as he does so, before turning to peer at her closely. "I'm going to show you the Playpen, my sweet."

The only positive from this response is that his words are slurred and he's having trouble focusing. "Then lead on," says Brenda, not wanting to muck about any longer. If the bastard passes out in the hallway, there's no way in hell she'll be able to move him on her own. Nope, for the plan to work, he mustn't keel over until they're safely in the viewing room.

She hadn't given any thought to where people would look from, but Eadie knew all about it and it's this new location that makes Brenda's nervous, even if the plan is stronger for it.

He starts forward again, using both her and the wall to keep going straight. Their route is convoluted, ridiculously so. Eadie's right, there are probably rabbit warrens with better town planning. After half a dozen rights and a couple of lefts, Benda doesn't have a sodding clue where she is and knows she couldn't find her way out with a map.

Eventually, they stumble into a room that isn't so much dark as completely lacking in light, especially so after Wallace slams the door shut after them. That he doesn't move gives Brenda hope. Only when her eyes are open wide and she's sure her pupils have sent her irises packing, does she see thin flashes of light on the wall opposite the door. Sliding her feet along the carpet, with her hands held out in front of her, she inches her way over to these, taking her time rather than smash herself into a random piece of furniture. After an age, her hands connect with what feels like a velvet-covered wall. Kinky or what?

Heaving a deep breath, Wallace stumbles his way across the room, with his lack of care letting Brenda know the room must be free of furniture for him to risk moving so freely. That is until she cracks her knee against something. "Bloody hell!"

"Ssshhh," slurs Wallace with theatrical quiet as he slides into place next to her.

He throws a meaty arm around her shoulders, nearly taking off one of her ears in the process. She stumbles and it's only by putting her hands on the piece of furniture she's crunched her knee into, that she manages to stay upright. This also identifies the offending item as a bar stool. And a bloody tall one at that.

"Sidown," whispers Wallace, his words running together in a most pleasing manner.

Shrugging the mountain of meat off her shoulder, Brenda does as he suggests and finds that when seated, she's at the perfect height to look through one of the slits. What had looked like lights, have revealed themselves to be small peep-holes allowing them to look into the room beyond.

Knowing who's in the other room, she resists looking through the gap. There are things that once seen, can't be unseen and she'd prefer her sex life wasn't screwed up by looking at what is most likely happening in the Playpen. She's still mulling this over when Wallace slams a glass into the side of her head, missing her hand by miles.

She's unable to stop a string of obscenities and is again censured by Wallace to keep it down. That he does so at twice the volume she used is further indication of how well the drugs are working. He opens a bottle of champagne without deadening the loud pop, reinforcing the impression.

Despite holding his hand and her glass, Brenda still gets a good slosh of bubbles poured into her lap, but rather than swear, she simply resigns herself to her fate before grabbing the bottle in hopes of drinking more than she wears. Her glass filled, she whispers to him "Let me fill yours, too."

She swings her seat so she's facing him, at least she thinks she is, and in doing so, smashes her knee into what she suspects is a ledge. The crack she'd received was too solid for it to simply be a fancy wall trim. Holding in her hiss of pain is difficult but she does so to avoid Wallace berating her again. Not that she cares as such but she may as well keep as quiet as possible, at least for appearance's sake.

Moving her hand with the glass of champagne in it, towards the ledge, she's rewarded by the sounds of glass scuffing on woodwork and sliding it back; she leaves it safely against the wall, before concentrating on filling Wallace's glass, shoving her thumb inside the glass to make up for the lack of visual clues.

Wallace proposes a toast to 'fun times' in a hoarse whisper and tries to clink his glass against hers. Instead, he shoves it into her shoulder blade, sloshing half of it down her cleavage.

She is so getting even with this arsehole once he passes out. If he ever does.

"Look," says Wallace, his mouth close enough to her ear for her to shudder.

Now that they've been in the dark for as long as they have, Brenda's able to make out his pudgy finger pointing towards the slit that's right in front of her. Damn.

Brenda duly puts her forehead against the plush wall, her eyes level with the peephole, but rather than look, she shuts her eyes. Now that she's this close to the slit, the sound effects are more than enough to paint a picture of what's happening the other side of the gap.

"Come, ma dear. I wouldn't have thought you a prude," slurs Wallace, again ickily close to her ear. "Open your eyes to a world of pleasure."

Why can't the bastard pass out? Until he does, she has to play along and so with reluctance, she opens her eyes. Damn it all to hell and back. The sight of Cecil Percy-Ryder strapped to a rack would be bad enough without the old codger being buck naked. Bleeding hell, the rumours are true; he's hung all right. Or maybe his length is as a result of all those weights?

Even more of a revelation is Stef's get-up. The girl has embraced the role of dominatrix with zeal, that's for damned sure and those whip lessons have sure paid off. Hopefully, the first-aid lessons won't be needed.

Brenda's so transfixed by the scene playing out in front of her that it's a moment before she twigs there are sausages crawling up her thigh, heading for her crotch. Sleaze-ball. With a deft twist of her hips, Brenda swings her chair away from Wallace to disengage him, not that he misses the opportunity to pinch her bum hard enough that she'll sport a bruise in the morning. Mind you, after she's finished with him, she won't be the only one who's black and blue.

There's the crack of a whip followed by a scream of pleasure from the Playpen and this, thankfully, takes Wallace's attention away from her. Unable to resist looking herself,

Brenda stares hard at the scene beyond. It's only when her chair shakes that her attention is brought back to where she's sitting. Ungluing her eyes from the red-lit gap to hell, Brenda looks to see what Wallace is up to, but he's no longer beside her looking through the other gap.

Actually, she can't see him at all.

Maybe that bang was the door shutting? She listens carefully for the sound of breathing but with all the B-Grade admonishments followed by 'yes, mistress' and moans of pleasure and whip-cracking coming from the other room, it's impossible to hear. Or even think.

Of course, when Wallace starts snoring loudly enough to rattle the champagne flutes, Brenda gives up on any effort to be quiet, or even to stay looking at Cecil Percy-Ryder's screwed-up idea of a sex life. Sliding down off the bar stool, she inches her way in what she hopes is the direction of the door. She arrives safely at the other side of the room and by running her hands along the wall, finds the way out. Opening the door, she's blinded by the light coming in from the hallway but can see enough to clock that there's someone standing there. Not knowing who the hell it is, she closes it again, but not so fast that she doesn't hear a hissed, "Brenda, it's us," that stops her locking it.

She opens it again and, after her eyeballs stop imploding, sees that it's Eadie and Julian. Julian is standing next to a sack barrow the likes of which are more commonly seen at the markets for lugging produce. That Eadie's next to him in the wheelchair is even more amazing. For one thing, how the hell did she even get down to this floor?

"Dumbwaiter! Used to sneak in that way all the time," says Eadie, before instructing Julian to push her into the viewing room.

Entering, Eadie gets Julian to pause just long enough for her to use her cane to turn on a light that Brenda hadn't known was there. Trust the Eton Mess lying on the floor to deliberately leave them in the dark. Not that the light is any great shakes. The feeble beams emanating from it struggle to be in the same league as the bulb in the supply cupboard at the hotel. Cheap bastards, the lot of them.

Eadie's laughter at seeing Wallace lying in a heap is full on and it's something that alarms Brenda. "Keep it down. You want to put Cecil off his punishment?"

"Hah, fat chance. The bigger the audience, the more he loves it."

Brenda wonders at whose eyes are glued to slits in other rooms. "Just how many are in tonight?"

"None thankfully, given the short notice of tonight's session, but we locked the outside door to keep it that way," says Eadie, jabbing Wallace in the forehead with her cane and leaving a black mark courtesy of the stopper on the end.

"Stop that!" says Brenda, fighting her laughter.

She has a lengthy discussion with Julian on how they'll get the besuited lump of lard onto the sack barrow but they're interrupted before a viable solution is settled on.

"Their session's over," says Eadie, causing them to turn in her direction.

"How—" says Brenda, but then comprehends that all is quiet in the other room.

A quick peek through the nearest slit confirms the room is empty.

"Go grab Stef," she says to Julian. "The three of us together might be able to manage it."

Julian leans the sack barrow carefully against the wall and stands in the hallway undecided which way to go, when Eadie instructs him to head to the right and not muck about.

He must have followed her orders because he's back with Stef, who, while she's more than likely strong enough to help, isn't dressed for it.

She's all for going and retrieving her bag from the Playpen and getting changed, but an interruption to Wallace's snoring pattern suggests they need to move fast if they want him trussed up like a Christmas ham before he's conscious again.

———

Bloody hell," I've pulled something, says Stef, "and not in a good way."

"Charge him extra for that," says Brenda, her laughter stopping her from putting in as much effort as is required.

"Will you two stop faffing about and put some welly into it?" says Julian, his shoulder hard against Wallace's back as he tries to roll enough of him onto the sack barrow that they have some hope of dragging his sorry butt into the Playpen next door.

It's like watching the sandal-wearing crowd trying to save a beached whale and it's only after Brenda gets her sniggers under control that she looks around and notices Eadie is no longer with them. "Where the hell has she gone?" she says, to herself.

"You can look for her after. Let's sort this tosser out first." After this, Julian gives a huge heave and Wallace rolls slowly over in an ungainly heap and thankfully comes to rest mostly on the sack barrow.

Only when their captive is lashed in place like a side of beef do they attempt to get the barrow upright. It doesn't take long to comprehend this is a complete impossibility, with the three of them simply incapable of lifting that much dead weight. Fortunately, the sack barrow is of the older design and has a couple of curved metal legs at the handle end that allows them to push and shove the whole thing as it is. That it's truly screwing up the carpet in the process is something they can live with.

It's no small task to get him along the hallway and into the Playpen, and it's there they find Eadie.

She's no longer in the wheelchair and is now dressed like a dominatrix, which is the least of their worries when she barks, "Strip him!"

26

Brenda thought seeing Percy-Ryder being given a good seeing to was reason to Ajax her eyeballs, but it pales compared with what she's looking at now. She knew Eadie had a shady past, but seeing it in front of you in glorious black and red leather, is another thing altogether. The corset is as stiff and cracked with age as Eadie and while it might once have been a snug fit, Brenda suspects the old girl could swivel around inside it now and you'd never know.

"Eadie, what the hell are you doing?"

"Something I've wanted to do for a long time." She says this while teasing the whip out and around various items in the room. Brenda finds this more than a little distracting.

"What about your arthritis?"

"All sorted."

"What?" says Brenda, her brow wrinkled for a moment. "How many did you take?"

"Four!" says Eadie, triumphantly.

"Four!" says everyone else in the room. Except for Wallace – he's still out cold after taking only two of those anti-inflammatory horse pills.

"Pffft, you get used to them. Now stop mucking about and strip him."

Doing as she's instructed is a lot easier said than done. If they'd thought it was difficult hefting the beached whale in front of them through from the other room, removing said whale's evening suit is a hell of a lot harder. Brenda would pay to see the crowd from Whale Watch taking care of this. By rolling him backwards and forwards they manage to remove the jacket. Next comes the shirt. The trousers require a lot of yanking and bouncing to get them free of his chubby cheeks that are as good as glued to the floor so loath are they to part company with it.

It's only after they've got rid of his grots and singlet that they get the biggest shock of all.

"He's wearing a corset," says Brenda, in disbelief.

"He's tiny," says Stef, also in disbelief, tending towards disgust.

"Stand back, ladies," says Julian, pulling a knife from his coat pocket. "This could get ugly."

Brenda doubts he's about to go all pig-sticker on them, but stands back as he's suggested. He applies only the slightest pressure to the corset laces, but it's all that's required. Physics takes care of everything else.

"Owww," says Brenda, putting her hand to her face. "I got pinged by an eyelet!" Only when she's finished rubbing the sting out of her forehead, does she look down at Wallace in all his glory. On the plus side, the belly flap has hidden his tiny todger from view. If you could call that a plus?

"How the 'ell are we supposed to get 'im on that?" says Stef, looking between Wallace and the rack so recently vacated by Percy-Ryder.

Brenda can see Eadie is itching to pull the girl up on her dropped aitches, but to forestall the elocution lesson, says "Eadie, you know this room. Any ideas?"

"Let me think? It's been a while." She stands there staring into space and replaying scenes in her head if the unconscious flicking of the whip is any indicator. "Yes! Julian if you check in that far corner, you'll find a pulley and harness."

"Bloody hell," spits out Brenda, when sounds of rusty metal screaming against rusty metal cleave the quiet of the room like an axe. Last time she'd seen something like this had been on a school trip to an abattoir. Who knows what the teacher had been thinking but it had put paid to luncheon meat sandwiches for some of the more squeamish in her class.

If the three of them had thought it was difficult getting Wallace out of his suit, getting him into the harness is like putting suspenders on a jellyfish, a sodding big one.

"This is truly disgusting," says Stef, adding, "Just as well I bought my camera," as she nips over to retrieve it from her oversized bag. Lord only knows what else she's got in there.

Photos dutifully taken, in which they stay safely out of shot even if it's tempting as hell to do bunny ears, and they're back to getting him safely onto the rack.

Thanks to a lot of ropes and pulleys, they slowly haul him into place and if Brenda thought he looked revolting while lying on the ground, now that gravity has taken hold, he's even more of a sight to behold. It's a travesty of droopy pink bits and lashings of leather cutting into any nook and cranny on offer.

"This deserves another photo," says Stef, following through.

"Right, he's all mine now," says Eadie, expertly cracking the whip and coming close to relieving Wallace of his foreskin.

"You sure?" says Brenda, still worried that Eadie might finally succumb to the anti-inflammatories and pass out.

"Yes! Go! Find my paintings. I'll meet you in the van."

Only by following the salt and vinegar crisps dropped by Julian earlier, are they able to find their way up to the main foyer. They enter stealthily, unsure who's still up and about, but the place is as quiet as the lounge in a gentleman's club. It's lit by one small lamp that casts an eerie glow about the place as though no one should be here, especially them.

Following a whispered confab, they decide to split up because they'll need to check every square inch of the place given they have no idea if the paintings are up on walls in plain sight or stuck in an attic room, facing a wall. Brenda's sure it will be the latter because Wallace hadn't taken the paintings because he's an art lover; he'd taken them purely for spite.

"I'll take this floor," says Julian. "You and Stef head upstairs and I'll join you when I'm done down here."

His tone is authoritative enough that Brenda doesn't think to question it. He's about to go through a door when Stef's "*Pssst*" stops him. Without a word, she hands him a heavy-duty metal torch that could easily take someone out. The red plastic piece of shit she hands Brenda is at the other end of the spectrum entirely, but it's bright enough.

No sooner has Julian disappeared than Brenda and Stef leg it to the upper floors. Walking up to the middle of the first flight, Brenda stops and scans the walls on each side, looking for Eadie's work, but all the paintings here are dour and dark and the work of people long since dead, of people even deader. She leaves Stef to check out the floor and keeps on climbing up to the next level but doesn't see anything that looks vaguely like Eadie's work. Even the third flight doesn't reveal anything.

"Sod it." Brenda's no chicken, but thoughts of rooting around in the attic, with only a cheap-arse torch to light her way, gives her the creeps. Never mind 'there be dragons' – 'there be dead relatives'. Problem is where the hell is the staircase for her to get up there? Nowhere bloody obvious, that's for damned sure.

If it's like the stairs at Eadie's place, the higher they go, the narrower they get. Brenda starts opening doors quietly and quickly, starting at her end of the hall and working her way down the left-hand side first. She hits pay dirt at the other end when she opens a door and is faced by a narrow, unadorned wooden staircase. There's a rope handle running up one side, strung between iron rings that would be of sod-all use if you took a tumble.

She closes the door quietly behind her and is at once assaulted by the staleness of the air. This place hasn't been visited in a long time. Cue dead rellies.

Shaking the tension out of her body, she forces herself to take the first step. The creak that emanates from this long-ignored tread is deafening in the silence and immediately she lifts her foot. For god's sake, it was loud enough to have roused Wallace in the blasted cellar. Hoping to reduce the racket, Brenda hitches the front of her dress up, tucks it into her undies and then places her foot two steps up and to the side and slowly puts her weight down.

There's creaking but it's low enough in volume that the dead up here can keep on snoozing. Stuffing the torch down her cleavage, she uses the rope bannister as a mountain climber would and slowly hauls herself to the top of the thankfully short flight of stairs, where there's another door.

It's locked.

This is at once both good and bad news. There's only one reason for the door to be locked: because there's something valuable behind it. The problem is, she hasn't got anything with her that she can use to pick the lock.

"Sod it," she hisses at the door, before turning and just as slowly retracing her steps. The chances of finding something she can use up here are zip, meaning she'll have to retrace her steps right back down to the bottom floor. If she can find a kitchen, there might be something in there she can use to jimmy the lock, or even attack the hinges with.

She's on the second floor when she sees a beam of light moving around in one of the side rooms. Doubting it's anyone who's meant to be there, she puts her head inside the door and gives a quiet, "*Pssst.*" It's enough for the torch to swing in her direction, blinding her. Instinctively, she puts her hand over her eyes.

"Sorry," whispers Julian, at the same time as pointing his torch at the ground.

"I've found something," she says, still dealing with the spots of light that are all she can see. Hell, that torch is bright. "But I need help. Door's locked."

"I'll finish this room, just in case," says Julian, before swinging a beam of light over every wall in the place as well as checking the wardrobe that stands sentinel against one wall.

Brenda thinks it might be overkill when he gets down on his hands and knees to check under the bed, but, hey, rich people are weird, so maybe he's got a point.

Conversation is sparse on the return trip to the top of the house although Julian lets her know he hasn't been able to search the whole ground floor because he could hear someone moving about towards the back of the house.

Once on the top floor, Julian makes short work of the length of the hall, his long strides forcing Brenda to hustle it. "I hope they are up here, because we're fast running out of time," he says, standing to the side so she can precede him and open the right door.

"I've got a good feeling about this," she says, inching open the door to the final set of stairs.

"Don't," she hisses out, just as Julian is about to put his foot down on a wooden tread, leaving him standing with one foot in mid-air.

"Creaky as all get out. Take them two at a time and if you walk on the edges of the treads, it's not too bad." With him on his way, she hikes her dress back up in front

Progress to the top is slow, although maybe not as slow as Brenda's first trip and she's not sure if it's her imagination or not, but the stairs aren't as squeaky and creaky as they were earlier. Maybe she's getting used to the racket? Hauling herself up onto the top landing, she cannons into the back of Julian, who isn't as far forward as she'd thought. He spins and catches her around the waist, easily stopping her from falling backwards.

"Careful," he whispers, close enough that she can feel his breath on her face.

Once sure she's stable, he turns back towards the door and although she can't see anything, the unmistakable sounds of a lock being picked come back to her. In an inconceivably short space of time, the door swings open on hinges that sound like they're being murdered.

"Screw it," says Brenda, her voice louder than it should be, although whispering seems superfluous after the din the door has just made.

Even so, they both freeze, waiting for the sounds of running feet, but after long enough that someone could have come up from several floors down, their breathing returns to normal.

Brenda doesn't know why, but she'd thought it would be split up into a multitude of small rooms. It's cavernous, with the sheer amount of stuff they need to look through, over-whelming. There are lightbulbs dotted around at regular inter-vals, but because of the small windows that pepper the roof line, there's no way they can risk turning them on and perhaps being seen from outside, especially as it's well after midnight.

Once again, they decide to divide and conquer with Julian heading towards one end of the house and herself towards the other, scanning everything on their way.

Progress around the attic is slow because, while there might not be any actual long lost kin up there, they sure as hell left all their crap behind. It's an obstacle course of high-end antiques and complete tat.

They're about half an hour in when Brenda hears a *pssst* from the other end of the space and she wastes no time in threading her way back over to Julian's side.

"Whatcha got?"

"These look familiar?"

"Bleedin' oath!" Brenda's voice echoes loudly around the space, but it's not so loud that they don't hear someone creaking their way up the stairs. The speed at which they're climbing indicates they're allowed to be up here.

Without a word, Julian and Brenda, click off their torches and drop to their knees where they're enveloped in a cloud of well-heeled dust.

After a lot of creaking, the unoiled door is thrown wide, crashing into the wall and making even more of an unholy din than it had earlier. Whoever it is, is allowed to be up here. They know it can't be Wallace, as there isn't a snowball's he could have freed himself from the set up where they'd left him hanging.

Waiting on the newcomer to move, Brenda is automatically shallow breathing, but the need to cough is overwhelming. She clears her throat as quietly as she can, fighting the spasms that want to explode and give away their hiding spot.

Julian appears to have his own battle going on. Given how croaky he'd been that morning, his battle is no doubt more full on than hers.

Eventually, she gets a good quantity of spittle collected in her mouth and swallows it. Sure it's gross, but it does the job.

With an absence of footsteps, she risks popping her head up above the trunk they're huddled behind and is shocked to see Rupert Smythe-Brown, clearly visible in the moonlight from the attic windows, and already halfway to their position.

He's creeping along in the gloom like something out of the Pink Panther movie credits.

Dropping back down, she turns to update Julian, but he's no longer behind her. Where the hell has he gone? Brenda risks another peek to see if she can spot him and is in time to see him sneak up behind Rupert and put his hand on his shoulder.

She's wondering what the hell he's up to, when Rupert crumples to the floor without a sound, other than that of well-fed pudge hitting uncarpeted floorboards.

She wastes no time in getting over there.

"What the hell did you do to him? It was like something out of Star Trek."

"A trick my father taught me," says Julian, not leaving her any clearer on the manoeuvre itself. "But he won't be out for long, so we need to get cracking."

Using old ties and belts they'd spotted earlier, Rupert is hog-tied, gagged and blindfolded rodeo style and then dragged to the far corner of the space, well out the way of them and their ferrying of the paintings down onto the next floor. They're about halfway through when Stef makes an appearance and things speed up with the extra pair of hands. They're still not finished when Rupert gains consciousness and so they make sure they don't say a word. For all Rupert knows, he's stumbled upon the world's largest rats, which is not that far from the truth.

It's over an hour before all the paintings are safely stowed in the van. Brenda's dress is ruined through a mix of champagne, buckets of sweat and seams giving way under the pressure exerted on them from the strain of carrying large paintings down three flights of stairs. Just as well it was reasonably cheap.

"Where is she?" says Julian, placing the last and largest painting carefully in the back of the van.

Stef and Brenda both shrug.

"Dammit, she should have been here by now," says Brenda. "What the hell's she doing to him that's taking this long?"

Stef starts to explain options but is silenced when Brenda holds her hand over the girl's mouth. "More than we need to know, thanks."

"Why don't you go and find her and I'll nip back up and untie Rupert's feet so he can get himself downstairs," says Julian.

"Too late," says Brenda, nodding towards the shuffling figure of Eadie, who's leaning on the back of the wheelchair and using it as a walking frame of sorts. Of immense relief is that she's once again dressed like a little old lady.

They rush to her aid and safely ensconce her in the front seat. The amount of creaking whenever she moves divulges that the corset is still in place under the mauve silk dress. Stef and Brenda climb in the back to join the paintings and the wheelchair and while Julian doesn't exactly lay rubber when they leave, he doesn't muck about either, getting them as far away from the Smythe-Brown residence as rapidly as he can.

"Did you get them," says Eadie, her voice edged with pain.

"The lot," crows Brenda from in the back.

"Good, we can store them in the cellar until I work out what to do," says Eadie, and Brenda understands dealing with them tonight is physically beyond the old lady.

"I wouldn't have them in the house, personally," says Julian.

"Why ever not?" says Eadie, her tone indignant.

"Because although he was out cold the whole time, you still have to be the prime suspect," says Julian. "Even if he can't legally pin it on you, chaps like him have friends who can make things happen."

27

From her spot in the back of the van, Brenda looks at Eadie in silhouette, watching the old lady's features every time they're highlighted by a streetlight. It isn't difficult to see the internal battle that's raging; her expressions as clear in their meaning as if they'd been spoken words.

At last, Eadie's shoulders droop in resignation. "Where do you suggest?"

"My family have a small weekend place in the country. I can take them out there after I've dropped you ladies home."

"May I keep one?" says Eadie, her voice trembling, although whether this is from emotion or fatigue isn't obvious.

"No, you can't," says Brenda, knowing her reply will cause more distress. "If we're going to get away with this, we need to let things cool down before hanging them at home."

"I've got an idea," says Stef, continuing only once she knows she's got everyone's attention. "Why don' I take photos of 'em? That way you can look at 'em whenever you want. Just 'til things cool down."

Eadie mulls this over for a couple of sets of lights before consenting and with the plan given the green light, Julian pulls into the next empty alleyway and they photograph everything in double-quick time, with Brenda incredibly grateful Stef has enough flash bulbs in her portmanteau of a handbag.

"I'll get the film developed termorra," says Stef, already in the process of rolling the film back so she can remove it. "Mate a mine has a darkroom so we don't need t'bother none with this 'ere lot garn to Boots."

It's only when Eadie doesn't reprimand Stef on this bastardisation of the English language, that Brenda sees how tired her elderly friend is. This becomes even more apparent when they get to the house and Eadie chooses to use the wheelchair again.

It makes it a hell of a lot easier to get her into the house and through to her bedroom, where Brenda is surprised to find Flo asleep on the bed. That Eadie isn't put out signifies this must have been pre-arranged by the two women.

Leaving Eadie to Flo's no-nonsense ministrations, she slowly makes her way up to her own bedroom. The old lady isn't the only one who's knackered after tonight's entertainment. Brenda hasn't involved herself in that much hard work in a long time, if ever. There are people for work like that and she sure as shit isn't one of them. After a quick trip to the bathroom, with no time wasted on teeth brushing, Brenda steps out of her once-beautiful dress. No need to undo the zip, it's screwed, pretty much like the rest of it. She doubts there's a dressmaker in London who can resurrect it after what she's put it through and so it's with reluctance that she rolls it up into a ball and stuffs it into the plastic bucket that she uses as a rubbish bin. It only just fits.

She crawls into bed exactly as she is and, despite a less-than-gentle pummelling from Charlie, is out cold in seconds.

28

It doesn't take much movement on her part the next morning to find herself living in a world of pain. My god, she's got muscles she didn't know about, well, none that has ever hurt this much.

"Ow, ow, ow. Left a bit," Brenda instructs Charlie, who's cat-massaging her back with a fervour usually only seen in Russian Olympic gymnastics coaches, although they might be more effective and have better-trimmed nails. Not that the snarky feline is out to ease Brenda's muscle tension. He needs someone to top up his bowl.

"Okay, okay. I'm getting up." She rolls to the side to dislodge him before throwing the blankets back so she can stagger to her feet. "Bloody hell!" If she'd thought her muscles were giving her grief in bed, now she's upright they've redoubled their efforts, making her feel like she's been a few rounds with Muhammad Ali.

After pulling on her daggiest tracksuit bottoms and sweat-shirt, she limps out on the landing in readiness to tackle the stairs that are all that's between her and what she hopes is a fry-up, if the smell of bacon wafting up from the kitchen is any indicator.

Wow, Julian must sure as hell be more bulletproof than she is with his bedroom door wide open, a sure sign he's already up and about. Not such a stereotypical queen, after all.

The stairs she tackles one at a time, with knees locked to stop them giving out on her. She continues this gait on the ground floor, inching her way along the hall, one painful step at a time. Charlie's already there; sick of her slow progress, he's scooted ahead, nearly tripping her up in the process. Brenda's grateful to the little bugger though when he pushes the door open. Not that he holds it open for her and when it swings back and collects her, it's all she can do to stay upright.

Brenda lowers herself slowly into her chair at the table, watched by Julian, who's already well on his way to finishing a 'full English'. "Oh god, I hurt. So bloody much."

"Do what I did," says Julian, sounding ever so slightly stoned.

Brenda takes her head out of her hands and looks at him, noticing for the first time that his pupils are unusually huge. "You didn't?"

"Trust me, after unloading that lot last night, I needed all the help I could get."

"Where the bloody hell did you take them?"

"Somewhere safer than downstairs." On seeing Brenda is getting ready to grill him, he presses on. "They're safe, that's all you need to know. Better that way."

Brenda thinks on this. Before last night, she wouldn't have trusted him but now he's up to his armpits in getting the paintings back, she's hoping he's on their side.

"How come you're not out cold?"

"Only took half of one."

Brenda doesn't pause, swallowing the other half of the tablet Flo offers her, along with a large glass of water. Bert slaps down a plate piled with bacon and eggs soon after, further helping her cope with the pain.

"How's Eadie?" says Brenda, to Flo, who's setting up a breakfast tray.

"None too good, but a couple of days in bed and a rub with my special liniment and she'll be tickety-boo in no time." Backing out of the kitchen with the tray held out in front of her, she adds, "She'll need company, though."

"I can spend time with her," says Stef, who's waiting in the hall for Flo to exit.

"I'll finish this lot and pop in and see her," says Brenda.

By late that afternoon, Eadie isn't the only one who's suffering from cabin fever. Brenda, who's spent the day watching the old lady sleep on and off, is fit to scream with boredom and the need to move, while the fug of wintergreen that hangs like a noxious cloud over the bed is hurting her throat. She's contemplating doing a runner, or more likely a hobble, when Eadie opens her eyes again.

"How are you feeling?" says Brenda, when the eyes regarding her gain lucidity.

"Much better! But what about you?"

"Just twinges," says Brenda, deliberately playing down how much she still hurts even after a couple of half anti-inflamma- tory tablets. The last thing she wants is Flo slapping that lethal brew all over her body. She'd be lucky to get laid in less than three months.

"You should take yourself off to the Turkish baths in Notting Hill tomorrow. They'll sort you out."

Stef, who's lying on the bed next to Eadie, adds her support to this suggestion. "That's a brilliant idea, my arse muscles are poked."

Brenda files the idea but doesn't ask any more about it, because to be honest the thought of being starkers in a room full of women, leaves her cold, even if steam is involved.

"So did Wallace rouse at all when you untied him?" says Brenda, asking the next question that pops into her mind.

"Untied him?" says Eadie, through an evil grin.

"You didn't!"

The horror Stef injects into these two words lets Brenda know the newbie dominatrix is more aware of the consequences of this than she is herself.

"He could lose something if the blood is too constricted. Those harnesses can be as tight as tourniquets," says Stef, proving beyond doubt that she's been paying attention in all those first-aid lessons.

"Shit, I've just realised, we never let Rupert go, either," says Brenda.

Later that afternoon, Brenda stands in the middle of the first-floor landing, slowly fills her lungs and yells, "Rooooooooad tripppppppp!"

It has the desired effect of Julian popping out of his room and Stef flying down the stairs. She's on her own with Rosie presumably around at Brian's place and Paula no doubt working on Parker to buy her some expensive bit of flash.

"Where we off too?" says Stef, her question bubbling with enthusiasm and curiosity.

"Bet I know," says Julian, looking closely at Brenda. "But I'm not sure that's such a good idea."

"We could park around the corner and wear disguises. If we dress as tourists, we can hide behind a big old map."

She knows this solution is a good one when Julian smiles

despite himself and Stef squeals, "I've got wigs!" before flying back up the stairs, to collect them.

"We look ridiculous," says Julian, tugging on the shaggy brown wig that covers his new military style haircut.

"No, we don't," says the newest redhead in the house, and dominatrix-about-town, Stef.

"I don't know, I like myself as a blonde," says Brenda, unable to stop looking at herself in the mirror. "It's not like the prick's gonna see us up close."

"I can use the zoom on the camera if we want to take a closer look at anything," says Julian, hefting the monster SLR that's slung around his neck on a sturdy leather strap.

His is the most impressive of the cameras each of them has. This coupled with shorts, socks and sandals and lots of maps has them firmly labelled as the type of American tourists who wouldn't be popular even 'back home', and not worth a second glance, unless you've got a thing for people who like to dress hideously.

On the plus side, traipsing into Eadie's room and showing her their disguises gets them a broad smile in return. Promising to get photos of anything happening, they leave the old lady humming contentedly to herself.

It's Sunday afternoon and the trip into Knightsbridge is fast and they have lots of parking spaces to choose from but Julian opts for a loading zone. This worries Brenda at first, but when he slaps signs on the side that make out the van belongs to a plumber, she can see the logic, proving yet again, that he's a handy guy to have around.

They're walking in the direction of the Smythe-Brown mansion when Brenda hears a loud pop from behind her. This is followed by a lot of swearing; none of it with an American accent. Turning, she finds Stef doing her best to pull the remains of what must have been a monster bubble of gum out of her fake red hair.

"Tone it down, honey," says Brenda, her twang vaguely southern. "We need to be believable."

"Kiss mah grits," says Stef, in true Southern style, although her main focus is still on the pink mess she's working on.

Julian doesn't speak, simply exhales a heartfelt sigh and pulls a penknife from inside his jacket. "Hold still," he tells the madly twisting Stef, "you'll only make it worse."

The tone he uses is one that works for small children and pets and Stef is rigid in a second, although that might have more to do with a knife advancing in the direction of her face than the instruction as such. Either way, she's stock-still, allowing Julian to cut the sticky mess free, although there's a lot of red nylon attached to it. Brenda's already noticed a tendency for the stuff to float in the direction of power poles.

Sorted, they continue on their happy-snapping, loud-commenting way, peppering their observations with comments like, "We've got nothing like this back home" and "Shoot, I've seen bigger at the State Fair."

Swinging the final corner on their way to their target, their steps falter, although not for long.

"Two ambulances?" says Stef, walking forward slowly as if on autopilot. "Who's the second one for?"

"What did you do to Rupert?" says Brenda, also inching forward. "I thought that Vulcan shoulder tap thingy only put him out cold."

"I did, it does," says Julian, his concentration more on the view through his monster camera than on what she's saying.

"Sheesh, I can't believe Wallace can't share with Rupert. He's not that fat," says Brenda.

Julian pulls on the lens housing, doubling it in length, and pointing it in the direction of the ambulance and what's being shoehorned into the back. Brenda swings her gaze between the flashing light on top of the meat wagon and Julian, with neither giving much away. Until Julian starts to shake. It takes a moment for Brenda to realise he's laughing, although he's trying his hardest to hold it in; for him to be caught laughing at someone being loaded into the back of an ambo would draw attention.

The ambulance driver shuts the back doors slowly and methodically, walks around to his door and climbs in. Once there, the flashing light on top is turned off and he pulls out onto the street at a rate that could only be called funereal.

"Shit, did she kill him?" says Brenda, equating the lack of urgency with there being no need to hurry.

"What?" says Julian, finally pulling the camera away from his eye and looking down at her.

"No siren means dead in my part of the world."

"Yeah, likewise at my end of town," says Stef, blinking rapidly.

"He was alive all right," says Julian, once again stifling his laughter. "Groin was weighed down by a pile of ice packs, though."

They're quietly discussing what the likelihood is that Eadie castrated Wallace when further movement over the road grabs their attention. Two ambulance people and a couple of cops are struggling with a stretcher at the top of the lavish front steps. Whoever it is hidden by that sheet is one fat bastard, thus ruling out Rupert as the patient. He's pudgy, but not that monstrous.

Observing them lug the oversized patient down the front steps is like watching a car crash, with it only being a matter of time before a spectacular impact ends the scene. It happens soon enough when one of the cops drops his corner of the stretcher. The other cop drops his side straight after. Whether this is to keep the stretcher reasonably level, or he wants to avoid his back being stuffed, who knows. The only thing in the patient's favour is that it's the uphill end that's been slammed down onto the steps with a loud crack; otherwise, he'd have slid off the end of the stretcher and landed in a heap on the ground.

Even with this small mercy, the yelling and threats coming from the patient tell of "heads rolling" and "this'll cost you your job." Whoever he is, he has friends in high places.

Either way, it's funny enough that the three American 'tourists' on the opposite side of the road are crying with laughter, but quietly to avoid unwanted attention.

"Who the hell do you suppose it was?" says Julian, after the patient is finally safe in the ambulance and taken to wherever it is they take fat bastards who aren't feeling too hot.

"Barry'll know," says Stef, confidently.

"Barry who?" says Brenda.

"The ambulance driver," says Stef, derision at Brenda's ignorance colouring her tone.

"Sod off, ya cheeky tart. He's just an ambo to me." She turns to ask Julian if he knew that was the guy's name, but he's MIA. "Where the …?"

"He's over there." Stef points in the direction of the mansion opposite them.

"What the hell?" Brenda watches in dread and fascination as Julian speaks to the elderly gentleman at the top of the stairs, who's been a silent observer to the preceding rescue operation.

They find out when Julian returns to their side. He's speaking loudly, more for the sake of his audience rather than any lack of hearing on their part. "Honey, the nice man says we can look through the place."

"What's ya name," whispers Brenda.

"Bob," returns Julian, as quietly.

"Now, Bob, I hope you didn't annoy that nice man." Brenda's accent is lousy, wavering as it does between Southern and something closer to 'Noo Yoik', but she doubts it's going to make any difference to proceedings. She makes a show of berating 'Bob' as she and Stef follow him across the road and up the stairs of the mansion.

Julian hands the butler a rolled-up wad of notes and as if by magic, the front door is opened for them. Julian keeps up a running commentary about the architecture and waxes lyrical about every painting they pass. Sure enough, the elderly retainer wearies of keeping an eye on them, tells them they can let themselves out and disappears through a small door at the back of the foyer, presumably to help himself to alcohol somewhere in the depths of the building.

Julian waits no longer than the door swinging into stasis, before he's off, opening doors and shoving his head through them with surprising speed. It's only when he's at the end of a hallway leading off the foyer, that Brenda hears a muted, "Eureka". Maybe she'll find out what the hell he's up to because she knows for sure they took all the paintings the night before. Eadie had confirmed this while Stef was taking the photos.

Following in his footsteps, Brenda finds herself in a library; the shelves that line the room are full to overflowing with dusty tomes whose pages haven't seen the light of day since rolling off the presses. And indications are that was a bloody long time ago. Deciding there's nothing to interest her, she slings herself into one of the well-upholstered chairs that dot the room. May as well be comfy while Julian gets on with whatever the hell he's up to. She's right that it's not paintings he's interested in, because he's ignored the ugly specimens dotted in alcoves around the room.

He makes for the large desk that dominates the centre of the room, sitting squat and fat in a pose reminiscent of Wallace himself; Rupert is too much of a lightweight to need a piece of furniture of this calibre. After rummaging in his jacket pocket, Julian takes out what looks like a manicure kit and places it on the top of the desk.

She's about to give him a hurry up when he unzips the

small leather case but, rather than pulling out clippers and a file, he retrieves what looks like a pair of tweezers. He makes short work of opening the second drawer down on the left-hand side, ignoring the others. He's up to his elbow in the drawer before Brenda hears a quiet, "Gotcha".

She's unable to see what it is he's retrieved without getting up and to be honest she's not that interested, although her interest is piqued when he walks over to what looks to be a bog standard panelled wall and slides whatever it is he's retrieved into a gap between two of the panels. After jiggling what must be a key, one of the panels clicks open to reveal a set of shelves.

With all the dexterous work out of the way, Julian pulls on a pair of thin rubber gloves and wastes no time grabbing a handful of manila folders and stacking them on the leather top of the desk. This is followed by another handful, and another, until there must be upwards of twenty or thirty of them sitting there. He flicks through them one-after-the-other with impressive speed.

"Whatcha looking for?" says Stef, wandering over to stand next to him.

"Proof."

This terse reply raises more questions than it answers and Stef looks at Brenda with raised eyebrows. Brenda interprets this as, "What the hell is he up to?" None the wiser than her student, she pulls a face in reply, deciding to let Julian get on with it and grill him afterwards.

"Huzzah!"

This short exclamation is loud enough in the quiet of the library that the girls jump. Even Julian, who's yelled the cry of discovery, flinches. He wastes no time folding the piece of paper he's pulled free, before shoving it into what must be a cavernous inside pocket. This is followed by a couple of small packets but there's no tell-tale bulge in the front of his jacket after he pulls his hand free. He continues to flip through the files and, if she hadn't been looking directly at him, she would never have known about the second sheaf of paper that disappears inside his jacket.

"Come on, let's get the hell outta here." Julian's accent is spot-on American, but his swearing is out of character for the real him.

"Aren't you going to put the folders away?" says Brenda, shuffling to the front of the chair in readiness to stand.

"No, it's better if I leave them exactly where they are," says Julian, smiling broadly and already on his way to the door. "More significant if he knows."

Fine, thinks Brenda, struggling to gain her feet with the sodding chair having swallowed her. "Come on Stef, stop sodding about over there."

"Be with you in a second," says Stef, distracted, while reading one of the folders she's picked up off the desk.

Even having prompted Stef to "move her arse", Brenda and Julian are still out in the hallway before the girl joins them and even though they hot foot it, they're still not fast enough. They're opening the front door when a booming voice comes from the direction of the stairs.

"And what the bloody hell do you think you're up to?"

Sod it. Brenda looks at the stupid little twat standing on the half landing, striking a lordly pose. It's Rupert Smythe-Brown, living up to the description made by Jennie's boyfriend, of a 'Hooray Henry who's missing a chin'. Looking up at the little git, Brenda has to admit it, the description's spot on.

"Oooh, look honey, a real lord," says Brenda, taking the offensive. She swings her camera up and blinds Rupert with the flash a couple of times before the soft cock knows what the hell's happening.

Not one to miss an opportunity, Stef is over and up the stairs where she stands next to Rupert, before calling out, "Quick, Bob, take ma picture. I got me a real lahv lord."

Her timing is perfect in that she has a good handful of cock and balls when the flash goes off. Rupert crumples, making it clear that Stef has executed a genital version of the Vulcan nerve pinch. Almost as funny is watching Stef skip down the stairs afterwards like a five-year-old anticipating a big slab of birthday cake.

She doesn't stop skipping until she's at the front door. "Come on, you two, let's get the 'ell outta here." She hefts her bulging shoulder bag higher on her shoulder and is out of the door a moment later.

"You want to tell us what the desk riffling was all about?" says Brenda, only once they're well on their way to Chiswick.

"A few bits and pieces a friend of mine wanted me to track down. I was going to grab them last night but I couldn't and so when I saw Shit-Brown being carted away I saw an opportunity and took it."

Brenda removes the itchy blonde wig and gives her scalp a good scratch. "What friend?"

Julian takes one hand off the wheel long enough to tap the side of his nose, before putting it back on the wheel; he concentrates on his driving with a lot more zeal than is necessary with traffic as light as it is. Brenda bristles in the knowledge that he's avoided her question. No, he hasn't avoided it; he's straight-out refused to answer.

If he thinks she's going to give up that easily, he can think again.

29

A second after the door shuts behind Brenda and her two students, her name is called from the direction of the sitting room. It's incredibly faint, indicating Eadie hasn't made it out of bed yet. Still, she only has herself to blame, hopped up on painkillers and whipping the bejeezus out of Shit-Brown.

Frustrated at Julian's lack of response to her on-going barrage of questions, Brenda feels torn between visiting with Eadie and following him up the stairs so she can continue the inquisition.

Eventually, loyalty to her elderly friend wins out and she turns away from the stairs. There's more than one way to skin a cat, or frisk a gay, as happens to be the case here. She'll search his bloody room if she has to.

Satisfied?" Eadie's expression is a touch on the curmudgeonly side. "Told you I didn't do away with that waste of space." She finishes this statement by crossing her arms over her chest and continuing to give Brenda the evils.

"Just wanted to make sure, because if that arsehole had done to me what he did to you, I'd have done him an injury of a permanent nature."

Somewhat appeased, Eadie unfolds her arms. "So, do tell."

After some well-placed pillow fluffing and topping up of drinks, Brenda sits down on the end of the bed and fills Eadie in on the developments that afternoon.

"What do you suppose the boy was looking for?"

"I'm more interested in *who* than what," says Brenda, casting her mind back over who Julian had mixed with at the various social functions they'd attended.

"Who's the boy talked to?"

"That's just it, I've only ever seen lots of 'haw haws'. The only person he talks to in any depth is Genevieve."

It takes a second, but both of them are talking over each other, agog at the possibility of this being the 'friend'.

"It makes sense," says Eadie, rubbing her hands together and causing herself obvious pain in the process, "If anyone wanted to have something on the elder Shit-Brown, it would be her."

By the time Brenda's on her way up to her bedroom, they've formulated a plan of attack. As Eadie mentioned on numerous occasions during their discussion, knowledge is power and it's something Brenda has found to be bloody useful in the past. If she and Eadie have something on Wallace, other than him stealing Eadie's paintings all those years ago, so much the better.

Anything to avoid retribution, as far as she's concerned.

Brenda knocks on Julian's door and is in his room a second or two later in hopes of taking him by surprise. He's not there. Damn it, she hadn't heard him leaving the house. She has a peep in the bathroom and, after a fruitless search of his room for the pieces of paper he'd stuffed inside his jacket, walks up to the common room, but he's not there either.

Stef is, but she's so busy reading the contents of a manila folder that it takes her a moment to look up and see Brenda standing looking at her. "Oh, shit!"

If she's expecting to be reprimanded for grabbing all the folders from the mansion, she's sorely disappointed because the last thing on Brenda's mind is telling off her student for doing what she should have done herself. Damn it all, she's losing her touch if she passed up an opportunity like this.

Brenda slings herself onto the couch opposite Stef, grabs a file and settles down for some light evening reading.

They're still at it three hours later when Julian walks in.

"Perhaps you'd like to tell us about the papers you took," says Brenda, not even giving him time to sit down. "For Ginny, was it?"

She knows she's onto something when his pupils shrink and he stiffens infinitesimally. It's the first reaction she's ever shaken out of the po-faced bastard, but it's enough and she goes in for the kill. "Something to do with the demise of that prick Wallace's father, is it?"

He doesn't answer.

But this isn't to say he confirms it either.

He'll keep.

Brenda goes back to reading the handwritten file in front of her. There's enough in here to keep her in funds for the rest of her life but for once, the thought of profiting from someone else's misery doesn't sit well. Far more entertaining to hand the files over to the people being blackmailed and sit back and watch them get even with Wallace and Rupert, for indeed the pudgy little toe-rag is up to his balls in the extortion racket, too.

"Aww, hell," says Brenda, in response to the pile of photos underneath the next sheet of paper. "Perverted little wankers!"

The majority of the photos are in black and white, which gives her an idea of how long the wankers have been at it. Even though she's not interested in the content of the sickeningly glossy eight-by-tens, Brenda makes herself flick through all of them, putting selected images to the side as she does so. Any that feature the old lady downstairs will not be handed over to the subjects.

"What about the negatives?" says Stef, tapping the growing pile of photos on the coffee table.

"Already got that covered," says Julian, not looking up from the folder he's working his way through with a lot more absorption than either Stef or Brenda.

"Were they in the stuff you nabbed?" says Stef, even if the answer seems obvious.

At least, that is, until Julian doesn't answer it, with his lack of words saying a lot more than if he'd answered the damned question. That he keeps his gaze on the piece of paper he's currently holding also says a hell of a lot, his avoidance being so obvious as to be audible.

Brenda only twigs he's folding said piece of paper when Stef jumps to her feet, sending the file on her lap flying. "Oh, no, you don't." She takes the sheet out of his hand, drops it on top of the others stacked on his lap and folds the whole lot up like something out of a magic show. "I lifted these, they're mine."

File intact, she puts it on the coffee table and sets about picking up the one she'd sent flying. While the tidy up is going on, Brenda keeps flicking through the files she'd managed to get hold of, worried that Stef might take these back, too. She comes across another couple of photos that still her hands. After looking at them closely, she adds them to the pile, hoping she can keep these with Stef's permission.

It's only when she looks up from her final file that she sees that Julian has left them to it. Closing the file and plonking it down on the coffee table, she nips out onto the landing and checks the bathroom. Nope, coast is clear. "Stef, you okay if I hold onto these photos? They've all got Eadie in them somewhere and I'd prefer they didn't see the light of day."

"With ya," she says, pulling photo after photo from the side of her seat cushion until she too has a pile of incriminating evidence.

The girls go through all the files again, methodically this time, putting any photo that has Eadie in it to one side. In the end, Stef gets a shoebox from her bedroom and they put them in there. The old girl had been busy in her middle years, a time when most were starting to take things easy.

They're also a lot more aware of how many important people have been, or are still being, blackmailed by the Smythe-Browns. It's not that they've come across any open signs of extortion, but there are a lot of scribbled notes that make no sense and look to be in a code of some kind. But with both father and son being complete and utter arseholes with no morals and no ethics, it's hard to imagine them showing these files to people and not using them to better themselves. Whether it's cash or favours, or both, is anyone's guess, but Brenda thinks Julian knows more than he's letting on.

A quick look at her watch shows her that it's too late to knock on his door now, but there's also no way she will let him weasel out of any more questions and so if that means trapping him in bed, so be it. She's not quiet when she stomps down-stairs after hiding the photos of Eadie under a loose floorboard in a cupboard up on the top floor.

Brenda raps on the door of his room, hard. Just watch him try to feign sleep with the racket she's making. It's obvious he's still awake when he wrenches the door open seconds later, fully clothed. So he wasn't in bed, either. If anything he looks as if he's about to go out. Walking past him as though she owns the place, her eyes flick around the room, quickly and instinctively.

"Hah, so you did have them." Brenda makes for the bed and

the stack of negative folders that sit on its neatly made surface. Before she can pick them up, Julian intercepts, holding her back with unexpected strength. The guy is full of surprises at times.

"They're not yours." Julian's tone is measured, his words evenly spaced.

"They're not sodding yours, either," says Brenda, all the while trying to get around Julian to the packets sitting there so tantalisingly.

"No, but they are evidence."

Evidence? This stops Brenda's struggle like nothing else would. That's a fuzz term if ever she's heard one. No longer putting up a fight, all Julian's forward momentum sends her stumbling backwards under his weight. Her heel catches on a fold in the rug and they're both in a heap on the ground. If it wasn't for the rug cushioning her landing, this could have proved painful, but even so, Brenda has the wind knocked out of her and is left gasping for air.

Panicking, desperately trying to claw air into her unresponsive lungs, she's about to freak. Julian pulls her into a crouched position, all the while telling her to take slow deep breaths. The calmness of his voice cuts through her anxiety so she does as he says, rewarded by drawing enough air into her system that she's less likely to kark it.

Only when her breathing has settled, does Brenda lie back down. She feels better but reckons if she gets to her feet now it will be all over.

"Just who the bloody hell are you? Because I'll be stuffed if you're some Hooray Henry who's on the pull for old guys."

Julian's humph of exasperation lets her know she's onto something.

"Police?"

Julian shakes his head, giving her a small measure of relief.

"Private dick?" She's unable to stifle an adolescent snigger after asking him this.

Again, Julian shakes his head.

Brenda sifts around in her memory for what else he could possibly be.

"Bond. James Bond?" she says, in a reasonable impersonation of the great man himself, although her question is deadly serious.

The corner of one of Julian's eyes twitches. She's hit a nerve but he blows her theory by saying, "Hardly. Bond doesn't even exist. He's fictional."

"Technicality. So, are you investigating me?" Even though she doesn't want to know the answer, there's no way she cannot ask the question. Knowledge is power, and all that.

"No. What you're doing isn't technically illegal, just immoral. It might be borderline, but it's nothing a good lawyer couldn't get you off."

"So you're investigating something?" says Brenda, smugly.

Again, Julian's eye flickers proving he's nowhere near as relaxed as he's making out. This is something that's confirmed when Brenda moves no more than a gnat's whisker. He jumps to his feet, sweeps the negatives up with surprising speed and slides them inside his jacket. He's out of his bedroom door and running down the stairs before she manages to stand.

"Bugger it!" The slippery bastard has managed to dodge her, again.

With nothing else for it but to go to bed, Brenda sets up a booby trap that would do a thirteen-year-old boy proud and hits the sack secure in the knowledge that no matter what time he gets home, she'll know about it.

It's only a little bucket.

Brenda is woken early the following morning by Charlie's yowling rather than Julian's yelling. Damn it, this can only mean he didn't come home last night. Maybe now he's got the 'evidence' and knows she's onto him, he'll give up the pretence and drop out of the school.

"Bugger it, we need that dosh," says Brenda, rolling in Charlie's direction to see what the hell he's on about with all the caterwauling.

"Aw, bloody hell. No! Don't cuddle up to me."

The cat is soaking wet and Brenda knows full well how he ended up that way; if the damp spreading across the counterpane is any gauge, his fur has the water-carrying capabilities of a sponge. What's weird is that she didn't hear the booby trap go off. At the least she should have heard the rubbish bin bouncing around on the ground.

"Off, off, off," Brenda screeches as Charlie climbs up onto her chest in readiness to lick himself dry, but he ignores her.

It's not long before the damp works its way through to her boobs making them feel decidedly clammy. She rolls sharply to the side, sending Charlie flying and then flips herself out of bed. It's hardly how she'd envisaged getting up this morning. But now that she's up, curiosity as to how the cat got wet without making a sound gets the better of her. She drags on her dressing gown and is across the hall in no time.

That's weird, the trap is still in place. She's looking up at it when someone comes up behind her.

"After you," says Julian, giving her a good nudge in the middle of her back.

It's enough to make her stumble forward into the door, springing the trap and drenching her in the process. She'd thought the dampness from Charlie was bad, but the soaking she's just received is in another league altogether. Damn it, there wasn't that much water in the blasted bucket.

Was there?

No, there wasn't.

"You arsehole," hisses Brenda, turning so she can get a good swing at him.

"What did I do?" he says, stepping back. "Wasn't me that set the trap." He eyeballs her, although he doesn't keep eye contact for long. His eyes widen and Brenda hears a hitch in his breathing.

She looks down to see what's got him gawping but is at a loss. Okay, her boobs are visible through the soaking wet silk of her dressing gown, but that shouldn't bother him. Wanting to check for certain, she crosses her arms over her chest and, sure enough, Julian's scrutiny lifts back to her face.

Shaking her head to centre her concentration, she's aware of how wet her hair is and so, putting her hands up into it, she gives it a good fluff up sending water flying in all directions, with Julian copping his fair share.

He isn't impressed.

Tough titties.

"You still got the negatives?" says Brenda.

He shakes his head, confirming her suspicions.

"Where are they? There are shots of Eadie in that lot."

"They're safe. That's all you need to know."

30

After a night spent stewing about Julian fobbing her off, Brenda is under the pathetic trickle of water that masquerades as a shower in the first-floor bathroom, hoping it will wash away her frustration. She'd asked him if he'd be leaving now that his cover was blown but he'd said it suited him to stay and with the merest non-committal *hmmm* on her part, he'd offered to double his already doubled rent.

There's no way in hell she'll turn that down. But neither does she feel comfortable with someone on that side of the law living so close to her. If he is from that side of the law. As far as she's concerned, the law is fuzzy in more ways than one.

It's only after breakfast that she gets time alone with Eadie so she can bring her up-to-date on this latest development. She also takes the opportunity to hand over all the photos that Stef had let her keep from the folders.

Brenda expects Eadie to want to check out the files themselves, but the old lady appears at best disinterested in their contents, other than the photos.

Tucked in her usual chair in the sitting room, Eadie slowly sifts her way through the stack of photos, alternating from looking bloody furious, right through to wistful and even tearful in one instance. Her manner when she's finished is business-like in the extreme.

"Burn them!"

"But, you could pad out your retirement with this lot." Brenda takes the photos from Eadie's hands.

"With a private detective or whatever he is living in the house? Goodness no!"

"Okay, if you're sure." Brenda's anything but. It's not a good idea to permanently destroy evidence like this, but if that's what Eadie wants, she's not going to argue about it.

She doesn't bother building a proper fire and instead burns each of them individually until there's a heap of ashy bondage and discipline in the grate. Thinking that's the end of it, she's surprised when Eadie asks her if she'll get Flo in to empty the fire's ash pan.

"I'll go get her," says Brenda, her misgivings clear by her tone.

"Too many memories," says Eadie, and on seeing the emotional hurt on her face, Brenda doesn't bother trying to understand further and instead hurries to get Flo, queen of clean.

They only strike up their conversation again, once Flo has gone and Eadie is sipping on a large sherry, purely for medicinal purposes.

"I'm still worried about the negatives," says Brenda, sipping on her own glass of the sweet stuff, purely to keep Eadie company.

"The boy says they're somewhere safe?"

"He does, but his idea of safe and mine might well be sodding poles apart."

They sip on their drinks for a while, before Eadie breaks the silence.

"I hope Stef finds out who the mystery patient is."

"Should be soon. She said something about catching up with the ambo driver today."

The rest of the morning is spent in companionable silence with Brenda reading *The Bitch* by Jackie Collin's, while Eadie immerses herself in *Juliette*, a book that looks to be of an altogether different vintage. Every now and then there's a chuckle from one or the other of them, but apart from that, the clock on the mantelpiece is the loudest thing in the room.

The din in the hallway when Stef stumbles in sorts that out. Apart from slamming the door, she's yelling at the top of her voice for everyone to, "Get yer arses down to the kitchen, quick smart."

"Sounds like this will be good," says Eadie, carefully marking her place with the book's ribbon and closing the tome with care.

Brenda folds the corner of her page, tosses the paperback on the coffee table and scrambles to her feet so she can help Eadie to stand. They're the last two to arrive in the kitchen; Paula is at the place in Chelsea and Rosie is out and about somewhere with Brian.

This leaves, Bert and Flo, who are privy to everything that goes on in the house, and Stef and Julian. By the time Eadie is safely in her spot at the end of the table, Flo is pouring boiling water into the biggest teapot and Bert is ferrying everything else over to the table.

They're all set, but Stef refuses to speak until everyone has a cuppa and selected a biscuit from the tin.

"You are not gonna bleedin' believe it." She pauses, for dramatic effect and it works with everyone at the table clamouring for her to continue. "It was none other than the right 'onourable Findus Bleakly, Tory MP for Croydon East," she crows.

There are reactions from everyone around the table to this

apparently juicy tidbit, apart that is from Brenda, who hasn't a clue who the fat tosspot is.

Eadie's sniggers turn into chuckles before escalating into full-blown belly laughs that are much louder than should be possible for someone so diminutive. Flo and Bert look simply look horrified, as though they've voted for the guy, or something.

It's Julian's reaction that is the most interesting. His laughter sounds forced, as though he's playing a part, which could be entirely possible given what Brenda had found out about him last night.

"Okay, you lot. Spill," says Brenda. "Who the hell is he?"

It takes a minute for Eadie to get her laughter under control, but when she's composed enough, she says, "Findus is a morals campaigner, who's so high and mighty he makes Mary Whitehouse look like a complete degenerate."

Even though she hasn't been in the UK for long, Brenda knows all about this paragon of virtue. The woman's on the telly and in the papers all the time, wanting to suck the fun out of anything and everything. But, if dear old Findus is getting away with pretending he's even purer than Mary, he's doing a bang-up job of hiding his murky secrets. Secrets right up the Smythe-Browns' extortion alley. It must be costing him a fortune, so no wonder he was so pissed off at being openly carried out the front doors of the mansion containing the infamous Playpen.

"Friend of your client?" says Brenda, looking closely at Julian so she can spot even his most subtle of reactions.

"No, actually."

Dammit, she can't read anything into his simple reply, as he regards her without emotion; although he goes off-plan by raising an eyebrow when her frustration shows. It's all she can do not to lean over the table and wipe the smile off the smug bastard's face. It is only thoughts of his quadruple rent that settle her back into her seat.

He'll keep.

"What injuries had he sustained?" says Eadie, to Stef.

"None that they could see."

"What about Wallace? What was up with him?" says Brenda, hoping that whatever it was, it's not enough to have the arsehole going all-out to find whoever was responsible. Still, that aside, for sure there'll be a witch hunt to find out who nicked all those files.

"Barry wasn't sure. He said there was nothing outwardly wrong with 'im, but 'e was in a lot of pain. They had to dope 'im up to the eyeballs to get 'im on the stretcher."

"Him, him," mutters Eadie, about Stef's dropped aitches, but loud enough to bring a smile to Brenda's face.

Only after Stef has had a thorough grilling on every little thing that Barry said, does Brenda help Eadie to her feet and back through to the sitting room. She holds her tongue until they're in there with the door shut, before speaking. Even then, she deliberately keeps her voice down.

Brenda helps the old girl back into her seat before resuming her own. "So, what's your take on this?"

Eadie doesn't answer immediately and instead clasps her hands together in her lap and leans back and closes her eyes. She looks like Yoda when she pulls this pose but Brenda knows from experience not to interrupt, because while it might look as though she's sleeping, the cogs inside the old lady's head are whirring at double their usual speed. She might be slow physically, but her mind is like the proverbial steel trap.

Eadie's eyes open after a few minutes. "I wonder?"

"What?" Brenda's unable to stop herself from leaning forwards on the couch.

"What if Genevieve is simply convenient?"

Brenda winds her hand in the air, indicating that Eadie should continue.

"What better way to get dirt on Wallace and Rupert than through the mother and grandmother who abhors them?"

Brenda agrees with this logic.

Eadie focuses on a scene that only she can see. "What if the real friend is the Conservative Party?"

Holy hell, this shit just got real. "But hang on. If Wallace is a rich prick, doesn't that make him a Conservative, too?"

"Most definitely, but that's not to say he doesn't have need of the occasional favour from those in power. There's never been the slightest whiff about him extorting money out of the chaps who've had reason to use the Playpen."

"But people must know it's going on. You can't keep that sort of shit under wraps."

"It would depend who Wallace kept dossiers on," says Eadie, once again closing her eyes to focus on the problem.

"Keep thinking about it, I'll be back in a second," says Brenda, already opening the sitting room door.

She flies up the stairs, taking them two at a time, gasping and puffing by the second landing, but curiosity has given her wings. There's no need to knock on Stef's door – it's wide open, the girl sitting in the middle of her bed, surrounded by the brown manila folders.

"Any chance I can take those down and show them to Eadie? She's got a theory as to what the Shit-Browns are up to."

"Sure, I'll come with you."

Stef uncoils from the lotus position, demonstrating herself to be a lot more flexible than most. She tidies the files into two piles and gives one of them to Brenda, who immediately clasps it tight against her chest to avoid any bits of paper or photos from dropping out the bottom. Stef is likewise engaged with her selection of files. Even so, they need to stop a couple of times to retrieve items that have wormed their way out the bottom of the folders.

Brenda thinks Eadie must have fallen asleep when she first opens the door to the sitting room; but no, her eyes snap open, regarding the files held by the girls with interest and maybe even dread.

"Okay, let's have a look at them," she says, reluctantly.

Brenda puts her pile down on the coffee table, takes the top one and hands it over to Eadie, who, now that she's committed to looking at them, wastes no time placing the file flat on her lap and opening it up like a good novel.

"Not sure if you'll get much outta them. Lot of it looks to be in code, or the bloke's handwriting is shit," says Stef.

Silence reigns as Eadie flips through the folders one after the other, to the point Stef gets bored and wanders off and Brenda picks up her book again. She's getting to a steamy bit when Eadie interrupts her.

"I knew Wallace was devious, but this lot takes the cake."

"What gives?"

"If the contents of these folders had been made public a year ago, the Tories might not have won last year's election."

"What would happen if the Shit-Browns went public now?"

"For starters, we'd most likely be facing at least a dozen by-elections."

"Why? A bit of the old spanky is hardly illegal."

"No, but allowing yourself to be blackmailed into swaying decisions in government, most assuredly is," says Eadie, closing the final file, her face grim.

"We need to get rid of this lot, don't we?" says Brenda, tidying the files up into one large pile.

"Most assuredly. This is the sort of thing that SO6 take an interest in."

"Who?"

"Diplomatic Protection."

"Bloody hell, and I thought the pigs were bad," says Brenda, staring down at the innocent brown folders with their incendiary contents.

"Well, technically, they are part of the police force."

It's all Brenda needs to know. "Here, give me this lot. We are getting them as far away from this house as possible."

Eadie tries to get her to divulge where exactly, but Brenda feels the fewer people who know, the better. She doesn't even bother telling Stef what she's up to and instead, bundles the folders up into a huge holdall and, after a quick trip to the dungeon, is out the door immediately after. She's paranoid on her walk to the tube despite her being incognito with a cap of Jennie's pulled low over her eyes and a jacket of Sam's that's like nothing on earth she'd wear normally. Hopefully, the girls who are currently in Italy with their fiancé and boyfriend won't mind. Tough if they do.

It's the first time she's visited the Swiss bank in months: continually checking for a deposit that didn't happen, had become depressing in the extreme. Sod Stefano and his dodgy investments. She should have been living it up in London and enjoying Martin's inheritance rather than racing around like a criminal. Maybe she should simply leave the bag on the steps of a cop shop and scarper? The only problem is Wallace might still slime his way out of it because of his connections in the upper echelons of government.

Organising a security deposit box is remarkably easy for someone who already has an account with the bank, even if there's sweet FA in there, and it's with relief that Brenda takes the folders out of her bag and stacks them neatly inside the metal box. Even though the bank had said the security cameras were for her own protection, she's careful to place her body between the lens and the deposit box; especially so when she puts the diamond bracelet on top of the folders.

After locking the box, she threads the key onto the gold

chain around her neck and tucks it down the front of her top, safe between her boobs. The key is nondescript enough that no one will know where or to what it gives access. And that's how she likes it.

Stepping out of the bank and around a corner, she removes the cap and jacket and stuffs them in the holdall before slinging it over her shoulder. Halfway to the tube station, she gets the distinct feeling she's being watched. She's had too many years of avoiding ex-boyfriends and current wives to know she's not imagining it.

Without breaking her stride, she throws herself at the revolving doors of a large department store, much to the horror of the elderly gent who's exiting at the same time. He's on the footpath a lot quicker than he expected, but Brenda doesn't bother slowing down to see if he's okay and instead works to bury herself among the racks of upmarket clobber.

Eventually, she's right at the back and safely ensconced behind a mannequin wearing one of the ugliest dresses she's ever seen. This spot affords her a great view of the front door that's still spinning following her hasty entrance. She doesn't need to wait long.

Why the hell is he tailing her? She knows he has to be following her because there's no way he's in here purely by coincidence. Much as she'd like to confront him, she prefers to leave him wondering where the hell she's gone.

It isn't just because of the ugly mannequin with its tent-like dress that Brenda's chosen this spot. Dropping down so she's hidden by a rack of the same ugly dresses, she spins around and heads through a door marked 'staff only' and once safely through, shuts it behind her. There isn't a lock on this side, but there is a chair that she slides under the handle. It will require considerable force to open it from the outside.

Assuming an 'I'm meant to be here' attitude she strides down the corridor before her, hoping like hell that it leads to a back entrance. She's not disappointed, although she has to brazen her way through the staff canteen and in and out of the ladies cloakroom before she finds the exit she's after. She peeks out and along the back alley.

Phew, that's a bloody relief.

Safely on the next street over, Brenda jumps on the first bus she sees. It's pulling away from the stop and she knows that even if Julian isn't too far behind her, he's never going to catch up now. As it is, her arm is almost ripped out of its socket as she hangs onto the upright pole with the rest of her flapping in the breeze. This risky manoeuvre gets her a *tsking* from the conductor, accompanied by a shake of his head. Tough.

She tosses herself onto one of the long side seats in time to see Julian when he runs out of the alley and onto the footpath. As tempting as it would be to wave at him, Brenda sits back in the seat so she's partially hidden by the chap sitting next to her. Only when they're a good way along the road does she check to see if she's away scot-free.

With him no longer in sight, she yanks on the leather cord to signal the driver to pull over at the next stop and alights with as much speed as she'd flown on with not much earlier. She's belting her way down a side road not long after.

She does this a couple more times all the while heading away from the last spot she'd seen the gay supersleuth, until the chances of him finding her are slim at best. Hell, she doesn't even know where she is. One thing's for sure, though, she needs a bloody drink and, in London, it doesn't take long to find a pub. Actually, there are three to choose from.

31

"W here the bloody hell did you get to?" Julian pounces on Brenda the moment she rolls in the door later that night

She hadn't meant to have that many drinks, but the crowd at the Plucked Duck had been generous to a fault and so she'd stayed on for dinner. She was lucky that one of them had put her in a black cab afterwards and thrown enough money at the driver to get her home safely.

Maybe it was the generous number of G&Ts she'd quaffed over the course of the afternoon, but she's no longer as concerned as she had been about Julian following her. It's kinda funny when she looks back on it, now.

"Gave you the slip!" crows Brenda, delighted at having outmanoeuvred him.

"Yes, me and, luckily for you, the other person who was following you," says Julian, cutting through the alcoholic haze that has her in its bosomy embrace.

"What other person?"

"Whoever he was, he knew what the hell he was doing. I

was looking out my window when you did a runner and I saw him fall in behind you. So I fell in behind them."

"Stuff it!"

"It must be someone sent by Wallace," says Eadie, now standing in the doorway of the sitting room.

"Damn it all. Surely Wallace isn't out of hospital yet?" Brenda can feel herself sobering up by the second.

"No, but Rupert would know about the paintings having been taken and said something to his father." Julian drops onto the bottom step, looking at Eadie and Brenda in turn.

"And now I've linked myself to both Eadie and the bank." Brenda leans her forehead against the wall in hopes of cooling her rapidly heating brain.

Eadie's "Oh, dear," is barely audible and a moment later, she's no longer standing in the doorway.

"The only thing in your favour is the bank you took the stuff to, is Swiss," says Julian.

She's about to ask about the relevance of this when she hears Eadie calling for them to join her in the sitting room.

"Can you describe him?" says Eadie, to Julian.

"Nondescript. Professionally so. Doubt I could pick him in a line-up if I tried."

As if realizing this avenue of questioning is a dead end, she turns to Brenda. "Which bank did you take the files to?"

"UBS," says Brenda, in unison with Julian.

"Well, there's a relief." Eadie sinks back into her chair. Seeing the old lady looking relieved, Brenda allows the tension to leave her own body.

"The only thing that concerns me is how much the tail overheard when they followed you into the bank," says Julian, ruining this respite for both women.

"But?" Brenda thinks back on her visit to the bank, going through each step in the process of getting a safety deposit box sorted out. "The middle-aged bloke in the muddy brown suit?"

Julian twitches his head briefly in response and Brenda lets loose with a string of expletives that, while not solving anything, make her feel better. Even Eadie is muttering under her breath, before spitting out a terse "Bugger."

"We might be okay," says Julian, getting their attention again. "UBS have a good reputation for confidentiality. And while he might know your name and that you've got a safe deposit box, that's it."

"True. I was alone in a small room when I put the files into the deposit box and I made sure I was blocking the view of the camera before I swapped them over from the bag."

"Did you see your box placed in the vault?"

"Not exactly. I had to put it on this Lazy Susan contraption and they it swung around and I couldn't see where it went after that. But I've got the key to the box," says Brenda, unconsciously fingering the gold chain around her neck.

"That's something, I guess," he says, with a lot less conviction than she'd like. "You do need to hide it but around your neck isn't ideal."

"What about in the garden shed," says Eadie. "Much safer than inside the house and there are lots of nooks and crannies out there."

"We could booby trap it, too," says Julian, smiling broadly at Brenda.

The pair of them waste no time and, after grabbing torches, hoof it to the shed that sits unobtrusively at the end of the garden. Eadie's not wrong about a number of nooks and crannies out here. For such a tiny shed, there is a multitude of places to hide a little key. The hard part is hiding it without disturbing the patina of grime coating every surface. Any scrape or smear they make will point the way to their hiding spot as effectively as neon lights.

They stand in the clutter-free patch in the middle of the shed and look, without touching, for the perfect spot. Having decided on it, they thread a piece of wire they've found on the dirt floor, through the bow of the key and secure it behind one of the wooden uprights. Not that this is an easy exercise in itself, as they first have to gain access to this hidey hole. Julian removes items with the clever use of pliers so as not to leave any smudge marks on the half-empty oilcans and garden sprays that stand sentinel around the perimeter.

"I reckon that should do it," says Brenda, as they illuminate the hiding spot from all angles to make sure the key isn't visible.

"Should be good," says Julian, putting the pliers back on their hook on the wall.

Even if someone searched the shed and was observant enough to see they'd recently been used, there's no indication to where or how.

"Should we booby trap it?" says Brenda.

"I wasn't serious about that. No, the likelihood of someone finding it down there is remote at best."

It's not until they're sliding the bolt on the shed door that the day catches up with her. It's been full-on that's for damned sure; the soaking she'd received courtesy of Julian so early that morning now feels like it happened days ago.

"I'm knackered." She doesn't bother with any more than this because to do so would take far too much bloody effort and all she wants to do is get horizontal.

"Right behind you," says Julian, "just need to get something out of the van and I'll be right up."

He veers off to the side of the house, leaving her to walk inside on her own. The lights are on in the kitchen but that's the only sign of life and Brenda flicks them off before pushing on the swing door and out and down the hall. Eadie is still up and so Brenda pops in to say goodnight and explain where they've hidden the key. It always pays to have one other person knowing where something like this is.

"Good, as soon as Julian's in bed, you need to move it."

"What? Why?"

"We still don't know he's one hundred percent on our side in this matter. You need to move it tonight. Somewhere in the garage might be good."

As dead on her feet as she is, this is the last thing Brenda feels like doing, but Eadie's got a point. She needs coffee if she wants to stay awake, and lots of it.

Walking back into the darkened kitchen, she's about to flick the lights on when she notices torch light at the bottom of the garden. That sneaky bastard.

Not wanting to alert him by opening the back door, Brenda races back down the hallway, out the front door and around the side of the house. It's only when she's part way down the side path that she realises she hadn't heard the gate open. The bastard must have oiled the hinges! Sure enough, when she opens it to enter the backyard, it swings silently instead of squealing in protest as it usually does.

She sneaks across the grass not bothering with her torch, the moonlight enough to keep her from tripping over any of the larger tufts of unmown grass. Might be time to pay Bert to take care of this, it's getting all Wimbledon Common out here.

She stands at the shed door, takes a slow and full breath and lets him have it. "What the hell are you doing?"

The sheer volume of her question is enough for the person ransacking the shed, to stagger backwards, trip over the lawn-mower and land in a heap amongst a whole stack of tomato stakes.

It's only when she's turned on her torch that Brenda sees it's not Julian who's in a heap at her feet, but a nondescript, middle-aged man in a grubby brown suit.

"Who the hell are you?" says Brenda, not for a moment stopping to worry if the guy is dangerous and maybe she should get the hell out of there.

He doesn't answer and instead gets slowly to his feet. He's bigger than he'd seemed in the banking chamber; this becomes especially apparent when he rushes her.

Boy, does he get a surprise.

Self-preservation kicks in and Brenda gets her foot up a lot quicker than Brown Suit is expecting, rearranging his nuts hard enough that the sound of the air leaving his lungs echoes, loudly, around the garden. He crumples in a heap on the grass where he rolls around, keening like a girl.

"Ya sodding prick," says Brenda, the adrenalin pumping. "There's plenty more where that came from."

"Hell's teeth, are you okay?" Julian has appeared from nowhere and is crouching down next to the robber, pulling his hands behind his back and cuffing him.

"What? Where the hell did you get those from?" says Brenda, eyeing the cuffs sitting snuggly about Brown Suit's wrists. They sure as hell don't look to be entertainment level without a single piece of fluff marring their shiny surface.

"Never mind that, perhaps you'd like to check there's nothing missing from inside the shed."

His tone is pointed but he's careful to keep his comment vague enough that he doesn't give anything away. Brenda is just as circumspect when she looks inside the shed, swinging her torch in all directions without specifically highlighting the actual spot. It only takes the merest swing of the torch in that direction to see the oilcans and weedkiller are sitting exactly as they were when they left the shed not ten minutes earlier.

"Bleedin' arsehole doesn't look to have taken anything, but I reckon we should strip search him, just to be sure."

Julian breathes in hard through his nose at this comment and Brown Suit's whimpering stops so suddenly that the quiet that descends has a spooky quality to it.

"Hmmm, sounds like someone has something to hide," says Brenda, gleefully.

"As entertaining as that would be," says Julian, "I'll settle for ID."

He makes quick work of patting down the writhing heap of brown tweed on the ground before rifling through every pocket he can find, but without results. "Nothing, not a goddam thing." Julian allows Brown Suit to settle back onto his stomach and stands next to Brenda.

They're looking down at him, wondering about the best course of action, when the lights go on in the kitchen illuminating the whole backyard.

"Damn," says Brenda, looking inside and watching Eadie slowly hobbling across the kitchen in the direction of the back door.

"I'll stay here if you go and help her," says Julian.

Brenda's at the back door well ahead of Eadie, even though the old lady had far less distance to travel. Opening it a smidge, she puts her head inside in an effort to block her mentor from stepping outside but Eadie is having none of it.

"Out of my way, young lady!"

Eadie slides her walking stick through the gap in the door and jabs in the general direction of Brenda's foot so that she has to step back to avoid injury.

"It's bloody cold out here, so don't bitch if it screws with your arthritis."

Eadie's sigh speaks volumes although she still follows it up with another order. "Fine. Bring the reprobate over here so I can get a good look at him."

This is easier said than done because when Brenda and Julian each grab an arm to drag him across the lawn for Eadie to have a gander, he puts up one hell of a struggle. Until Brenda offers to rearrange his family jewels again, then he simply goes limp, offering no resistance other than his dead weight.

Once there, Julian flips him over so that he's facing Eadie, who's leaning against the door jamb.

"Oh, my god. Ernie Palmer, is that you?"

Brown Suit closes his eyes in acknowledgement but doesn't go to the bother of speaking.

"I see you're still running around playing Wallace's pet thug. Aren't you a little old for it?"

Ernie's reaction to being called old is comic in the extreme. Brenda wouldn't have thought it possible for a grass-stained and handcuffed thug to look indignant, but he manages it with aplomb.

On the plus side, he's not government. On the downside, he knows where Brenda's taken the files.

"Shit, we can't let the arsehole go until I've moved the files tomorrow."

"We'll have to keep hold of him until then," says Julian.

"I know the perfect place." Eadie breaks out into peals of laughter that elicit quite the reaction from the turd on the ground.

"I'll go get the key," says Brenda, before retracing her steps to the garden shed. She doesn't bother trying to hide her tracks, and instead kicks all the cans out of the way and grabs the key from its hiding spot. She's on her way back when the lights go on in the studio up in the attic.

It takes the combined efforts of Julian, Brenda and Bert, who's since arrived with Flo in tow, to drag Ernie downstairs and lock him in the B&D dungeon. After supplying him with water, blankets and a bucket, Julian undoes the handcuffs while Flo stands at the ready to rearrange his bits with a rolling pin if he makes a run for it.

"Don't know about you, but I need a drink after that," says Brenda, when they're back up in the kitchen and Bert, Flo and Eadie have retired.

"Not if you want to get up early enough to be at the bank when it opens, you don't," says Julian, already filling the kettle.

"What's the rush? It's not like Ernie's going anywhere."

"No, but he might well have told someone about USB before coming over here."

"Shit," says Brenda, putting the cask of wine back in the fridge, "I'll have tea, thanks."

They enjoy their cuppa in a companionable silence, which is only interrupted by the occasional thump from the cellar.

"Do you reckon the lock will stand up to the punishment?" says Julian.

"I've been in holding cells that are flimsier," says Brenda, provoking a smirk from Julian.

Brenda's head feels heavy in the morning, liking a hell of a lot more sleep than she managed last night. She'd been awake for hours worrying about how her haven has been breached. Despite the dodgy state of her finances, she's felt safer living with Eadie than she had since Martin was looking out for her. It's a feeling she'd grown used to; having it ripped away has her beating herself up for becoming complacent, for not looking out for number one to the exclusion of all others.

"Stupid, stupid, stupid," rattling around in her head like a loose screw had made it impossible to sleep. Charlie having abandoned his usual spot snuggled up next to her, is testimony to her having spun like a lump of meat in a kebab shop for most of the night.

It's both a curse and relief when Julian knocks on her door, telling her she needs to get up. She has a shower, but it's no good, she's drained and her eyes feel like the sandman has chucked a couple of bucketsful in each one; no amount of rubbing clears her vision. She's sure she looks as bad as she feels.

This is confirmed when she stumbles into the kitchen.

"Holy hell," says Bert, unable to stop himself.

"I know," mumbles Brenda, before plonking herself down at the table. She's relieved when a steaming hot cup of instant coffee is plonked down in front of her.

It's only after half a dozen sips that she's able to face the others at the table. Julian looks reasonably well rested, but Eadie must have had as good a night's sleep as Brenda herself. If anything, the old lady looks smaller than usual, as though her vitality has been drained.

"Are you okay," says Brenda, forgetting her own woes for a moment.

"I'm fine," says Eadie, briskly.

"Yeah, you look it."

After an unladylike *humph*, Eadie says, "I didn't like seeing my past sitting in my backyard like that. I thought that era was finally behind me, especially with my paintings back."

"We'll sort it out," says Julian. "Soon as we uplift the files from the bank and put them somewhere safer, we can let Ernie go."

"Are there any more where he came from?" says Brenda.

"I doubt it. He was the youngest by far. Any of the others would be long gone or too decrepit to bother us now."

As if he knows they're discussing him, a series of loud bangs come from the cellar.

"Time for more porridge," says Flo, slopping some into a bowl.

This explains why their prisoner is upset. Flo isn't a great cook with those duties usually taken care of by Bert. But she'd insisted on several occasions that porridge was her speciality. As far as Brenda could tell the only thing special about it was its ability to set like concrete. If you didn't rinse the bowl a second after the last spoonful had been gagged on, the stuff would stick to the plate so hard that binning it lock, stock and barrel was the only way to clean up.

"Flo," says Eadie, stopping the old char from putting the bowl onto a tray in readiness to carry it downstairs. "Perhaps you should crush a couple of my painkillers and mix them through his porridge. Help keep him calm."

Calm? Comatose would be more like it. But if Brenda and Julian are back from the bank quickly enough, he'll still be out cold. They can drag him upstairs and take him somewhere in the van and dump him. Preferably next to a pub so he looks like he's sleeping off a bender.

They waste no time jumping in the van and heading into the city. Traffic is a bitch, but Julian's fairly certain they're not being followed, especially after evasive manoeuvres on his part. In their favour, they're not the only white van on the road at this time of the morning and if you've seen one white van, you've seen them all.

Even allowing for all the dodging and swerving, they're there when the large double doors open at nine. They're taken through to the viewing room and left under the careful eye of the security camera. If she hadn't been looking directly at the Lazy Susan, Brenda wouldn't have even realised the security box was in the room with them. That's one well-oiled turntable.

Lifting the deposit box, Brenda knows they've got problems.

32

E ven though she's only hefted the full security box once, she knows it's far too light to still contain the folders. What if they've taken her bracelet too?

"Shit!"

"What?"

Rather than answer, Brenda puts the security box on the small table in the middle of the room, unlocks it and flips the lid back.

"How is that even possible?" Julian peers into the box as if hoping for a false bottom.

"I'm stuffed if I know, but it's not your standard robbery." Brenda lifts her precious diamond bracelet out and slides it onto her wrist. No way in hell she's leaving it here when the security is a complete piece of arse.

She's still staring down at the sparkling stones when she hears Julian knocking on the door for it to be opened. The two of them are more secure right now than the files had been overnight. Sod it, that weasel-dick Ernie had obviously spoken to someone between losing her in the city and them catching him in the garden shed.

After she's finished with him, he's going to be singing like a girl for the rest of his miserable life.

Brenda's roused from her nefarious thoughts by sounds of the door unlocking.

Julian doesn't give the officious chap much time to stand to the side before he strides out into the main banking chamber asking to see someone in authority, his tone deliberately benign.

The portly gentleman who shambles his way from a back office is obsequious in manner. But Brenda's not buying it. She's seen that pattern on a tie before, usually when Wallace was smoothing it down over that gut of his.

"We need to speak privately," says Brenda, fighting to keep the anger out of her voice.

She knows she's been believable when the sad sap says, "Follow me," and waddles in the direction of what must be his office. They follow close on his heels with both of them far less relaxed than they're making out. They settle in visitor chairs in front of a sarcophagus-style desk where the fat twat also takes his seat. Ringing a buzzer located somewhere under his desk, a less fat, less old, less fawning assistant pops through a side door. Tea orders taken, he disappears again.

Damn, they're going to have to wait for that before they can get stuck into the blighter. Only once the English version of a tea ceremony is set up will the assistant be able to leave. Brenda's a twitching heap before this finally happens and they're left alone with the Eton old boy. She stands quicker than she'd meant to and his hand strays towards the buzzer under his desk.

"It's so hot in here," she says sweetly, shrugging out of her jacket to reveal an incredibly sheer shirt, under which sits an equally sheer bra. Thank god all her clothes were bought for her by lovers.

Fat twat's hand drops back into his lap and well clear of the buzzer.

She makes a real production out of looking at a particularly ugly oil painting that hangs on the wall above the target, before gushing, "What a gorgeous piece."

The bull that's the subject matter of the work is as overweight as the prick sitting under it and she hopes he buys her enthusiasm about its artistic merits. But instead of looking doubtful about her praise, he beams with pride. Jeez, he's the one who must have chosen it, although it's bad enough he might even have painted it. Jennie would hate it.

Either way, it gets her safely over to his side of the desk where she wastes no time spinning his chair around so that his pudgy fingers are well away from buzzing for assistance. She slams her hand hard over his mouth, stopping any yelling and screaming on his part.

While she's doing this, Julian shoots around the desk and pulls the mostly for show hanky out of the manager's top pocket before loosening the old school tie that had given him away in the first place. Julian then stuffs the balled-up hanky in the manager's mouth and keeps it in place by wrapping the tie around the now trembling man's head and knotting it securely at the back. Following this, he removes the manager's belt and uses this to secure his hands behind him and to the chair. That's one long belt.

Despite Julian's rapid-fire questions, the bank manager stays mum, but this has nothing to do with him being gagged and more to do with him refusing to even look in any particular direction.

Brenda's had enough. Casting her eyes around the oversized desk, she finds what she's after. "You remove his pants and grots and I'll see if I can't skewer his balls to the seat of the chair," says Brenda, casually tossing the letter opener from one hand to the other.

All it takes is for Julian to undo the top button of the pinstriped trousers and the manager jerks his head towards the bottom drawer in the mahogany filing cabinet, tucked between the door they'd come in and the one the assistant had left through after sorting out the cup of tea.

"Are you sure, because I get pissed off when people muck me about?" Brenda drives the opener through the ink blotter and into the desk beneath.

Damn, she hadn't thought it would make such an unholy din.

She freezes where she is and all three sets of eyes flicker between both doors, but after a minute or so without interruption, she relaxes a little and bends down to open the bottom drawer of the cabinet.

Dumb prick, he should have hidden them further away than this.

"Count them," instructs Julian. "There should be thirty-three of them."

"How the hell?"

She doesn't bother interrogating him further and instead gets on with counting them out onto the desk.

"Thirty-one, thirty-two. There's one missing."

"Anything we should know," says Julian, spinning their captive around so he can lean in menacingly.

The manager must see something in Julian's gaze, because his own eyes are wide with fear. Hah, who knew Captain Camp had such hidden depths?

"You'll need to get rid of the tie if you want any sense out of him."

No sooner has she said this, than the manager's eyes go all squinty and she knows the second the old school tie is free of those sloppy lips, he'll yell fit to bust.

Well, screw that.

"If you so much as squeak," says Brenda, quietly, before

wrenching the letter opener out of his desk, "I will ram this through your cock and balls so they look like a shish kebab. We clear?"

She knows she's been convincing when even Julian winces in reaction. But it's only after the manager has acknowledged he understands that she allows Julian to remove the gag.

"The missing file is mine," whimpers the manager, the tears rolling down his face giving him a woebegone expression. "I burnt it."

"You better sodding be telling the truth, mate, because if I hear otherwise, you're done." Brenda punctuates this threat by slapping the letter opener against the palm of her hand, leaving the old boy in no doubt his goolies will be Middle Eastern cuisine if he's telling porkies.

He doesn't answer, just nods at her and Julian, in case he needs to appease him, too.

They re-gag the manager, bundle up all the files, and shove them in the canvas bag that Brenda had delivered them in only the day before.

She's turning the door handle when Julian puts his hand on her shoulder, stopping her. He walks over to the corner where the bank manager has been wheeled, well away from the panic button, and spins him a couple of times before bending down so he's face to face with their captive.

"If you give Wallace even the vaguest description of either of us, I'll send prints of the photos I took of your file to head office in Geneva. If you so much as squeak before we're out of the building, it'll mean the same thing. We clear?"

Fatty nods vigorously, desperate to get his promises around the Eton tie bisecting his florid face. It'll have to do.

They're out on the street before they hear yelling from inside the bank and waste no time legging it around the corner and into the plumber's van that's waiting for them in a loading zone. Only once they're a couple of streets away and sure they're not being followed, does Julian pull over long enough to remove the fake signs.

"Where to now?" says Brenda.

"My parents' place in the country. No one can link you to that address so we should be good there for a couple of days until things calm down. We can also hide the files where they'll be safe from Smythe-Brown and the Old Boy network.

It takes bloody ages to break away from the gravitational pull of greater London, with both of them keeping a wary eye out for anyone following, even if only by coincidence. Paranoid? Hell, yes, after this morning's debacle!

They're trundling along the A24 before Brenda relaxes, with most traffic heading in the opposite direction. Other than the weekend away at the house party, she hasn't been out in the country. Not that they're in the middle of nowhere yet.

"Where exactly are we headed?"

"Isle of Wight."

This reply leaves Brenda's none the wiser and Julian isn't forthcoming with anything further, concentrating instead on his driving. She'd grill him, but the combination of last night's lack of sleep and the soporific rumbling of the wheels has her slouching back into her seat and, after going through the stage where even insignificant sounds are weirdly magnified, she's out for the count.

Julian shaking her hard wakes her with a start, and it takes a moment to process her surroundings. Wow, she must have been knackered for him to drive them onto a ferry without her knowing about it.

"Wake me when we get there." She closes her eyes and is concentrating on going back to the happy place she'd been in, when Julian interrupts her dreams again.

"I'm heading upstairs for a drink."

As good as that sounds; the thought of sinking back into oblivion is far more appealing to her. "Wake me when we get there."

Julian takes her at her word, meaning she misses both disembarking in Fishbourne and the drive to his parents' country place.

"You are bloody kidding me?" Brenda looks up in disbelief at the tumble of soft grey stone and mullioned windows sitting before her. Sure, it's not as massive as the place where the house party was held, but neither is it the country cottage she's been expecting. There are three floors for Pete's sake.

"Are your parents here?"

He shakes his head. "They only come down once a month."

"You are sodding kidding me?" Brenda knows she's repeating herself, but she's having trouble believing that anyone could have a house this amazing and only visit once a month. "Are there live-in staff?"

Julian's confirmation doesn't surprise her. Without staff on site, his mother would spend every bloody visit strapped to a vacuum cleaner to avoid the dust bunnies turning feral.

She follows him into the house and is impressed as all hell with the humungous, carved front door. The damned thing has to be at least ten feet in height.

"Come on, I'll show you to your room."

"Before we do that, I need to phone Eadie and let her know where the hell we are."

"The phone's in there," says Julian, pointing to a glassed-in phone booth at the back of the wide hallway.

Brenda has to stop herself from saying "You are kidding me?" sufficing with a simple, "Thanks."

The phone isn't as archaic as the booth it sits in and Brenda has no trouble connecting to Eadie's place in London but it takes an age before the call is answered to the point Brenda's about to hang up.

"Eadie speaking."

"Eadie, it's Brenda."

"Thank goodness. Where on earth are you? I've been worried sick."

Brenda fills Eadie in on everything starting from the bank doors opening, right up until her placing the call although she stops short of telling Eadie exactly where in the country she currently is. "Will Bert be okay to take care of Ernie?" She's unable to stop the Muppets' theme tune starting up after this question, but she shuts it down so she can concentrate on Eadie's reply.

"No need. The young ones arrived back from Italy, so Mark and Chris took care of it. Flo slipped the prisoner something in his soup and he was sleeping like a baby when they carried him out to the Combi van.

"Are they back yet?"

"Not yet, but we're expecting them anytime soon."

"Is Sam there?"

"Up in her room, I believe."

"Can I speak to her?"

In answer to this, she hears the phone put down and a bell ringing. The connection is good enough that Brenda hears Sam running down the stairs and all the explanations when she arrives in the sitting room, before her old flatmate from Melbourne picks up the receiver.

Brenda wastes no time bringing her up to date on what's been happening, leaving nothing out and continuing to talk even when Sam is gasping and asking questions until there's nothing left unsaid and her Kiwi mate is fully conversant with everything, including bits and pieces that not even Eadie is aware of.

"We should be back in a couple of days," finishes up Brenda. "I can't wait to see you and Jennie again."

Not giving Sam the option to waffle on, Brenda hangs up and opens the booth door.

Julian's nowhere to be seen, but she can hear him talking to another guy and so walks in the direction of the voices, eventually finding him and a besuited elderly gentleman chatting like old family friends. The sitting room they're standing in is inviting, filled as it is, with big squishy chairs and couches.

The room is dominated by a fireplace big enough to roast a whole cow, if you were so inclined; a small fire burns merrily away, filling the room with a welcome, flickering glow. Even though it's hardly cold enough to have a fire, Brenda's drawn to it and before she's aware, she's sitting on the wide stone hearth, poking extra twigs in any gaps she can see. There's something so reassuring about fire.

"All sorted?" says Julian, leaning on the wide, wooden mantelpiece.

"Should be good for now. Mark, Eadie's nephew, and his mate arrived back from Italy with Jennie and Sam. The guys are taking the trash out right now."

It takes Julian a moment to understand what she means, but she sees the comprehension in his eyes.

"You hungry?"

Until he asks, Brenda hadn't thought much about it, but now she's ravenous. "I could chew my arm off!"

"Probably don't need to go to those lengths. There should be something in the kitchen more palatable than that."

"I hope you can bloody cook," says Brenda, swinging around and onto her hands and knees, ready to stand, "because I sure as hell can't."

Julian proves himself adept in the kitchen, which comes as

a surprise given the hired help around who could take care of it for them. It appears that he does it because he actually enjoys it. Like he thinks he's Delia Smith, or something.

They eat at the large oak table in the kitchen, which Brenda is happy about. She hadn't fancied the idea of them being marooned in some toffee-nosed blasted dining room where she'd be scared she was going to scuff something. Nope, the kitchen table is familiar territory to her with this one having enough dings and nicks to make her feel positively at home. Interesting that Julian appears similarly relaxed.

"Shit!"

"What?" says Julian, his forkful of omelette poised in mid-air.

"Just realised these are the only clothes I've got with me."

"It's too late now, but we can go into Ryde tomorrow and pick up some things."

Brenda's so focused on how likely her knickers are to dry overnight that she's surprised when she sees Julian is on his feet.

"I know you had a nap in the car, but I'm going to call it a night."

Him calling her passing out for several hours a nap is typical of how polite the English can be, something Brenda finds more than amusing. As far as she's concerned, she'd prefer to call a spade a sodding shovel and let everyone know where they stand.

"I might hit the hay, too." She also stands and is ready for him to show the way when he looks pointedly at the plate she's abandoned on the table. "Oh, right."

Having her knuckles rapped like this pisses her off, but if she bitches about it, she'll come off looking like a complete cow rather than just a lazy one and so she dutifully picks up her plate, takes it over to the sink and washes it before putting it in the rack next to his.

She follows him up first one flight of stairs and then another looking closely at everything on the way. The place is beautifully decorated and a lot less ostentatious than many establishments she's been inside. Homely, but loaded, is the best way to describe it, with the quality of everything in the place more than evident. His parents must be rolling in it, meaning he is, too.

Damn, she should have charged him a truckload more rent. He can obviously afford it.

They stop outside a nondescript white wooden door that he opens wide, allowing her to enter first. Not that she gets far, with her feet failing her after a single step. The room is gorgeous but in a different way to her accommodation at the house-party weekend. The room looks lived-in and not just for show as her room at Lady Preston's had been.

"Is something wrong?"

"No!" Brenda doesn't try to articulate how she's feeling about spending the next few nights sleeping in a room that's like something she's only ever dreamed of. She doesn't like to expose her weaknesses to anyone.

"Right, I'll leave you to it. Bathroom's across the hall and there are fresh towels on the shelf above the bath."

Brenda's about to say thank you, but he's nowhere in sight.

Only after shutting her door tight, does she allow herself a broad grin. She takes a running jump at the bed and even indulges in an uncharacteristic giggle. She's living the dream, all right.

33

They've been on the island a couple of days and Brenda's over it. Julian has been the perfect host, but she's bored out of her tree; she's used to a hell of a lot more action than this. It's like being buried alive except that coffins are more flattering than the crap clothing she's been forced to wear.

Looking down at today's godawful outfit, she's sure the stock must have been in the shops longer than is profitable, leaving her feeling like an extra in *Little House on the Prairie*. Screw you Laura Ashley and your dumb tiny floral prints. The yellow and cream of the current number make her feel like a head of cauliflower. Something Julian had taken delight in pointing out at breakfast earlier that morning.

Black, there's a colour that suits her and the colour she'll wear when they return to the city. She's kept the clothes she'd travelled in clean rather than wear them now. The cauliflower and cabbage dresses can be burned or used to clean toilets, for all she cares.

"Everything all right, miss?" says Carter, the elderly gent who'd been there on their first night at the lodge.

Until she hears this, Brenda hadn't even been conscious of

the sighs that were her constant companion while sitting in the conservatory reading some boring-as-batshit country magazine.

"Yeah, I'm fine. Where's Julian?"

"I believe he's in the sitting room, miss."

Sheesh, what is it with this guy and the 'miss' gubbins? She'd given up telling him her goddam name because he didn't use it anyway. Tossing the magazine with its preserving tips on the wrought iron table next to her, Brenda hoists herself to her feet and goes in search of her gay handmaiden.

"I need to get out of this place, or I'm going to lose it." Brenda's opening gambit is designed to leave Julian in no doubt that she's had enough and she wants to get back to London. If he stalls her again, she intends to hitchhike to the ferry and get the bloody train back on her own. She'll sell the Laura Ashleys if she hasn't got enough for the blasted fare.

"We can catch the morning ferry," he says, much to her relief.

"Before we go, is there any chance you can show me where Eadie's paintings are stored? I know she'll ask me about them when we get home."

"They're not here. They're at my father's hunting box in Essex."

His father sits in a box to hunt? Brenda doubts she'll ever understand the aristocrats in this country. Too much inbreeding that's for damned sure.

"Does Eadie know that?"

"She does. You fancy a drive out to the oldest pub on the island this afternoon?"

Does she ever! "Just let me change. If I turn up dressed like this, I'll be banned."

Brenda sleeps well that night. A combination of knowing she's escaping purgatory in the morning and a good amount of cider on board and she couldn't stay awake if she tried. Waking the next morning is another story. She bounds out of bed, and is in the bathroom not long after, determined to enjoy plenty of hot water for a shower.

Pulling the curtain over the bath, she turns on the ancient plumbing and waits while the water wends its way up from the ground floor. There's a fair amount of banging of pipes before the water eventually makes its way out of the spout over the bath. Not one to look a gift horse in the mouth, Brenda leaps under it, determined to be in there as long as possible before the cistern gives up the ghost and the water turns icy.

Maybe it's the volume of her singing, but it's not until Julian's yelling at her through the shower curtain that she hears him.

"Sod off, I won't be much longer."

"If I turn the water off now, I should get at least three minutes of hot, if I'm lucky."

Brenda doesn't understand what he's on about, until the water that had been sluicing down her back stops.

"You cheeky bastard. Get out of here!" Brenda turns towards the taps ready to turn them back on again, but Julian's hands are still on top, having foreseen her action.

A sharp rap on his knuckles with a shampoo bottle and he yanks them out of the way but when she turns the taps on, he rips the curtain to the side and wraps it around her where it sticks in place.

Leaving her done up like a kebab, he again turns off the water.

"I need some hot water and while I appreciate you've got more hair than me, I'll be damned if I'm going to suffer another cold shower," he says, indignantly.

If it were anyone else, Brenda would be self-conscious

about standing there only wearing a clingy shower curtain, but given it's Julian, her main concern is finishing her shower. "I've still got conditioner in my hair."

"You should have thought about that before simply standing there for half an hour before you started shampooing it, shouldn't you?"

"What, were you standing outside the sodding door with a stopwatch," she yells, managing to free her arms of the plaster-like qualities of the shower curtain. No sooner has she done this than she pulls the curtain back into place, ready to get the water going again.

But Julian's having none of it. Man, he's peeved.

"Fine, have your sodding shower, I'll rinse off after you've finished."

Brenda wrenches the shower curtain back, steps out of the bath not bothering with a towel and stalks back to her bedroom where she immediately freaks out about dripping all over the expensive carpet. In the end, she uses one of the butt ugly Laura Ashleys to dry herself off, wrapping another around her hair until she can rinse it properly. It's all they're fit for.

The knock at her door is unfailingly polite and for a moment, Brenda thinks it must be Carter, the old chap who takes care of everything around the manor house. It's for this reason only that she opens the door just wide enough to peek through. It's Julian and he's washed and dressed.

"It's all yours," he says, pointing in the direction of the bathroom.

"Thanks a bundle," says Brenda, throwing the door wide and marching buck-naked across the hall and into the tiled room. She is not looking forward to rinsing off in freezing cold water, knowing from experience it'll have her nips hard enough to take out someone's eye.

Yep, the temperature is every bit as arctic as she's been expecting, although yelling, screaming and cursing does make it more bearable but she stays under its icy embrace for no longer than necessary. After wringing the worst of the water out of her hair, she puts her hand above her head to grab a towel to find the shelf empty.

"For god's sake." Not only had that tosser used the last of the hot water, he's nicked the last towel. Good bloody job they're returning to the city this morning, she's ready to do him some harm.

An image of hitting him repeatedly with a handbag pops up, with him retaliating in kind and it's enough for her to go from blinding anger to laughing. In between the occasional titter, she dries herself as well as she can with the hand towel before checking if the way is clear and returning to her bedroom with the occasional guffaw accompanying her.

The trip back to London is as cold as her shower had been that morning and Brenda chooses to stay in the van for the forty-five-minute ferry ride to Portsmouth. After that, she feigns sleep rather than openly ignore Julian.

The first thing she intends to do on getting home is to have another shower. Even standing under the freezing water for as long as she could stand it hasn't rid her hair of that slimy feeling only made possible by leftover conditioner.

Without bags to weigh her down, she's out of the van a second after Julian's pulled on the handbrake. He hadn't been able to pull into the driveway because of Chris's Combi van. Leaving him locking the van, she marches up the front path, opens the door and is upstairs in seconds. She doesn't even bother looking for Eadie to say hi.

She feels so much better after a proper rinse, that walking back downstairs in search of Eadie, she's feeling positively chipper. She never wants to go to the country again. Ever. First port of call is Eadie's sitting room, but the old lady isn't there and neither is she in her bedroom.

Now that she thinks about it, Sam and Chris hadn't been upstairs either. Opening the kitchen door, her gaze is met by those of Mark and Jennie, Sam and Chris, as well as Eadie, Stef, Bert and Flo. None of them are smiling; it's more like a sitting of the Privy Council than afternoon tea.

Screw it all, what now? "What gives?"

"We need to talk," says Mark, his tone as no-nonsense as his expression.

Brenda looks at Eadie for a clue as to what it's all about, but she looks to be as pissed off as her nephew, leaving her worrying that she's done something that she's not aware of.

"Okay, spill it." Brenda folds her arms and leans against the side of the fridge, ready to leave at a moment's notice if needs be.

Eadie picks up on this. "Don't fret, this isn't about you."

"Thank god for that. I thought I'd screwed up."

No longer in the crosshairs, she takes the only empty seat at the table, thankful that with Paula having 'popped over to the continent' and Rosie down in the depths of Cornwall on an official visit to the 'family pile', that there's actually a spare available.

"What's up," she says, around a mouthful of homemade biscuit.

"The police were here earlier," says Mark.

If Eadie hadn't said that this wasn't about her, the Brenda of old would have been legging it by now. Not that she would have been able to get out the kitchen with the doorway, now full of Julian. There's a pause in proceedings while he's introduced to the four recently back from Italy, and then Mark starts up again.

"They wanted to speak to Eadie about swindling money out of Wallace Shit-Brown."

"What? How the hell do they figure Eadie is the one at fault here?"

"Friends in high places," says Eadie, positively vibrating with anger. She spits out "Effing bastards," and Brenda understands how angry her mentor is. "Yes. They had a search warrant and the fact they knew about the hidden dungeon at the back of the cellar clearly points to Wallace putting them up to it."

"Dungeon?" say the four recent returnees, horror evident on their faces.

"Never mind," says Eadie, waving her hand airily about, "nothing to concern yourselves with. Go on Mark."

"Shit," Mark shakes his head slowly to compose himself. "Yeah, well anyway, they ripped the place to bits and couldn't find a damned thing. From what I overhead, they were looking for some files."

"They didn't mention the paintings?" says Julian, saving Brenda the trouble.

"No," says Eadie, "he can hardly accuse me of stealing my own paintings, especially when there's no record of him ever having bought them."

"Where to from here?" says Brenda, looking at Mark, who's appointed himself chairman of the board.

"Not much the cops can do now. No evidence means they haven't got a case for Eadie to answer."

"I wouldn't be so sure about that," says Julian, no longer leaning back against the doorframe. With all eyes on him, he continues. "It wouldn't be the first time Wallace and his ilk had manufactured evidence to support their case."

"Just who the hell are you again?" says Mark, twisting around in his seat so he can eyeball Julian.

"And if you tap the side of your bloody nose like you usually do," says Brenda, also eyeballing him, "I'll deck you!"

"It doesn't matter who I am, what matters is what you're

going to do about the Wallace situation," he says, neatly avoiding the question.

"How about we give him a taste of his own medicine?" says Jennie, surprising the hell out of Brenda.

Living in Italy and being shagged around the clock by someone like Mark must have loosened her up a bit, although the air of nun still hangs about her. True, she'd retaliated on Rupert Smythe-Brown after a lot of prompting from Brenda, but surely that was a one-off?

"What have you got in mind?" says Sam, who Brenda knows from experience is all for revenge if it suits her.

"I'm presuming you have the files safe somewhere?" Jennie looks first at Brenda and then Julian.

Brenda isn't exactly sure where in the manor house Julian had stuffed the bloody things but confirms they're safe in tandem with him.

"Right, we need pen and paper."

It's dark before they've hashed out a rough plan. Bert had offered his stool to Julian, but he was having none of it and had instead gone and grabbed a chair from the dining room. It's only after all the biscuits are demolished and Chris's stomach gives a loud and long gurgle that they see it's gone nine.

"That explains why I'm so bloody hungry," says Brenda.

Flo gives Bert a good whack on the arm, looking pointedly at the stove.

"Who fancies a fry up?" he says, getting to his feet, all the while rubbing his hands together with relish. The man does love to fry things in lashings of lard and tonight he's got a captive and willing audience with everyone yelling out "Me!" There are even hands held aloft.

It's while they're carving their way through their meal, that

Sam's head pops up from concentrating on her bacon and eggs. She stares through the back windows and out into the garden, before shaking her head and going back to cutting up a piece of bacon.

"What?" says Brenda, looking at the backyard rather than Sam.

"Nothing. I'm imagining things."

Julian, who's next to Mark at the end of the table away from the back windows, doesn't say a thing, and instead eases off his chair and onto the ground rather than stand and risk being seen. "You fancy a hunting trip," he says to Mark, who, to give him credit, catches on quickly.

"You want me along?" says Chris from his spot near the windows.

"Best you stay there," says Julian. "If you move it might be too obvious to our unwanted guest."

Mark and Julian adopt stealth mode, sneaking through the kitchen door towards the front of the house where, presumably, they'll go outside and around the back so they can take their visitor by surprise.

Despite the seriousness of the situation, it's all Brenda can do not to laugh and eventually she loses the battle and guffaws loudly.

"What's going on?" says Eadie, her back to the windows. "I don't dare turn around."

"Nothing happening out there so far, what I'm laughing about is this lot opposite me."

Three pairs of eyes swivel back in her direction. "What?" says Chris.

"It's looking at the three of you with your eyes so skewed to the side that you must be looking out through your ears," says Brenda, through small outbursts of the giggles.

Before they can defend themselves, there's a loud knock on

the back windows; all of them levitate in their seats for a fraction of a second.

Eadie looks pale and has a hand over the region of her heart.

Brenda looks at her with concern. "Are you okay? Bastards scared the crap out of me."

"I'll be fine, I might just need a small drink to calm my nerves."

"Good as done," says Flo, already heading to the cellar for the top-up flagon.

There's more knocking on the back windows, although more controlled this time. Obviously, they haven't moved fast enough for the jailors outside with their captive. Chris hops up and opens the back door and Julian and Mark drag their prize inside as though they've won the Pools.

"You know this sorry piece of shit?" says Mark to Eadie, holding their captive's chin so he can spin it in Eadie's direction for better viewing.

"Good god, you're still alive?" says Eadie, confirming she knows who it is. "Bit long in the tooth for this malarkey aren't you, Maxwell?"

On face value, Brenda would have to agree with Eadie. The guy looks ancient, even borderline cadaverous and better suited to being at home with cocoa than skulking around in the middle of the night.

He doesn't respond to Eadie's questions, until he's given a good shaking by Julian and Mark. Even then, they don't get a lot of sense out of him no matter how loudly they shout their questions at him.

"At least we don't need to worry about him overhearing anything," says Jennie, spotting what the others haven't.

"Whatcha mean?" says Brenda.

"Flo, try banging a pot loudly right behind his head," she says, rather than answer.

The chief cleaner and bottle washer does as she suggests and is rewarded by both Julian and Mark yanking their heads away from the din, unable to cover their ears. The old bloke's only reaction is to continue standing there looking miserable.

"Check he doesn't have a recorder on him," says Sam.

They do and he does and it's still recording. Not that it carries on once Bert grabs it and tosses it in the dirty frying pan where it slowly sinks into the still cooling fat. Bugger, Brenda wouldn't have minded listening to it to see what was on there, in case there was something before he started recording them.

"Sorry mate, but you're going to have to stay right here until we get our plan underway," says Mark, for all the good it does. In the end, he writes it out and shows it to the old chap.

Rather than look upset about it, he's happy. Relieved even.

That is, until he sees the dungeon, then he kicks up such a ruckus that it's decided to lock him in the common room on the second floor with a bucket and a few blankets. Bert even fixes him something to eat and a hot drink, meaning never has a captive been so happy.

34

The next night, the chap Wallace sends is younger and one not known to Eadie. He's fitter and stronger than Maxwell, their new addition to the household, and it takes the combined abilities of Chris, Mark and Julian to take him down. Even Bert gets in on the act, kneeling on the captive's back until they have him safely trussed up like a pig. This image is particularly strong after Bert shoves an apple in the bloke's mouth to stop the string of invective directed at them.

This is only removed to force-feed him a sandwich made with butter laced with a couple of Eadie's painkillers. After that, he sleeps like a baby and they're able to load him into the Combi. With him comatose, Brenda, Sam and Jennie all clamour to be taken on the outing, too.

"Come on, we can take care of ourselves," wheedles Sam.

Jennie doesn't voice her plea, but her request is evident in the way she's looking at Mark. He buckles and the three girls seize the opportunity and pile into the back of the van before Chris or Julian can voice any objections. Wallace's latest emissary takes up most of the floor space so they have to step on him to get themselves onto the seat folded out to form a bed.

Meanwhile, Chris is driving, Mark's in the passenger seat, and Julian's jammed in the middle. He must be in heaven right now, sandwiched between the other two, not that he's obvious about it.

"What are we going to do with him?" says Brenda, already running through options in her head. Stripping him is obvious. But what else?

"Same as the last guy," says Chris, looking over his shoulder to check if the way is clear before he backs out of the driveway. "We'll dump him somewhere near a pub so that anyone finding him will assume he's passed out from too much booze."

"What? Where's the bloody fun in that? Isn't it about time we sent that prick Shit-Brown a message."

"She's right," says Sam, "It won't interfere with the plan."

Although not voicing her agreement, Jennie has a slow nod going on.

Stopping the Combi after backing it out on the street, Chris puts it into first and pulls forward, only to stop again next to the curb. "What do you guys think?"

"If we go about it the right way, it'll let S-B know we aren't taking it lying down, but won't ruin the set up for the sting," says Julian, his tone vague, as though he's still going through the implications in his mind.

"Screw it, let's deal with the prick," says Mark, to whoops from his cheer squad in the back.

"You want us to strip him now?" offers Brenda.

"It'll save time down at Turnham Green," says Sam.

Jennie pulls her feet up onto the bed, well away from any potentially squidgy bits.

"Turnham Green?" says Chris, pulling out onto the road. "Why there?"

"There's a LOT of fence to tie him to," says Brenda, as if speaking to a child.

Chris doesn't argue the point, but they know he's bought

into this plan when he steers in the direction of open ground in the middle of Chiswick.

"High Street side," says Brenda, when he's about to pull up on the quieter side of the Green.

"Is that wise?" says Julian, "the fewer people who see us, the better."

"Stuff it, if anyone asks what's going on, act drunk and say it's a stag do," says Brenda.

"Sounds good to me." Mark receives more cheers although these are interspersed with grunts as Sam and Brenda work to relieve their captive of his clothes. It's a lot harder than stripping a willing victim. Almost as hard is untying the ropes. Shame Stef hadn't been home tonight, she was a whiz at the quick-release knot following some serious study of an old Boy Scouts handbook Eadie had given her.

He's so floppy!

Everywhere, it would seem when they finally relieve him of his underpants. Those anti-inflammatories do what they say on the bottle, thinks Brenda, before sniggering to herself.

"What can you possibly find funny about this," says Jennie, from atop her high horse.

Brenda points at the guy's family jewels and simply says, "Anti-inflammatories. Get it?"

Jennie does, but rather than get frostier as Brenda's expected, she giggles and soon the three of them are laughing so hard their eyes are watering and they have to hold their sides. They hardly notice when the boys open the side door ready to drag sleeping beauty out and onto the footpath.

Mark tries to move the guy but drops him back down again. "Jeez, he's a heavy bastard."

"We should tie him in place in the bus shelter," says Julian.

"Where's the bloody fun in that?" says Brenda, sensing her entertainment is about to be curtailed. "Not enough people will be able to gawp if we shove him in there."

"Also less chance of him suffering from hypothermia and ending up seriously ill," says Julian.

"It's not that cold," says Sam, rubbing her bare arms.

"It is if you're naked and sitting on concrete," says Julian, emphatically.

"He's got a point," says Chris. "If we do the guy some serious harm it could come back and bite us on the arse."

"Fine." Brenda folds her arms and taps her foot on the back of the guy's head. "Fine."

Chris restarts the engine and they move slowly along until they're right at the bus stop; Julian and Mark walked alongside. The naked thug is dragged out from the back of the van and into the bus shelter in double quick time. Meanwhile, Chris moves the van out of the stop before a double-decker rolls up.

With the creeper all tied up tickety-boo, Sam nips back into the van and grabs the Polaroid camera, taking three good photos before they leave him sitting there starkers and at his ease in the middle of the slatted wooden seat more commonly used by those waiting for the bus to Richmond.

Not until they're safely rattling down Chiswick High Street, do the girls talk again, although with all of them talking at once, it's impossible to make any sense out of it.

"Stow it!" yells Mark, at such a volume that they all stop mid-sentence. "Let's discuss it when we get home, Eadie will want to be in on it all."

Before they've travelled the short distance home, the three girls are fit to explode. Sam, in particular, is having a tough time and has even taken to using sign language. That is until Chris sees her in the rear-view mirror and *tsk-tsks* stopping her mid-gesture.

Eadie's still sitting at the head of the table when they tumble back into the kitchen en masse with the girls talking over each other a second after the swinging door has stilled.

"One at a time, one at a time," says Eadie, holding her hand up like a cop on traffic duty. "Brenda, off you go."

Before she can, Brenda has to stop laughing at the expression on Sam's face over not being the one to talk first. Jeez, that girl can be such a motor mouth.

"Right. We stripped him and tied him to the bench at that bus stop next to Turnham Green. Sam's taken photos. A letter to Wallace is in order."

Brenda sits down and relaxes, confident that her plan is a good one but this conviction is scuppered when Eadie, Chris, Julian and Mark all yell "No!" to her suggestion.

"Why not," she says, crossing her arms, and frowning.

"Because, antagonising Wallace any further at this stage isn't a good idea. We've survived one visit from the police and I, for one, don't want to endure some pimply youth in a uniform rummaging through my underwear drawer, ever again," says Eadie.

"Are you serious?" says Brenda, who hadn't realised the extent of the search. "Did they go through my stuff like that?"

"They would have," says Mark, laughing and continuing to do so, until he's laughing so hard he can't speak.

"Charlie stopped them in their tracks," says Jennie, also smirking. "He was lying in the middle of your bed when they went into your room but rather than attack them, he stayed exactly where he was, just did that deep growl in the back of his throat. The cops gave him a wide berth after that."

Mark, back under control, continues, "It wasn't until they left that he got up and we saw he'd been lying on a notebook with your name on the front."

"Bloody hell, if they'd got their mitts on that we would've been screwed," says Brenda, a fine sheen of sweat popping up on her forehead.

Thinking back to what she's written in there, well, the consequences didn't bear thinking about. But, hang on?

"What about the plan I'd written out for us retrieving the paintings? How come they missed that?" Brenda tries hard to remember where she'd last seen it.

"Because I still had it on my bedside cabinet from that night," says Eadie. "Soon as I heard it was the police I popped it inside my nightgown."

"Your nightgown? What time did they arrive?" says Brenda, wondering if it was early or late.

"Bloody six in the sodding morning," says Mark, still manifestly peeved about being rudely awoken. "It took us bleeding hours to find all the bugs they'd left behind."

"Bugs?" says Julian, his brow creased with worry. "Are you sure?"

"Yep," says Mark, getting to his feet and retrieving an ice cream container from the freezer. He places it on the table and peels the top back to reveal a solid block of ice with a lot of small metal devices frozen in its depths. "We put them on ice."

Lame as his joke is, it gets a good amount of laughter.

"You sure you got all of them?" says Julian, stopping the laughter dead.

Only after he gives the house a good going over, and returns with a couple more bugs sitting in a glass of water, do they relax. These join their counterparts deep inside the freezer.

"Where were they?" says Sam.

"Sewing room and the studio at the top of the house."

"Thank the stars for that," says Eadie.

"Might pay to avoid using the phone for the time being," says Julian, regaining his seat.

"We are so getting even with that arsehole for this," says Brenda.

It takes a good week to finalise the details of the plan and put everything in place. The plan is simple like all good plans, but timing will be everything and so when it becomes apparent the bait they plan on using is busy at his constituency, toadying up to the voting public, they need to delay everything for a couple of days.

It hadn't been difficult to decide on the tastiest morsel to dangle in front of the parliamentary security team, with the file held on Findus Bleakly being the fattest one of all, like that exemplar of ethics himself. If Wallace's notes are to be believed, the Conservative member for Croydon East couldn't get enough of someone in a corset thrashing the living daylights out of him. No preferences on what sex either, with him happy to be tied up and spanked by whoever was willing. He'll be putty in Stef's hands. Well, at least bits of him will be.

Wallace was asking after you tonight," says Stef, putting her head around Brenda's bedroom door on her way up to bed. "Grilled me on what the 'ell happened after 'e passed out, before being taken away in an ambulance, 'a broken man'."

"Broken? In pain, for sure, but hardly broken according to our pet ambo, Barry."

"Been developments on that front, too. Word on the loading bay at the hospital is that Wallace's old fella took a beating all right and it couldn't hack it."

She follows this up by pantomiming herself snapping a twig.

"Ouch," sniggers out Brenda. "I'd have loved to see them trying to put that in plaster!"

Only once Stef stops laughing does she continue with her story. "Yeah, you an' me both. 'E kept asking me what I knew about 'is 'unfortunate accident', but I played the dumb card and said I hadn't even realised 'e was there that night. 'E still wouldn't leave it, so I accused 'im of being a peeping tom. 'E shut up after that."

"How did you get on with Findus?"

"Piece a cake. All I 'ad to do was 'ave him overhear me talking to Paula about the chaps in London not being able to take a good whipping. 'E was all over me like a rash after that, practically begging for it."

"How can you be sure he'll use the Playpen?" says Brenda, absently smoothing her hand over the top of Charlie's head.

"Didn't give 'im no choice. Told 'im I liked the Playpen because of the rack. It was a doddle after that. I've said Saturday night is the only night I'm free, so that'll give 'im time to arrange it with Wallace.

Stef goes on to explain that after plying him with drinks and whispering what she planned on doing to him on Saturday night, he'd told her they'd have to be circumspect as he'd nearly been caught last time and a chap with a reputation like his couldn't be too careful. "Stupid arse, telling me that. Just asking to get 'imself blackmailed."

"So how come he ended up being carried out with Wallace?"

"Apparently he knew Wallace was 'eading out of town for a coupla days and so 'e planned on visiting the Playpen on the sly. 'E was standing in front of Wallace, wondering what to do when Barry's lot arrived, so 'e faked passing out, and told 'em he didn't know where 'e was when 'e 'came to' after they dropped 'im on the front steps. Lucky for 'im, 'e still had 'is kit on and 'is dom 'adn't arrived, else 'e'd have had some s'plaining to do. 'E still thinks Wallace was writhing in ecstasy."

Brenda watches Jennie make short work of producing the two ransom notes the following morning, even hampered as she is by the washing-up gloves she's wearing to avoid fingerprints. While she might be safe from leaving evidence, the gloves are on the big side, making her less than dexterous, resulting in a couple of the letters she's cut out of the newspaper ending up stuck to them.

Finished with the second note, she has a good go at trying to get the letters off the pink gloves, but in the end simply stuffs them into a large brown paper bag along with the decimated newspapers. The glue she's used is her own recipe and Brenda, who's been watching her friend construct the notes, knows from experience it's capable of mounting a Hooray Henry securely to a gallery window for the duration and so there's no way a couple of bits of newspaper will be a challenge.

Jennie rolls the top of the paper bag shut tight and hands it to Bert who immediately heads outside to burn it in the large rusting drum that sits forlornly at the end of the garden. This makeshift incinerator is already full to the brim with dry leaves and garden waste, so he has a blazing fire going in a jiffy. The flames bursting out of the rusty sides of the drum mean Bert has to constantly move farther and farther away to avoid cooking his bits.

With the fiery display over, Jennie picks up the notes by their corners using eyebrow tweezers. "I'll put these in the studio until they're dry. Any more cops drop by and one of us will need to beat them to the top of the house and flush them pronto."

"How long before they're dry enough?"

"Should be fine to fold and put in envelopes in the morning ready for Julian to deliver."

Brenda's still nervous about the final destinations for those two missives.

35

L ater that day, Brenda wanders into the kitchen to make
yet another cup of tea. Never mind turning Japanese, as
steeped in tea as she is after so many days lying low, she's
feeling decidedly English. She has even suggested this pot of
tea to Eadie, rather than the other way around.

Flo's the only one in the kitchen, sitting perched on her bar
stool. "What on earth are you doing?"

What's different this time, is that rather than the stool being
next to the kitchen bench as is the norm, it's smack bang in
front of the door leading down to the cellar. There's also something no-nonsense about the way the char's got her skinny
arms crossed high over her chest, as though she's trying to look
staunch and bigger than she is.

"Julian's set up a darkroom downstairs. I'm his red light."

Brenda confirms her understanding of this random
comment.

"He say what he's developing?" Brenda's got a fairly good
idea if the threat he'd made to the bank manager is for real.

"No, but he grabbed a lot of kitchen stuff before he went
down there. Bert's helping him," says Flo, looking over her

shoulder to the closed door. "Said if Julian was using his tools of trade, he needed to keep an eye on them."

The fresh pot of tea forgotten, Brenda takes a seat at the table where she waits for the 'red light' to officially be turned off, allowing her to grill Julian on what film it is he's been developing down there.

In the end, simply waiting for Flo to move proves more boring than hours of reading and tea drinking, so Brenda gets on with making the cuppa that Eadie must surely be wondering about. Either that or the old lady will have given up and moved on to pouring herself a large sherry.

"Shit," says Brenda, dropping the teapot on the counter, making Flo bounce on her bar stool.

"If I've left her this long, she'll be close to having the decanter over again."

"Go, go!" says Flo, unfolding her arms long enough to flap her hand in the general direction of Eadie's sitting room. "That stuff's the dickens to get out of the carpet."

Brenda makes it through to the sitting room, but only just in time. Eadie is on her feet, her frail grasp attempting to choke the neck of the decanter.

"I'll sort that for you," she says, fighting to keep her tone light. The decanter is close to full and Eadie's grasp around the neck looks tenuous at best.

Returning to the kitchen, she finds Flo and her bar stool are back next to the kitchen counter and Julian is carefully laying two black and white photos out on top of the kitchen counter where they join a couple of dozen others.

"Shouldn't they still be hanging up?" says Brenda, understanding at least the rudiments of developing photos from watching spy movies.

"Dry enough if I'm careful. Wanted to have another quick read through this lot before tomorrow."

Brenda only needs to look at them briefly to confirm her suspicions. "When did you take these?"

"I figured while it was safe to have the original files at the manor on the Isle, it'd be handy to have some reference with us here in town. I photographed the lot while we were down there."

She bends over so she can examine the photo more closely. "But there have to be more photos than this."

"There are, these are Findus Bleakly's notes."

"But you've still got your other negatives of the other files, right?"

"Safe and sound!" Julian's tone is so emphatic that it negates any further discussion.

Well, that's what he thinks, Brenda could chew over the subject for hours, but she leaves it, for now.

"Will they be dry soon?" says Bert, already filling the sink with hot soapy water in readiness to wash the odd assortment of kitchen paraphernalia stacked on the other side to Julian's impromptu photo display. "I need to get dinner under way."

"They're dry enough that I can move them upstairs. Brenda, you want to give me a hand?"

Without waiting for her to respond, he slides his hands under two of the slightly curved photos before leaving the kitchen, moving slowly with his precarious cargo. Brenda waits for the swinging kitchen door to get itself under control before she picks up another two in similar fashion. It's not until she moves that she twigs why he was walking so slowly. Any faster risks the photos floating to the ground. Jeez, this is going to take bloody ages.

Picking up the last photos from the kitchen table they take them up and lay them carefully on Julian's bed, Bert is all but hopping from foot to foot in his desire to get on with preparing dinner, a roast being on the menu tonight.

Not that Brenda's got much of an appetite.

As if by unspoken decree, one by one, everyone trails into the dining room with the boys even having to fit an extra leaf in the table to accommodate them all. The only people missing from this final council of war are Bert and Flo who are finishing the dinner.

This leaves Eadie, Sam and Chris, Jennie and Mark, Stef, Julian and Brenda sitting around the polished mahogany. Stef is the last to arrive, announcing triumphantly that Findus Blakely had confirmed he's booked the Playpen for the following evening.

"His double chins positively jiggled with the excitement of it all," she says, with revolted groans from the table in response. "An' he lives in Knightsbridge."

"Whereabouts," says Sam, leaning forward in her chair.

Jennie is also poised on the edge of her seat.

"Hang on, I wrote it down."

She retrieves a dog-eared scrap of paper from the back pocket of her Lurex trousers and hands it to Sam without bothering to look at it herself.

"The Maidstone." Sam examines the note, flattens it out, and continues as though reading is a newly acquired skill. "Cliveden Place." Any hesitancy on her part vanishes a second later. "Countess Harrow! He lives close to Countess Harrow."

"That old trout?" Resorting to calling the woman names says a lot about how peeved Jennie still is.

However, Eadie brightens considerably at this news. "Of course, Bunty's place."

"Who?" says Brenda, looking at the three of them, with her question getting support from the others, who are as much in the dark as she is.

"Countess Harrow is one of my clients," says Sam. "Got a purple poodle called Quincey who dresses better than she does."

"She's also Rupert Smythe-Brown's auntie," says Jennie.

"And Wallace's sister," adds Eadie, with what can only be described as glee.

"Don't you remember her standing in front of Rupert to cover his, ah, bits, the night of his exhibition?" says Jennie. Brenda still looks baffled. "He was glued him to the outside of the gallery's front window at the time?"

"Oh, right," says Brenda, comprehension at last dawning. "I was outside, looking at his arse flapping in the breeze, so I missed all that."

"So," says Julian, drawing this single word out long enough to get everyone's attention, "what you're saying is that Findus lives near someone known to you."

"Yes!" cry Eadie, Jennie and Sam in unison.

"Would you be able to get access to a phone in that building," he says.

"Of course," says Eadie, at the same time as Sam and Jennie shake their heads.

"That could work," says Mark, grasping what Julian is only hinting at.

Even Chris is in agreement.

Eadie's nutted out a solution a second later. "I'll drop by unannounced and take a bottle of the good stuff. Bunty likes a tipple in the afternoon and she'd never turn me away if I'm bearing gifts."

"Even after what happened to Rupert because of me?" says Jennie, her gaze firmly locked on the placemat in front of her.

"Bunty likes a drink a lot more than that," says Eadie, confidently. "And if she's still cut up about it, I'll say I'm there to apologise."

"Jeez, you do want to get even with Wallace, don't you?" says Brenda.

"You don't know the half of it," mutters Eadie.

They look at each other, not sure what to do next, but Julian fills the void, by insisting they need to go through the plan again, amending it to allow for this new development and ensuring they've ironed out any other wrinkles. He keeps them at it with all the aplomb of a drill sergeant until everyone can answer his rapid-fire questions without hesitation and Brenda's stomach is a swirling pit of acid.

It's one thing doping the bastard and giving him a jolly good thrashing, quite another thing setting him up to be arrested for extortion and fraud. Even if the bastard is guilty as charged. The plan they've spent the evening fine-tuning involves far too much contact with people who carry badges as part of their job for her to feel truly comfortable.

Brenda waits until the others have left before voicing her concerns to Eadie.

"Don't let it bother you," says Eadie, her words slurred from one too many post-prandial ports. "He's had it coming a long time and there are those in power who've been itching to see him get his just desserts."

"It's not just you itching for revenge?"

Eadie's eyebrows loft indignantly and her feathers ruffle before she says, "Most definitely not!" All trace of a slur is gone.

"Okay, okay, I just wanted to make sure."

Brenda waits for Eadie to calm down before saying, "Any chance I could have a half of one of those anti-flams of yours? I doubt I'll get much sleep tonight without it."

Half an hour after taking something pink that Eadie had said was equally as good, and it's all Brenda can do to get her sorry self upstairs to bed. While she's feeling dead on her feet, she's also got the strangest urge to sing.

'Waterloo' by Abba of all things.

She doesn't realise she's given into this urge until she hears hammering on her bedroom door. That's weird. She doesn't remember walking into her room, or getting into bed. And where Charlie? He's usually glued to her side for most of the night.

"Come in," she sings out, only then noticing the overhead light is still on. Huh, weirder still.

She's still staring at it when her door opens and Julian walks in. He's right next to her bed before she thinks to look at him. His eyes appear scoured, and he's looking grumpy, although he's as beautifully turned out as always, this time in pyjamas and a silk dressing gown. Even stranger than him turning up in her bedroom like this, is that Sam and Chris are right behind him.

"What is wrong with you?" says Julian, leaning over and peering at her in such a way that his image shimmers.

Brenda doesn't answer him right away; she's too busy wondering why he's gone all fuzzy. "You have such a gorgeous body, shame you're gay." The words leave her mouth of their own volition. Brenda smiles, pleased they came out properly, given her voice isn't fully under her control.

"Stone the crows," says Sam, moving forward, "or just plain stoned."

"I'll put some coffee on," says Chris.

"I wouldn't bother," says Julian, chuckling, "that only works with alcohol."

Brenda's eyes close and she's going back under when she hears the three of them talking out on the landing. "Why is she under the impression you're gay?" says Chris.

Sam backs him up. "Yeah, why is that?"

Even falling asleep as she is, Brenda's aware of the suspicion in Sam's voice.

Julian says something in answer, and she wants to hear what he says but is unable to resist the dreams any longer.

The next day, Brenda can't believe what a good night's sleep she's had all thanks to that little pink pill Eadie had given her.

She feels prepared for the challenges she has to face today. Sure she'd had some weirdo dreams, but no weirder than usual.

"Okay, why is everyone smiling?" she says looking around the kitchen table.

"You don't remember?" says Sam, incredulous.

"What?" says Brenda, looking at her and then Chris and Julian, who are the only others at the table.

"You were quite the dancing queen last night," says Chris.

"Stop yanking my chain, you guys."

Julian doesn't say anything, simply looks at her, speculating; she feels something that's familiar and unfamiliar in turn. She doesn't like it.

There's not much for any of them to do for the rest of the day with everything scheduled to happen from late afternoon onwards. It makes for a long day and Brenda gets twitchier and twitchier by the second. For one thing, she's not keen on seeing Wallace Smythe-Brown that evening: there's no way of knowing how he'll react to her story of what happened that night. It's plausible, but will he buy it? There's also the niggling worry that she's missed something. That they all have.

"For goodness sake, will you stop jiggling about and go for a walk or something," says Eadie, without looking up from the book in her lap.

Brenda stills, not realizing she's been fidgeting. It's as though her body is full of ants trying to escape so they can get at Eadie's sherry. Maybe a walk would be good. Mind you, a marathon would be more effective.

"You're right. It's driving me nuts lying around here waiting for kick off."

Glad to have a plan of action, Brenda slams her book down on the coffee table, causing Eadie to flinch and spill her sherry.

"Sorry, I'll get a cloth."

"Get Flo and get yourself out of here."

Brenda's zipping up her jacket when Julian walks down the stairs. By the looks of his mussed hair, he's been asleep. His eyes have that just woken up look about them.

He pauses on the final step. "Where are you going?"

"For a walk, I've got cabin fever."

Her hand is on the doorknob when he announces he'll join her.

She's not sure how she feels about this. There's something about him that's bugged her all day, but she's damned if she can work out what it is. Having him along might have her discovering what it is.

They're not even at the end of the street before she finds out.

36

They're outside the church on the corner of their street, when Julian drops his bombshell and Brenda doesn't so much stop, as freeze.

But not for long.

The haymaker she aims at his head only misses because of his quick reactions.

"You bastard!"

"Come on, it's not that bad," he says, holding onto her fists, to stop her having a second go. "I've only seen you naked once. No, hang on, make that three times."

A frantic search of her memory and she can only come up with two occasions and both of those were on the Isle of Wight.

"Twice at my parents' place and again last night. I don't know what Eadie gave you but you were off your chops."

Keeping hold of one of her hands, Julian urges her on and she stomps alongside him, taking out her anger on the pavement. She's never been sucked in by a guy like this before. What the hell happened to her being able to spot a gay at twenty paces? She could have sworn he was at most playing for both teams, but to find out he's straight is a shock, especially feeling on edge as she is today.

It's only when she's sure her words won't all be profanities that she says, "So what the hell are you?"

"Um. Straight, 33-years-old, own teeth, dress to the right," says Julian, his eyes alight with laughter when he turns to look at her.

"No, not that. Are you a cop or what? Because that's the only reason I can see for this whole charade."

He doesn't answer and so she stops in her tracks, jerking hard on his hand to get him to do the same, forcing him to turn in her direction.

"I'll say it again, what the hell are you?" This time, if he doesn't give her a direct answer, she'll smack him so hard, he'll see stars.

It must be something that shows on her face, because after a heavy sigh, he brings her up to date.

"So, you are a sodding cop!" her tone is stridently fishwife in nature, her hands on her hips merely reinforce how hacked off she is.

"No! I WAS a cop!" says Julian, riled himself. "I got sick of seeing bad people getting off because of good lawyers and so I threw it in."

"To do what?" Brenda taps her foot to hurry him along, but now the dam's broken, he's no longer reticent.

"Private security. I put the skills I learnt on the force to use, I work fewer hours and I make more money."

Begrudgingly she acknowledges that it's a work ethic she could embrace.

"Who are you working for now?"

In a flash, he's cagey again, so she starts guessing, throwing names at him all the while looking closely for a reaction. But, as on previous occasions, the guy's poker face is well and truly in place and no matter what she says, his demeanour doesn't waver.

Stumped, she walks in small circles around him while working through various scenarios in her head. She'd thought the files he'd taken that afternoon in Wallace's library were something to do with Genevieve and her dear departed husband. What if it was the dirt on some sucker who simply had a penchant for being racked and spanked on a regular basis?

"Tory or Labour," says Brenda, knowing it has to be one or the other because that had been clearly marked on every file she and Stef had skimmed through that night in the common room.

"Does it matter?"

Brenda completes a couple more circuits of him. "I guess not."

"So we're okay?"

"We will be when you back-pay a rent increase for the time you've been staying with Eadie."

He doesn't quibble, or even ask the sum, confirming the file holder is paying him a bloody shedload. Although he does wince when she simply says, "Double quadruple, whatever that's called," before swinging wide in yet another circuit around him and heading back to the house. It's as well he's behind her because this way, she doesn't have to smother the wide grin she's enjoying at his expense.

Unlike the inertia of earlier in the day, from mid-afternoon onwards, the house is in an uproar, with all of them going out that evening, in one form or another. There are fights over who gets to use the shower first, outfits to check and recheck and last minute discussions. Brenda relishes this chaos as it takes her mind off Julian's revelations of earlier in the day. She hasn't said anything to anyone about them since coming home. This isn't because Julian has said not to, but that to discuss it with someone else would mean her having to face it more fully than she does by ruminating on it all afternoon.

Julian is the first to announce his departure. He does this from outside Brenda's room so that she knows and, after pulling her sleeve down to form a glove of sorts, she picks up the two envelopes sitting innocuously on her bedside table and carries them out into the hall.

"You sure you're good to deliver these?" she says, holding the ransom notes out towards him. After drying properly overnight, they're safely stowed in no-frills envelopes, wiped for prints.

He nods briefly and then takes the envelopes from her and slides one each into the front pockets on his tweed jacket. He doesn't need to be as careful as she has because he's wearing black leather gloves, of the kind with a big hole on the back of the hand and smaller ones over his knuckles. Even for him, today's ensemble is conservative, but neither will he stand out. Brenda suspects his clothing choice is specifically designed to blend; in certain parts of the city, it would be hard to tell him from hundreds of others.

He picks up the canvas holdall sitting at his feet and is off down the stairs. He's not using the van for this particular delivery; instead, he leaves it parked in front of the house and walks briskly towards the tube station. He hasn't told them where he's dropping off the notes and knowing what she does about him now, part of Brenda doesn't want to know anymore. He's assured her he knows exactly which department and which desk to leave it on and in such a way the cops will be none the wiser who dropped it off. As to who is destined to receive the other ransom note at SO6, it's all too MI5 for Brenda to even contemplate.

She's torn between relief that he knows what he's about, and worry that he knows what he's about. He's still too cop-like for her to fully relax and all this insider knowledge of his doesn't sit well with her, at all. While she's waiting for the other shoe to fall or the pigs to turn up, or whatever else could go wrong, she and Sam go through Eadie's script with her one more time. The call she'll make to the cops has to be specific in its wording and the last thing they want is for Eadie to deviate and leave them up shit creek without a paddle. For all that Brenda loves the old biddy, she can be a handful at times.

———

Eadie frowns at the page of handwritten notes sitting in her lap. "Why do I have to say it like this?"

"Because this way, you can't be done for impersonating someone else," says Sam, who's next to Brenda on the couch. "We know you don't like playing the doddery old lady card, think of it as being a part in a play."

"Yeah, what she says," adds Brenda.

Neither girl says anything further while they wait for Eadie to cave. She finally gives an undignified *humph* before going back to reading her script.

There are several more fits and starts before all three of them are happy with the final composition, with it mostly being Eadie who's had to be talked around. In the end, the script is as close to the original as Brenda could have hoped for. Only thing will be to make sure Eadie sticks to it once she's on the phone, but that's for Mark to do.

37

Eadie's in her usual spot in the sitting room sipping on a sherry young Brenda had poured for her earlier. Where on earth are Jennie and Mark? They should have been down by now and if they take much longer they'll be too late to call on Bunty given her propensity to be out cold by five in the afternoon.

She's working hard to remain calm and composed, if only for appearances sake, while inside she's roiling with emotions that she's successfully kept at bay for over twenty-five years. But, with Wallace's charade so close to being shattered, it's hard for her to keep a lid on things. It would have been so much easier if she could have called from here, but if Julian is right and there is a tap on the phone, then they'd be scuppered for certain. Damn Wallace and his network of old boys.

Hearing someone coming downstairs, she gulps the rest of her sherry, hoping this will have some anaesthetic properties. It works and as the door to the sitting room opens, she feels her usual sense of calm slot back into place.

"All ready," says Jennie, her voice uneven as though she, too, is struggling with nerves.

"I am indeed. If you'd be so kind as to get my green coat from the wardrobe," says Eadie, shuffling forward on her seat in preparation to get slowly to her feet.

Everything she does is slow these days because whenever she moves, her joints feel as though they're smashing and then crunching on broken glass. Even with the worst of the pain kept at bay, courtesy of the ever-stronger pills the doctor doles out like lollies, it's not a pleasant sensation

Jennie helps her into the coat while Mark holds her cane. It's a painfully slow trip out the front door and down the path to the Jag that's parked at the curb as close to the front gate as possible. For all he looks like a thug at times, he's a most courteous boy.

The journey to Knightsbridge is completed in silence, apart from Mark abusing the occasional driver he doesn't feel is adhering to the letter of the law, or his idea of it. He double-parks outside the large brick and soft grey stone building that Eadie hasn't set foot in for many a year. Not that she's been avoiding it as such, but her joints make her a virtual prisoner in her own home. If it weren't for putting that upstart Wallace in his place once and for all, she'd be happy to be at home nursing an aperitif.

Mark slowly pulls the handbrake on and, leaving the engine running, gets out and runs around to Eadie's side to help her out of the car. Meanwhile, Jennie crawls between the front seats and takes her place ready to drive laps of the square to avoid them worrying about finding a parking space. She's pulling away before Eadie and Mark are even halfway up the front steps.

"Just give me a minute," says Eadie, leaning heavily on Mark's arm.

He takes this time to check out the building they're about to enter and Eadie can't help but smile at his muttered, "Bloody huge," although she doubts she's meant to hear.

Her breath caught and the crunching in her joints given enough of a rest to allow her to carry on, she nods a fraction. This is enough for Mark to move on, until they're making their way slowly between the columns guarding the entrance.

"Could you be a dear boy and ring the bell," says Eadie, her head inclined towards a

porcelain button that's surrounded by gleaming brass. He does so and is rewarded by a bell ringing inside.

Not long after there's a Cockney, "Can I 'elp you?" from beside them but down a level causing Mark to look for who's asking.

"We're here to see Countess Harrow," he says, his tone brooking no argument.

"'Ave you got an appointment?" The Cockney voice is now brimful with officious self-importance.

Eadie moves from behind Mark. "Jack, stop messing about and let us in. I haven't seen Bunty in ages and we were passing."

The change in the little twit is immediate, with the suspicion lifting from his gaze, replaced with warm regard. "Eadie Cadwalader, is that you?"

"Well, who else were you expecting? Door, now!"

"Oh, oh, right," he stutters before disappearing inside. Moments later the door opens and he darts to the side to let them enter. "It's so good to see you again," he says, sounding like he genuinely means it.

While she's pleased someone remembers her from the good old days, that he does remember her could prove problematic if push came to shove.

He scoots across the marble-lined foyer in front of them so he can press the button by the lift doors and there they wait. Eadie had forgotten how blasted slow this lift is and it hasn't improved with age. She knows how it feels.

There's rattling from somewhere above them, corroborating that it is indeed moving in their direction although when it will arrive is anyone's guess. She hates waiting like this; there was a time when she would have eschewed the lift and bounded up the stairs two at a time. Not anymore.

After an acutely flat *ding*, the lift doors open slowly as if they're stuck on something. Just what it is becomes apparent and Eadie has to dip her head to hide her smile on hearing the "Bloody hell," that escapes Mark before he can stifle his reaction to the visage before them. The inside of the lift is wall-to-wall Findus Bleakly, although what the repulsive man is doing here, lord knows. The only thing that's obvious is that he's wearing the lift like a straitjacket, so tight is the fit.

If it weren't for the wide overhang of his gut, the lift doors would surely have circumcised him and whoever said stripes were flattering had never seen someone this size decked out in enough pinstriped suiting to swallow three normal-sized chaps. He truly is enormous; poor Stef will have her work cut out for her getting this one safely strapped to the rack. Even with his co-operation.

Despite the fat man squirming and huffing in an effort to free himself, Eadie worries they'll need to resort to a tub of margarine and a tyre iron if the Conservative MP for East Croydon doesn't extricate himself, soon. After a particularly valiant struggle, he wrenches himself free of the confines of the lift and shoots across the foyer nearly bowling over Jack, the doorman, in the process. He's in a hurry, which she for one is thankful for because it's all that stopped him from recognising her. Mind you, she's changed an awful lot since they last met and while he's twice the man he used to be, she's a shadow of her former self.

Only after the lift doors have closed and they're in its snug embrace, does Eadie speak. "But what on earth is he doing in this building? He lives across the road and down a bit if the address he gave Stef is the correct one."

"Search me. Maybe he was visiting Bunty?"

Mark says this with a fake accent spot on for Sean Connery, which makes Eadie chuckle although this peters out when she thinks the boy might be right. What if Bunty is involved in the extortion racket, too? It would make sense if the money were paid to someone other than Wallace and double that for a different address.

Shaking her head a little to clear these thoughts, she responds, "Let's hope he's on his way home because the last thing we need is for me to call the constabulary about a kidnapping and them turn up to find the supposed victim swanning around the neighbourhood as right as rain."

"Shit! Here's hoping he was hurrying to keep his date with Stef."

The trip to the sixth floor is agonisingly slow with every shake of the iron coffin they're crammed in doing nasty things to her joints. She'd do anything to sit down but it's simply not possible. She sighs in relief when the doors finally open on the top floor, allowing them to escape and head to Countess Harrow's apartment.

"You ready," says Mark, his hand poised to knock on the wood next to the large brass 6A that dominates the door.

"As I'll ever be."

Even prepared as she is, when he raps his knuckles against the wooden door, she gets a shock. It's so surprisingly loud in the marbled hush of the foyer with the echo bouncing around and around until the remnants of the last knock eventually die away and silence reasserts itself. That is apart from their quickened breathing.

Heels clacking down the hallway inside announce someone's on their way, so when the dark blue door swings open, it's not a surprise. However, the woman who answers it is. Eadie had been expecting Anne, drudge to Bunty since time immemorial and a part of the furniture. This girl's a stranger, which all things considered, is a plus given half the inhabitants of the building appear to know her in one way or another.

Somewhere in her middle thirties, the woman's hair is pulled back so tightly, her look of surprise has nothing to do with Eadie and Mark turning up unannounced. That she's a maid is obvious by her plain grey dress, the design being exactly the same as that worn by Anne for all those years. Stylishly non-descript, leaving no doubt the wearer is subservient to the lady of the house.

She stares at both them in turn, her elevated eyebrows enough of a question for Eadie to speak.

"We were passing and I thought I'd pop in and see Bunty so we could talk about old times," says Eadie, deliberately not giving her name and plumbing her voice up as much as she dares. She's never been one to flaunt her background, but in this instance, it will be the difference between the Countess being at home, or not, with the 'or not' meaning she'll be in her drawing room waiting for whoever it is to be shown the door.

There's a discreet cough from a room at the end of the hall, confirming for Eadie that increasing her volume on the word 'Bunty' has worked.

"Please, do come in," says the crispy starched help. She steps to the side allowing them to enter. After she's taken their coats and hung them up, they follow her down the wide hallway with its Oriental runner and parquet flooring. But Eadie's not up to the speed set by the girl and they're falling farther and farther behind until she realises and pauses, allowing them to catch up. She starts up again at a much slower pace, allowing for Eadie's ungainly shuffle. Mark also walks slowly so he can support Eadie on her caneless side.

The girl swings to the left at the end of the hall and leads them into Bunty's private sitting room with its large oriental-patterned Aubusson rug sitting smugly in the middle of yet more gleaming parquet flooring. She always was a stickler for the niceties.

Shame about her family.

It's hard to believe the exemplar of upper-crust breeding sitting primly on a glorified confection of gilt work and over-the-top self-stripe gold fabric, was a complete bitch at school. The shame of it is, that despite her outwardly benign exterior, she still is. Bunty's dressed in her usual At Home outfit of twinset and tweed skirt with its *de rigueur* coating of dog hair.

The donor of this fine mantle of canine chic is Quincy, a toy poodle sitting patiently beside his mistress's feet, no doubt looking for another treat. Bunty dotes on the dog but, who in god's name would deem it a good idea to dye their blasted pooch purple? It clashes horribly with the colours in the room for one thing.

There's no acknowledgement of their presence other than a genteel flaring of Bunty's nostrils. Subtle, but visible to another society gal like Eadie, that she's got some grovelling to do if she's to carry out her part of this afternoon's plan. While it might work without her phone call, any doubts on the part of the police will be scotched after she speaks to the Chief Inspector, whose details Julian had given her.

"Thank you, Vivienne. That will be all," says Bunty, her tone dismissive in the extreme.

As if sensing they're about to be lambasted, Mark chooses the perfect time to reveal the gift carton of the good stuff he's been holding behind his back. He places it carefully on the coffee table in front of Bunty, and close enough that she can see it without putting on her glasses.

Eadie had had a devil of a job persuading him that it couldn't simply be any whisky and that it had to be a bottle of single malt Glenlivet older than he was. It had taken him all of Friday to find it, and he hadn't stopped going on about the price of it since.

"Vivienne!" says Bunty. Her voice is raised to carry down the hall with acknowledgement it's been heard taking the form of the footsteps coming to a halt. "Come back here."

To Eadie, the absence of please and thank you in this request is a sad indictment of her entire class. Bunty is a plonker of the first order.

"Yes, ma'am?"

Eadie's not sure if it's her imagination, but there appears to be a slight edge to the girl's tone, but not enough that Bunty can bitch about it.

"We'll need glasses. And if you could decant this." Bunty gestures arrogantly in the direction of the Glenlivet.

Decant it? Eadie's unable to stop herself from throwing an I-told-you-so look in Mark's direction before getting an okay-you-were-right eye-roll in return.

"I suppose you're here to apologize," says Bunty, having taken the bait like the lush Eadie knows her to be, even if it's only on the sly.

Her unspoken 'you've taken your bloody time about it,' hangs heavily in the air but rather than acknowledge that it has been an age since the unfortunate incident, Eadie says, "Of course I am. I felt so bad about what happened to young Rupert. I'm still not sure what occurred. I'm so pleased he's shaken it off and got on with his life."

And indeed it's true, but this is more likely due to the English aristocracy having a high tolerance when it came to bonkers behaviour, but if Rupert is anything like his father, it'll still be eating him up inside.

Eadie sprinkles faux apology liberally with lots of fluttering of hands and headshakes in order to sell it to Bunty, who never was the sharpest knife in the drawer. Lord, she hates acting as though she's on the verge of losing her marbles, but needs must when the devil drives. Petering out of platitudes, she's grinding her teeth to keep her mouth shut because of the look of sympathy she receives from Bunty. It's only when Mark coughs loudly that she realises it's audible and stops.

They're waiting for Vivienne to return with the whisky and the glasses and Mark gets to his feet. He moves over by the mantelpiece, staring hard at the painting hanging there conspicuously.

"It's marvellous, isn't it?" booms out Bunty, pride evident in every word.

"It's something all right," says Mark, not concentrating on his words.

Before he can put his foot in it by telling Bunty exactly what he thinks of the appalling painting, Eadie gets his attention by calling his name. But even when he's looking at her, she can see he's still slightly dazed.

"That's one of Rupert Smythe-Brown's pieces," she says, deliberately enunciating her words. "You've seen his work before, remember." Seeing cogs finally click into gear behind his eyes, relief settles back on her shoulders. That was close.

"It's wonderful," he says, so enthusiastically that she has to muffle an errant guffaw. Maybe not as well as she could have. Bunty's gaze swings back in her direction, her eyes narrowed in suspicion.

"I've always loved your nephew's work," says Eadie, only just managing to keep a smile at bay. "It's so raw and, ah, primitive."

It's primitive all right; a blasted monkey three sheets to the wind could produce something of a similar standard; if not better.

Now it's Mark's turn to stifle his laughter.

The clinking of crystal in the hallway alerts them to Vivienne's return. The woman glides through the doorway soon after, her arms full of a large silver tray with glasses and decanter atop.

She places this carefully on the coffee table and is dismissed by Bunty with a snooty wave of her hand.

Twenty minutes later, half the contents of the decanter have been demolished, mostly by Bunty. Eadie simply pretends to drink and Mark is still on his first glass. Eadie had forgotten what a fish her old school chum is. At this rate, they'll finish the whisky and Bunty will be no closer to taking a nap.

"Mark, you should go and check the car is all right."

It takes him a moment to get her drift, but when he does, he puts his glass down.

"You're right, I'd forgotten for a moment. I might see if I can find a better parking spot. Just you stay put, I won't be long."

If ever there was a loaded comment, it's this. Innocuous to the casual observer, the cheeky blighter is telling her not to do anything while he's away. She nods to get him moving but if he thinks she's going to sit here like a little girl in Mass, he has another think coming.

He leaves after getting her visual assurance; the pace of his steps down the hall making it obvious he'd forgotten about Jennie driving laps in the neighbourhood. It's something she'll keep to herself, should Jennie ask. No need to rock the boat unnecessarily.

"Here, let me," says Eadie, on noticing that Bunty has finished yet another glass.

Hopefully, with the decanter half empty, she'll be able to manage it with these useless hands of hers and, with Bunty half cut, she should also be able to slip something extra into the glass.

She's lucky on both counts and a mere five minutes later, the snores emanating from the small, round woman on the throne are those of a man and a much larger one at that. Seizing the opportunity, Eadie rises painfully to her feet and, shuffling as fast as she's able, makes for Bunty's bedroom where she knows there's a phone, mainly because the supercilious woman made such a song and dance when it was installed.

It's with relief she sits on the bed, allowing herself a moment's respite before taking the piece of paper out of her pocket with the special phone number on it.

———

Hanging up, Eadie chews her lip. Maybe she should have stuck to the script as the girls suggested, but the opportunity had been irresistible and so she'd made the most of it. Take that, Wallace Smythe-Brown.

She's back in the hall on her way to the sitting room when a knock comes at the front door. It'll most likely be Mark, but his timing is awful: no way does she have the physical wherewithal to get along the hall and be sitting before Vivienne appears to answer the door. What to do, what to do?

While her body might not be as responsive as it once was, there's nothing lacking in her mental faculties. As quick as she can, she turns to face the front door rather than the sitting room and it's like this that Vivienne finds her, although her puzzlement at finding one of the guests standing in the middle of the hallway is evident.

There's another knock and her gaze swings away from Eadie, back towards the door.

This could work.

It's opened, to reveal Mark. "Oh, are we leaving already?" he says, misinterpreting her standing in the hallway like this.

Eadie crows inside at having gotten away with it. "Yes. Vivienne dear, Bunty's all done in. She maybe needs a nap."

"Isn't she already?" says Mark, under his breath, but loudly enough that Vivienne hears. She giggles, revealing a side of her that isn't all grey and starched.

"Mark, can you help me with my coat?"

"Allow me, ma'am," says Vivienne, once again conscious of her role in this establishment.

"No, no, that's fine. You go and look after dearest Bunty and we'll be on our way. Tell her we had a lovely time."

In the lift and down a floor, laughter gets the better of them.

"Dearest Bunty? Wasn't that was pushing it?"

"Maybe I over overcooked the pudding a trifle," says Eadie, laughter again catching at the back of her throat.

"And speaking of over doing it. Did you do it?"

"Most assuredly and then some."

"What did you do?" says Mark, but before she can answer, the lift drops the last few inches to the ground floor and the agony that explodes through every one of her joints renders her mute.

38

Hair and make-up complete, Brenda slips into the all-in-one jumpsuit she's chosen especially for tonight, before laboriously doing up every one of the little buttons down the front. It's the most bulletproof outfit she owns and as she's deliberately putting herself in the same space as Wallace Smythe-Brown, the more that's between her skin and his, the better. She steps into her shoes and looks at herself critically in the mirror.

Good, there's nothing to show she's right royally shitting herself. Of some comfort is that she won't be on her own tonight; Chris and Sam are accompanying her to the private party that it had taken using every one of Eadie's connections for them to be invited. Julian hadn't made the exclusive list, but he'd already told her he had things to do other than delivering the notes and that he'll join them at the Smythe-Brown mansion when the time is right. As to when exactly that is, Brenda's in the dark, part of the reason she's feeling so freaky.

If he abandons them because he decides there's nothing in it for him, she'll find him, rip off one of his arms and beat him to death with the soggy end. She still hasn't decided on which arm she'll use, when she hears the front door opening followed by the sounds of Mark and Jennie in a heated discussion with someone.

Something's not right.

Kicking off her stilettoes, she tackles the stairs at a speed not possible with them. Her steps falter when she's part way down the final half flight.

"Eadie, what's wrong."

Mark is carrying the little woman; she's pale, frighteningly so, as if most of her blood has been siphoned off. Mark and Jennie, on the other hand, are highly coloured, agitated and berating Eadie, each other and themselves.

"I need to get into bed," says Eadie, her voice wispy and insubstantial.

"Flo!" yells Brenda, relieved when the swinging door to the kitchen opens.

Brenda doesn't even need to explain what's going on. Flo takes one look at Eadie's face and she's a woman on a mission. If Brenda weren't so worried about her old mentor and friend, she'd laugh at the look on Mark's face when he's bulldozed through the sitting room door along with instructions to take Eadie through and put her on her bed, immediately. Jennie is firmly told to go and instruct Bert to get one of her special brews on.

Instantly, Eadie looks alarmed. "No, no, no! I don't need THAT!"

But Flo's having none of it and steers Mark and his precious cargo slowly and surely through the sitting room and into Eadie's bedroom with Brenda following closely behind. Not that she gets much farther than the entrance to the bedroom, with Flo telling her in no uncertain terms to stay exactly where she is. Once Mark has carefully deposited his aunt on her bed, he's sent packing. Flo shuts the door firmly in their faces to "give Eadie some privacy".

The two of them are pacing around the sitting room when Jennie returns from giving Bert his instructions.

"Any ideas what it is that he's brewing up?" says Brenda.

"No, but he whistled through his teeth in a manner that makes me think Flo must be pulling out the big guns in the painkilling department."

"Is that's what's wrong?" says Brenda, not sure if she's relieved it's this, rather than something having gone wrong with their plan, or distressed that her elderly friend is in pain because of said plan. "I knew we should have asked someone else to do this."

"Good luck trying to stop her," says Jennie, who Brenda knows is well aware through personal experience of the stubbornness of the little lady.

"We were doing okay until the lift dropped a couple of inches when we got to the ground floor at Bunty's place," says Mark.

"That death trap!" says Jennie, with feeling.

They're still waiting just outside Eadie's door when Bert arrives with a pot of something that smells suspiciously like burning tyres. No mystery why Eadie would prefer to put up with the pain. He knocks tentatively and waits.

Flo opens it only wide enough for one of her whip-corded hands to snake out and take the pot off him. A second later, she recloses the door on them.

"What's wrong with her usual anti-inflammatories?" says Brenda, to Bert.

"This stuff is much stronger than them," he says, seemingly incredulous that such a thing is even possible, with him having seen first-hand the effects of those yellow monsters on Brenda and Julian as well as a couple of their unwanted visitors.

Brenda's wondering if it will be possible to speak to Eadie before they head off to the party when the door is opened and Flo walks out. "She's wanting to speak to you."

She tiptoes into the room, not sure what state Eadie will be in after swallowing something that smells of a recently used drag strip. Burning rubber and then some.

"Whoa, are you okay?"

"Pain'sall gone," slurs Eadie, already showing the effects of Flo's brew, with her eyes dark orbs and exceedingly possum-like.

Brenda sits carefully on the side of the bed. "I was so worried when I saw you earlier."

"S'all fine. Made the call, sorded Wallace. Thas for sure."

"What do you mean?" There'd been no mention of Wallace in the script they'd rehearsed that afternoon. None at all. "Eadie? What did you do?"

There's no response.

The old girl's eyes have rolled up in her head and her mouth hangs open with drool already forming on the bottom lip. Brenda doesn't breathe until she hears Eadie is doing the same. Dammit, what's she gone and done?

Mark and Jennie are still in the sitting room, waiting for an update, which Brenda gives them, such as it is. Pain-free, out cold.

"She was rambling on about sorting out Wallace in that phone call. Any ideas?"

"She mentioned something to me before the lift dropped and she fainted, so I don't have a clue either," says Mark.

Jennie backs this up. "Nothing she said in the car made sense. Even when she was out cold, she kept muttering 'twenty-five years'."

Back in her room, Brenda slips on her shoes and finds the handbag she intends taking. She thinks briefly about taking a coat, but the less clobber she has with her, the better it'll be to make a clean getaway. She paces like an animal that's outgrown its zoo enclosure, chewing over this new development and wondering if what Eadie has done will screw up their whole plan. What if continuing with it means they're walking into a trap?

These ruminations are further exacerbated by having no clue whether Julian has delivered the ransom notes or even if he will bother meeting up with them later. Her thoughts are getting darker by the second when there's a knock at her door.

"Come in!"

It's Sam, with Chris waiting behind her. Both of them, like Brenda, are dressed head to toe in black giving the three of them a sombre appearance as though they're off to a funeral, which hopefully it will be for Wallace.

The death of his extortion plan.

The death of his reputation.

The death of his power over others weaker than himself.

Sam looks Brenda up and down. "Good choice."

Brenda likewise checks out Sam's dress, with its bias-cut panels and deep vee neckline. "I like yours, too. Designer?"

Brenda doesn't care, but chatting about clothes feels normal as though they are simply heading out for a night of fun.

"It is, but no one you'll have heard of, yet. This guy's only just started out."

"Are you ready to go?" says Chris, interrupting the forced discussion.

Even though her stomach says otherwise, she responds, "As I'll ever be."

Chris finds a parking space for Julian's van around the corner from the house where the party is. Although, it's far enough away that Brenda's shoes are pinching well before they walk up the marble front steps with their elaborate iron railings. Apart from this small affirmation to up-market architecture, the house is reasonably modest from the outside when compared with the over-the-top establishments she's frequented of late.

She can see why it was so bloody hard to get an invitation. Numbers would have to be strictly limited purely from a logistics point of view.

Not that the numbers feel limited when they step inside the hallway. The place is packed. Uncomfortably so, with the crowd different from any Brenda's seen in London so far. For a start, the first three women she looks at closely have their nipples out. Not overtly, but definitely on closer inspection.

"Jeez, I haven't seen this many knobs in one place since visiting parliament as a kid," says Sam, causing Brenda to also drop her gaze.

"I'm feeling overdressed here," says Chris, patting his fly as if to ensure it's closed, unlike a lot of others around them.

"What the hell?" Despite Brenda's rough and ready upbringing and the sights she's seen since being in London, this crowd is something different altogether and she's having difficulty coming to terms with her reaction.

Maybe it's because at first glance, they look to be your usual bunch of upper crust twats and not a slice of debauched reality. The English could be weird at times and the richer, the weirder.

"Apart from wearing black, we stand out like sore thumbs," says Sam, before worrying her bottom lip.

"Stuffed if I'm airing my old fella in public like this lot."

Brenda's hand unconsciously runs the length of the buttons down the front of her jumpsuit. "I'm with you on that." Not that she has an old fella, but she knows exactly what Chris means.

"Short of cutting holes in the front of my dress, I'm stuck as I am, thank god," says Sam.

"Come on, let's circulate. If we keep moving, perhaps no one will notice we're not flaunting our bits," says Brenda.

After a small council of war, they decide on working their

way through the room the movement of the crowd is steering them towards, before exploring the rest of the ground floor. Brenda's hoping to hell they don't have to venture upstairs, because if their fellow guests are this brazen in the front hall, who knows what's going on up there.

This stops her for a second. Sod it all, when did she become such a prude?

They're out the back in the conservatory before they spot their quarry, although the expression that mars Wallace's ugly features when he spots them, has Brenda feeling that she's the quarry. It's something she doesn't like.

"Show time," whispers Chris, from right beside her.

She's flanked on the other side by Sam.

Wallace's journey over to them is slow through a combination of the crush of people and the fact he's moving awkwardly, as though in pain. Hell's bells, Eadie did a number on him, all right. On the plus side, it means he won't be trying to poke that thing anywhere near her tonight.

If he as much as sniffs at hurting her, she's going to bust his balls to match his dick. Thoughts of him being vulnerable like that go some way to bolstering her confidence and when he pops up next to three of them, Brenda steps into her role for tonight; one that's been as carefully scripted as Eadie's phone call, for all the good that did.

She waits for a beat until she sees him taking in air and she lets him have it. "Passing out on me once is bad form, Wallace. Twice is just plain insulting!"

She says this with as much scorn as she can muster, channelling Genevieve Smythe-Brown to get the right amount of vicious bitch.

Unfortunately, he's had a lot of practice with that old bat and it doesn't affect him in the least.

"Pass out? Pass out? You drugged me, you little bitch."

"No, you willingly took the same pills as I did, you couldn't handle them," says Brenda, going off script.

"But, but, but," says Wallace, floundering for a response and looking pissed off enough that she hopes to hell he never finds out she doped him to the eyeballs. "What about what you did to me afterwards?"

Brenda takes her time to respond, looking Wallace up and down in such a manner that he stiffens everywhere not recently broken.

"You mean leave you lying in a heap snoring in that blacked-out room, while I had to pay for my own cab home? You mean that?"

She's back on script, if only slightly.

"You mean you didn't ..." Wallace peters out as though he can't bring himself to recount the injuries he'd sustained that night.

"Didn't what?" says Brenda, mustering as much scorn as she can.

She watches him closely as the wheels inside his head whir frantically before she sees him coming to a decision. "Oh, my dear, I've wronged you horribly."

It's all Brenda can do not to whoop that he's accepted her version of events. Or has he? For a split second, she sees something other than contrition deep inside his scrutiny. But when she looks again, it's gone.

During this interlude, neither Sam nor Chris has said anything, simply given her moral support by standing close to her. Wallace saw the pair of them, albeit briefly, on the opening night of Rupert's infamous exhibition they have no desire to put his memory to the test. The less they say, the better.

"And who are your lovely friends," says Wallace, looking at Brenda's bodyguards with interest.

"This is Isabella and this is Sebastiano, Seb for short," says Brenda, using the names suggested by Sam and Chris themselves. "They're Italian friends of mine."

"Strange, they look familiar," says Wallace, suspicion clouding his words and Brenda's heart rate picking up. The adjustment in the posture of the other two, suggests they're experiencing a similar reaction.

In an effort to shore up their cover, Chris spouts forth with a stream of Italian, that Sam answers in kind. Their hand waving is as Italian as Stefano's, that money-losing wanker back in Melbourne. There isn't a jot of reaction from Wallace to this, letting her know that Julian's assurances that Wallace couldn't speak Italian are bang on. Brenda can only presume that information came from Genevieve.

Chris's next line is pure theatre as he asks with a strong Italian accent if it's true that Wallace has a *prigione di dolore*. Skewered by Wallace's blank look, Chris flounders as though looking for the correct words. He has a conflab in what sounds like Italian with Sam, who eventually stutters out in equally appalling English, "'E ask if you 'ave dungeon of pain," before she ices the cake by turning beet red.

Wallace takes the bait, cuffs, whips and spanker and shows a remarkable ability to organise those around him. They're outside on the steps and ready to leave in a remarkably short space of time. Chris offered to hire the space, but given the any-friend-of-Brenda's-is-a-friend-of-mine line.

While 'Isabella' and 'Seb' are to travel to Wallace's abode under their own steam, he will take Brenda there in his Rolls. "But no pills this time, you naughty minx."

The high-pitched giggling he lets loose results in an urgent need to spew; it's all she can do to keep up the pretence of enjoying his company.

It doesn't get any easier once they're tucked up in the back of his car, although by using the glass of whisky he offers her, she keeps some distance between them but it's only a matter of time before he'll be all over her like the proverbial rash. She keeps him at bay by partaking in a second glass of the golden spirits, holding this safety shield in place right up until the car glides into the side entrance as at his mansion. Only once he's outside the car and waiting for her, does she put her glass down inside the drinks cabinet built into the back of the driver's seat.

He holds his hand out to her to help her out of the car and she's surprised to find she needs him to keep her upright once she gains her feet. They're halfway up the stairs when she trips. Bloody shoes, she should never have worn her highest pair, even if the added height gives her confidence.

Leaving her sitting on a small hard-backed chair in the foyer, Wallace walks over to the front door and opens it and Sam and Chris walk in a moment later. The light in the foyer is ridiculously low and Brenda has trouble focusing on them as Wallace escorts them across the marbled space and through the hidden panel in the back wall.

"I'll be back to get you in a moment, my sweet," he says, before the panel swings shut silently behind him.

He takes forever to come back and get her and it's all she can do to keep her eyes open. So frigging tired. All those sleepless nights have caught with her. Wallace needs to shake her awake to escort her downstairs to the viewing room and she's leaning hard against him when they pause outside the door into that secret room.

"We're in for a treat tonight, my dear. Not only will we see those luscious young Italian friends of yours in action, but we have The Walrus himself on the premises?"

"You've got a sea lion down here?" says Brenda, mightily confused.

"Close enough," says Wallace, chortling, although he stops when he opens the door and ushers Brenda into the stygian dark of the room before them.

If anything the room is even darker than the last time she'd been here. Strange, but she thought she'd be nervous being in here with Wallace, but, he's not such a bad chap. Even with him helping her, she manages to trip over the lush carpet and if it weren't for his firm grip on her arm, she'd have taken a tumble.

He helps her onto a bar stool and even places her forehead against the viewing slit so she can see through into the other room. Rather than Sam and Chris, as she expected, she's subjected to Findus Bleakly in all his naked glory and can do nothing about the bile that bubbles up in her throat. It's a relief when blackness claims her a second later.

39

R egaining consciousness, it takes Brenda a moment to work out what the hell has happened. That sneaky, underhanded, effing son of a bitch. This thought has only just finished skipping across her brain like a pebble on a pond, when she realises she can't move.

Not because she's paralysed: because he's tied her up, with ropes cutting into both her wrists and ankles. She can feel the caress of the lush carpet against her back – not a good sign. The only plus is that she's still in the viewing room as far as she can tell. It's dark enough and there are tell-tale slits of light on the wall above her. Consciously slowing her panicked breathing, she listens carefully.

The arsehole's still in there with her, she can hear his laboured panting. Whether this is due to stripping her and tying her up or from watching Findus Bleakly get the crap beaten out of him is anyone's guess, but Brenda's opting for the latter.

What the hell is she supposed to do now? What if Julian has left them hanging? No cops or SO6, or whoever the hell they are, coming storming through the door means she's at that peeping arsehole's mercy. She's so busy mentally berating herself for getting into this mess that she's surprised when a sob escapes.

"Ah, I see that you're awake. I had hoped you'd stay under until I could get you safely installed next door, but Findus always did have staying power." His voice is barely above a whisper but she hears every word with terrifying clarity.

She pauses only for a heartbeat before putting everything she can into both abusing the wanker standing over her and screaming for help. Even if it does go against her principles, she'd be stupid not to know she's in deep shit and needs all the help she can get. Her only hope is the others can hear her through those skinny viewing slits.

A moment later, she's seeing stars but, despite him continuing to smack her around the head, she keeps on screaming. He slams his hand over her mouth, silencing her. His meaty hand slapped over her wide-open mouth, she can't even bite him.

She struggles against both him and the ropes, but it's no good. Not only is she tied up, she's also tied down, although she can't imagine to what. She's sure she could move furniture if that were all it was, but no matter how hard she pulls, her restraints don't budge an inch. All that happens is she rubs her wrists and ankles raw.

She listens hard, but there's no indication her cry for help has been heard by any of the others. Wallace shoves something in her mouth to gag her and then tapes it in place. With her silenced, he wastes no time roughly groping her breasts and twisting her nipples hard enough that no amount of breathing in through her nose helps ease the pain.

"I'm going to have so much fun showing you the joys of the flesh," he says, before staggering to his feet and going back to his peep show.

Brenda lets her head flop to the side and concentrates on

not retching, while trying to ignore the tears that are slipping sideways down her face. She's well and truly wallowing in her misery when movement in the weak light filtering under the door to the hallway captures her attention. There's someone out there, but there's stuff all she can do about it. Even if she banged her head on the floor, all that would happen would be that she'd give herself a concussion.

The small spark of hope that had flickered into life inside her chest snuffs out when the light in the hallway is extinguished along with any hope of rescue. That prick Julian has left them to it because the place should surely have been crawling with cops by now.

A small puff of air cools the tears on her face as the door opens; if whoever it is, is being this quiet, she doubts they're friends of Wallace's. A moment later, there's a comforting squeeze to her shoulder. A moment after that, two hundred pounds of aristocratic wanker lies on the carpet next to her.

It's only when the dim light in the room is turned on that Brenda is able to see her rescuer.

He didn't abandon them after all.

And doesn't he look very 007 in all that black.

He makes short work of untying her from rings set into the floor and helping her to dress as best she can. Wallace had used a knife rather than waste time undoing all those buttons down the front of her jumpsuit. Not so bulletproof after all.

"What happens now?" says Brenda, unable to stop the trembling that is consuming her body. Julian notices and pulls her into a tight embrace with the heat of his body thawing the chill that had settled deep inside her chest. He gently steers her head down and onto his shoulder, before kissing the back of her neck. This small act of kindness is enough to have her tears seeping into the soft wool of his turtleneck sweater.

"You're okay, you're okay." Julian's tone is deliberately

soothing as though she's a small frightened animal, which isn't that far from the truth.

"I've never been so scared in my life," mumbles Brenda, admitting it to herself as much as to him.

He puts his hand under her chin and lifts her head so he can look at her. His face is serious when he says, "With good bloody reason."

He looks closely at her and, as if some internal battle has been fought and won, he drops his lips to hers for a kiss that scatters all thoughts of the unconscious prick lying at her feet.

She's giving herself over fully to the kiss when the practical part of her brain gets in on the action.

He's not old.

He's not rich in his own right.

He's sure as hell not easy to control.

She wrenches her mouth free and pulls out of his embrace, all the while screaming 'stupid, stupid, stupid' loudly inside her head.

He looks as though he wants to say something, but the sound of booted feet thundering down the stairs leading to the cellar alerts them to the imminent arrival of the cavalry and his face is once again poker ready.

"Unless you want to be found in here with him, I suggest we skedaddle," says Julian, quietly. They waste little time locating her shoes and handbag and he leads her out of the viewing room and down the hall in the opposite direction of the all those booted feet.

"What about the others?" says Brenda, unable to simply leave them behind.

"Already out of here."

"Even Stef?"

Julian nods while executing a hard left turn into a short hallway that looks to be a dead end. He runs his hand down the side of the back wall and after a barely audible click, the wall swings open to reveal another small room full of recording equipment. Inside, he closes the wall, making the space claustrophobic.

Julian checks the labels on the tape decks crammed on a shelf to one side of the room until he finds what he's looking for. "Best we take away any evidence the others were here." He hits stop buttons on two of the machines, removes the reels and shoves them into a small backpack Brenda hadn't even noticed.

After a worrying length of time, in which he checks each and every boxed spool on the floor to ceiling shelves on the other side of the room, he's down on his hands and knees looking at those on the bottom shelf. His backpack is now bulging with all the tapes he'd been after, while she's taken the opportunity to try to tie the front of her jumpsuit together so her tits are no longer hanging out. Only once it's as secure as she can make it, does she step into her shoes and sling her handbag over her shoulder so it hangs on the diagonal.

He stands and scoots around her, and reopens the wall panel. Rather than swing it wide, he opens it a sliver and listens. Brenda can't hear anything, and Julian mustn't either, because he deems the coast clear enough for them to leave.

She's pulling the panel closed behind them, when he looks over his shoulder at her and whispers, "Don't make it too hard for the boys in blue."

This has the opposite effect of what he's after, with Brenda looking him dead in the eye and before shutting it.

"Don't you want them to find that evidence against Wallace?"

"Shit!" says Brenda, as quietly as is possible for a curse, before she stands to one side so he can locate the secret switch again.

Leaving the small room wide open, they slip quietly out into the main hallway, with Julian running his hand along one side of it, as though feeling their way forward. It's hardly necessary; the meagre light is enough to see where they're going. He stops and runs his hands all over another panel and Brenda realises what he's up to.

There's only one person who knows their way around these subterranean passages well enough to tell Julian where he should be going and which spots to push.

Eadie!

Once they're on the other side of the panel, they inch their way forward in the space that is dark as pitch. Even after her eyes get used to it, Brenda still has to slide her feet forward rather than walk properly. Her hands skim along the walls on either side of her until they walk through a doorway and negotiate their way up half a dozen steps into a large open area.

"Wait, I can't see a thing," she hisses, in what she hopes is Julian's direction. The guy is cat-like in his movements.

"I'm right in front of you," he says, with his breath whispering on her forehead.

"Where are we off to now?"

"We can watch the show from in here. Better take your shoes off, though."

Given he'd saved her not much earlier, Brenda doesn't question this and slips out of her uncomfortable footwear and luxuriates in the feeling of the lush carpet for a moment, before bending over and picking up her heels. Apart from not wanting to leave any clues behind, they cost a bleeding fortune.

Holding onto them with one hand, she puts her out the other until she encounters Julian's chest. He takes hold of it and she blindly follows him across what feels like a large room. At what she assumes is the other side, she's aware of light coming through some decorative latticework.

Julian puts his finger to his lips – whispering is out of the question now. Observe and stay mum. Okay, got it.

The room they're looking down into is luxurious in the extreme, decorated with an over-the-top oriental feel to it.

Brenda hasn't seen this much gilt in one room, ever. Not that Wallace seems perturbed to be surrounded by London's finest. Simply seeing that many uniforms in one place and Brenda's experiencing nasty flashbacks.

It takes a while to put things together and she doesn't like what she's seeing. For a start, all the pigs have glasses of spirits in their hands, as does Wallace. Nor is he in handcuffs. Of even more interest is the fat brown envelope on the gold filigree table sitting in the middle of the circle of chairs on which the assembled players are lounging.

He's paying them off. No!

The large red blob on top of the envelope looks to be a wax seal, presumably to stop sticky fingers going where they shouldn't. Lord only knows how much is in there.

It takes all of Brenda's reserve to keep quiet, but when she looks at Julian and sees him smiling in the dim light, she buttons her lips, although staples would do a better job. She isn't even aware she's growling deep at the back of her throat until he squeezes her arm.

"Well, gentlemen, it's been a pleasure doing business, again," says Wallace, watching one of the cops pick up the envelope. "Give my regards to the Super."

Even from their hidey-hole, Brenda can see the cops aren't happy about it either. Maybe it's because the money's going to their Super rather than them?

A couple of them are already on their feet, when the door to the room opens and out of the corner of her eye, Brenda sees Julian leaning ever closer to the latticework. If he gets any nearer the damned thing, he'll be visible from inside the room. She puts her hand on his chest and applies enough pressure for him to move back.

Who the hell are these guys? They're not more cops if the sharpness of their suits is anything to go by. Despite the lack of official insignia, the three of them exude power. It's as though their civilised exteriors are simply a thin veneer that's in danger of cracking with the merest provocation.

"Excellent work, Sergeant, we'll take it from here."

Given the new arrivals aren't in uniform, Brenda's as confused as the cop holding the large brown envelope.

"Collins, SO6," says the dark-haired chap in the severe navy suit, who's at the front of the group. Then, like something out of a magic show, he pulls ID from an inside breast pocket and holds it up for all to see, before it disappears as magically. He holds his hand out for the envelope.

It's a fight to see who it is, the cops or Wallace, who loses their colour the fastest, with Wallace winning and lucky to be sitting by the looks of things.

Collins, still with his hand out ready to accept the evidence, beckons with his fingers to prompt the cop to hand it over.

"Just following orders, sir," says the cop, as he hands it over. "Not sure what's inside."

"Let's have a look, shall we?" Collins makes short work of the seal and has a peek inside the envelope, with a lot of *tsking*, before he empties the contents out onto the small table for all to see.

Now the cops are challenging Wallace for top spot in the pale stakes.

So, it isn't money after all. But who the hell are the photos of? Bloody shame she can't see from here. She turns to Julian to ask him in sign language and finds him smiling more broadly than ever. She taps his shoulder and when he looks at her, uses her best Christmas charade skills to mime that she wants to know who's in the photos.

He brings his mouth right up next to her ear, and whispers, "Their Super," before placing a gentle kiss on her neck.

"Stop it!" says Brenda, wrenching away from him.

"Did you say something, Sergeant?" says Collins.

Damn Julian for making her screw up.

Wallace stares directly at her through the latticework, although she's sure she's far enough back that he can't see her. "We have rats."

Julian has also moved farther back into the room as a precaution, but rather than them sneaking off as she's expected, he stays right where he is and once again puts his fingers to his lips.

"These old places are full of them," says one of the other SO6 chaps, inducing a sneer from Wallace that his mansion is an 'old place', even though that's exactly what it is.

The atmosphere in the room changes considerably when the sergeant reads Wallace his rights. Wallace flares from pale but composed to fire engine red and agitated.

"There's no need for that sort of thing amongst friends," says Collins from SO6, but the sergeant ploughs on until he finishes his prepared piece.

The sergeant produces a search warrant and Wallace is ashen again. Interestingly, this time the SO6 guys share his colour.

After a call for back-up, the mansion has more cops on the premises than some stations, meaning Brenda and Julian are stuck where they are, until the point she fears her bladder's going to explode.

Every time the room below them is empty of uniforms or badges, Brenda asks another question of Julian.

Seems as though Wallace has friends in high places in more than one department, which was why Julian had asked for two ransom notes. By delivering them both on the same night, to friends he knew were 'clean' but didn't have the power to do anything about the corruption higher up, he hoped to get around it. With both groups turning up at the same time, they couldn't very well risk it getting out that they'd let Wallace get away with extortion.

I need to pee. Bad!" says Brenda, keeping her voice low, even though there isn't anyone in the room below them. Wallace has been taken away for further questioning at the station. Brenda's hoping he's in a cell with someone who's even more into pain than that nipple-twisting arsehole. Unfortunately, the place still appears to be crawling with police and SO6 personnel, each keeping an eye on the other, according to Julian.

"Hang on," says Julian, stating the obvious, "let me see what I can sort out." He leaves her side, she hopes in search of a bucket. She's desperate enough that a large serving platter would do and to hell with any splashing while slashing.

The room floods with light, forcing her to cover her eyes. She hears curtains closing but it's a moment before her eyes adjust and she can look around to take in her surroundings. The curtains have covered up the latticework, effectively blocking the light to anyone in the other room. They still need to keep quiet, though.

The only stick of furniture in the room is a large and sumptuously appointed bed.

"I hope there's a chamber pot under that thing," she hisses, as much to herself as Julian, all the while undoing the knots down the front of her jumpsuit.

"We can do better than that," says Julian, opening a door opposite to the one they'd entered through.

It doesn't smell good, it doesn't look good, but it's a toilet and by the time she's shut the door on Julian, she's jiggling around and thinking dry thoughts to keep the pee where it is for the moment.

The relief is immense. But this is short-lived when she pulls the chain. The noise is deafening.

"For god's sake, give me a break," says Brenda, roundly abusing the ancient cistern high above her head.

Her hand is on the door when it's opened abruptly by Julian, who grabs her hand and pulls her along in his wake. He has her shoes and handbag in his other hand.

"We need to get out of her now," he says, no longer bothering to keep his voice lowered.

40

Julian doesn't need to tell Brenda to stay close, if she was any closer she'd be inside his bloody backpack. Without him to show her the way through the labyrinth that is the Smythe-Brown cellar, she'd be screwed for sure.

After unlatching the wall panel they'd come through hours and hours earlier and opening it a mere slit, he listens for a couple of seconds. His flurry of action leaves Brenda feeling faint. They shoot out into the hallway, and along it for a few feet before scarpering through another panel a moment later and into yet another secret room, then out into another hallway, through what looks to be a broom cupboard and, finally, out onto an unadorned wooden staircase.

It's as though he has an inbuilt map inside his head, so certain are his movements. Not once does he hesitate about which way to go next, although he pauses again on the landing. He tilts his head to the side and swivels it backwards and forwards and up and down like a radar. Without warning, he grabs Brenda and drags her up the stairs at a rate of knots. Going up feels counterintuitive, but he hasn't steered them wrong so far and when there's shouting a couple of floors below, she knows this time is no different.

He's taking the stairs two at a time now, with fear giving Brenda the strength to keep up. Thank god she's not wearing any shoes and is in a jumpsuit rather than a dress. It's also a good bloody thing she's had a pee or it would be running down her legs by now.

Brenda's concentrating so hard on keeping herself upright that she isn't even aware they've gone through yet another wall panel until Julian stops suddenly and she canons into him, sending him flying. He wastes no time getting up, swinging the panel closed and locking it.

His quiet "*Shhh,*" comes just in time, leaving her scared to move. She shallow breathes through her mouth, conscious of keeping the flow of air as quiet as possible. The person on the other side of the panel isn't as cautious and the laboured breathing is loud enough that he could be in the small room, too.

"See anything, Sergeant?"

"No, sir. There was definitely someone ahead of me, but I'm buggered if I know where they've gone. It's all dead ends up here."

Even with her bladder running on fumes, when the panel next to her squeaks, as someone on the other side pushes against it experimentally, she comes close to pissing her pants. Thank god Julian locked the bloody thing.

"Come on," says the senior cop. "We've got a load of evidence to bag up downstairs. The sooner we get on with it, the sooner I can get home to my bed."

"Do we know who the tip off was from, sir?"

"No, but without her we wouldn't have found half those concealed rooms."

Not until their footsteps have faded does Brenda feels she can take in a decent lungful, but Julian squeezes her shoulder.

With her mouth open and not enough oxygen on board to make a sound, let alone sustain her, she's seeing spots before there's movement right outside the door, followed by someone thundering off down the stairs. That sneaky bastard. If it hadn't been for Julian they'd have been collared for sure.

They wait for a couple more minutes, with the only movement from Brenda being the hammering of her heart in her chest. If she gets out of this safely, she is never, ever going to put herself at risk like this again.

Oh so slowly, Julian gets down on his hands and knees and looks through the sliver of a gap under the hidden panel. The coast must be clear because he is far less concerned about making noises as he regains his feet.

"Right, let's get the hell out of here."

———

It wouldn't be the first time Brenda's climbed out of a window, but it's the first time it's been on the third floor. Actually, stitch that: it's a window in the attic, so they're higher still. She's more of a ground floor kinda girl.

"Isn't there another way?"

"Yes! The front door."

"Hah, bloody hah," says Brenda, threading her arms through the strap of her evening bag and wearing it like a small backpack. She's still not sure how she's going to carry her stilettos, because she sure as hell can't wear them on those slippery looking roof tiles.

"Come on, chicken, I wouldn't mind being home in time for breakfast."

"My shoes," says Brenda, holding them up as though she'll miraculously discover pockets in her jumpsuit big enough to hold them.

"Give them here!" Julian takes them off her and, without

ceremony, shoves them up the front of his jumper before tucking the bottom of that into his trousers. "Right, I'll go first."

He makes short work of climbing up onto a chair and out the window where he disappears from sight so quickly that Brenda fears he must have slipped. She's on the chair a second later, scanning the roof below the window, expecting to see him hanging on like grim death. For someone who's in mortal peril, he's remarkably relaxed. She sees that while he has done a bit of sliding, it's been controlled and he's standing on a flat section of roof that's tucked inside a parapet that runs across the back of this house and the next one and the next, and so on. All they need do is walk along that until they're a couple of doors down the road, break in somewhere and get the hell out of there.

Easy.

Unless you happen to suffer from vertigo.

Then it's a bloody nightmare.

Standing safe and sound on the parapet, Brenda's shocked at how cold the roof is on her bare feet, but this pales when she realises just how high up they are. She dries her hands on her already ruined jumpsuit. They don't stay that way for long.

"You okay?" Julian peers at her in the dark.

Rather than admit to being shit scared and unable to speak, she forces a grin.

He does likewise in return, although his is less contrived. "Right, let's get out of here."

He takes off at a speed that makes her head spin, or maybe that's the vertigo. He's back just as quickly when he twigs she hasn't followed him. It's not that she doesn't want to, but her feet appear stuck to the tar paper used to waterproof the flat gulley they're standing in.

"You're not okay, are you?"

She shakes her head, while wiping her hands down the side of her legs.

"Do you trust me?"

She can't answer that, but when he holds his hand out towards her, she wipes her right hand again and puts it in his.

"Shut your eyes," he coaxes.

"Are you nuts!"

"Shhhh, you want the whole neighbourhood to know we're up here?"

Eventually, she closes her eyes and has to admit, it's better. The head spinning decreases and the sweat glands on her palms halve their production.

"Okay, we're going to move slowly, if there are any obstacles, I'll let you know."

He's true to his word and the more confidence Brenda has in his leading abilities, the faster they go.

But it still feels like hours before Julian says, "You can open your eyes now."

Brenda doesn't comply "Are you sure?"

"Scout's honour," he says, and Brenda can imagine him saluting.

Opening her eyes, she's immensely relieved. Like something out of Mary Poppins, they're still up on the roofs of London but they're in the dip between two roofs, so there's no longer a heart-attack-inducing drop on one side.

Julian almost loses his footing when she throws herself into his arms and appears shocked when she plants a loud kiss on his lips. He is one handy guy to have around.

"If you've finished, we should get out of here."

Fine, if he's going to be like that thinks Brenda, struggling to hold her shoes that he's just shoved at her. Rather than look him in the eye, she looks past him to the small service door that's behind him in an unspoken, 'Well, what the hell are you waiting for?'

He stiffens, before turning abruptly and leaves her standing there. He's already using his lock-picking gear when she joins him; the door clicks open a moment later. They don't say another word until they're safely through the house and in a black cab and that's only so Julian can give the address to the driver.

It's not one she recognises, but rather than talk to him, she sinks into her corner of the seat and looks fixedly out of the window.

The building they pull up outside is sixties housing estate right down to its dingy exterior and the walkways that run the length of the building on every level. This impression is enhanced when they get out of the cab and Brenda notices the trash banked up behind the low brick wall marking the front boundary. The smell of urine in the stairwell is par for the course and eye-watering in strength; she automatically takes shallower breaths. He lives in this dump? That makes no sense whatsoever given how well off his parents are.

After unlocking and unbolting the door of the third floor flat, he stands to one side to allow her to enter. Inside, the place is as bad as she expected, but at least it doesn't smell of piss, just the olfactory remnants of too many fry-ups and having never been vacuumed. It's obvious no one lives here now.

She's tired, her feet hurt, and she's over everything. She doesn't bother dusting off the vinyl couch before throwing herself down into its unforgiving depths, only to discover any springs had long since sprung. Her knees are up around her ears, folded up like a sodding deck chair! She's working out how the hell to get up again when Julian starts to laugh.

She struggles to free herself, which renews his laughter, so much so he's holding onto his stomach and bending over. She slams her hands down hard on the seat on either side of her, whilst glaring at him. Controlling his laughter, he pulls her free of the couch's embrace.

The moment her feet are back on the ground, she wrenches herself free from his hold and stomps as far away from him as possible to stare unseeing at the view through the grimy window above the sink.

Rather than talking her around as she expects, he ignores her. She's surprised to see he's not even there when she turns to face the room. The open door on the other side of the room, explains his whereabouts. Must be a bedroom.

Damn, she so doesn't want to go there, especially after his reaction to her giving him a celebratory smack on the lips. Jeez, young guys were so touchy and too much bloody trouble all round as far as she's concerned.

But she'd give anything to lie down and there's no way she's going anywhere near that fungal carpet. Although, who knows, the bed might not be a lot better. There's only one way to find out for sure.

Stalking across the room, she looks through the door and is relieved to see that not only is the bed in far better shape than anything else in the flat but that the sheets look reasonably new and, more importantly, clean. The only issue is that Julian is spread out across the bed in full ownership and already out for the count.

Dammit. If she weren't already dead on her feet, she'd high-tail it now.

Jeez, Charlie, ya fat bastard, get off me." Without opening her eyes, Brenda shoves at the cat in hopes of relieving the pressure on her bladder. "What the hell?"

Even after opening her eyes, it takes her a moment to work out where the hell she is and why she's close to wetting the bed for the first time in around 23 years. Julian's still comatose, which explains the dead weight of his arm when she moves it as slowly and carefully as she can to execute her plan of sneaking out of bed and doing a runner. Luckily, she's got enough cash on her to spring for a cab.

"Five more minutes," mumbles Julian, without coming around.

She stops moving his arm only long enough for him to resume his gentle snoring. She slides out from under him, into an ungainly heap on the floor before putting his arm down gently on the spot she's vacated.

So far so good.

Much as she'd like to leave immediately, thoughts of bouncing along in a cab when her bladder is so full that her eyes are probably yellow, isn't her idea of fun. Stuffed if she'll flush this time, though. Apart from a distinct lack of toilet paper, she manages to have the world's longest pee before grabbing her shoes and handbag and sneaking out of the flat. She shuts the door behind her as quietly as she can, but even then it sounds deafening to her. Torn between waiting to see if she's got away with it, and legging it, she legs it. Well, as fast as she can in her damned stilettos. Stopping on the bottom step, she listens carefully for sounds of someone in pursuit, but all is quiet. It's crazy quiet. Even creepily quiet.

A quick flick of her wrist shows her it's only five in the bloody morning. For god's sake, she'll be lucky to get a cab. There's also the small fact that she wouldn't have a clue where she is. Other than finding a cab, her best hope is to stumble across a tube station or at least someone she can ask for directions. Although given the state of her, she's likely to send any good Samaritans running for the hills.

The only thing in her favour is that she's managed to tie the front of her jumpsuit in such a way that her tits aren't hanging out. Shame about all the grime and carpet fluff she's covered in: she looks as though she's been wrestling all night.

She's hobbling in pain before she finally sees a black cab sitting outside a tube station with the night bus pulling into a stop on the other side of the road. Typical! Nothing for ages, and then all three of them turn up together.

She aims for the cab, although when he sees her, the driver looks as though he's ready to drive off. He changes his tune, thankfully, after she starts shoving money at him through the window to show she's good for the fare but it takes every penny she's got to get her home.

Never has Eadie's house looked so good.

Shame there's a cop car parked out front.

"Keep going, keep going!" she yells, along with a lot of hand waving in case he can't hear her through the glass.

He either doesn't hear her, or he does and figures he's already got all her cash. The upshot is that he pulls into the curb right behind the cop car and sits there giving her no option but to get out.

41

Brenda's never been one to back down from a challenge and that's exactly how she faces the prospect of walking brazenly past the cop car. Act as though you're meant to be here. For god's sake, don't act guilty. Going for the jugular, she raps hard on the passenger window of the cop car, startling the officer who's leaning against it and fast asleep. Not anymore, he's not, thinks Brenda swallowing a smile.

While he's composing himself, she waits with her hands on her hips, tapping a toe impatiently. If she can ignore the fact that she looks like she's been dragged through a bush back-wards, maybe he can, too.

She steps back to allow him to open his door and get out but she doesn't give him a chance to speak.

"Has there been a break-in, officer, because that's the only reason I can see for you being parked out here at this hour of the morning." Inside her head, she's envisaging her dearest Martin's bitch of a wife. If anyone could take the cops on and win, it'd be that woman.

"Are you Brenda Munroe?" His demeanour is professional in the extreme.

Damn.

She doesn't answer and instead glares at him as if he's something she wouldn't want to step in, until he gets fidgety. But he doesn't back down.

"Miss, can you please confirm if your name is Brenda Munroe."

Brenda's still summing up her options when another cab pulls up and Julian piles out, throwing money at the driver and joining her side at a fast trot.

The change in the cop is immediate. He lifts his cap up, runs his fingers through his sleep-tousled hair and replaces it again. While not standing at attention, he's more upright than he was a moment earlier. Damn it, Julian said he wasn't on the force any longer. What the hell is going on here?

"Sir, I have instructions to ascertain the young lady's where-abouts for the past twenty-four hours. She'll need to come down to the station."

"I can vouch for her until about half an hour ago." There's a distinct edge to Julian's voice which makes Brenda feel sorry for the cop. Almost. "I'll take it from here, Hawkins."

He's closing the front door when the cop car pulls away from the curb and motors slowly down their street.

"You want to tell me what the hell that was about?" she says, quietly so as not to disturb the household. This takes a fair amount of willpower because all she wants to do is scream at him at the top of her voice. A bit of shaking and some smacking wouldn't go amiss either. She's so angry.

Rather than answer, he methodically looks through the mail on the hall table as though to stall for time. He even hands her an envelope with an unfamiliar logo on it before climbing the stairs, beckoning her to follow. As if she's going to let him simply mince off into his room without telling her what gives. She slaps the envelope against her leg a couple of times, before racing up the stairs until she's close on his heels and in his bedroom a second after him, wasting no time in closing the door behind her. Even then she can't let loose, conscious of Sam and Chris, presumably asleep on the other side of the wall.

"Don't leave anything out," she hisses at him.

He sits down on his bed and pats it invitingly, but she ignores him and stalks over and sits in the chair. No way does she want to cosy up with him.

"First off, I was telling the truth when I said I'm no longer a cop. What you saw out front was residual power. Also, he's working the Smythe-Brown case, and so he knows that I've been helping them out because of my case overlapping theirs. They're not all bad, you know."

Brenda sniffs in response rather than admit he might have a point. "Hang on a second, if you were working with them, why the hell did we have to escape over the rooftops?"

"Because I wasn't *officially* helping them, and if Wallace had a sniff of anything not being above board, his lawyer would have had a field day with it. I left the force to stop the bad guys getting off and I wasn't about to jeopardise this case in the same way."

"What will happen to Wallace?" says Brenda, looking absently at the envelope she's still holding.

"He'll go away for sure. He's been blackmailing far too many people in power to be allowed to get away with it any longer. I suspect it's cost some government departments millions over the years."

"Millions!"

"How else did you think he maintains that lifestyle of his? Genevieve got all the money after her husband was killed."

"So he was done in?"

"It's looking that way."

"Holy molely!"

"Shocking, I agree."

"Not that," says Brenda, staring at the bank statement she's taken from the envelope. While the name of the bank is unknown to her, the name on the account sure as hell is, but there's nothing to explain why she's the proud owner of a bank account with a closing balance of several million. "This!"

She leans forward in the chair, holding the statement out to him, desperately wanting a second opinion on what she's seeing. Having passed it over, her hand drops to her stomach to calm the fluttering.

Julian checks the statement meticulously, doing everything but taste the damned thing. "It's legit as far as I can see."

"But, but ..." Despite her half-arsed reply, Brenda knows exactly where the money has come from, but is shocked that not only has it arrived, but the gold-plated investment Stefano had rabbited on about, appears to have paid off beyond her, and sure as hell his, wildest dreams. While the bank statement might be legit, she doubts the investment and final pay out are. Not that she's bothered, with no dental explorations planned for this particular gift horse. She's never seen that many zeros in one place before.

Julian interrupts her plans for her new-found wealth when he taps the statement, looking thoughtfully at her. "You invest this properly and it could grow into a sizable nest egg."

"Grow? It's bloody humongous now. I'm never working again!"

"Ah, Brenda."

"And you can pack your bags and all." She stands, grabs the statement from him and is already skipping out the door when he verbally trips her.

"It's in lira!"

"What?" She swings back into the room, dread attacking her stomach lining.

"That's an Italian bank. Best guess, it's around five thousand pounds."

"Shit." She sinks slowly to the floor so that she's as low as she's now feeling. For a moment, the worry that has been her constant companion since childhood had been shown the door. Now it's back with a vengeance. She'll need to recruit more students because she sure as hell is not getting a job.

She's wracking her brains for the best places to go to for recruits when Julian hands her a bundle of crisp ten-pound notes.

"You're staying?"

"No, that's your cut."

"Of what?" Brenda crushes the notes hard against her chest while waiting for him to reply.

"Of my fee for stitching up Shit-Brown. Trust me, you earned it."

She's stuttering for a response when he continues. "You're devious, underhanded, sly, street-smart and conniving. You're a natural."

"Thanks! I think."

He breaks into a broad grin before going for her Achilles' heel. "You'd make a great cop."

She has no trouble responding to this insult and rearing up, she puts him in a headlock quicker than either of them are expecting. "Take ... that ... back!" She increases the pressure with each word.

She's not sure how it happens, but one minute she has the upper hand, the next she's pinned to the bed.

"So, how about it?"

Does he mean what she thinks he means? "How about what?"

"I'm offering you a job in high-end security. You'll have a lot more fun than you are now and make a damned sight more to boot."

"Plus benefits?" says Brenda, thinking she'll need a clothing allowance if she continues ruining clobber at the rate she has of late.

"Oh, definitely plus benefits," says Julian, but she's not sure he's talking about the same thing she is.

All it would need is for her to arch her hips.

THANK YOU

For choosing my book from all those fantastic Chick Lit stories out there! It's readers like you who allow me to pursue my career as a writer.

Lastly, don't be a stranger. I'm mostly online at Twitter, but I'm also on Facebook, Instagram (so many sunset and cat photos) and Pinterest. Because my name is as unusual as it is, you should be good simply searching for that.

www.andrenelowauthor.com

ABOUT THE AUTHOR

Andrene's love of writing was instilled in her by her mother, although if her mum was still alive, she'd be smacking Andrene across the back of the head given the direction some of her writing has taken. Irreverent, cutting and reflecting her background as a stand-up comic, it's edgy with humour that's very dark in places.

Her That Seventies Series, which was relaunched in August 2017, comprises Friday Night Fever, Brush With Fame and Strapped for Cash. The series explores the wild ride the seventies was for anyone lucky enough to be young and single during this craziest of decades. Imagine a mash up between Sex in the City and That Seventies Show and you're half way there.

Andrene's currently working on a cozy paranormal mystery series about Frankie B, a jinxed witch with Bruce Lee moves and Dex, her Jack Russell familiar. Andrene lives in New Zealand with Jasmine, a neurotic, geriatric cat who should be bald given how much fur she sheds.

Printed in Great Britain
by Amazon

57703660R00241